"I don't play games," she said.

Now that wasn't exactly true. Whether Sophie knew it or not, she'd been playing with his head since he'd first laid eyes on her. "Three truths and a lie," Jacob said.

She stared at him. "As in you tell me three truths and a lie, and I pick out the lie?"

"Yes."

She considered this. "What do I get if I win?"

"What do you want?"

For the briefest of beats, her gaze dropped to his mouth. *Oh hell yeah*, he thought. *Want me...*

"My first boyfriend taught me that game," she said.

"What did the winner get?"

"A kiss."

Definitely still playing with his head..."Is that what you want, Sophie? A kiss?"

Again she stared at his mouth before dropping eye contact and wrapping that eye-stopping pink robe tighter around her body. "Do *you*?" she asked.

"Hell yes."

Her gaze flew back to his.

"Problem is," he said conversationally. "If I kissed you, I don't think I'd be able to stop..."

High Praise for Jill Shalvis

"Jill Shalvis will make you laugh and fall in love."
  —Rachel Gibson, *New York Times* bestselling author

"Shalvis never disappoints with her witty, comical, and überromantic reads."
                    —*RT Book Reviews*

"Ms. Shalvis has a gift for writing down-to-earth yet quirky heroines and swoonworthy, honorable heroes."
                    —HeroesandHeartbreakers.com

"One of my go-to authors of contemporary romance. Her writing is smart, fun, and sexy, and her books never fail to leave a smile on my face long after I've closed the last page…Jill Shalvis is an author not to be missed!"
                    —TheRomanceDish.com

"I always enjoy reading a Jill Shalvis book. She's a consistently elegant, bold, clever writer."
                    —All About Romance (LikesBooks.com)

"Whenever I'm looking for a romance to chase away the worries of life, all I have to do is pick up a Jill Shalvis book."
                    —RomRevToday.com

Second Chance Summer

"Sassy, funny, and down-to-earth sexy, this lively romance is one readers won't be able to resist. A hands-down winner and a terrific launch to the author's latest series."

—Library Journal (starred review)

"4 ½ stars! Top Pick! Flawless. This author knows romance and readers can always expect her to deliver humor, heat, and a kick-ass story."

—RT Book Reviews

"Plenty of love, laughter, and deep and long-lasting friendships to keep this lively tale moving along at just the right pace."

—ReadertoReader.com

"Top Pick! *Second Chance Summer* is sexy and packs a powerful emotional punch."

—FreshFiction.com

It's in His Kiss

"Shalvis combines humor, sparkling repartee, believable characters, and highly sensual sex scenes to make this book work on every level."

—Publishers Weekly (starred review)

Once in a Lifetime

"Readers will cheer."

—*Washington Post*

It Had to Be You

"Engaging writing, characters that walk straight into your heart, and a town you can't wait to revisit make this touching, hilarious tale another heart-warmer worthy of Shalvis's popular series."

—*Library Journal*

Forever and a Day

"4½ stars! Top Pick! Shalvis once again racks up a hit"

—*RT Book Reviews*

At Last

"A sexy, romantic read...What I love about Jill Shalvis's books is that she writes sexy, adorable heroes...the sexual tension is out of this world. And of course, in true Shalvis fashion, she expertly mixes in humor that has you laughing out loud."

—HeroesandHeartbreakers.com

Nobody But You

JILL SHALVIS

GRAND CENTRAL
PUBLISHING

NEW YORK   BOSTON

Copyright © 2016 by Jill Shalvis
Excerpt from *Second Chance Summer* copyright © 2015 by Jill Shalvis
Excerpt from *My Kind of Wonderful* copyright © 2015 by Jill Shalvis
Cover design by Diane Luger. Cover photography by Shirley Green. Cover background images © Shutterstock.

Grand Central Publishing
Hachette Book Group
1290 Avenue of the Americas
New York, NY 10104

forever-romance.com
twitter.com/foreverromance.com

First Edition: March 2016

Grand Central Publishing is a division of Hachette Book Group, Inc.
The Grand Central Publishing name and logo is a trademark of Hachette Book Group, Inc.

The Hachette Speakers Bureau provides a wide range of authors for speaking events. To find out more, go to www.hachettespeakersbureau.com or call (866) 376-6591.

The publisher is not responsible for websites (or their content) that are not owned by the publisher.

Printed in the United States of America

OPM

10 9 8 7 6 5 4 3 2 1

ATTENTION CORPORATIONS AND ORGANIZATIONS:

Most Hachette Book Group books are available at quantity discounts with bulk purchase for educational, business, or sales promotional use. For information, please call or write:

Special Markets Department, Hachette Book Group
1290 Avenue of the Americas, New York, NY 10104
Telephone: 1-800-222-6747 Fax: 1-800-477-5925

Nobody But You

Chapter 1

Sophie Marren parked her ex-husband's boat, tied it to the dock with knots she copied off a YouTube video on her phone, and flopped to her back on the fancy sundeck, trying to will away her seasickness.

And yes, she was well aware that *parked* wasn't the correct boating term, but then again, neither was the word *husband*, at least not as it had pertained to her marriage.

She'd made vows and kept them, but her ex? Not so much...

Old news, she reminded herself, and let out a long breath. That was something she was working on, new choices—such as living without the fist of tension around her heart, the constant pressure and fear to try to be something, some-one, she wasn't.

Her glass was going to be half full from now on, dammit, even if it killed her. And it might.

"And yet you now live on a damn boat." She shook her

head at herself. Week one of the new digs and it looked like she wasn't going to make it to week two.

The early morning was quiet, the only sound being the water rhythmically slapping up against the hull of the boat, then the dock. Boat…dock…boat…dock—"Dammit!" she cried, quickly sitting up before she got even more seasick. She had to get ready for work. But the air was cold—she was cold—and with the boat rocking as it was, she hadn't yet risked losing an eye to put on mascara.

From somewhere nearby came the song of the morning birds, all chipper and happy, making her wish for a shotgun. She put a hand to her stomach, but it kept doing somersaults. This was because she could get seasick in a bathtub.

Sophie groaned, hoping death came quickly. Cedar Ridge Lake was one of the larger high-altitude lakes in Colorado, and it didn't help that the winds had kicked up this morning, causing rolling waves across the entire surface.

When yet another gust hit, brushing the strands of hair from her damp face, she risked cracking open an eye. From her vantage point, she could see the impressive Rocky Mountains shooting straight up to the limitless, shocking azure sky marred only by a single white fluffy cloud that resembled a pile of marshmallows.

Her stomach, normally in love with marshmallows, turned over again. "Gah," she managed, and quickly squeezed her eyes shut just as her cell phone buzzed from the depths of her pocket. She pulled it out and hit ANSWER without looking, since looking would mean opening her eyes again and facing that all of this wasn't just a bad dream but her life. "Hello?"

"I just wanted you to know I had your car towed to the scrapyard."

Lucas, ex-husband and the bane of her existence.

"And I had a bonfire with whatever clothes you left in your closet too," he went on. "So I hope it was worth taking my boat."

She knew neither of these things was true, because he was too cheap and also a little bit lazy. He simply wanted to punish her for taking his boat. The irony was that she'd wanted nothing from the divorce. Nothing but out. Nothing but the chance to find herself again and not just be an extension of Lucas Worthington III, hotshot lawyer on the rise.

Hindsight being twenty-twenty and all, she now knew she should've asked for a small portion of money instead of taking a moral stand and refusing a penny of spousal support or any of their assets. But she'd gone into the marriage with nothing, and in the end she hadn't wanted anything from Lucas but out. Not a single thing.

When she'd said so to the judge, he'd called her aside and admonished her for cutting off her nose to spite her face, because she was entitled to not walk away penniless.

Hurt at the realization her marriage had been nothing but a sham from the get-go, she'd said fine, she'd take *one* thing, the one thing she knew Lucas had loved far and above anything he'd ever felt for her—his damn boat.

Petty? Okay, yes. But given that Lucas had managed to have the boat tied up in "renovations" for the past six months since their divorce, and that he'd also managed to get her fired from her office managerial position at a local inn so she'd had to give up her apartment, the joke was on her.

Karma was such a bitch.

Why couldn't he have loved his huge house? Or the Lexus…Neither of which would be affected by the morning breeze, bobbing up and down and up and down and up and down—

"Oh God." Clamping a hand over her mouth, she breathed slowly through the nausea.

"I want my *Lucas* back," Lucas said, and if she could have, she'd have laughed at the ridiculous ego it'd taken for him to name the vessel after himself, including painting *The Lucas* on the hull of the boat for all to see.

"Are you even listening to me?" he demanded.

Nope. She wasn't. She didn't have to; she had a sheet of paper saying that they were consciously uncoupled, thank you very much. And to prove it, she disconnected the call and then let out a long breath, hoping to die before he called again.

"Hey, what are you doing?" a male voice called out from the direction of the dock.

From flat on her back, Sophie froze. Maybe if she didn't move he'd assume she was dead and move on.

"You can't moor here, ma'am."

Right, *moor*, not *park*. She'd known that. But *ma'am*? What the heck was that? Her mom was a *ma'am*. Her grandma was a *ma'am*. *Ma'am* was for old people, not for twenty-five-year-old women who were desperately trying to get their lives together. Very carefully, Sophie sat up and narrowed her eyes at the guy standing on the dock staring at her.

He was tall, broad, and had the benefit of standing in front of the sun, which meant she could see his outline and little else. But his stance seemed aggressive enough that she felt herself wanting to shrink a little.

Which, for the record, she hated.

But there was a bigger problem. The motion of the boat bobbing up and down, compared to the guy standing on the end of the dock *not* moving up and down, made her want to toss her cookies. In defense, she lay down and closed her eyes again. "Did you really just call me 'ma'am'? Because I'm not even close to a damn 'ma'am.'"

Nope, ask anyone. They'd tell you Sophie Marren was fun and chill, though she didn't tend to stay the course. She was a starter, not a finisher, as her mom would say, and she was absolutely not grown-up enough to be a *ma'am*. As proof, she was living on a damn boat, illegally parked while she was at it—oh wait, excuse her, *moored*.

"Fine," the guy said. "You can't moor here...Red."

At the recognition of her long, wavy, deep auburn—okay, fine, *red*—hair, she choked out a laugh. He got a point for having a sense of humor. And ah, finally the wind seemed to be settling down. Around her the morning fell silent again. Even the birds shut up. Had the guy left too? Did it matter? Apparently it did, because she sat up—slowly—to look, and then groaned.

He hadn't left.

He'd shifted, though, coming closer, allowing her a good look at him. Military-short, sun-streaked light brown hair. Square jaw at least two days past needing a razor. Wide shoulders stretching an army T-shirt to its limits. Flat belly. Lean hips encased in camo cargoes. As she watched, he pulled off his reflective sunglasses, revealing eyes the color of one of her favorite things when she wasn't seasick—chocolate.

Damn.

But if he felt any insta-attraction for her, he was really good at hiding it, because he looked at his watch like maybe he was in a hurry.

The story of her life, men being in a hurry to get away from her, and she decided right then and there she didn't like him, hot or not. "This is a public lake," she said.

"Yes, but you're tied up to a private dock that belongs

to that cabin." He jerked his chin to the side, indicating the home just behind him.

The lake was multiuse. The west and east shores were owned by the state and were national forest land. There were public campgrounds on the northeast side, with houses on the north shore only.

The cabin that he pointed to was indeed privately owned, but she knew for a fact it was deserted because it'd been up for sale for months. Although—troublesome—the FOR SALE sign had been taken down. Even more troublesome, the shades were raised and the front door was open.

Huh. Her bad.

"I was just taking a short nap," she said.

One of his eyebrows took a hike nearly to his hairline. "At seven in the morning?"

Yes, well, that's what happened when one had to keep moving one's boat so as not to get cited for illegal overnight mooring. Not that she was about to admit *that*. "Didn't sleep last night," she said. The utter truth. "The winds were crazy and the boat never stopped rocking."

"Using two tie-downs instead of one would help stabilize the boat quite a bit," he said. "At the bow and at the stern."

Something that Lucas hadn't bothered to tell her, of course. "Thanks," she said, slightly mollified.

"You can moor overnight. You just have to buy a permit for one of the public docks at the campgrounds, or tie up at a private dock—with permission of the owner."

He was lake patrol, she realized. And a stickler for the rules. Not that she was surprised. The entire male population was on her shit list. Sometimes higher on the list than other times, but that was another story. "I'll move the boat," she promised, hoping to appease him enough to make him vanish.

He nodded and…continued to stand there.

Perfect. Still not feeling steady, she managed to get to her feet and sat behind the wheel. That she did so without puking was somewhat of a miracle. But before she could fumble the keys into the ignition, there came the *click-click-click*ing of heels running down the dock. Sophie turned her head in time to watch with the same muted horror she would've watched a train wreck.

A tall, leggy blonde was doing her best to run in painted-on leather pants and matching corset, vastly hampered by her store-bought double D's bouncing up to her chin with each step of those five-inch stilettos.

"Lucas," the woman called out. "Oh, Lucas…I've got the day off. We can play pirate and captive maiden again!"

Sophie managed to stand up and make herself seen over the windshield. Yep, it was one of Lucas's regular sidepieces, which made her see red. On the positive side, though, apparently a brain couldn't be both furious and sick at the same time, because she momentarily didn't feel like puking up her guts.

"Whoops," the woman said, skidding to a halt, tugging down the corset a little and very nearly causing a wardrobe malfunction of epic proportions. "I'm looking for Lucas."

What was her name? Sophie wondered, trying to remember. Brandy? Candy?

"I'm Mandy," Ms. Camel Toe said, sliding a side glance at Mr. Lake Patrol, who actually scored another point in Sophie's eyes when he took a quick, dismissive glance and then refocused on Sophie herself.

"I don't understand," Mandy said, confused, staring at Sophie now too. "Who are you? And don't even think of moving in on me. Monday mornings are mine and Lucas's.

Well, every other Monday, because he has very important meetings on the other Mondays. But he's going to leave his wife for me, so back off."

"Okay, I've got both good news and bad news for you," Sophie said. "The good news is that he did indeed leave his wife. Me."

Mandy did a double take. "*You're* the coat hanger he dumped?"

Jeez, give up college and then your own life to run your husband's busy schedule for him and suddenly people see you as a worthless extension of the man instead of being your own woman.

Good thing she was over that and back at work on herself.

Having no idea what she wanted to do for a living had her in temporary stall mode, but she was working on that too. She was doing the best she could at every job she tried. So far things hadn't exactly panned out, but all she could do was keep looking forward.

Mandy crossed her arms. "So where the hell is Lucas?"

Later Sophie would feel bad for what popped out of her mouth. Much later. "He…passed." Which, actually, wasn't a total lie, because if a Mack truck didn't run her ex over by week's end, she might just do the deed herself.

Mandy blinked. "Passed as in…*passed*?"

You're helping her out here, Sophie told herself. *Saving her future heartbreak*. So she did her best to look suitably grief stricken as she nodded and braced for hysterics.

But instead Mandy got all red in the face and stomped a stiletto on the dock. "Why, that bastard! He said that he'd had a lot of personal growth lately and he'd come to some life-altering decisions about us! And then he ups and dies? *Are you kidding me?*"

Sophie didn't think that a hard-on counted as personal

growth. She also felt she deserved a medal for sainthood for refraining from mentioning it.

"I had the diamond ring all picked out, with a matching necklace and bracelet and everything." Mandy blew out a sigh. "Men suck."

Now, *there* was something they could agree on.

"I need to board the boat," Mandy said, her breasts quivering in indignation. "I left a few things down there that the asshole doesn't deserve, even in death."

"Such as?" Sophie asked.

"Lucas gave me a drawer."

Sophie stared at her for a beat, then whirled and went belowdecks. She indeed found the drawer filled with lingerie and—ew—something in fluorescent pink that required batteries. Rather than touch anything, she yanked out the entire drawer and stormed on deck.

And tripped.

The contents of the drawer flew free and scattered across the dock. Lacy thongs, garter belts, skimpy bras…And last but not least, the fluorescent-pink battery-operated toy, which rolled to a stop at Lake Patrol Hottie's feet.

And then began to vibrate.

Lake Patrol Hottie stared down at it. "You have a license for this?" he asked.

"It's not mine!"

Mandy gave a big huff and gathered it up along with the rest of her lingerie, glaring at Sophie like this was all her fault. "I'll have you know, Lucas loved me *and* my Rabbit more than you." Then she whirled and headed up the dock, her heels *click, click, click*ing, her vibrator humming along in accompaniment.

Sophie sighed into the awkward silence between her and Lake Patrol Hottie. Actually, it was probably just her who felt awkward, because he stood there looking perfectly comfortable and at ease.

"I'm sorry for your loss," he said.

"Don't be. He didn't really die." She backed to the bench next to the driver's seat and dropped onto it in sheer woozy exhaustion. "What I said was that he'd *passed*. As in he passed on *me*."

And that was all she planned on saying on the subject.

Ever.

But apparently he didn't get the memo, because he crouched on the dock so that they were eye level and said nothing.

She grinded her teeth. The wind was back, dammit, and the boat began to rock. "Look, I said I'd move. I just need a minute."

He nodded and...stayed right where he was.

"You don't believe me?" she asked.

"Just waiting to see if you need any help."

She eyed him suspiciously, but he seemed to mean it. He really would assist her if she needed it. But she didn't need it. Not from him. Not from anyone.

Somehow she crawled behind the wheel. She started the boat before suddenly remembering she had to untie it first.

But her lake patrol guy was already on it, handling the ropes like he'd been born to the task, using his foot to push off on the hull so it didn't scrape against the dock and get damaged. He then tossed the rope into the boat. "You're good," he said.

She stared at him. Was he kidding? She wasn't good. She was a hot mess, and they both knew it. But then again, he'd meant the boat, not her, and she knew that too. Still, she appreciated his unsolicited help. "Thanks," she said.

He nodded. Waited a beat. "Need help finding the throttle?"

This actually made her smile. "You're a real charmer, you know that?"

"Yep. I'm fresh off the boat from charm school."

"Where was it, Timbuktu?"

"Close," he said, offering no further explanation.

Fine. Whatever. Over mysterious men, over men *period*, she hit the gas. When she glanced in the rearview mirror a minute later, he was still standing there on the dock, hands shoved in his pockets, watching her go.

Chapter 2

The very last thing Jacob Kincaid had expected on his first day back in town was a run-in with a mysterious, temperamental, green-eyed cutie. Somehow she'd managed to pull him out of his own head while also irritating and amusing him.

She'd also made him feel alive.

Since that messed with his head more than a little bit, he got in his new Ford truck and took a ride. The truck had been a present to himself for making it stateside in one piece. It drove great, but his attention was distracted by his first view of Cedar Ridge in a long time.

It felt like a lifetime since he'd walked away from his family—his mom; twin brother, Hud; and the rest of the Kincaids—when he was an eighteen-year-old hothead. He hadn't been home.

Until now.

He'd been a lot of things in his lifetime: brother, son, friend, Army Special Forces officer.

He was none of those things at the moment, though he intended to change that. He had begun by leasing a small cabin on the lake only a mile outside of town, a place that had once upon a time been the only true home he'd ever known.

Not that he'd admitted this until recently, and then only to himself.

The cabin sat on the northeast line of the lake and was quiet and peaceful—two things his life had most definitely *never* been.

Something else he intended to change.

When he'd arrived late last night, he'd picked up the keys and spoken briefly to the Realtor, who'd tried to convince him to buy the cabin instead of renting it.

But Jacob no longer made quick, rash decisions.

Although he *had* chased away the first civilian woman he'd had contact with in a while, and he'd done it pretty quickly and rashly.

Yeah, he could've definitely done better there, he admitted. Clearly he was *way* out of practice at being sociable. Maybe he was more messed up than he'd thought, because he'd actually gotten a kick out of the way her eyes had flashed temper at him, at the world. It'd been like trying to deal with a fiercely angry, beautiful, injured feline, and in spite of the sharp claws, she'd given him something he hadn't felt in a damn long time.

Adrenaline. The good kind. And after nine years in the military, also a taste of the real world.

Town was…the same. It was small, geared to the tourists who came through to ski. The streets were filled with expensive clothing boutiques, art galleries, jewelry shops, a few cafés, bars, B and Bs, and the like. At age eighteen, Jacob had been climbing the walls here, bored, slowly suffocating.

Now, after having been overseas and seeing more shitholes than he cared to remember, he could see in Cedar Ridge what others did, a unique quaintness and charm.

He didn't want to take the risk of running into anyone he knew before he told his family he was home. They deserved to be told he was here, from his own mouth. But the need for caffeine overruled self-preservation. Striding into a coffee shop like he was on a mission, he bought coffee and a bagel to go and headed to the cabin.

Unscathed.

Red's boat was still gone, and relief filled him. And if there was also a twinge of something that felt suspiciously like disappointment, he didn't examine it too closely.

Instead, he found several paddleboards leaning against the side of the cabin and decided what the hell. He took one out onto the water, paddling himself into oblivion so that maybe he'd sleep that night instead of trying to figure out how to reach out to his family after all this time, now that he was on leave, or thinking about the reason he'd been given bereavement leave in the first place.

The next morning Jacob woke up to find his arms pleasantly sore from all the paddleboarding he'd been doing to clear his head. The morning's chilly June air sliced through the window he'd left open and right through him as well, sharp and pine scented. From flat on his back he could see a sliver of the lake, the surface littered with whitecaps, much rougher and choppier than the past few days.

He lay there a minute, unable to get his mind to shut off. It kept flashing images. Images of his closest friend, Brett, dying in his arms in the desolate wasteland that was Afghanistan. Images of the look on his twin's face when they'd fought that long-ago day. Jacob hadn't seen Hud since. Images of his mom, who with her dementia couldn't keep time or place or people straight but never forgot who he was.

Even Red had somehow wormed her way in; she was tough and snarky, and yet she'd shown him a fleeting glimpse of vulnerability too. The combination had caught his interest.

And attracted him.

Not that he had time to go there. Nope, he was concentrating all his energy on figuring out how to approach his family. Day two and he was still drawing a big zero on that front. He'd given no advance warning of his arrival because, hell, what did one say after nearly a decade of radio silence?

But today was the day. He'd stalled enough. And at the thought of what lay ahead for him, his gut tightened.

Nerves. Crazy. It'd been a damn long time since he'd been nervous about anything.

Rolling out of bed, he showered, dressed, and headed out, once again on the hunt for food he didn't have to make himself. Halfway to his truck, he glanced through the clumps of trees lining his property to the lake.

The Lucas was moored at his dock again.

Changing directions, he headed down there and eyed the boat. No sign of Red, but he heard something from below-decks. A...moan?

Walk away, soldier.

But hell. He couldn't do it. "Hello?" he called out. "Red?"

The ensuing silence was so thick that he could tell she'd stopped breathing. "I'm boarding," he said, and when she didn't respond, he went for it, hoping she wasn't aiming a gun his way. As he did, she struggled on deck.

She wore a short, flowery skirt that flirted with her thighs and a white tank top, a forest-green sweater in one hand and a pair of high-heeled sandals dangling from the other.

With one look, she perfectly conveyed her annoyance as she sagged to the captain's chair and dropped her head to her knees. "Why you?" she moaned. "I mean, seriously, what the hell is up with my karma? It's like the bitch went on vacay. On another planet."

"Nice to see you again too," he said dryly. "You wanna tell me what's wrong?"

"Nothing. Nothing at all," she said to her knees, more than a little hint of the South in her tone. "I always talk to my knees while a stranger asks me twenty questions. Nope, I'm great. My glass is totally half full."

This made him smile. Call him sick, but he loved snark in a woman. "Are you okay?"

"Fan-fricking-tastic. Only way today could get better is if I were scheduled for an appendectomy. Without drugs. In a third-world country."

Snark and a bad 'tude, like she wouldn't hesitate to kick someone's ass if she needed to. Didn't get hotter than that. He crouched next to her so that he was level with her face, not that he could see it since it was still pressed to her legs. "You're not supposed to—"

"—moor here," she said, very carefully not moving a single inch. "Yes, you ever-so-helpfully mentioned that yesterday."

"I was going to say you're not supposed to look down when you're seasick. It makes it worse."

"Oh." She hesitated and then turned her head to look at him. "And you're not supposed to be nice when I'm not. But thanks—oh crap. Oh shit," she whispered miserably as the boat rocked.

Jacob instinctively reached out and rubbed a hand over her back. "Have you tried Dramamine?"

"Yes. It doesn't work. I'm getting a patch today."

"That'll help," he said.

She nodded and sat up. "I'm sorry I'm here. I just need to stay docked for the day, okay? I know the cabin's for sale and no one lives there, so I don't see a problem with that."

Other than she was getting off not having to pay the fees, which he suspected she couldn't afford. "Just so you know, the cabin's no longer empty," he said, fully intending to also say that she could keep her boat on his dock as long as she needed.

But she made a sound that might have been a snort of laughter or a sob. A little terrified it was the latter, he rose to his full height just as she gasped, and then moaned, and…and threw up.

An inch from his shoes.

Welcome home, he thought, reaching for her, supporting her with one arm while with the other he tried to gather her hair. Problem was, she had a lot of it, and more than a few of the silky strands stuck stubbornly to the stubble on his jaw as she tried to weakly shove clear of him.

"So much for improving on your first impression of me," she gasped. "Looks like you were lucky enough to draw the short straw on my crazy. Again."

"Shh." Her skin was waxy and green, so he held on to her, afraid she'd slide overboard and drown. "Give yourself a minute," he said.

She sighed miserably and didn't look at him. "How many Dramamine do you think it'd take to just kill me?" she asked.

Jacob couldn't make a return quip, not on that. Not since just about every time he closed his eyes these days all he could see was Brett's coffin being lowered into the ground.

"I'm so sorry." She sighed and straightened, still looking wobbly. "But hey, it must be your lucky day. I missed your shoes. Don't worry. I'll clean this up and be gone in no time."

If only he believed that. "Wait here," he said. He left the boat and strode to the cabin to get her some water and also to find a hose to help her clean up.

But when he got outside again, she and her boat were gone.

Which left nothing to distract him from what he had to do today, and at the thought, the unwelcome nerves returned with a vengeance, tap-dancing in his belly again.

She'd thrown up on the hot guy. Good Lord, Sophie thought weakly as she quickly cleaned up and then maneuvered the boat as far from the little cabin as she could get.

Easier said than done.

They'd had a violent summer storm over the past few days, which had made her seasickness so much worse. Especially since she'd had to move around, aka *sneak* around, to find places to moor.

The waves were larger than she'd ever navigated before. Feeling naked without a seat belt, she wrapped her ankle around the seat base so she wouldn't go flying out.

Because that would be more embarrassing than what had just happened. If that was even possible.

The problem was that she was crap at driving the boat. It was nothing like a car. When she steered, it didn't immediately react, and that guaranteed that she was always in the middle of correcting her previous maneuver. Compounding the problem was that because of the way the wind hit the water, she had to steer into the waves, riding up and over them just as the wave crested.

Not good. Several times *The Lucas* became airborne for a moment before slamming down, rattling her teeth. She did her best to battle her way through the brutal onslaught of choppy water, but every time she hit a bump, the shock of it jerked her hand on the throttle, speeding her up, slowing her down...

And in five seconds she was nauseous again.

None of which mattered right now because hello, she'd *thrown up on Hottie Lake Patrol Guy.*

And yes, he was hot. Very hot. The first time she'd seen him, she hadn't gotten a good look, but today she had. He was big, built pretty badass, and had stood there steady on his feet and stoic in army-green cargoes and a black T-shirt stretched to its limits across his broad chest. Eyes hidden behind those dark sunglasses, he'd held her hair back for her.

Oh God. It was possible she'd just hit an all-time low, but really she shouldn't underestimate herself.

As she drove, she searched for any other dock that looked deserted. Not that she was in a hurry to try to park this mother-effer. Because if she had trouble gliding across the water at speed, maneuvering the boat into a slip required skills and luck she didn't have. And something else she seriously lacked as well—patience.

But she had to get to work. Up until a few weeks ago, she'd worked at one of the local hotel chains, running the concierge crew for five locations, and she'd been great at it.

Then Lucas had slept with the CEO's wife and...well, Sophie had once again paid the price. Now she was temping, taking on every job that came her way out of desperation, because she was getting damned tired of ramen noodles, apples, and peanut butter.

And...she couldn't find a damn open dock. Finally, she turned and headed back, ending up right where she'd started—at the cabin. She stared at the empty dock and thought of the twenty bucks she'd save in campground day fees, which was good because she was currently so broke she couldn't even pay attention.

She slowed and eyed the dock, chewing on her lower lip. *You can't moor here...*

That's what Hottie Lake Patrol Guy had said to her, but she'd heard so much more than that.

You can't major in "good times."

You can't quit college. You're supposed to become someone.

You can't just casually flit your way through life being a fetch-it girl at a motel.

Life isn't always happiness. It has to mean something.

If you're not going to become someone, then at least marry Lucas, who will take care of you.

She shrugged it all off the best she could, because she was done listening to people. Her well-meaning parents. Her past bosses. Her so-called friends, who'd all gone AWOL since she'd left Lucas.

Nope, she was on a listening-only-to-her-heart kick.

And with that, she took the boat to the campgrounds. She managed to maneuver close to the dock and then brought up her bookmarked YouTube video on tying down a boat. And thanks to Hottie Lake Patrol Guy's advice, she used two tie-downs. She then scrounged up the cash for day fees—there went lunch—and rushed belowdecks.

It wasn't quite as pristine down here as it had been when it'd belonged to Lucas. This was because one, she wasn't an OCD cleaning fanatic who'd had it scrubbed with a tooth-brush. And two, she resented the hell out of her accommoda-tions. She hated the small porta-potty she couldn't even use because she didn't know how to hook it up.

This had forced her to always park—er, *moor*—the boat near one of the two campgrounds on the lake so that she could use those facilities. What she did have were seats for six and a bed that barely fit one. The seats and bed were done up with the same leather-like material as the seats above, white with red trim, making the compartment appear more spacious than it was. Much more. There was a top-notch stereo system and entertainment center that had probably cost more than she'd made last year tucked into the cabinets. Everything was compact and efficient.

And it all drove her crazy.

She hurriedly brushed her teeth in the small galley sink, tamed her hair, and changed her clothes, digging into her last clean outfit. She would have made herself breakfast, but the sole electric burner on the tiny stove would light only about half the time she tried, and this morning wasn't one of those times.

Forty-five minutes later she stood outside the hospital, switching out her running shoes for heels. Not that she'd run here from the lake. Nope, the only time Sophie did any running was if a bear was chasing her, and that hardly ever happened.

She'd walked the three miles to work, reminding herself that in return she could now have dessert with both lunch *and* dinner as a prize. She shoved her running shoes into her tote and headed into the building adjacent to the hospital, where for the next few days she was running the front office at the special-care facility while the regular office manager recovered from a root canal.

The job was stressful, but she loved the people. They were either elderly or a little loony tunes, but she fit right in. A shrink would have a field day with that, but she was making new choices these days, and one of them was not worrying about what people thought of her.

She waved at Dani, the receptionist, and then at the two accounting clerks in the staff room as she punched in. She moved to the front desk to see that everything was on track and froze as a man came in the front door. Given how the day had gone, nothing should have been able to surprise her at this point, but this did.

Hottie Lake Patrol Guy was striding directly toward her.

She opened her mouth and then closed it, gaping like a fish. What the hell could he possibly want? To sue her for getting seasick and throwing up? For leaving her boat in a spot no one else wanted anyway? Heart pounding, she narrowed her eyes. "Seriously?" she asked. Maybe yelled. "I didn't do anything wrong! Well, okay, other than parking my boat illegally, but throwing up—while unfortunate—is not arrest worthy, especially since I didn't even get it on your shoes! So just get over it already!"

He pulled off his dark sunglasses and met her gaze, his mouth tilted up in the barest hint of a wry smile.

"This is harassment," she said. "I could sue you, but I'm not that girl. Especially if you agree to compensate me by letting me use the dock for one more night." Holy crap, she couldn't believe the stuff coming out her mouth, but she was backed into the proverbial corner, her heart trying to beat its way out of her chest.

Without saying a word, Lake Patrol Guy reached for the pen on the sign-in sheet they used for visitors of their patients and…

Signed in to see a patient.

Then he set the pen down, quirked a brow at her, and walked away.

Unable to help herself, she watched his very fine ass as he went. "So I can stay one more night, right?" she called after him.

Dani came up beside her and joined in the ass watching. "You threw up on his shoes?"

She sighed. "It's a long story."

Chapter 3

Jacob was still shaking his head as he made his way up the stairs of the rehab center to the second floor. Turned out Red from the lake had a name, which he'd seen on her name tag just now.

Sophie Marren.

She'd been wearing a different outfit from the one he'd seen her in before, now a pencil skirt and a sleeveless blouse. Not looking pale and green, not throwing up…Instead, she'd had her hair twisted up on top of her head, with a few long, wispy strands falling out. There was a flush to her cheeks, and her lips were shiny. Her pretty green eyes were behind a set of reading glasses, and the overall look screamed sweet, cautious, reserved librarian.

It was a look he'd never given much thought to, but suddenly it was sexier than hell. Especially when he added in the slight Southern accent he detected every time she got sassy, which around him seemed to be a constant.

He was thinking about that and smiling a little because

she'd pretty much yelled at him, and it'd been a damn long time since he'd been called out like that. In his world, people respected him, feared him, avoided him…They most definitely did not put their finger in his face like a schoolteacher and take him to task.

His smile faded quickly enough when he remembered why he was here—to visit his mom. From there he'd figure out how to see Hud.

But then he turned the corner and came face-to-face with him.

Once upon a time they'd been mirror images, exact replicas of each other while also being opposites. Hudson was right-handed, and he was a southpaw. Hud's cowlick was on the right, Jacob's on the left. Hud reacted with his emotions, Jacob with his brain.

Except for the one time he hadn't.

The fight with Hud had been the worst day of his life, and that was saying something, as there'd been a few doozies before and since. But that day they'd each said things, and Jacob had no idea how to make it right again.

They'd grown up hard and fast. Carrie, their mom, had been a sweet but troubled eighteen-year-old whom their father had taken advantage of one night. Later they'd find out that Richard Kincaid was something of a serial sperm donor. And that *monogamy* wasn't a word he knew the definition of.

So growing up, it'd been just Hud, Jacob, and Carrie, raising each other. Actually, Hud and Jacob had raised themselves while doing the best they could to raise their mom too. But when they'd turned twelve, Carrie had fallen apart completely, leaving her unable to hold a job.

Jacob and Hud had done everything they could, working when they could get jobs, conning when they couldn't, but eventually they hadn't been able to keep a roof over their heads anymore and had landed here in Cedar Ridge, thanks to the generosity of Char Kincaid.

Char had been another of Richard Kincaid's rejects. She'd had two boys with the guy, Gray and Aidan, both a few years older than Hud and Jacob.

All of that had meant that once they'd landed here in Cedar Ridge, for the first time in their lives, they'd had a support system. Family. Carrie had been nearby in the home, and they'd had a roof over their heads and three squares a day.

And though he and Hud had taken an oath to leave together the moment they turned eighteen, to go off and explore the world and be all the other needed, Hud had taken to Cedar Ridge and their newfound siblings like a fish to water.

Jacob had tried. Or maybe he hadn't. What he for sure had done was carry his resentment and anger over his father's abandonment and the frustration of his mom's health in the form of a huge chip on his shoulder. He'd been a punk-ass kid who'd deserved to get kicked out.

Instead, Char had been sweet and kind and mothering. Aidan and Gray had ignored his dick-ness. They'd treated him and Hud better than they'd ever been treated before. So had Kenna, their baby sister—from yet another woman of their father's—who'd come to Cedar Ridge shortly after Hud and Jacob.

And yet still, when graduation had come, Jacob had packed as he and Hud had always planned.

Only Hud had steadfastly refused to leave.

When Jacob had insisted, Hud had let loose of his rare temper and said that if Jacob wanted to go, then he should. But if he did, they were no longer brothers.

Jacob's eighteen-year-old bluster and ego had kicked in

hard at that ultimatum, and he'd walked, breaking up the tightest bond he'd ever had with another living soul.

He'd gone into the army. In boot camp, he'd met Brett, who'd lost his family to a drunk driver. Very different from losing a family due to pride and stupidity. But the two of them had been each other's support system and family through basic training, specialized weapons training, and several tours of duty.

And then Brett had died in a stupid roadside bombing they'd never seen coming. That's when the "no man left behind" mantra had hit him hard. Really hard. He'd never have walked away from Brett, and yet he'd done just that to Hud.

He hated himself for it.

Which was the biggest reason he was here. He'd been wrong and had to tell Hud that. Had to tell everyone. He had no idea if he'd even be welcomed. But blood or not, family was family—or so he hoped. And he had to do right by his.

When he'd walked away all those years ago, he'd been a self-righteous, selfish prick. He didn't want to be that guy anymore. He had no idea what kind of a man he'd be instead, but it was past time to find out.

Hud had stopped walking, just stopped on a dime in the middle of the hallway. Slowly. He pulled off his sunglasses and stared at Jacob, relief and joy evident on his face.

Jacob nearly hit his knees at that. With his heart suddenly feeling way too big to fit inside his rib cage, he took a few steps toward his brother.

Hud met him halfway, wrapping his long arms around Jacob, clapping him hard on the back.

For the first time since Brett's funeral, Jacob felt emotion, hot and all-consuming, swell up and block his throat.

Arms still tight around him, Hud lifted Jacob off the ground—not easy to do—squeezing the hell out of him while he was at it. "Holy shit. How much does all this muscle weigh?"

Jacob shrugged. It was his job to be big and bad, which, yeah, was pretty much a complete turnaround from the too-skinny, too-scrawny kids they'd once been. Which reminded him all that was between them.

And given the look on Hud's face, it'd hit him too. His twin schooled his features into a blank mask so fast Jacob's head spun.

"What the fuck, man?" Hud said, taking a step away.

"Hudson Kincaid, you watch your language!" came a woman's shocked voice, a voice that Jacob would know anywhere.

His mom.

He and Hud turned in unison to the patient room where Hud had come from. Carrie sat on her bed wearing black leggings with bunny slippers and a huge bright pink sweatshirt that said NEVER STOP FIGHTING. Her hair was as it always had been, so light blond it looked like a cotton ball, the flyaway strands doing whatever they wanted. Eyes locked on both Jacob and Hud, she slowly set down her tablet. "It's not a dream." Her mouth fell open. "Oh my goodness, it's not a dream," she whispered, and her eyes filled. "Jacob?"

Jacob managed a nod. His voice, when he managed to speak, was low and rough. "Yeah, Mom, it's me."

She brought shaking fingers up to her trembling mouth.

He let out a breath, feeling like he'd been stabbed in the gut. "Please don't cry."

She closed her eyes, and a few tears spilled out down her cheeks.

Hud sent him a fulminating look, and Jacob knew he deserved no less. "Mom—" he whispered hoarsely, letting out an *oomph* of air when she launched herself off the bed and flung herself at him. Since she was at least a foot shorter than he was, it wasn't all that hard to catch her. Holding her tight, he pressed his face to her shoulder.

"Did you think I wouldn't find out?" she asked in a hurt voice. "Did you?"

"Uh…" Lifting his head, he eyeballed Hud, who was a granite statue and no help at all.

Carrie pulled away and shook a finger in his face. "How many times have I told you, cutting school is bad. Baby, you need your education. You're so smart. You're going to make something of yourself. I just know it. But Mrs. Stone called me and said you missed her math test…"

Mrs. Stone had been Jacob's sixth-grade math teacher.

And he had absolutely ditched her class often, usually to get to a card game at a neighbor's house, where he'd used his considerable math skills to count cards and make their rent money. "I'll make it up."

"Yeah, well, see that you do," his mom said, looking very much the same as she always had, which was a little bat-shit crazy and a whole lot wonderful, the warmest, sweetest woman on the entire planet. And as she always had, she brought out conflicting emotions in Jacob. Rough memories of being a kid and yet having to be the adult, relief that she was exactly the same, the only person on the planet to un-conditionally love him even if she didn't know what year she was living in.

She hugged him again. "It's just that you can do better," she whispered, squeezing him, her small hands patting him gently. "You can do so much better, Jacob. Please try."

He closed his eyes and held her. "I will," he promised.

"Hud can help you. I know you've been doing all his English and history papers." She gave Hud a long look before turning to Jacob. "Let him pay you back by helping you in math, okay?"

Jacob met Hud's gaze, which was cool and assessing. Nope, there wouldn't be much help coming from that direction, for anything.

"Now shoo," Carrie said, pushing them both to the door. "I've got book club to get to." She picked up a book from her bedside table.

Fifty Shades of Grey.

Hud choked and then turned it into a cough when Carrie looked at him.

"*That's* the book you're discussing at book club today?" he asked.

"Yes," she said, her cheeks a little pink. "And don't ask me to tell you about it. There's nothing in here for thirteen-year-old boys, trust me. I'm raising you right, so I'd best not ever hear in the future—*way* in the future, when you're grown men—that you treat your women anything like Christian Grey treats his. You got me?"

Hud lifted his hands in a surrendering pose. "Jacob's the one with authority issues," he said. "Not me."

And then the rat-fink bastard darted out of the room, leaving Carrie to stare at Jacob.

He stared back, finding himself starving for her sweet warmth and affection. He flashed a smile.

She let out a breath and shook her head. "You always were the charmer."

No. He wasn't a charmer. And in fact, he was the worst sort of deserter. Yes, he'd sent money every month to support her, not that he'd ever looked at her as a financial burden. He didn't see her that way. Just as he knew she didn't see him as a grown man. In her eyes, he was still a child. The dementia had taken a lot of time from her.

And he'd wasted even more.

That was his cross to bear. He bent and brushed a kiss over her jaw. "I'll come tomorrow, okay?"

"You'd better. No more missing school, Jacob. I mean it."

With a nod, he left her room.

He'd expected Hud to be waiting for him, but the hallway was empty. He reminded himself that he'd seen Hud's face light up at the first sight of him. The rest would come.

Or so he hoped.

He felt eyes on him as he left the center but wasn't in the mood to interact with Sophie, even if she was the only thing that had made him feel better since returning to Cedar Ridge.

The warm sun hit him as he went outside. He thought about the paddleboards at the cabin and could admit he'd hoped to get out on the lake with Hud. It'd been a damn long time since he'd been carefree, with time to do whatever he wanted.

A damn long time.

He headed toward his truck and then slowed when he saw Hud leaning against the driver's door, arms casually crossed, sunglasses in place. "How did you know which vehicle was mine?"

"It's the only new truck in the lot and it looks like you."

"You waited for me," Jacob said.

"It's what I do," Hud said evenly, giving no visible indication of an emotion one way or the other. He didn't have to. His tone said it all. He'd gotten over being happy to see Jacob and had moved on to the pissed-off portion of the reunion.

Jacob got that. He deserved that. "Hud, I'm—"

"If you're going to apologize to me, fuck you."

Jacob cut off the words he'd been about to utter, which indeed had been an apology.

"Too little too late," Hud said. "I called. I emailed. I texted. I—" He shook his head and pushed away from the truck. "Never mind."

Jacob blocked Hud's escape and met his brother's eyes. Not easy when he didn't exactly know how to defend his own actions. It was complicated, far too complicated for a parking lot. "I have things to say to you," he said. "Things you're going to have to hear eventually, but Mom first."

Hud closed his eyes briefly. "Yeah. She's not doing good."

Jacob nodded, a fist tightening around his heart.

"Sometimes we're eight," Hud said. "Sometimes we're teenagers. She's stuck on those early teen years the most, probably because that's when she first began to lose it." Hud lifted a shoulder. "I just go with it. She's happiest that way, and the doctor said that was best. To keep her happy."

Jacob nodded again.

"I gotta get to work," Hud said.

Another nod. He'd become a fucking bobblehead. Not knowing how to move on, get past this, he held out his hand.

As far back as he could remember, the two of them had had a private language all their own, often able to communicate without words. They'd also had a ridiculously complicated handshake, one they'd used every time they'd greeted or left each other. So Jacob's hand went out automatically, an action born of reflexes.

But Hud just looked at Jacob's hand.

He didn't remember.

Jacob had known it wouldn't be easy to come home, but hell, he hadn't expected to look into Hud's eyes, so like his own, and feel like a complete stranger to his own twin. He dropped his hand to his side.

Hud swore, stared at his feet and then looked up again,

running a hand through hair the same light brown as Jacob's, though it was longer, curling nearly to his collar. "When the hell were you going to tell me you were home?"

Shit. Jacob hadn't felt so helpless since that time he and two others in his unit, including Brett, had been caught and tortured for two days. "I was going to come see you."

"When?"

"I don't know."

Hud turned away, and Jacob felt like he was in enemy territory and didn't know the terrain. Fucking lost with no one to watch his six, not with Brett dead and gone. "Hud."

Hud shook his head. "I have to go." Then he walked away, giving Jacob what he supposed was nothing but a taste of his own medicine.

Chapter 4

Sophie was still at the front desk when Lake Patrol Guy came down the hall a little bit later, his face blank, way too carefully blank.

She knew what that expressionless facade meant. It meant he'd been deeply affected by whatever he'd seen.

She watched him go. Correction, she watched his leanly muscled bod move effortlessly in faded-to-buttery-soft Levi's that so lovingly cupped his…assets.

And then she was flanked by the girls in the office.

"He's so damn hot," Dani whispered. "I mean, he just oozes testosterone and badassness, you know?"

The other office helper, Shelly, hummed her agreement. "Just like his brothers."

Sophie divided a look between them. "There's a pack of them?"

"The Kincaids," Dani said. "That one's Jacob, the missing Kincaid brother. He's back."

Shelly nodded. "Hud looked pissed off about it too."

"They're twins," Dani explained to Sophie's blank look. "I'm pretty sure they haven't spoken in years. Not even when Jacob called or came into town to visit his mom."

"Wonder if Jacob's seen the new mural at the resort yet," Shelly mused. "It's got all the Kincaid siblings on it, including him, which has gotta be weird, coming into town and seeing yourself painted on the side of a building."

"Yeah," Dani said dryly. "'Cuz that's what he's worried about. Not that he hasn't seen his twin or his other siblings in years, but what he looks like painted on a wall."

"Hey, you've seen that wall. You know how good he looks."

Sophie was flummoxed. She knew of the Kincaids; everyone in town did. They ran the ski resort up the road. She'd temped in the business office there for two days last week, answering phones, and she'd seen all of them several times. Gray was the oldest, then Aidan, Hudson, and Kenna.

And now that she thought of it, Hudson and her Lake Patrol Guy—Jacob—had looked alike, very much so. But Jacob was broader and more built, and his hair was military short—a direct contrast to the several-days-old scruff on his jaw. But more than anything, what set the twins apart was the air of danger and authority Jacob emitted.

Not that Hud was a pussycat by any means. As a cop and head of ski patrol at the resort, he was tough in his own right, but Jacob was a whole new level of badassery and testosterone.

"Those brothers are hot," Dani said. "And now that the resort has leased North Beach for the summer to host events, there's going to be hot guys everywhere—better than any online dating app out there."

Which meant that Sophie should put the boat up for sale. North Beach's campground was where she'd been showering, but once summer got into swing with these events and Kincaids everywhere, including Lake Patrol Jacob, it'd be too crowded for her to be able to lie low. And if she sold the boat, she could go anywhere. Except...

She didn't want to go anywhere. She loved Cedar Ridge.

"You okay, Sophie?" Shelly asked. "You've been looking a little green lately."

No, she wasn't okay. She was mad at the entire male population, thank you very much, not that she was about to admit such a weakness. Or her secret shame—Lucas had closed her accounts, forced her from her apartment, and as a result, the once-upon-a-time enviably chic, had-her-shit-together Sophie Marren had sunk just about as low as she could get.

So low that all her married friends had—politely, mind you—ditched her for Lucas. And just today she'd been dumped by her book club. On Facebook.

Humiliating.

But she'd made a choice not to care what others thought of her, including Lucas. And yet another choice, she decided on the spot, would be to fix her life. She didn't need a knight in shining armor. Especially not one with dark, melting eyes who made her feel far more than she wanted to feel.

"Sophie?" Shelly asked, sharing a worried look with Dani.

"It's nothing," she said. "I'm fine. I just need caffeine."

But caffeine didn't help.

Late that afternoon, Sophie walked to the marina and stared at *The Lucas* where she'd left it. "I hate you," she told it.

The kid standing in the booth at the marina gate about twenty feet away started laughing. "Lady, you don't know your boat very well. *The Lucas* is *awesome*."

"You think?"

"Well, sure," he said. "She rides real sweet. Or that's what your husband always says when he gets on it with—" He slammed his mouth shut and flushed a beet red. "I, uh…" He pulled his cell phone from his pocket and stared at it with desperation, like he was hoping it'd ring.

Sophie just shook her head and headed down the dock.

"Hey, wait! You forgot to pay your day fees," the kid called after her. "Twenty bucks."

Dammit. She strode over to him, shoved her hand in her purse, and pulled out her wallet. It took her a moment to scrounge it all up, but she slapped the money on the booth's counter between them.

"Remember you have to be moored by sundown or risk a fine," he said.

"I remember." She climbed onto the bane of her existence, kicked off her heels, sank to a vinyl bench, and closed her eyes.

And then jerked them open when the wake from another boat came along and jostled her. Before she could start to feel sick again, she moved to the wheel, started up the boat, and pulled out of the marina.

She'd implied to Jacob that she would be mooring at his place tonight, but hell if she really would. It took her an hour to find a stretch of beach that looked quiet. She knew she could get a ticket, but it was late enough that she hoped Jacob Kincaid had already made his patrol.

Days went by but Sophie was able to ward off further motion sickness with a prescription patch she wore on her neck. She also somehow managed to get to work and moor the boat secretively every night.

It was killing her. The constant moving around, the feeling like a thief in the night.

She'd spent the last two days working at a high-end interior designer shop that catered to the rich and wealthy second-home owners in the area. She was exhausted when, after being on her feet and running around for ten hours, she boarded the boat where she'd left it at the day dock at the campgrounds on the south side.

She levered the throttle and let the sun and wind hit her face, and for a moment, just a single beat of a moment, she enjoyed herself. But eventually reality sank in. She needed to find a place before nightfall. She'd used up all her secret spots and after half an hour ended up at the cabin where everything had started. It took her a few minutes to tie the boat properly, but a lot less time than it used to.

She was out of options and had nowhere else to go, no one to turn to—at least no one she was *willing* to turn to.

She could leave town entirely. She knew this. She could sell the boat and go. But it wasn't Cedar Ridge making her unhappy. In fact, she loved it here. She wouldn't let Lucas take this town from her. He'd taken enough, and she was over it.

Besides, where would she go? Back to Dallas? Brooklyn, her sister, was a few years older than Sophie. She had her life together and didn't need the hassle of a baby sister whose life was in the toilet. Her parents were in Dallas, too, but she couldn't go there.

It wasn't until she'd left for college at age eighteen with two hundred bucks in her pocket and an ancient VW that she'd realized there was nothing normal about a father who, on good days, would sit like a zombie on the couch with a month-old beard, unshowered because he was too "tired of living" to get it together to help his daughter with her math homework—even though once upon a time he'd been a brilliant physicist. And on bad days…She closed her eyes at the memory of having to shut all the shades in the house and keep the lights off, not making a single sound for sometimes forty-eight hours or more at a time, not even the creaking of the wood floors beneath her feet, because her dad's migraines had been so bad.

No, she was satisfied with the semiannual visits she made to put in her time, to help out however she could. But more than that and she was afraid she'd end up like her dad and forget how to be happy, afraid she'd return to that shell of herself.

She was over doing that, for anyone.

The sun had begun to sink behind the mountain peaks now, casting the water in a brilliant glow, making it glitter like a bed of diamonds. In a single heartbeat the air shifted from warm to chilly, and she shivered.

She hadn't been able to get the heater below deck going, not once. And since she wasn't at the campground, her shower would be short, have the water pressure of an eye dropper, and be holy-shit icy cold. But she'd been saving something that would cheer her up.

She went to the tiny galley and grabbed the bottle of Glenlivet she'd found hidden on her first night out here. It'd been shoved way in the back of a cabinet, forgotten, though the moment she'd seen it, she'd known what it was.

The Scotch that Lucas had purchased on the same day he'd bought the boat and kept on board to show off to his guests. She'd asked him once why he never drank it, and he'd barked out a laugh.

"It's special," he'd said mysteriously. "I'm saving it for something special."

She had no idea what that *something special* might've been, but she suspected divorcing her had been high on the list of options.

Good thing the last laugh was on him. "Finders keepers," she murmured, and grabbed it, along with the small can of paint she'd purchased at the hardware store on the walk home.

Knowing it would be cold on deck, she searched for her jacket but couldn't find it. Then she remembered she'd had it in her car—the one Lucas had taken back.

Shrugging, she pulled her fuzzy, thick pink bathrobe on right over the sundress she'd worn to work and headed up to the deck.

She went out to the dock and eyed the words on the hull—*The Lucas*.

Who named their boat after themselves? Asswads with egos bigger than their dicks, that's who.

She opened the can and very carefully made an adjustment. *The Lucas* became…*The Little Lucas*.

She stood on the dock and eyeballed it with a pleased smile. Better. Much better.

She'd just finished with another extra swirl and was feeling righteous when someone with very long legs crouched at her side.

She looked up, and her gaze collided with Jacob of the dark sunglasses and darker smile. He stood there in a white long-sleeved Henley and an unbelievably fine-fitting pair of faded jeans. "You I'm not speaking to," she said.

He didn't appear in the least bit bothered by this. "*The Little Lucas*," he read. "I like it. How have you been?"

Not wanting to think about how his nonjudgmental smile and words warmed her. "Great." She went to smash the bottle of Glenlivet against the hull, but he caught her wrist.

"What are you doing?" he asked.

"Rechristening the boat."

"That seems like a waste of a very good twenty-five-year-old Scotch."

She gave him a long look.

He smiled. "Right. You're still not speaking to me. And just for curiosity's sake, why is that again?"

"I'm into making new and improved choices for myself," she said. "And not repeating any bad patterns is one of those new choices."

"I'm a bad pattern?"

"The worst."

He seemed amused by this.

"And plus, you didn't tell me you were one of the infamous Kincaid brothers," she said.

He shrugged. "Been away long enough that I don't necessarily feel like one of them right now."

This stopped her. Up until now she'd seen him as only Lake Patrol Guy, an authority figure she could happily and easily resent. Dislike.

But suddenly he was also a real man, and given that carefully blank look on his face and the hint of pain in his eyes, he was also much more. He was flesh and blood, with feelings and emotions, no matter how well hidden. It shamed her a little bit because she realized she wasn't the only one hurting. He was just better at hiding it than she.

Proving it, he gestured to the bottle. "I can drink without speaking," he said. "How about you?"

Sophie thought about that for a minute. "I was going to watch it dump into the water with great enthusiasm."

He cocked his head, his eyes hooded, a slight curve to his lips. "Why?"

She decided to answer only because he wasn't judging her, not because he had focused those warm chocolate-brown eyes on her. "It belonged to my ex-husband, and he's the king of all the assholes in all the land."

"A good reason," he said agreeably. "Except for the flaw."

"The flaw?" she asked mistrustfully.

"That bottle probably cost close to four hundred bucks."

Shocked, she stared at him. Lucas had cut her off without a penny to her name. She'd been dodging lake patrol because she couldn't afford a boat pass for going on two weeks now. He'd made her a criminal. "That asshole," she finally whispered around a tight throat. But oh, hell no was she going to cry. She refused to shed a single tear over the disaster she'd let a man make of her life.

But damn. Letting out a breath, she jerked from Jacob's hold and struggled to open the bottle. The alcohol was so going down.

Again he reached in and stilled her frantic movements. Slowly, like he was dealing with a deranged chick—which he totally was—he pried the bottle from her clutches and opened it without straining in the slightest, although the muscles in his arms moved quite enticingly. Then he offered the bottle to her.

She accepted it, lifted it in a mocking toast, took a tentative sip, and promptly choked.

Grinning, he took the bottle.

"Are you allowed to drink on duty?" she asked.

He gave her an odd look. "I'm not on duty right now." He gestured to the cabin behind her. Now that it was becoming dark, she could see the cabin was lit up from within, looking homey and inviting. And she'd somehow missed the fact that there was a new truck parked in the driveway next to it.

"I saw you from the front porch," he said.

"You bought the cabin?"

"Rented it." And then he took a pull of the Scotch as well. And didn't choke.

She watched his Adam's apple move as he swallowed. She stared at the stubble on his jaw and the way the corners of his eyes crinkled when he relaxed a little bit. And then there was his mouth. Pulling the bottle away from that mouth, he licked his lips, and from deep within her came a…quiver.

Not good. So. Not. Good. She already knew she couldn't make a smart decision to save her life under the best of circumstances, of which this most definitely wasn't.

"Something I said?" he asked wryly as she backed away.

"No." *Yes*. She paused, because in truth she had no idea.

What she *did* know was that he churned her up, big-time—though she'd go to hell and back before admitting such a thing. "I've gotta go," she said, and bolted below-decks. She closed the door and then pressed an ear to it, listening, hoping to hear his footsteps moving off.

She heard nothing.

But then again, she hadn't heard him coming either. For such a big guy, he'd sneaked up on her several times now, and that made her nervous, very nervous.

Lucas had been big too, and also sneaky.

And sometimes mean.

Which was why Jacob's obvious virility was a problem. He moved like a cat. A big, sleek, lethally sexy cat…

She froze at that. She backed up the thought and ran it by herself again. A big, sleek, lethally sexy cat…? No. No, no, no, no. Jacob was *not* sexy, not in the slightest.

Except he was.

The truth was, Jacob was so damn sexy she couldn't see straight for all the wanting and yearning he'd caused inside her, and that was the biggest problem of all.

Did she want to rediscover herself and reclaim her sexuality? Sure. And if that happened, great. But she didn't want more than that. She didn't want to get emotionally invested, or worse, fall for him. Because falling was dangerous and made her stupid, and she'd made a conscious choice not to do either of those things ever again.

Chapter 5

When she was gone, Jacob stayed where he was. She'd made him smile. She'd made him laugh. The muscles around his mouth had pulled like they were rusty, and they were. Smiling had felt foreign and odd and...

Good.

"Sophie," he said to the door, knowing she was listening. He could feel her nerves through the wood. It bothered him that he made her nervous. He wanted to make her smile. Maybe make her want him as much as he wanted her. But he didn't want to scare her. "It's considered rude to leave a guest out here drinking alone," he teased.

She didn't bite. The door remained firmly shut.

He couldn't hear anything from the other side, but he was pretty sure her emotions could supply enough energy to light up the entire western hemisphere. Thinking about her reaction to the price of the Scotch, he stood and moved to the door. She'd seemed far more hurt than mad, and that sucked.

"Come out," he said quietly, knowing she could hear every word. "I'll help you waste some more of the Glenlivet."

Nothing but a very loaded silence.

Willing to wait her out, he sat again, leaned his head back, and watched the last of the day's light vanish behind an entire spectrum of blues and purples streaking across the sky. Been a damn long time since he'd caught a Rocky Mountain sunset. There'd been a lot of "been a damn long times" here in Cedar Ridge since he'd returned.

And none of it was exactly comfortable.

The water slapped against the dock and the boat. Insects hummed. The air was scented with pine, and all of it evoked more memories than he knew what to do with.

He and Hud had ridden around this lake on their bikes. Made rope swings in trees and judged their own crazy entries into the water. Had climbed the peaks and camped out as often as they could. When they'd hit fifteen, they'd gone to work at the resort their father had deserted, making it their own. Had spent the next three years getting closer to their half siblings Gray and Aidan. And then Kenna, as well, once she'd come along.

He realized he was smiling again, though it faded when he remembered what had come next.

Him leaving.

Walking away.

He turned his head at the sound of someone approaching on the dock, a tall, pretty brunette in painted-on jeans shorts and a white tank top, her high-heeled sandals defying logic and gravity as they carried her to the boat.

She eyed the bottle of Glenlivet and her eyes lit up. "Is it a party?"

"Excuse me?" he asked.

She smiled, extremely friendly-like. "Is Lucas having a

party? He didn't mention it." She looked around. "We have a long-standing once-a-week date here in front of the empty cabin. Where is he?"

He could almost feel Sophie stop breathing from below-decks. Could imagine her green eyes narrowing, see the steam coming out of her ears. Damn, that would be hot. But that wasn't why he did what he did. Nope. It was because he felt like he owed her one. "First of all, the cabin's no longer empty. And second, Lucas...passed," he told the woman.

"Like...gas? He passed gas?" she asked, confused. "That's nothing new. He always does that."

"Not gas," Jacob said.

The woman stared at him and then gasped, hand to her chest. "You mean he's...?"

Jacob nodded.

"That asshole!" she yelled. "He promised me a diamond bracelet!" Whirling, she went running—and loudly sobbing—up the dock.

Sophie stormed out. "Hey," she said, every bit as magnificent as he'd known she would be, eyes flashing, all that wild red hair in uncontrollable motion around her face. "That's *my* lie! You can't lie about someone you don't even know!"

Jacob shrugged. "I just gave her the information I'd been told."

"You didn't even have to say the words."

"That would've been mean. If she misunderstood my silence, that's on her."

She stared at him for a beat. "Are you saying I'm mean?"

"Yes." He smiled. "But I like mean on you. It's sexy. Kind of like your pink robe."

"You're a sick man."

"There is no doubt."

She shook her head at him, but he could tell she was smiling on the inside. He'd meant what he'd said about the robe, the one that should have made her look fifty years old but instead made him want to pull her to him and nuzzle her.

Crazy. She was crazy. And so was he. Because he wasn't sure what it was about her that had him so interested. He had no idea why he wanted to keep whatever this tentative connection was that they had going, but he did.

He offered her the bottle of Scotch.

She met his gaze, her dilemma evident. She couldn't reach it unless he stood. He didn't, hoping that instead, she'd move closer.

She hesitated, but he waited her out, doing his best to look harmless. When she finally took the few steps, he felt like he'd won the lottery and casually nodded to the bench for her to sit.

Instead, she crossed her arms. That bathrobe hid what he knew was a God-given figure with curves that could make a grown man forget he didn't know how to love.

She eyed the bench a long beat but did eventually sit, perching primly as far from him as she could get and yet still be close enough to grab the bottle.

Smart woman.

She took the Scotch and drank. Her eyes watered and she coughed as she handed it to him. With a sigh, she leaned back to study the night sky. Her bared throat was slim and creamy smooth. An unexpected temptation. Remembering the flash of pain and vulnerability she'd unwittingly revealed, and that for whatever reason he'd somehow added to it, he spoke. "I'm sorry."

She glanced at him as if she'd never heard a man apologize before in her life. "For…breathing?" she asked. "Having a penis? What?"

"You were upset because you didn't know I was a Kincaid."

She sighed. "That was just me looking for a reason to be mad at you so I wouldn't…" She bit her lower lip, clearly not wanting to go on.

But now he had to know. "So you wouldn't what?"

"Nothing," she said. "It's just that I'm trying to make better choices."

"Of which I wouldn't be one."

"It's not necessarily your fault," she said. "It's that you're a man."

"Guilty as charged."

"And I'm off men right now."

"And on…women?" he asked with admittedly more than a little fascination.

She rolled her eyes. "I'm on *no one*, but thank you for proving my point on men."

"I get that," he said. "But being off men doesn't seem to be making you very happy, or sound like a whole lot of fun."

"Maybe I don't need fun."

He understood that. He'd felt the same way since Brett died. "What *do* you need?" he asked, honestly wanting to know more about her.

Instead of answering, she reached for the bottle. He waited until she met his gaze before letting go.

"Nothing," she said a little too quickly. "Everything's… perfect."

"And your glass is half full," he said. "So you've said." But he didn't believe her. "How about a game?"

"I don't play games."

Now, that wasn't exactly true. Whether she knew it or not, she'd been playing with his head since he'd first laid eyes on her. "Three truths and a lie," he said.

She stared at him. "As in you tell me three truths and a lie, and I pick out the lie?"

"Yes."

She considered this. "What do I get if I win?"

"What do you want?"

For the briefest of beats, her gaze dropped to his mouth. Oh, hell yeah, he thought. *Want me…*

"My first boyfriend taught me that game," she said.

"What did the winner get?"

"A kiss."

Definitely still playing with his head… "Is that what you want, Sophie? A kiss?"

Again she stared at his mouth before dropping eye contact and wrapping that eye-stopping pink robe tighter around her body. "Do *you*?" she asked.

"Hell yes."

Her gaze flew to his.

"Problem is," he said conversationally, "if I kissed you, I don't think I'd be able to stop."

Her mouth literally fell open. The pulse at the base of her throat jumped. And she seemed to lose her words.

He went on. "But you should know, I don't lose. That means you'll have to tell me three truths and a lie."

And he'd hopefully get to know more about her.

She closed her mouth to bite her lower lip in what could've been indecision or excitement. Obviously he was hoping for the latter. "But hey, if you're not sure you can handle losing, we can just forget about it," he said.

The challenge lifted her chin and put sparks in her eyes. *That's it, babe. Show me what you've got.*

"Bring it," she said. "Three truths and a lie, and if I guess the lie, I…" Again, she tortured her lower lip.

"Say it, Sophie."

She squirmed a little bit. "I kiss you."

"And in reverse?"

She paused, and he cocked a brow. "You kiss me," she said softly but with unmistakable interest.

Christmas in June.

"Another drink first," she said, and took hers before giving him the bottle. Holding her gaze, he drank too.

"You go first," she said.

"Hell no," he said on a low laugh.

"Why not?" she demanded.

"You're a flight risk."

"How do you know that?"

"Because you've already run away from me at least twice now. Plus, you're eyeing the alcohol like it's a Hawaiian getaway."

She tilted her head and studied him frankly, not playing shy or coy in the slightest. She'd been right—she didn't play games—and he realized he was smiling again. Clearly she was down but not out, and he liked her attitude. He liked it a lot.

"Fine," she said. "I'll go first, you big baby. But there's no way you'll be able to pick out my lie." She said this smugly. "No one can ever tell when I'm lying."

He knew that was probably true. For all her fiery temperament, she was all talk, no go. She hid behind the tough-girl facade, and clearly the people in her life had let her.

But he knew a little something about hiding, too, and it hadn't ever worked out well for him. He was changing that. And if *he* had to, well, they said misery loved company. He smiled. "Try me," he said. "And no 'my favorite color is red and I like long walks on the beach and I'm a natural blonde and I hate ice cream' bullshit either. It's gotta be something good. In fact, I think the other person gets to set the topic. And the topic I set for you is…reasons you're on this boat you hate. Go."

She rolled her lips together, eyes on his as she thought so hard he could practically hear the wheels spinning. "Okay," she finally said. "One, I love this boat very much. Two, I happen to think it's very freeing to live out here on the water, very freeing. Three, there's nowhere else I'd rather be. And four, I'm just waiting for my overnight boat pass to be approved and then I can better settle in and won't bother you again." She turned her face skyward and closed her eyes, like all was right in her world and she hadn't just fed him four fat lies.

He took another drink, and when she finally opened her eyes and looked at him, he handed her the bottle to do the same.

"Well?" she demanded.

He nudged the bottle to her lips and watched as she took a sip. "You cheated," he said.

She choked on a laugh and coughed.

And coughed.

Thinking she was going to lose a lung, he leaned in and rubbed her back firmly, absolutely not noticing how soft her skin was or how she felt beneath his hand.

Much.

Finally, she swiped her eyes and gave him a look from beneath lowered lashes. "I don't know what you're talking about."

"You cheated," he said again, "because *all* of your answers were lies."

Her eyes widened in surprise. When she opened her mouth, he shook his head, cutting off whatever she might have said next. "Don't make it worse for yourself by adding yet another lie," he teased.

She let out a low laugh. "No one's ever been able to tell—"

"Oh, you're good," he assured her. "I'm just better."

She looked intrigued at this, like maybe she was realizing they both had their ghosts. "Hmm," she said.

"Cheaters pay a penance. You know that, right?"

She gave him a sideways look. "Do they, now?" she asked, voice softer. Playing a little, he thought, which made his night.

"Yes." His voice was husky now too. Jesus. This had gone from a playful game to something hot and seductive in a blink. "Maybe you'd like to reconsider some of your answers rather than pay the price."

She thought about that and…didn't change any of her answers.

Chapter 6

Sophie's mind was scrambling like a cat trying to get purchase on slick linoleum. Her heart pounded hard against her ribs and her breath caught in her lungs.

How had he known that she was just one big, fancy liar?

And more importantly...*what now?* Still as stone, she eyeballed him, considering her options. Run like hell? No. This was her boat and she no longer ran from anything. Let this play out? That seemed...terrifying, especially given their unexpected nuclear sexual chemistry.

And then there was the smart thing to do. Hold back.

But she'd never been all that good at self-restraint.

In direct opposition to her inner panic, Jacob was relaxed as he gazed at her, waiting patiently for her to...what exactly?

Lucas had been in perpetual motion, always moving with high-strung nervous energy that had made her own nerves leap.

Jacob was the opposite. He sat there, long legs sprawled out in front of him, one arm out along the back of the seat, the opposite hand—large and capable-looking—easily holding the bottle steady on a thigh. He was relaxed and utterly still.

There was no hiding from him, and that was new for her. The people in her life had always let her retreat, mostly because it'd been an easy way to not have to deal with her.

Jacob smiled at her prolonged—and let's face it, unusual—silence. "Scared?" he asked.

"Hell no," she said. *Lie number five…*

His smile turned into a grin. A Cheshire-cat grin. Had she been cold only a few minutes ago? Because suddenly she was sweating and fumbled to drop her heavy bathrobe.

"A striptease isn't going to save you, but I'm game for you to try."

She froze in the act of shrugging out of the robe and choked out a laugh. "Do lines like that ever work for you?"

He grinned that lethal grin, and instead of answering, crooked a finger at her, the universal sign for *Get your ass over here*.

A part of her wanted to flee, but apparently a bigger part wanted to throw herself at him, because she heard herself say, "Just tell me the penance already."

Good Lord. Not *Take a hike* or *Eff off*…just *Tell me the penance*.

Seriously? she asked herself, and perfect, now she was actually sweating. Around them, the temp had dropped, but she was sweating.

Unlike her, Jacob showed no sign of sweating, or being ruffled in the slightest. Instead, he cocked his head and studied her like a bug on a slide. Except she didn't feel like a bug. Not with his eyes so dark and warm, his lips curved in a way that made her own mouth dry.

She wanted that damn kiss. Wanted it bad too. Which

settled it—she needed to sell the boat and get her own place with a nice hot shower that had a handheld showerhead so she could go back to taking care of her own business, business that she'd sadly neglected lately.

When the corners of his mouth curved further, more panic filled her. What if he could read her mind?

Reaching out, he wrapped his hand around her wrist, tugging until she stood directly in front of him, looking down at his big, hard body sprawled out on her bench.

"I want four straight truths," he murmured softly, staring up at her. "And then I want my original reward."

The kiss.

Her knees quivered. Other parts did too. And an intense heat flashed through her, but she had a decent sense of self-preservation, and her inner alarm was going off now. This man was a danger to her mental stability. And maybe her heart too.

And yet she still didn't run. "My truths are ugly," she said.

And they were. She'd grown up with a father who'd been ill a lot of the time, and when he hadn't been ill, he'd been deeply depressed. She'd spent most of her childhood trying to get his attention, to please him, but neither had ever happened. So what had she done? She'd fallen in love with the first guy who'd turned his head for her and given her an ounce of attention—a guy who'd been rich and charming and utterly unreachable.

And she'd never been able to reach or please him either.

Of course, she'd then compounded her error and had married him young. Not even twenty-one when she'd given him her vows, she'd spent the next few years knowing she wasn't good enough for him and never would be, no matter how much she tried.

And she'd tried it all. There'd been a lot to do as Mrs. Lucas Worthington III. It'd been exciting for about a month and then…completely overwhelming.

Sophie'd had a life before she'd married Lucas. She'd worked at a law firm, heading toward becoming a paralegal, and had loved the demanding work. She'd had her own friends. But being Lucas's wife had come with a lot of demands. Too many to half-ass it. Needing to make him happy, she'd given up her own ties *and* the job she'd loved to do the Stepford wife thing. She'd joined the Junior League for Lucas's business, doing everything she could to make his life easier.

While losing her own. "*Very* ugly," she added softly.

Jacob ran the pad of his thumb over their entwined fingers. "We all have ugly truths," he said.

She knew that. And though she didn't trust him—she didn't trust *anyone*—she somehow knew that if she was honest, he would be too. She had no idea how she knew this about him, a perfect stranger, she just did.

Unable to think clearly with his hand on her, she pulled free and sat down. She pulled her legs up close and wrapped her arms around them. "One." She sucked in a deep breath, and there in the dark of the night, admitted her mistakes. "I married the first man to give me the slightest bit of attention because I was young and stupid and way too trusting."

Jacob nodded, noncommittal, not judging, and somehow that gave her the courage to go on. "Two, I compounded my error by giving up my life to help him live his." She paused, but Jacob still sat there, calmly, quietly, like he had all the time in the world for her.

"Three," she went on. "Predictably, I couldn't please him, and it was like with my dad all over again. The harder I tried, the worse it got, until I completely lost myself—my own fault." God. This was hard. "And four…" She paused. Four was the worst one to admit because it made her an active participant in what had proven to be the lowest point of her life. She closed her eyes and dropped her forehead to her knees, not wanting to see what he thought of her when she made the confession. "In retribution, in the divorce I took the one thing he loved above all else. I wanted to hurt him, and now I'm the stupid one who has nothing but this stupid boat."

Jacob didn't speak.

Sophie let out a slow breath and stayed still, telling herself there was no reason to be embarrassed. What did she care what he thought of her? But oh, how she wished he'd speak.

She startled when one of Jacob's big hands stroked up her back and settled on the nape of her neck. Warm. Sure. "Did he hurt you, Sophie?" he asked.

God, the care in his voice, layered with absolute steel. "Not the way you think," she managed. "Not…physically."

His thumb stroked over her skin, rough with calluses but somehow comforting. "There's a lot of ways to hurt someone," he finally said. "To make them bleed."

The utter truth. And since she didn't trust herself to speak, she didn't.

"Little Lucas is an idiot," he said.

A shocked laugh bubbled out of her, and she lifted her head as her heart began a heavy beat. Because she knew what was coming next.

The kiss.

Her gaze fell to his lips, which seemed to curve slightly. "You going to give me a topic?" he asked.

She blinked. "Topic?"

"For *my* three truths and a lie."

Oh. Right. He'd just given her a stay from paying up. Even if she wasn't all that sure she wanted one. "Your topic is..." There were so many things she wanted to know about him. Where he'd been, what he'd been doing, if he was staying...But he'd been good to her, so she started with what she thought might be the easiest for him. "What brought you back to Cedar Ridge?"

He took a long pull on the bottle and offered it to her. She drank, too, incredibly aware that her mouth was right where his had just been.

He appeared to think about his answers for a moment before speaking. "One," he said quietly. "For the past nine years, the military's been my family. Two, I just recently lost someone close to me there, someone I thought of as a brother. Three, afterward I realized I had blood family that I'd walked away from and shouldn't have. Four..." He shrugged. "So I came back. It was natural for me to do so. There's a lot for me to do here, work-wise and family-wise."

She was pretty amazed at his work ethic, that he'd take on lake patrol shifts while on leave...and also impressed that he wanted to make things right with his family. That said a lot about him.

And he'd been right when he'd said he was good at this game. He was good. But maybe because pain recognized pain, she could easily see his lie.

A few minutes ago Jacob had wanted nothing more than to have five minutes alone with Sophie's ex for ever making this warm, sweet, sexy, *amazing* woman hurt, however he'd hurt her.

But then she'd switched the game up on him, put *him* beneath the microscope, and that sucked. He waited while she studied him, but it sure wasn't easy, not after he'd just unintentionally stripped himself bare-ass naked for her.

Or maybe it had been intentional. Maybe he'd wanted someone to hear him, to forgive him.

Turning the bottle in his hand, he studied the way the light from the boat's control panel shined through the liquid, which was how his legs felt at the moment. Liquid. Good thing he was sitting down.

Her voice washed over him. "Four's the lie."

He didn't ask how she knew. Somehow, as the night had fallen, the sky going black, cocooning them into the illusion that they were entirely alone on the planet, creating a sensation of intimacy, it didn't matter that she'd seen right through him.

"And you cheated too," she said. "Because it was only half a lie. You came back, but it wasn't natural at all, was it?"

He slowly shook his head.

Unbelievably, she used his own tactic against him and waited him out. He couldn't remember anyone ever doing that before.

Nor had he ever cared. He told himself he didn't care now, that the Scotch had just gone to his head. But the truth was that *Sophie Marren* had gone to his head. Sophie of the sharp yet somehow vulnerable eyes, Sophie with the sweet laugh and sexy body, just out of arm's reach… "I made a mistake in walking away from my family like I did," he said. "At the time I thought I had no choice, but I was wrong, something I didn't realize until…" Christ. He closed his mouth, unable to spell it out.

Sophie slid her hand into his and squeezed as if she was willing her strength to become his. "Your brother-in-arms died," she finished for him gently.

"Brett," he managed. "Killed in a roadside bombing."

Soft green eyes cradled his. "I can't even imagine," she said. "But you know it wasn't your fault, right?"

"Yeah." He paused and then admitted the rest. "But I feel guilty all the same."

"Life's unfair," she said. "Bitterly so. But being home again must be a bittersweet silver lining?"

Because her gaze was so clear and deep, making him feel exposed, something he didn't do ever, he closed his eyes. "Coming here is about guilt too," he said. "I just kept thinking if it'd been me who'd died, Hud would've gotten a letter or someone at the door. After all those years of not seeing him, a stranger would've had to say good-bye for me. I was selfish to stay away from him for so long."

"What about your mom?"

He opened his eyes and stared at her. Shit. She was a sharp one. "I've seen her," he said, admitting a truth he'd told no one before, not even Hud. "I came into town whenever I was on leave to check on her."

She raised a brow. "Hud didn't know?"

He shook his head. "We fought right before I left, when we were eighteen. He said…"

He let out a breath, remembering it as if it were yesterday.

"What?" Sophie asked quietly. "He said what?"

"He said if I left, I should stay gone because we were no longer brothers."

"Oh, Jacob," she breathed. "And you believed him?"

"I absolutely believed him then," Jacob said. "And by the time I didn't, too many years had gone by. It was too late."

"I believe it's never too late." She cupped his face and stared into his eyes, her own glossy and a little bit crossed as she focused in on him with such fierce concentration that he had to smile.

"What are you doing?" he asked.

"I don't want to take away from this conversation we're having," she said slowly, "but I think I'm maybe a little bit drunk. And you should know, when I'm drunk, I'm always right."

That wrung a low laugh out of him.

"No, I'm serious. I know I'm responsible for what happened to me, for letting my emotions take over, for choosing this boat over the house. I was stupid and childish, but luckily, I learn from my mistakes. And part of what I learned is that love isn't for me. I just don't have the same level of emotions I used to have. It's…broken. I'm broken. But I know that about myself and I'll use that knowledge, making sure I keep relationships light. Open. *Not* love." She paused and looked at him from beneath hooded eyes. "What did you learn from your mistakes?"

He stared at her, aching that she believed that she wasn't meant for love. But he wasn't either, so he wasn't one to talk. "I learned that walking away was bullshit. I went to see my mom and ran into Hud before I could call him."

"How did it go?" she asked, looking like she already knew the answer.

"Not well," he admitted. *And how did you expect it to go, genius? You didn't even call him. You just happened upon him at the hospital.*

It'd been cold. And wrong. "So actually, no, I haven't learned from my mistakes, but that's going to change."

"How?" she asked.

"You know, you're a little…"

"Pushy?" she asked. "Annoying?"

"Different," he corrected. "In a good way." A very good way…He paused. "You said you can't do love, not ever again. But for me, it's not that I can't. It's that I won't." He thought of how it felt to walk away from his family. Like he'd ripped off a limb. And losing Brett had nearly killed him. He shuddered. "Love isn't for me, never will be."

She took that in, looked like maybe she'd argue the fact, but then changed her mind. "So are you going to go away again?"

"I'm on leave," he said. "I still have to go back to finish. I don't have a choice there."

"And then what? After you finish? And truth," she said with a small smile. "Or *you'll* owe *me*."

He wouldn't mind that one little bit, but he surprised himself by answering honestly. "I'll be back. To stay." He met her gaze. "Now you. Why do you stay here, in a town where you were so badly hurt? What holds you here?"

She hedged, biting her lower lip, tipping him off to yet another truth.

She hadn't told him her entire story.

Somehow she'd pulled off what no one else could, getting him to let down his guard and open up. A little terrifying. "Where's your family?"

"Dallas."

He smiled. "I knew I heard the South in you."

"You do not," she said with a definite twang.

He smiled. "It comes out when you're especially irritated."

"It does not," she said, twang heavier now.

He laughed, and she crossed her arms. "There's nothing wrong with that," she said.

"Of course not. And the accent's hot."

She looked torn between being embarrassed and pleased.

"Tell me about your family," he said.

She reached for the bottle. He obliged.

She tossed back another gulp and then proceeded to nearly cough up another lung.

"You all right?" he asked.

"Never better." She let out a long exhale. "Okay, let's see. My mom and dad live in a house they got from my grandparents, who also grew up in Dallas. My sister lives close by with her husband and two kids. She's a nurse and has the perfect life. My mom's a saint who takes care of my dad."

"He sick?"

"Depressed," she said, surprising him. Her voice had changed to practically a whisper, like it was hard to say. Hard and painful, and he wanted to pull her in close and hold her. Not because he wanted to bury himself inside her—which, for the record, he did—but because he felt compelled to ease her pain.

"It's debilitating," she said, "and he can't take care of himself."

She'd already told him she'd been unable to please the guy, and he ached for the little girl she'd been, for the young woman who'd been further hurt by the next man in her life because her husband hadn't given her himself either. If she were his, Jacob thought, he'd make damn sure she felt loved. But she wasn't his. And given that he'd told her he didn't do love, she never would be.

And she told you she couldn't love. But he didn't want to believe that, didn't want to think of her so beautiful, so animated, thinking she was incapable of love.

"My dad worked for NASA as a physicist," she said. "He was under a lot of stress. Something cracked deep inside him at all the pressure, and now he does…well, nothing, really." She shrugged again. "I think that's why I stay on the boat for now. I've learned that when you don't know what to do, you do nothing. Otherwise you get yourself in bigger trouble. The boat…me living on it…it's me not doing anything until I know exactly what to do."

He wanted to argue, wanted to tell her she deserved more, but who the hell was he to judge? "It'll come to you," he said.

"Yeah. I know." She chewed on her bottom lip, belying her confidence, making him ache for her because she didn't know if it would come to her.

"It's no biggie," she said with false cheer. "I'm like a rubber ball. I always bounce back. It's a hard-earned talent." She stood up. "Look, it's late. Game's over, and we're both big losers."

"No, we're not."

Slowly she turned to him, her eyes lit with challenge as she silently dared him. "No?"

He rose to his feet. "No."

She tap-danced in place, looking torn between running for the hills and dying of curiosity, and Christ, she drew him in like no other.

"Are you talking about…the kiss?" she whispered.

"You know I am." He took one of her hands and slowly reeled her in, keeping his hold on her light, making it clear that she was the one in control here.

But she shocked the hell out of him by not resisting in the slightest, in fact using her momentum to tumble into him. Balancing herself with her hands on his arms, she went up on tiptoes, her entire weight braced on his chest like she trusted him to keep her from falling.

The realization stunned him.

"Problem," she whispered.

Yeah, there was a problem. Hell, there was a big problem. She felt way too good against him. He was already hard and had been since they'd first said *kiss*. And then there was the sobering fact that she was a mess, and so was he…

She didn't take her eyes from his. They were so close, they were sharing air.

"The problem?" he reminded her.

"Right." She cleared her throat. "Technically it's more than one kiss owed. I owe you one and you owe me one, so that's…"

"Two," he said, tightening his grip on her. "Two kisses."

"Yes." She took a step back and came up against the captain's chair.

Worked for him.

Still holding her hand, he planted his other palm against the chair at her hip, pinning her in place. Then he lowered his head and brushed her mouth with his once. And then again. And as he pulled free, she followed with a soft whimper for more.

With a surge of sheer, unadulterated lust, he captured her mouth again, swallowing her soft moan, taking his time now, letting himself sink into the first real pleasure he'd felt in…too damn long. The feel of her hands on his chest egged him on as she slowly fisted her fingers in his shirt, a low whimper coming from deep in her throat. She tasted like the Scotch, warm woman, and the very best kind of trouble.

Ending the kiss, he stared at her. She was breathless, her eyes revealing what he knew was in his as well—equal parts lust and shock.

"Uh-oh," she whispered.

Yeah. No shit.

"Jacob?" She licked her lips. "Remember how you said you weren't going do love, not ever again?"

"Yeah."

"I'm going to need you to promise me."

He would have sworn nothing could surprise him, but this woman continually did. "What?"

"I just need to make sure," she said. "Because if you

promise me, then I know I can't hurt you. And I don't want to hurt you."

There was an endearingly earnest—almost desperately so—look in her eyes that made his chest feel too tight.

"Sophie." He pressed his forehead to hers. "You don't need to worry about me."

"No, you have to *promise*," she said with a level of urgency that had him cuddling her to him and giving her what she wanted.

"I promise," he said.

"You promise not to fall for me," she said seriously. "No matter how lovable I am?"

He wanted to smile at that but didn't want her to think he was making fun. She wanted his word, and he could give it easily enough, confident that as adorably sexy as she was, he could refrain from falling for her, since his heart felt dead in his chest. "I promise."

Chapter 7

Jacob's words relieved Sophie so much that she nearly collapsed. There was freedom in knowing that this thing between them couldn't go anywhere.

Except hopefully to bed.

He was on leave, and his time here wasn't his own. He was working lake patrol shifts and he was here to make things right with his family. He was too busy for a relationship, other than a sexual one.

It'd been a long time since she'd felt like a sensual creature of any kind, but need and hunger were rolling through her now, nudging at her good spots. And actually, it was more than nudging. It was washing over her in waves. Need. Hunger. *Desire.*

And best yet, she saw the way Jacob's eyes had darkened, the way the same need and hunger she felt had tightened his body.

Still not speaking, he caressed the hair falling over her

temple, drawing his finger slowly along her jaw to the corner of her mouth. He paused and then once again leaned in.

She didn't hesitate to press in to him, or to moan when he kissed her again. He kept things gentle, his hands warm at her back, his lips caressing hers.

But she didn't want gentle. Little shocks of need were racing through her, and she leaned in to him, finding his hard body in complete opposition to the softness of his touch. She could feel how restrained he held himself and wanted to rip at that tight control, unleash the power he was so clearly working hard at keeping reined in. "Jacob."

"Yeah?"

She bit down on his lower lip and then slid her mouth slowly across his.

He pulled his mouth away a fraction and stared into her eyes. She stared back, seeing the reflection of her own heavy-lidded expression. His eyes darkened, flamed, telling her he could read her like a book, which made her stomach clench with excitement. "You in a hurry?" he asked, voice low and sexy as hell.

"Yes!"

He flashed a smile and then kissed her again, this time deeply, hungrily. The night, the moon, the stars, everything spun around her in a delicious whirl.

It was the alcohol, she told herself, but she knew that wasn't it.

It was Jacob, and right then and there her entire belief that this kind of chemistry didn't exist went up in smoke—just poof, gone.

And she was okay with it because, holy cow, this crazy heat had a lot going for it. As long as they were doing this, she could let herself go just a little bit. Because lust was okay. She could handle lust. *Was* handling it just fine, as both of her hands were full of Jacob. She wanted to touch everywhere: his broad shoulders, the biceps that were hard as rocks, his chest so warm and solid and pressed to hers. God. God, she couldn't get enough, and she was thinking of ripping her clothes off when he used the hand he'd entwined in her hair to pull free of her.

"What?" she gasped.

He stared into her eyes. "Just making sure we don't take this further than you bargained for."

A sexy, alpha gentleman. She'd never wanted anyone like she wanted him. Slowly she shook her head.

"No, it's not more than you bargained for?" he asked. "Or no, you want to stop?"

"If you stop, I'll cry."

He looked at her for a beat and then easily lifted her up and deposited her on the instrument panel, which put them face-to-face.

And body-to-body.

Mmm, yes. She spread her legs and he stepped between them. She wanted him to shove her dress up to her waist and admire the last pair of pretty undies she had before laundry day tomorrow. She wanted him to dip his fingers beneath the lace and remind her of all she'd been missing since she'd stopped loving Lucas, since she'd shoved her feminine, sexual side deep down and refused to let it out.

But he didn't. Instead, he slowed the kiss, gently turned down the power of his sexuality and brought her slowly back with him, calming her—not easy since she could hear herself breathing like she'd just run the entire length of the mall to get to the opening of a Macy's shoe sale. Her entire body yearned and burned and ached.

But though he was still touching her, it was the kind of hold that wasn't going anywhere, and suddenly she felt...

exposed. She shoved him, and he immediately took a step away, looked into her eyes.

The bastard even had the nerve to smile. "Yeah, you're back."

She crossed her arms.

His mouth quirked as he turned and started to walk away.

She stared after him, still breathing heavily, still aroused beyond belief. *"Hey!"*

He turned away, hands in his pockets, the night breeze plastering his shirt to his torso like a second skin.

"I suppose you think it's funny, leaving me in this state?" she said.

His mouth curved, but his eyes were serious. "You think you're the only one feeling it?"

This had her pausing. "I don't know. What state are you in?"

"State Wrecked," came his quiet answer, and then he was gone.

She was still standing there contemplating what had just happened when her cell buzzed an incoming call. Seeing it was her sister, Brooklyn, she blew out a breath and answered as casually as she could, considering she was in, as Jacob had so helpfully noted, State Wrecked. "You okay?"

"I don't just call you when I need you," her sister said.

"Okay, I'll rephrase," Sophie said. "Hi. I've already heard from you this week and I know how busy you've been, so I'm guessing something's come up."

Her sister laughed. "You could say so. Listen, I have this idea for you. It's a little crazy, so I don't want you to say no until you've heard me out."

"Uh-oh," Sophie said. The last time her sister had come up with an idea, it'd been for Sophie to go out with some gorgeous, rich dude named Lucas...

"Okay," Brooklyn said. "Remember Jimbo?"

"The guy who graduated in your class who was arrested for being a pimp the week before you got your diplomas?" Sophie asked. "Yeah, I remember. He was my middle school current event that week."

"Yes, but technically he wasn't a pimp," Brooklyn said. "He was just keeping a few of his friends…organized. Business-wise."

Sophie laughed. "You should've been his publicist. Let me guess, you ran into him."

"Facebook. He's in Vegas now, running a legit business, making big bucks. And he's got a job opening for you. One you can do from home."

"I can hardly wait to hear this," Sophie said.

"It's easy. You can do it from the comfort of your own home—er, boat—and you would make big bucks per call."

Sophie blinked. "Phone sex?"

"Well, it's not like it's real sex," Brooklyn said.

"No."

"You didn't even think about it," Brooklyn said.

"Yes, I did. I gave it great consideration. It's a terrible idea. And it's not just phone sex anymore. It's also video sex. They live stream themselves."

"Do I even want to know how you know this?" Brooklyn asked. "And anyway, you don't have to do the live streaming part. And did you not hear the big bucks part? Look, it's mostly late-at-night work. All you've got to do is sigh and pant a little bit, mention a few body parts and do it in a breathy Marilyn Monroe voice, and you're golden."

This time Sophie paused. "No," she said less convincingly.

"*Big bucks*, Soph."

She sighed. "Okay, maybe I'll think about it."

"You're welcome."

"I'm not thanking you yet," Sophie said. "And for God's sake, don't tell Mom and Dad."

"Duh."

Body still humming with the need for something he wasn't going to get tonight, Jacob left Sophie's boat and strode toward the cabin.

He could taste her. Feel her. And it hadn't been enough.

He'd had to forcibly remind himself he wasn't here for this. For her. He had a limited amount of time before he had to go back to his duty, and he needed to get on with what he'd come to do. In light of that, he pulled out his phone and stared at his list of contacts.

At one contact in particular.

Hud.

He hit the number before giving himself a chance to change his mind.

Hud answered on the first ring, sounding a little breathless. "Jacob?" he asked.

"Yeah." Jacob scrubbed a hand down his face. "Uh, you busy?"

"I'm at the Slippery Slope. You remember it?"

"Yeah," Jacob said. "I—"

But Hud had disconnected. Okay, then. He walked. It wasn't far, maybe two miles. When he opened the door to the bar and grill, he was hit by the scent of fried food and the sounds of loud country music and a boisterous, happy crowd.

He was also hit with his past and present as they collided inside his chest.

Across the room, Aidan and Gray were bent over a pool table, in the midst of what looked like a vicious game. Kenna was on the other side of the table, darts in her hand, staring intently at the dartboard. Next to her was a man Jacob didn't recognize.

Hud stood at the bar, pushing forward money for a pitcher of beer. As if he could feel Jacob's presence, he quickly turned, and his eyes went straight to his twin.

Jacob took a deep breath and started toward him. He'd never in his life felt more out of his comfort zone, and he wasn't good at that. It made him itchy, as itchy as if he'd headed into combat without being loaded up with weapons.

At the pool table, Aidan hit a shot that had him shoving his fist in the air and pumping it in triumph. Gray snagged Aidan, hooking his arm around Aidan's neck and giving him what looked like a painful noogie.

Aidan pushed free, put his hand on Gray's face, and shoved.

Gray fell back, the two of them laughing.

A beautiful blonde came up behind Gray and slipped her arms around him. Turning in her arms, Gray nuzzled her in close while Jacob did a double take. It was Penny. She'd gone to school with them and Gray had always had a huge crush on her. She was wearing a big, fat diamond.

Seemed Gray had gotten his wildest dream to come true.

Nope, Jacob thought, standing still, he wasn't any good at this. He'd manned up to come home and he had a lot more manning up to do, but at the moment all he could think was that he was an outsider.

Your own fault…

Hud left the pitcher at the bar and started toward him. Jacob took a deep breath and did the same. When they were each halfway to the other, Hud cocked his head, gesturing to the back. There, another room held more dartboards and pool tables.

They met at an open dartboard. Once upon a time, darts had been their game. Neither could lose, and with the help of fake ID's, they'd used the skill to their benefit.

Jacob met Hud's gaze. "We playing?"

Hud shrugged and casually picked up a set of darts.

Oh, yeah. They were playing. Jacob did the same and gestured for Hud to go first.

"Five-oh-one?" Hud asked.

"That's a pussy game," Aidan said. He and the others had come up behind them. Everyone but Kenna and the guy she was with.

Penny jabbed an elbow into Aidan's stomach, hard by the choking cough Aidan let out. "Excuse me?" she said. "*Pussy* game?"

Aidan grimaced. "You know what I mean."

"No," she said. "I don't. Maybe we should call it a dick-head game."

"Kincaids play crickets," Gray said over the ensuing battle. He stepped past Penny and Aidan, right up close to Hud and Jacob.

Jacob assumed his oldest half brother was going to reach for some darts, but instead he came toe-to-toe with him, eyes swirling with emotion.

"You're home," Gray said, voice a little thick.

Jacob managed a nod.

"Hud told us," Gray said. "But I needed to see you with my own eyes. You staying?"

"I'm on leave," Jacob said. "I have to finish my stint."

"So this is what, a onetime thing, then?" Gray asked.

Jacob heard someone suck in a breath. Penny, he thought, because not one of the four of them—the brothers—appeared to be breathing.

Up until Brett died, he'd never allowed himself to imagine coming home and staying. But from the moment he'd set foot on this mountain, he'd wanted nothing else. He shook his head. "Not just a onetime thing."

Hud's shoulders fell from his ears, and when that happened, Aidan and Gray relaxed as well.

Not Jacob. He felt like he'd been strung up on tenterhooks and left hanging.

But then Gray stepped up to him, wrapped his arms around him, and lifted him in a huge bear hug, feet hanging off the floor.

The air left Jacob's lungs forcibly with an "oomph" and he caught a flash of Hud's grin.

"Jesus," Gray said, dropping Jacob. "What the hell did they feed you over there? You're as big as a mountain."

"That's what I asked," Hud said, casually reaching out and giving Jacob a shove that had him bumping into Aidan.

Aidan was solid enough to keep them both upright as he made a show of looking Jacob over. "I don't know, man," he said to Gray. "Still looks a bit scrawny to me."

"I'll fatten him up!" Penny cried gleefully, jumping up and down. "With my fabulous homemade double-fudge brownies!" Shoving her way through the four big men, she stood in front of Jacob, her hands on her hips. "Hi," she said. "Remember me?"

"You were my hottie English tutor," Jacob said. "And Gray used to try to get me to ask you if you liked him. He'd bribe me with whatever cash he had, and I'd promise to do it. Instead, I pocketed the money and told you he was an idiot and that you shouldn't look at him twice."

Penny laughed in delight. "I'll have you know, I married that idiot." She flashed her diamond at him. "Eight years ago. He's *my* idiot now."

Gray slid his arms around her from behind and kissed her

jaw. They all had a groove, a pace. They all knew each other so well and he…didn't.

That was when Penny flung herself at him.

Jacob barely caught her and let her hug him for what felt like a damn long time. Finally, with a sigh, she pulled back and sniffed, swiping at a tear. She pointed at Jacob, her mascara slightly smudged. "If you leave and don't come home when you're finished, I'm coming after you myself, you hear me?"

"I hear you," he said quietly, his chest feeling tight. For years, his life had depended on his instincts, and they were honed sharp. Survival had been harshly ingrained. Emotions had no place in that life.

He'd gone a whole lot of years purposely feeling nothing. And then Brett had died and had set off a tsunami of all he'd been holding in. He wanted to be here and was gratified Aidan, Gray, and Penny were receptive to that, but Hud hadn't said a damn word.

And it was Hud he needed to hear from the most. He forced himself to look at his twin.

Hud's eyes were closed. Once upon a time that wouldn't have mattered. They'd been able to read each other blind. They'd shared everything. But Jacob couldn't get a bead on him now to save his own life. "Where's Kenna?" he asked, hoping to give Hud a minute.

Aidan and Gray exchanged looks.

"What?" Jacob asked.

"She's got plans," Aidan said. "She had to leave."

"Or she's pissed at me," Jacob said.

"Or that," Aidan agreed.

"Don't sweat it," Gray said. "She's always pissed at one of us. She'll come around."

Aidan nodded.

Hud still didn't speak, making it clear that Kenna wasn't the only one pissed at him. "I'll go see her in the morning."

"That'd be good," Penny said softly, not missing the silent and tense exchange between Hud and Jacob. "She could use some one-on-one time with you, I think."

Awkward silence while everyone divided a look between Hud and Jacob.

"So we playing darts or standing around holding hands?" Hud finally asked.

Penny sighed. She didn't say anything, but the sigh spoke volumes, mostly that she thought men were ridiculous.

"Crickets," Jacob said decisively, and palmed the darts.

"Now, see, *that's* what I'm talking about," Gray said, slinging an arm around Jacob's neck, hooking him in. "Crickets. Kincaids play crickets." He jostled Jacob. "Missed you, man." And with that simple sentence slaying Jacob straight through, Gray let him go, snatched the darts, and stepped up to go first.

Jacob didn't move, couldn't. "So…we're good?"

"Yeah," Aidan said. "Though you're still a dumbass."

Gray nodded.

Penny beamed.

But Hud didn't speak, didn't give any indication that he'd heard Jacob's question at all, and Jacob knew.

They weren't all good.

Chapter 8

Sophie dreamed about hot, drugging kisses and Jacob's warm, hard, perfect body. She woke up at the crack of dawn overheated, and for a bonus, also sporting a splitting headache. Thank you, Scotch.

Not.

No, scratch that. She blamed Lucas. For everything.

Feeling better about reassigning the blame, she pulled on sweats and did the only thing she knew to do. She walked to McDonald's, because nothing fixed a hangover like a carbo-load of greasy hash browns and pancakes.

She doubled the order and walked to the lake, making excellent time because she was hungry. She was on the dock when her phone rang with a number she didn't recognize. "Hello?" she answered warily.

"Sexy Sophie…"

She sighed. "Hey, Jimbo."

"How's it shaking, babe?"

"Terrific, great, couldn't be better."

He laughed.

And she sighed again. "Okay, so I know I told Brooklyn to give you my number, but it was a weak moment. I don't think I could ever really go through with this sort of thing."

"Trust me, sweet cheeks, it's easy. All you've gotta do is be encouraging. And maybe let out a few moans here and there."

"Encouraging?"

"Yeah," he said. "Talk 'em through it. Tell them what you're wearing—that's always a conversation starter."

Sophie looked down at her sweats. And they weren't the cute Victoria's Secret kind of sweats either. More like the Walmart midnight shopper kind. "Well…"

"Lie," Jimbo said, reading her mind.

"And the encouragement part?" she asked.

"Just say stuff like…" He affected a woman's voice. "'Oh, I've been hoping you'd call. I've been bad, so very bad. I need a spanking,' and then you throw in a 'Thank you, sir, may I have another' and you're golden."

She was nearly boggled right out of her hangover. "You're kidding, right?"

"I never kid about business."

"But…people don't say any of that stuff in a real life, do they?"

He just laughed. "Look at it like it's an acting job, all right? It's all just a gig. Like playing *Fifty Shades* with your boyfriend. And don't even try to tell me you haven't done that."

If Lucas had tried to play *Fifty Shades* with her, she'd have killed him and no one would have ever found his body. And thinking about Lucas reminded her that even thinking of phone sex as a job was all his fault, making her groan.

"Yes!" Jimbo said with glee. "Just like that, only a little louder. Also, it helps if you pant a little. And add in a soft, helpless whimper once in a while, like you're totally into it."

Sophie sighed and nearly fell overboard when Jimbo laughed and yelled, "Yes! That's it, baby, just like that. Come on, give me just one little 'do me harder!' and I'll know you're ready for the big league."

There was no way she was going to do this, but she had to laugh at his enthusiasm for his job. Must be nice to love what you did for a living. "People can't be serious about this."

"As a heart attack." But he was laughing, too, teasing her. He knew she wasn't going to really take this job.

And because he was being a good sport, and because she was hungover and feeling a what-the-hell 'tude, she teased too. "Oh, Jimbo, I've been a very, very bad girl," she said in her best frog-in-throat, can't-catch-my-breath voice, throwing in a ragged, broken moan that might have sounded like a cat in heat. "Please, sir, I need a spanking."

She waited for his laugh, but it didn't come. In fact, there was nothing but static. "Hello?"

"Da-aaaamn, woman." He sounded seriously impressed. "You're a natural. You sure I can't talk you into this? I mean, there ain't no insurance coverage with this gig or anything, but I could get you some good, cold, hard cash."

Sophie managed a laugh that hurt her aching head, and disconnected. That's when she felt it, a disturbance in the force field. She'd felt it the other day, too, an odd tingle of awareness as she slowly turned and, yep, found Jacob standing on the dock only a few feet away, staring at her.

He was in board shorts and a T-shirt, snug across his shoulders, loose across his abs, looking like an ad for Hot Lake Living. If she hadn't known better, she'd say he looked surprised as hell behind his dark lenses and stern but sexy mouth, but she did know better. Jacob Kincaid didn't do surprised.

What he did do was stealth. She hadn't even heard him coming. "How do you do that, walk on the dock without a sound?"

"'I've been a very, very bad girl'?" he asked.

Shit on a stick! Her brain raced for something to say, anything. "Wow," she said. "I didn't peg you for having a drug problem."

He arched a brow. "So you didn't just also moan, 'Please, sir, I need a spanking'?"

"Okay," she said. "Fine, you caught me. I'm a porn star. I know, it's a huge disappointment, right? Get in line behind my mother."

He smiled.

"Hey," she said. "I could totally be a porn star if I wanted to be!"

At that, he out-and-out laughed. And if she hadn't been hungover as shit, hot and sweaty from the walk for food, and maybe still a little turned on from last night, she might've been able to find the humor in this. Instead, she narrowed her eyes. "Was there a reason you were eavesdropping on me?"

"Is it eavesdropping when you're having public sex?"

"I wasn't—" She cut herself off and took a deep breath. "I wasn't having public sex!"

"Asking for a spanking, then. I especially liked the 'please, sir' part." He shifted closer and then closer still, so that he blocked out the early-morning sun with his broad shoulders and she could see nothing but the dark of his eyes. "I'll be happy to put you over my knee," he said in a voice of pure sex. "If you asked real nice."

"Bite me," she said, even as her pulse raced.

"That too."

"Argh!" She slapped a hand against his chest. "You're annoying as hell—anyone ever tell you that?"

His lips twitched. "Not exactly the 'thank you, sir, may I have another' type, I see."

"In your dreams." Deciding to ignore his sexy ass, she boarded the boat and sat, digging into the hash browns. "Oh, my God," she murmured, this time in sheer pleasure. So good.

He just stared at her. "Are you having sex with the hash browns now? Do you need a moment alone with them?"

She flipped him the bird.

He grinned and boarded, sitting next to her without asking.

"Is that all you men think about?" she asked. "Sex?"

"No." He paused. "Maybe."

Outwardly she rolled her eyes. Inwardly she quivered.

"Who were you on the phone with?" he asked.

"My sister's got a friend who has a…lucrative business out of Vegas. She knows I need more work, so she told the guy I was looking. That was my audition."

"Define lucrative business."

"Phone sex."

"No," he immediately said.

She stared at him in disbelief. "I'm not taking the job. Although I have no idea why it would matter to you."

She never even saw him coming. All she knew was that in the next heartbeat, he'd slid a big hand to the nape of her neck and pulled her in and kissed her.

His mouth didn't feel stern now. It felt warm and giving, and she made an utterly involuntarily helpless little murmur and pressed against him, seeking more, seeking things she hadn't even realized she wanted.

And then suddenly his mouth was gone.

She staggered back a step and stared up at him. "Wha…?"

"Do you know now?" he asked in a low, sexy voice. "Why it would matter to me?"

She bit her lower lip.

"Do you, Sophie?"

She closed her eyes and then opened them and pointed at him. "You are a big complication, you know that?"

"Ditto, babe." Reaching out, he lightly tugged on a strand of her hair. "Thanks for sharing last night."

"I didn't mean to," she said. "I didn't mean to drink that bottle at all."

He smiled. "I meant you. Thanks for sharing some of you."

"Oh," she said brilliantly, both annoyed at him for making her talk about it and also oddly pleased and moved by him saying so.

"Don't look so surprised," he said. "I like you. I like you a lot."

If him saying thanks for sharing had stunned her, this just about paralyzed her. And then there was the way she reacted to his body, his touch, his voice. She offered him one of her two bags.

Sitting back, he opened his and peered inside, breaking into a smile. "Hash browns and pancakes," he said reverently.

She took a deep breath. "For the hangover," she managed, maybe a little more defensively then she'd have liked.

"My favorite," he said. "Even if I don't have a hangover."

"Bastard," she said, and reached out to snatch the bag back, but he held it out of her reach.

He smiled. "I'll let you keep the boat moored here tonight."

"Two nights," she said instantly. Hell, she might be a sucker for a hot guy, but she wasn't stupid.

He smiled. "Two," he said so easily she wished she'd asked for a week. She opened her mouth and then hesitated.

"What?" he asked.

"We're really not going to talk about it?"

"You wanting a spanking?" he asked. "Sure, but I'm much more an action guy than a talker, so…" He patted his knee.

She narrowed her eyes. "Try it and you'll be walking funny. Forever."

He laughed. And dammit, he had a really great laugh.

"And I meant the kiss," she said.

Jacob was quiet for a beat, and she started to get more than a little annoyed. That annoyance kicked up a notch when he finally spoke.

"Thought it best to leave it alone," he said, calm as you please. Like maybe he hadn't been driven nearly as crazy as she by said kisses.

I like you. I like you a lot…

Confused, unsettled, she got to her feet, but he did the same, wrapping an arm around her to halt her progress. His eyes, intense and hungry, fixed on her mouth. Her skin came alive with hot pleasure, and her bones liquefied. He kissed her then, deep and hungry and powerful, his hips sliding against hers.

He was hard. For her. And at that realization, the stupid boat, her money troubles, her entire screwed-up life all faded away.

It was like she'd never been kissed before him. Like a dormant part of her had been waiting all her life for this one kiss to wake her up.

His fingers slid beneath the hem of her sweatshirt, settling against her bare midriff. They were long and callused and warm. She could feel the latent, easy strength of him, at rest now, but she was very aware that beneath his surface was a power she didn't understand and wasn't sure she could handle.

She could also feel his palms just beneath the curve of her breasts. He was waiting for something. He was waiting on her, she realized. This big, alpha guy wasn't going to make a move unless she gave him a sign that she wanted him to.

And oh, she wanted. That wasn't the question. The question was…did she trust her own judgment right now? Honestly, she didn't know, which must have shown in her eyes, because with a small, wry smile, he pulled free. "Looks like you have yet another choice to make," he said. "You'll let me know when."

"When what?" she asked, her voice raspy.

"When you're ready for me."

We're ready. We're ready, her good parts screamed.

But her brain wouldn't shut up. *It's too fast. You don't want to be just a hookup.*

But why not? her good parts argued. *You tried love and got kicked in the teeth! Let's try something new. Let's try him.*

She was still just staring up at him when he playfully tugged a strand of her untamed morning hair and said, "We'll have to play another round of three truths and a lie sometime." He smiled. "Unless you'd rather play *Fifty Shades.*"

"Seriously," she said, even as she felt the heat of her blush rush up her face. And if she was being honest, other parts too. "Walking funny for a very, very long time."

He grinned.

She pointed to the food she'd given him. "Consider that payment for today's parking pass. I'm going to want a receipt."

He laughed and surprised her by hauling her to him again. She hadn't realized she was chilled, but at the way he touched her, something deep inside her warmed. Then her thought process derailed completely, when he kissed her again, slow, deep, hot. She felt immersed in him, in his scent, the feel of his hard body against hers, the sound of his breathing…the feel of his heartbeat beneath her hands.

"Receipt received," she murmured, dizzy with desire, so much desire. She licked her lips, wanting a last taste of him, though it wasn't enough.

Not even close.

It'd been so long since someone had touched her like she was so sexy he could do nothing else, like she was worth something, like she meant something to him. She knew there was more to life than a sexual connection, but sometimes a sexual connection was good, really good. God, she needed this, needed him, and she decided right then and there not to let herself worry about what-ifs or later or anything but *now*. Especially because now was all she had. The rest of her life was in complete flux. And Jacob…well, he was here for his family and that was it. He too had only the now. It was perfect. And how often had anything in her life been perfect? "Jacob?"

"Yeah?"

"*When*," she whispered.

He stilled for a beat, searching her expression. She hoped he found everything he needed to know there, because she'd lost her words. All she had was that hunger and need burning her up from the inside out.

Holding her gaze, he took her hand in his and brushed his mouth over her palm.

Her thighs quivered.

His fingers squeezed hers. "Be sure, Soph."

"I'm the one who said 'when,'" she reminded him, and then paused. "Are *you* sure?"

He hauled her against him, wrapping her up tight in his warm, strong arms and then rocked his hips to hers.

He was hard.

Yep, he was sure.

"I told you I wanted this," he said. "That I wanted you."

"Yes, but you were under the influence." She stared into his eyes. "Maybe I wasn't sure you meant it."

"I mean everything I say." His voice rumbled quietly in his chest, vibrating against hers. "Always."

She shook her head in automatic denial. "I don't buy into promises. I don't want anything like that from you. From anyone."

"We'll circle back to that later."

"No," she said. "We won't. No need. I know what this is, and I especially know what this isn't."

"So you have a crystal ball, then," he said.

Stepping back, she crossed her arms over her chest. "This isn't going exactly the way I expected."

"You expected what, a quick fuck, no words?"

"Yes, please," she said. "You going to deliver or not?"

He laughed low in his throat. "Now she says the 'please,'" he said, apparently to no one in particular. Then he met her gaze. "I can deliver." This was a low, husky, confident vow.

She shivered in anticipation. "You keep saying stuff like that, but I'm still standing here waiting for you to prove it."

"Our first kiss wasn't proof enough? Or our second?"

She shrugged, feeling overheated and uncomfortably aroused and a little bit like he was just teasing her. "A kiss is a kiss. They're all the same to me."

"Liar."

She felt herself flush, the heat rising all the way to the roots of her hair. *Caught.* Because she knew exactly how good it'd been when he'd taken her in his arms and kissed her. She couldn't forget a single second of any of it, all indelibly imprinted in her brain, every brush of his mouth, every touch of his fingers, every rough male sound of appreciation torn from his throat.

She started to turn away, but he pulled her back to him, her spine to his chest, her butt to his crotch.

He was still hard, deliciously so, and she couldn't help but wriggle into him.

He whipped her around to face him, and his eyes were dark and flickering with something much more than amusement now. Challenge and heat, both of those things licking along her every nerve ending. "Let me show you," he said, and lowered his head. But he surprised her when he spent a moment nuzzling at her jaw, murmuring softly against her ear. "We're doing this."

She clutched at him. "Yes." God, yes.

Wrapping his hand up in her ponytail, he gently but firmly tugged until she lifted her face to his. "If I'm going to be in your bed, Sophie, you're mine for the duration."

And hell if that didn't set back her inner feminist when her entire body quivered at the thought of being his. "But not in a *Fifty Shades* way, right?"

He flashed a grin. "Scared?"

Terrified. "You should know a few things about me," she said. "One, I really am good at shoving a guy's balls into his throat."

"Duly noted," he said. "And two?"

This was the hard part. She swallowed. "I'm really pretty vanilla."

His eyes softened and he kissed her gently. "One of my favorite flavors," he murmured.

Something inside her melted. "One more thing."

"Name it," he said.

"It's going to have to be your bed. Mine's too small."

He smiled a very naughty smile. "Then I guess that makes me yours."

She quivered at the thought. "Tell me you get hot water in your shower."

"The hottest."

"Jacob?"

"Yeah?"

"Hurry."

Chapter 9

Sophie barely registered Jacob taking her hand, pulling her from the boat, the both of them moving up the dock, across the beach to his cabin.

Remembered nothing of the interior of his place or how they got to his bedroom. Remembered nothing but him kicking the door closed and pushing her up against it and kissing her.

He was hers, she thought with dazed marvel. Hers for the duration. A thrill raced through her as she fought to get even closer to him. Oh, the things she wanted to do to that hard, lean, perfect body holding her to the door, starting with licking him from chin to the waistband of those sexy board shorts and beyond. Just thinking about it had needy whimpers escaping while their mouths tangoed.

"I've got you," he whispered roughly, his teeth scraping her throat as his hands slid down her thighs and lifted her up so that she could wrap her legs around him. "I've got you."

She had no idea what that meant exactly, but she was racing to her first orgasm in far too long and she was very busy trying to get her hands beneath his shirt, needing his heated skin on hers. Her fingers danced over the sculpted landscape of his sleek back and then came around to his chest, where she could once again feel the beat of his heart, not nearly so steady now. With a soft sigh, she went up on tiptoes and nipped his lower lip between her teeth, tugging at it before letting go.

His dark eyes blazed with promises of the retribution she wanted. She wanted him so badly she was shaking, wanted to be held, and for just a little while, wanted to lose herself. And she wanted the same for him, wanted him to be able to lose himself in her too.

Their bodies strained to get closer, but a sheet of paper couldn't fit between them. Her racing pulse throbbed so loudly in her own ears she couldn't hear anything else. But then Jacob smiled that incomparable smile and she did hear something, her inner voice saying "uh-oh" in a dazed voice. *You're going to get more than you bargained for. Remember, every good thing that's ever come into your life has cost you in blood, sweat, or tears...*

"Shut up," she said.

Jacob pulled back, a brow raised.

"Not you!" she said quickly. "My inner voice." She shook her head. "Ignore her. She's a bitch."

He laughed low in his throat and caressed the mad curls at her hairline, drawing a finger down her cheek to the corner of her mouth. "I like her," he said, and then covered her mouth with his again, possessing her with sweetness and ferocity, the carnal intensity of it knocking her for a loop.

When they broke apart to breathe, Jacob held her gaze as he let her legs slide to the ground. He hit the lock on his bedroom door. Reached behind him for the hand she had pressed low on his back, taking her cell phone from her weak fingers, setting it aside. His phone was removed from his pocket and suffered the same fate.

Then he pulled off his shirt, and while she stood there gawking at all the mind-boggling hotness—those shoulders! that chest! the abs!—he kicked off his shoes. This left him in those low-slung board shorts, which were just loose enough to gap away from mouthwatering abs, giving her a tantalizing, teasing glimpse of a treasure trail.

Before her fingers could reach out and touch, he unzipped her sweatshirt and discovered her secret.

She had nothing on beneath.

"I was in a hurry to get food," she said in explanation.

His growl was low and appreciative as his big, warm hands slid up her bare torso and cupped her breasts. "Make my day and tell me you're completely commando," he said hoarsely, his fingers rasping over her tight and aching nipples.

"I might be—" She broke off with a gasp when in the next beat her sweatpants were at her ankles.

Note to self: maybe not quite ready for prime time with Jacob Kincaid.

"Yeah," he said, voice filled with so much heat she nearly collapsed. "You went completely commando."

"Food, Jacob! I needed food!"

He laughed low in his throat, and his hands moving over her, slow and sure and igniting flames wherever they touched, which was *everywhere.* "Still need food?" he asked.

He had one hand on her ass and the other slowly gliding down her belly, heading south. "I…"

Those talented fingers of his slid between her thighs with a gentle but knowing stroke, and she forgot what she was going to say.

"Soph. Food? Or this?" *This* being a very naughty, very knowing glide of his fingers.

She opened her mouth to tease him and say food, but he did something diabolical with the pad of his thumb and she gasped and clutched at him. "Your shorts," she managed. "You're still wearing them."

A wicked smile crossed his mouth as he stripped free of them in a single economical movement.

Before she could get a look at the goods, he wrestled her onto his bed. "I fantasized about this last night," he said, crawling up between her legs and pinning her with his delicious weight.

"About me going commando?"

He smiled, intense, *dangerous*. "About you beneath me on my bed," he said, and then rolled so that she now straddled him. "And over me. Scoot up, Soph."

"Um, what?" Scoot up? To where?

Jacob didn't repeat himself, just slipped his arms beneath her thighs and physically lifted her farther up his chest and then…

Oh God, and then.

His hands were on her ass, his mouth on ground zero.

She did her best to pretend she'd been in this position before, but the truth was she had absolutely no idea what to do with herself. She was literally sitting on his face! Deer in the headlights, she stilled, her hands fluttering in the air.

Beneath her, he let out what might have been a low laugh—she'd kill him later, she promised herself—and grabbed her hands, bringing them to the headboard above him, waiting until she'd taken hold of the wood spindles to squeeze, letting her know he wanted her grip on them tight.

Since she was on an unknown roller-coaster ride without a harness, she could do little else.

Nudging her legs wider with his shoulders, he settled himself in. When his tongue caressed her in just the exact right spot, her every available brain cell not involved in basic life support honed in on the action. "Ohmigod," she gasped completely involuntarily as his tongue and lips teased her sensitive flesh, his shoulders holding her open for him, his hands on her ass. She'd never been quite so open and vulnerable before.

"God, you taste good," he murmured, shifting gears, going from nuzzling to kissing and making her tremble. Her hands started to slip from the headboard, but his eyes met hers and she tightened her grip—just as he captured her tender flesh and sucked.

It drove her straight to the very edge, even past it, just enough that she hovered there over the precipice, in that stomach-dropping heartbeat just before the free fall.

Had she ever felt like this? So wild, so completely, utterly out of control? So…close to another human being?

That answer was easy.

No.

Which brought its own terror. Because what the hell was she doing, allowing him to see her like this? Hell, allowing him to take her like this, turning her into a panting, whimpering, overheated ball of messy lust?

And that's when she froze, too open, too exposed, too damn…scared about what it might all mean. "Wait—I can't," she panted, her fingers white-knuckling a death grip on the headboard. "I can't—"

Jacob immediately reached up, covering her hands with his large warm ones, using his fingertips to run between hers and gently pry hers from the wood. "I've got you," he murmured huskily, squeezing her fingers. "Sophie, I've got you."

She nodded wildly. Good. He had her. That was really good, because God knew, she didn't have herself.

"Breathe," he ordered quietly, running his hands up and down her thighs—which were hugging his ears! "Just breathe."

Right. Breathe. She sucked air in and out, in and out, even as he kissed one inner thigh so gently and then the other. And then in between. She moaned, and he did it again.

And again, slowly driving her back up.

And then her fingers were in his hair, holding tight because he took her someplace she'd never been, someplace completely outside of herself, and when she came, she came long and hard. Afterward, her entire body collapsed. She just went completely boneless, unable to pick up her pieces and put herself together again.

But it didn't matter because Jacob scooped her in close, wrapping his arms tight around her, murmuring some sweet nothings in her ear. When she finally returned to herself, he smiled and kissed her, and then rolled, tucking her beneath him. "Now," he said. "Let's review the 'I can't.' Because you just did."

She laughed. "Show-off."

His smile faded, and he cupped her face. "Any more reservations?"

She couldn't think of a single one, so she slowly shook her head. He smiled again as he reached over her for something in his nightstand.

A condom.

Okay, good. Really good. One of them still had an operating brain. Because all she could do was run her hands over his chest, over the ridged muscles of his abs, which quivered beneath her touch as she headed south to the promised land. When she stroked him, he let out a very male sound of appreciation and thrust into her hand.

"Hold that thought," he said. He tore open the package with his teeth and then rolled the condom down his length, leaving her practically panting as she watched. This was lust on a seismic scale. It was something more, too, but she shoved that way down deep. She had no idea how, but he was making it impossible for her to resist him, or even remember why she'd wanted to. "You keep forgetting to hurry," she complained.

With a half laugh, half groan, Jacob sank inside her. Weight braced on his forearms, he cupped her face as he moved, taking his time, going so deep she gasped and her eyes threatened to roll back in her head. And then again. And yet again, and she felt her toes start to curl as she rocked up, cradling him between her thighs like he belonged there. "More," she moaned.

He thrust again and she tightened in anticipation, but instead of more, he pulled his mouth from hers. She opened her eyes, and in his dark gaze she saw her own heavy-lidded look reflected.

"I'm not really into hurrying," he said.

"What are you into?"

"Slow. Long. Hard. Hot. Dirty…" His teeth sank into her earlobe. "You still in?"

She took a breath to steady herself and rocked up, seating him even deeper inside her, clenching her inner muscles at the same time.

He groaned out her name. "Yeah, you're in."

"No, *you're* in," she said, making him snort.

Then he gripped her hips and took her. Slow. Long. Hard. Hot. Dirty…She was gasping, panting, begging for more in thirty seconds, but he continued to take his sweet-ass time, remaining buried deep and rocking gently, only to pull out and push in slowly, stretching her, reaching deeper with each stroke.

When she arched up into him and dug her nails into his back, crying out his name, she finally unleashed the beast. He set a pace that had her writhing beneath him, desperate as he moved over her, holding her head between his hands, kissing her with the same intensity that their bodies moved together.

When she burst again, crying out as the pleasure took her, he came with her, mouth to mouth, his eyes holding hers through the shocking pleasure. He stayed with her, over her, buried deep, leaving no part of her untouched, and when she finally caught her breath, she realized she was clinging to him like he was her security blanket. She quickly let go and gave a tentative wiggle, thinking he'd roll off of her and then the awkward aftermath could be had and gotten over with.

But he didn't move except to nuzzle at her jaw.

She wriggled again and this time added a little shove.

He let out a low, rough laugh, giving her one of those little post-sex body shudders that was practically another orgasm. "You make a man forget he's got obligations," he murmured, and rubbed against her like a big ol' cat.

Oh God. He was getting hard again. And even more shockingly, her body had twined itself around him like she was the salt to his pretzel. "Oh no," she said, slapping her hands to his chest. "Nope."

Lifting his head, eyes heavy-lidded, hair tousled, a bite mark on his neck—holy cow, a bite mark on his neck? She'd bitten him? When had she bitten him?—he gave her the full view of his post-coital expression, and damn. Damn, he was so effing hot. "I mean it," she said weakly as he brushed a kiss over her temple and then her cheek.

He gave one last lazy thrust, and though she would deny this until the end of time, she nearly came from that alone.

"What are you," she asked, "one-hundred-proof testosterone and pheromones? You've had your fun, now move."

So he moved.

Inside her.

"Like that?" the bastard asked sinfully.

She gasped and clutched at him. "You know that's not what I meant."

Giving another soft laugh, he kissed her, soft and sweet, and finally, thank God, he moved off her.

She felt the loss like she would a missing limb…Not that she would admit that. Ever.

But he took one look at her face and flashed a knowing grin.

Chapter 10

Sophie opened her eyes and realized she was wrapped up in a pair of strong, warm arms, which were curled possessively around her. Pulling back an inch, she found Jacob watching her from those fathomless dark eyes.

"Welcome back," he said.

Oh God, she'd dozed off in his big, deliciously comfy bed. She would blame the damn boat, the stupid lake, too many sleepless nights in a row, but she could tell her denials would fall on deaf ears because, given the smug look on his face, he knew the truth. It was the orgasms.

"Tell me I wasn't snoring," she said.

"Nope." He paused. "Drooling, yes. Snoring, no."

"I did not drool!"

He just smiled.

"You should know," she said, "I'm only here for your shower."

His lips twitched. "Sure."

She jabbed a finger into his chest. "I mean it. I slept with you because you have hot water. Sure, the sexy times were okay, but don't mistake this for something...*mushy,* because I won't put up with that."

He tipped his head back and laughed.

She stared at him. "You're supposed to be insulted."

"And you're supposed to be honest. Stop trying to scare me off."

She huffed out a sigh. "It's my thing."

"Your thing?"

"Yes, and I'm good at it." She frowned. "Why didn't you believe me?"

"The sexy times were just okay...?" he repeated, heavy on the disbelief.

She blushed. "That could've been true."

He laughed again. "Babe, you came, like, twenty-five times."

"Fine." She struggled with something to insult him with, but the guy even woke up looking hot. "You farted in your sleep," she said.

"Try again."

"Fine, you did something else. You...talked," she said, rather brilliantly, she thought. "You totally talked in your sleep."

It was subtle, his reaction, especially since not an inch of him moved, but he definitely...*retreated*?

"Hey, I'm kidding," she said. "You didn't talk." She paused. "But if you had, what is it you think you'd have said?"

He closed his eyes.

"Okay. So I'm assuming it wouldn't have been 'I know where the bodies are buried,'" she tried to joke.

His eyes opened, and she realized her mistake instantly. This was a soldier, a Wounded Warrior even if his wounds were on the inside. He probably knew where *lots* of bodies were buried and her joke had been in poor taste. "I'm sorry," she whispered. "That was thoughtless."

He didn't speak for a moment, just let out a slow, deep breath like he was gathering his thoughts. "I think I probably do sometimes talk in my sleep," he said. "Or dream badly. It's like that for a while after a rough tour."

"I can imagine." Unable to help herself, she sifted her fingers through his short hair and shook her head. "Actually, I can't imagine what it must be like to come home after all you've been through and try to fit into regular civilian life."

"I didn't expect to come home."

He met her gaze when hers flew to his face.

"I didn't," he said. "I thought I'd be a career soldier."

"What changed your mind?"

"Brett's death."

The pain, sharp and dark, was buried deep in his words, pain he was clearly fighting to hide, and it slid right through her, taking her a moment to find her voice. "Were you hurt in the explosion? Is that why you're on leave?"

His profile was tight, the corners of his mouth hard. "Just a few scratches and a concussion, no big deal," he said. "Another buddy was hurt far worse. Chris Marshall. He broke every bone in his left leg and lost his arm." He lifted a shoulder. "I can't complain. But I'm not crazy about the idea of going back."

Neither was she. "What will you do when you've finished out your tour?"

"Something quiet," he said.

She gave him a little nudge. "Like maybe live in a cabin on a mountain lake?"

His eyes warmed as he let his gaze roam over her face. "Something like that, yeah."

She got lost in his eyes a moment and then reminded herself that she had to get out of here and to work before she did something she regretted—like lick him from head to toe. "I gotta go."

"How much time do you have?"

She eyeballed his clock. It was nine. "I don't have to be at work until ten thirty today."

"Good to know." He pulled her beneath him and settled himself between her legs, his hands roaming, warming her up and revving her up, too, until she arched into him, already halfway to heaven. "You mind?" he murmured, mouth at her breast.

She slid her fingers back into his hair to hold his head to her. "Only if you stop…"

A while later, she was drifting again, mind blank with all the pleasure, when, from Jacob's dresser, the alarm on her phone went off. With a groan, she closed her eyes.

"Someone dying?" Jacob asked, not moving an inch.

"Just me." She sighed. "That was my alarm reminding me to call my sister."

"You set an alarm for that?"

"We talk on her days off when she needs a moment from her kids."

"At least you call her," he said, something in his voice. But his eyes were closed, so she couldn't tell what.

"Feel free to talk to her now," he said, his chest rising and falling with his slow, even breath.

She loved the sound of his morning voice, rough and gruff. An octave lower than usual. Heart-stopping. As was the sight of him in the bed, covered only by a sheet that had pooled low on his ripped abs. She blew out a sigh and reached for her phone.

"Oh, my God," Brooklyn answered. "I was having the best sex daydream about Chris Evans!"

"Sorry to interrupt that," Sophie said. "Hard to compete

with sex and Captain America." Then she realized what she'd said and slid a look at Jacob.

He was paying her no mind, seemingly not listening. In fact, she thought maybe he'd drifted off to sleep.

"Listen," Brooklyn said. "Dad's birthday is coming up. I thought we could do a surprise b-day visit."

"Are you kidding? Dad hates surprise visits."

"No, he doesn't."

"Yes, he does," Sophie said. "Remember the time I flew home for Father's Day and brought him a kitten because his therapist had mentioned it'd be good for him to have something to take care of?"

"Well, who'd have guessed he was violently allergic?" Brooklyn asked.

It'd been a disaster of epic proportions. "At least I called nine-one-one in time to get him an epi shot before his throat closed up completely," Sophie said on a sigh.

"And you did try to make it up to him by sending him and Mom to dinner the next year at that new fancy restaurant downtown," Brooklyn said.

"You mean the time they got stuck in the elevator and the paramedics and firefighters had to rescue them? No. No more surprises, not from me."

Brooklyn laughed, and Sophie laughed a little, too, but deep inside she couldn't help thinking that she was tired of always being the joke in the family. Then someone yelled "Mom" in the background of Brooklyn's call, followed by a bellow of "*wipe me!*"

Sophie laughed, genuinely this time.

"Please come visit?" Brooklyn asked.

Sophie sighed. "Yeah. I'll come." When they disconnected, she tossed her phone aside, flopped back to the bed, and stared at the ceiling.

Jacob peered down into her face. "I can see the wheels turning."

"I don't want to be like this," she said.

"Naked?" He stroked a hand from her belly to a breast.

"No," she said, and snorted, rolling to her stomach so she wouldn't feel so…exposed. "I don't want to be like this to my family. The one they laugh at."

He palmed a butt cheek, squeezed. "Then don't."

She craned her neck, cutting her eyes to his. "You make it sound easy."

"It is," he said in the way of an alpha man who'd never given a single damn about what anyone thought of him.

And maybe there was something to that. Maybe she was holding herself up to an impossible standard, like to Brooklyn, who was a really great person but had a very different life from Sophie. Different life, different needs.

And what are my own needs exactly?

Her alarm went off again.

"You have another sister to call?" Jacob asked.

"No, that's my get-my-ass-ready-for-work alarm," she said, and got out of bed.

Jacob came up on one elbow, hair mussed, eyes heavy-lidded and sexy, the sheet slipping down to his lean hips, watching in amusement as she raced around putting on her clothes, swearing a little when she hopped into her sweatpants and nearly fell over.

"What's today's temp job?" he asked, smirking, the sexy ass.

"I'm going to be a sous chef for a lunch shift. The regular took a few days off."

"Really?" He looked impressed. "You're a chef?"

She shrugged. "I love to cook. And I'm good at it."

"What restaurant?"

She hesitated. "Cooking tacos at Paco's." Where the hell had she kicked off her shoes?

"The Mexican taco truck that parks at the City Building?" Jacob asked.

"Yep."

He stared at her for a beat and then laughed.

She stopped looking for her shoes and went hands on hips. "I know you're not laughing at me because I'm as white as they come and everyone else at Paco's…isn't."

"I wouldn't dream of it," he said, and got out of bed.

Naked, he stalked her, catching her up against his dresser, pinning her in, nuzzling his face against hers until his mouth brushed her ear. "Think of me today," he said in a voice that was pure sex.

"Wh-what should I think of?"

"About where my mouth was a few minutes ago," he whispered, and slipped a hand between her legs.

Her knees wobbled. With a chuckle, he caught her. "I'll be thinking about how good you tasted." He sucked her earlobe into his mouth, and she shivered.

"I can't cook and think about sex," she said. Liar, liar…

"Try. You can practice right now. What are you thinking about right this minute?"

How his amazing tongue had made her squirm in the very best of ways. How even remembering it made her squirm again. "Are you fishing for compliments on your technique?" she asked. "Do I need to stroke your fragile ego?"

"Not my ego, but if you're looking for something to stroke—"

She pushed him. With a laugh, he released her. "Have a good day making tacos. They have the best tacos in the state."

"Yep," she said, "and today's are going to be the best in the nation."

"I'd never bet against you," he said. "And now I know what I'm having for lunch."

She found herself staring at him with a dopey smile.

"You know," he said, "you're pretty cute when you're being nice."

"What am I when I'm not nice?"

"Hot as fuck."

Something went through her at that, something warm and…dangerous. He believed in her, without question, when he had no reason in the world to do so.

I'm yours for the duration…

And for the first time, she wondered just how long that could possibly be.

Jacob watched her go, watched her run up the dock to her boat. Feeling like maybe his heart had shifted in his chest, he rubbed it.

What had just happened?

Either he'd been hit by a Mack truck or he'd been flattened by one Sophie Marren. He'd just experienced the hottest, most erotic sex of his life, and he was pretty sure he wasn't going to get a repeat. Which made him pretty much screwed, because it'd been the best thing to ever happen to him.

Fifteen minutes later she rushed off her boat, heading up to the road. She was wearing skinny jeans rolled up her calves, a halter blouse, and damn, a pair of FMPs.

He shook his head, smiling. Her glass was definitely half full. And here was the thing. He always saw his as half empty. He was in a dark place and just trying to survive, and yet here was this crazy hot woman who was his opposite. She was funny and light and…the highlight of his entire day.

And somehow, even as screwed up as he was, he knew

that much. Maybe they weren't opposites after all. They'd found lots of common ground in his bed. And at that, memories assaulted him, the length of her curvy body undulating beneath his, arching up as he cupped her breasts in his hands.

"Better bring your A game tonight," she yelled over her shoulder as she got into…a cab.

The one and only cab in town.

That made him laugh as he sat on the porch and ate the breakfast she'd brought him hours before. It had long gone cold, but he didn't care. Hell, compared to some of the shit he'd eaten, this was a five-course meal. Halfway through, he pulled out his cell phone and did what he'd been doing every single week for the past nine years.

He called his mom.

She answered on the second ring. "Darling, you're an hour late on your check-in. Everything okay?"

"Yes, sorry, just got detained." By the best sex he'd ever had. He looked down at the McDonald's food and shook his head, still having no idea what the hell he thought he was doing with Sophie.

"Well, I know I've taught you that it's rude to be late," his mom said. "Now I've got to write you a note for school and for your teacher. Make sure to also apologize in person."

Jacob leaned his head back against the railing of the porch and let the early-morning sun bring him some warmth. "I plan to apologize to everyone."

"You're a good boy," she said softly, warmly. "And, honey?"

"Yeah?"

"You sound different this morning. More…relaxed."

When he closed his eyes, he could still see Sophie naked and over him in his bed, head back, mouth open, the sexiest little whimpers escaping her while she rode his tongue. Yeah, he was most definitely feeling more than a little relaxed.

"Is it a girl? Because if so, you tell her that you can't afford to be distracted right now. You have grades to pull up."

He pressed his fingers into his eyes, a knot tightening in his chest. "I know. It's going to be okay, Mom." Even if he didn't know how.

"Well, I know that," she said, and paused. "Honey? I sure wish you'd undo our pinkie promise."

The one where he'd convinced her not to tell Hud that he'd been checking in with her every week for the nine years he'd been gone and that he'd managed to visit at least once a year on leave. "Someday," he said.

Carrie sighed. "Love you, baby."

"Love you, too, Mom."

"Don't forget to do your homework!" she said, and hung up.

Jacob blew out a breath and closed his eyes. The nurses had assured him she was physically healthy and doing fine, but no one could tell him when or if she'd ever figure out she was living in the past most of the time.

Shaking it off, he stood and stretched for a minute or two and then went for a run along the lake, heading north. Hell, maybe Carrie was the lucky one, not having to live in the moment, in the present, facing life's harsh realities every day. He wouldn't mind the same once in a while.

Five miles later he found himself at the resort. Unable to help himself, he walked around, refamiliarizing himself with the place that seemed at once exactly what he remembered and yet so different.

They'd grown, he'd realized. The day lodge had once housed the cafeteria and several shops, but now those shops had been pulled out and sat in another building adjacent to the lodge. The outside eating area had a beautiful overhang to allow shade, and the huge north wall of the place was no longer just a plain wall.

A mural had been painted on it. A huge mural that had been done like a gorgeous 3-D tapestry, depicting the brand of Kincaid family that was the five siblings: Gray, Aidan, Hud, Kenna, and…himself. Bigger than life.

He was still standing there staring at himself when Kenna came up to his side. She didn't say anything, but he could feel the emotions coming off her in heavy waves. He drew a deep breath as he stared straight ahead, just as she was doing. "I know you're mad at me," he said. "And you have good reason. I shouldn't have left like I did. And I shouldn't have stayed away."

She didn't say anything, and he realized with a hot poker-like stab of pain to the gut that she stood there silently, tears pouring down her face. Gutted, he closed his eyes. She'd been sixteen when he'd left, and he'd known her for only a few years before that because his dad, their dad, was an asshole. But Jacob had known damn well that Kenna had worshipped him.

And she was crying.

She never cried. Once she'd broken her arm riding on Hud's shoulders on his skateboard and hadn't shed a tear. She'd crashed on Devil's Face skiing and broken her leg. She'd become a world-champion boarder. And she'd had a very public meltdown.

All without shedding a single tear.

"Kenna," he whispered hoarsely, devastated when he turned his head and found her big eyes swimming with emotion that nearly drowned him.

"I loved you," she whispered, and punched him in the gut.

Chapter 11

Nice right hook," Jacob said.

"I've got a left hook too," Kenna said, her voice still broken. "And unless you want to see it, start talking."

He turned to face her and—very carefully—put his hands on her arms and pulled her in.

She resisted for a beat and then stepped in to him, burrowing deep with far less hesitation than he'd shown, slipping her arms around his waist and pressing her face to his chest. And then her shoulders started to shake and she slayed him dead.

Her overwhelming emotions spilled onto him, making him remember everything he'd so carefully buried. Walking away from those he loved so thoroughly that he'd lost them. Then losing Brett, and everything he'd shoved so deep he'd hoped to never feel again came barreling back, stealing his breath. All he could do was hold on.

Finally she shoved free, swiped a hand under her nose,

and jabbed a finger into his chest. "You just walked away, like…like I was *nothing to you*."

He shook his head. "No," he managed. "Not like that. Kenna—"

"You never even looked back! I mean, how could you do that, Jacob? You devastated me and I'm so…" She blew out a breath and tossed up her hands.

He took one of her hands and pressed it against his chest.

She stared up at him, slowly letting her fist open to set her palm over his heart. "Mad," she whispered. "I'm *so* mad at you." She paused. "But I'm also so very, very, very, VERY glad to see you." She shoved him again. "How could you?"

He didn't budge, which made her let out a sound of frustration. "And what the hell did they do to you? You're built like one of the Avengers now." Just like that, she threw herself at him again. "Were they mean to you? Did you get hurt? Are you okay?" She lifted her head. "Why didn't you want us at your six, dammit? We're *family*. We're all we have."

He was a man who'd learned how to react quickly, function under the worst of circumstances, and survive everything that was thrown at him.

But none of his training had prepared him for this. He had no idea what to do, so he let her cry, let her hit him a few more times and yell at him, too, until she just threw herself at him and held on for a long, long time.

When she finally pulled back, she took a moment to wipe her nose on his shirt—like she used to do when they skied together, and it made him laugh past the lump in his throat. And when she lifted her head and gave him a watery smile, he knew the storm had passed.

At least for now.

"I've gotta go," she said. "Got a board meeting. And since you're here, guess what. You do too."

"Hell no," he said immediately.

"Hell yes."

He crossed his arms over his chest, but she stared up at him, eyes narrowed. Once upon a time she'd been one of his very few weaknesses. She'd been able to get him to do whatever she wanted, drive her off the mountain when she needed an escape, stand up to her crazy mother when she needed backup, buy her the clothes she'd needed to compete on the ski team when she couldn't…Those things had been easy for him.

But this, facing everyone he'd wronged…

"For me," she said.

Damn. They both knew he'd never been able to deny her a single thing. He blew out a breath. "If I go, no more tears?"

She swiped at her eyes. "Gone."

"No more yelling at me?"

"Well, I wouldn't go that far," she said demurely. "You're bound to piss me off again."

"No more punching me," he said firmly.

"Oh, like you felt a thing." But she shrugged. "Fine, no more tears and no more punching you. And you—" She stared up at him, smile gone. "No more leaving without saying goodbye, without a plan to come back. Without a plan to keep me and the rest of us in your damn life. You hear me?"

"The people in China can hear you."

She rolled her eyes. "Tell me about the cabin you've leased." She smiled when he went brows up. "People talk. I drove by last night actually, but you weren't home. I saw you have a boat in your slip. You didn't have to buy one. We still have ours. It's moored at South Lake Campgrounds right now, but we'll be moving it to the north shore for several upcoming lake events we're running."

"It's not my boat," he said. "It belongs to Sophie Marren.

I'm just letting her moor there while she figures out where she can live on the lake without paying fees."

"Wait—really? Sophie Marren's living on her ex-husband's boat?" She grinned. "Serves that asshole right."

"You know him?"

"Yeah, and soon enough, so will you. Lucas Worthington's our new attorney for the resort. We needed a high-profile, bottom-feeding, soul-sucking lawyer to help us outthink Dad and the mess he left the resort in."

"Mess?"

She sighed. "You'll see soon enough."

Right. One problem at a time. "Sophie was married to Lucas Worthington?" Jacob had gone to high school with the guy. He'd been class president, taken the debate team to three state championships in a row, had enough charisma to light up everything on this side of the Continental Divide. He'd used that charisma to his benefit, sleeping with more girls than all four of the Kincaid brothers combined.

And that was saying something.

"Yeah, and he raked her over the coals too," Kenna said. "How's she doing? I thought maybe she'd left town."

Jacob thought about how Sophie had looked striding up to that cab to get to work earlier. Strong. Beautiful. Determined. Gutsy. "She's not cowed by this, and she isn't going anywhere."

Kenna stared at him.

"What?" he asked.

"So you and her…?"

"No."

She arched a brow but wisely didn't say anything more. In fact, she made him love her all over again when she changed the subject. "The meeting's at two. I'm keeping you in my sights until then."

"I've got a thing for lunch," he said.

"No problem," she said. "I'll come with."

He grimaced, knowing he'd never be able to shake her. Which was how he ended up standing in line with her for tacos at Paco's taco truck.

And there was a line. There was always a long line because the food was so great, but today it seemed even longer than usual. When they finally got up front to order, Sophie stuck her head out of the server window with a polite smile and froze.

She was wearing a GOT TACO? apron, and Jacob wanted to offer to eat her taco all day long—

"Hi," Kenna said brightly to Sophie. "Are you the one responsible for the goofy-ass look on my brother's face today?" She hitched a thumb over her shoulder at Jacob, as if there were any question of who she was talking about. "Because if so, I totally could kiss you."

Sophie opened her mouth, but Jacob shoved his sister behind him. "Ignore her," he said. "You look good up there."

Sophie blushed and glanced around her to see if anyone was watching.

Everyone was watching.

Jacob leaned in close. "You're all flushed."

"I get like that when I'm cooking. Or irritated," she said meaningfully.

He smiled. "That isn't the only time you flush."

She went a little redder. "Are you ordering something?"

Kenna pushed in front of Jacob. "I need three chicken tacos, an iced tea, and the scoop. How did you two meet?"

Jacob managed to get in front, placed his order, tipped Sophie for double the price of the food, and yanked Kenna away.

"Fun sucker," she said.

* * *

The "board meeting" was a family gathering in a large room at the head offices of the resort. Each of the Kincaids were there, and when Kenna walked in with Jacob, both Gray and Aidan grinned like he'd just made their day.

Hud glanced up from his iPad to see what was going on. He met Jacob's eyes briefly, nodded once, then went back to the iPad.

Jacob sat, and the meeting began.

An hour later, he excused himself and made his way out of the office, stunned. *Pissed.* Predictably, there'd been a lot of yelling inside the boardroom—they were, after all, the Kincaids—but there'd been a lot of solid decisions made and fires put out. None of which was what had him in shock.

No, that went to the knowledge that the resort, left to them by Richard Kincaid before he'd vanished years ago, had been mortgaged through the roof five years ago, leaving a huge balloon payment due at the end of the year.

Everyone had clearly had some time to get used to this betrayal, used to the hurt on top of hurt from the father who'd not given a single one of them the time of day in years. But Jacob actually had to leave the room in the middle of the meeting to try to absorb it.

He stood in the hallway, the offices around him buzzing, thanks to a Tough Mudder event going on and also an upcoming Wounded Warriors competition.

There were pictures on the walls of events that had gone on over the years. Jacob took them all in, moving slowly down the hall, anything to clear his head. He'd managed to keep pretty updated on things via the Internet, but he'd missed a lot.

Too much.

He'd been through hell overseas, a couple of times over. He'd thought there'd been some self-righteousness in that. Like because he'd been putting his life on the line for his country, it might excuse him for being a dick and going non-communicative for so long.

But his brothers and sister had been through hell too.

To his shock, Hud came out of the conference room and put a hand on his shoulder. "Look, Dad sucks. We all know that. Don't let yourself get caught up in anger over it now."

Jacob turned and met his brother's gaze. "Are you kidding me?"

Hud's expression stayed even. "Anger is a useless emotion."

"Is that right?"

"Yes," Hud said. "It takes away your ability to think straight, and we all need to be able to think straight to get out of this mess."

"So you're saying you don't do anger," Jacob challenged.

Hud shrugged. "I get over it."

"And how about me? When are you going to get over being angry at me?"

From Hud's pocket, his phone went off. When he pulled it out and looked at the screen, his entire face softened, telling Jacob who was calling.

Bailey.

Kenna had filled Jacob in on the love lives of the Kincaids, which Jacob was still a little in shock about. If he hadn't been looking right at Hud's face as he talked to his girlfriend, Jacob would never have believed it.

His hard-ass brother had fallen in love.

Immediately following Bailey's call, Hud's phone continued to go off in quick succession. Jacob went into the meeting since Hud was obviously not going to answer his question. He stood at the head of the table and eyed his siblings. "I want in. I want to help."

"Yes!" Gray said as Kenna and Aidan high-fived each other.

Jacob didn't know what he'd expected, but it wasn't this easy reception.

Gray cocked his head at Jacob. "Why do you look surprised that we want you here?"

"I don't know." But he was. He was also relieved, making him realize he'd been braced for a rejection that wasn't going to come.

Kenna had moved on and was simultaneously playing a game on her phone and eating a donut. Sensing his interest, she offered him a bite.

When he'd been overseas, Jacob had eaten fairly strictly, mostly because that's all that'd been available, but also because he needed to stay in shape. That discipline was deeply ingrained, but he wasn't trying to save the world at the moment. He was just a man, one who'd stopped being a machine the instant he'd stepped into Cedar Ridge and gotten one look at Sophie and let himself want her. Feel for her.

Have her.

He eyed the old-fashioned glazed chocolate donut and heard his stomach rumble in anticipation.

Kenna waved it enticingly, teasing him. Wrapping his fingers around her wrist, he guided the donut to his mouth and took a huge bite.

Kenna laughed in delight and set her head on his shoulder. He slid his arm around her and squeezed, and that's when Jacob realized everyone was watching them with varying degrees of shock. "What?" he asked.

"Kenna just laughed," Gray said in the kind of voice you use at the zoo when you don't want to startle the animals. His gaze was warm and filled with a silent thank-you.

Aidan's too. "Looks good on you, babe," he said to Kenna.

Kenna rolled her eyes. "I smile."

"Yeah, when you're planning the slow, painful death of one of us," Aidan said.

Kenna threw a donut hole at him. It bounced off his chest and into his hand. Not one to waste an opportunity, Aidan tossed it into his mouth and winked at Kenna.

"Time for the board," Gray announced, and everyone groaned.

"The board?" Jacob asked.

"Wait. I smile and now we have to do the board?" Kenna asked. "Remind me to never smile again."

"What the hell's the board?" Jacob repeated.

"Each week there's a list of jobs that none of us wants to do," Gray said.

"We handle the situation with a process that would've made our founding fathers proud of their hard-won democracy," Aidan said. "We play darts."

Gray slapped a handful of darts onto the table and gestured to the wall behind Jacob. It'd been divided into three categories: *Asshat-ery*, *Craptastic*, and *Shit Even Yo Mama Don't Wanna Do*.

Gray spun Aidan in his chair three times and handed him a dart. Aidan threw and got *Craptastic*.

"Tough break," Gray said when Aidan groaned.

Gray pulled a sheet of paper from the *Craptastic* section and handed it to Aidan.

"What did you get?" Kenna asked.

"I'm in charge of the fifty preschoolers coming to learn about living green on the mountain," Aidan said with a frown. "*Fifty?* Who in their right mind would want to handle fifty preschoolers?"

"You," Gray said, clapping him on the shoulder. "Oh, and

I wouldn't feed them too much. At that age they still need help with the paperwork in the bathroom, if you know what I mean."

Aidan stood and pushed Gray into the chair. With huge enthusiasm, he whipped Gray around three times and then slapped a dart into his hand.

Gray threw and got *Shit Even Yo Mama Don't Wanna Do*.

Aidan gleefully handed him a piece of paper, which Gray read out loud. "Make a sweep of the employee locker room—*Shit*," he muttered.

"Sorry," Aidan said, clearly not looking sorry in the slightest. "But we've been told that the room smells like skunk, so someone's broken the no-drugs rule. The stash has to go, and if we let Hud do it, he'll have to arrest the idiot."

Gray sighed again, then pointed at Jacob.

Jacob craned his neck and looked behind him.

"Nice try," Gray said. "But you're a part of this family, like it or not, so move your ass."

Jacob sat in the chair, and Gray spun him while the words sank into his head.

Like it or not…

Fact was, he did like it.

When Gray finally stopped his chair, Jacob narrowed his eyes on the board, but aiming the dart Gray had given him wouldn't help. First, he was dizzy as shit. And second, he didn't know which of the jobs were the shittiest. And the truth was, he was actually enjoying being included.

When his dart landed on *Craptastic*, Aidan grinned. "Nice," he said, and slapped a piece of paper to Jacob's chest. Jacob pulled it away and read, "Bring in a new load of firewood for the weekend bonfires."

Aidan whistled. "Tough break," he said, not sounding sympathetic in the least.

"This doesn't look so hard," Jacob said.

Aidan snorted. "We'll talk when you're done."

He looked at Kenna, who explained, "We can't get anyone to deliver firewood because it can't be driven in past the parking lot. It has to be carried in from there to the fire pit by wheelbarrow, which as you know, is a good hundred yards."

Jacob pocketed the paper, and when the meeting was over, he started thinking maybe this whole family gig was like getting back on a bike. Not easy, not always a good fit, but worth the trouble. "I can do more than load wood."

Kenna immediately claimed him. "Me! Me! I need his help. I'm in over my head and losing my mind."

"Spoiler alert," Aidan said. "You lost your mind a long time ago."

This caused a momentary rubber band fight. When they each had at least one welt, they got back to it.

"No, but seriously," Kenna said. "It's summer season, so you guys all have it easy right now. I'm the only one doing the work of five people—so I claim Jacob."

"Works for me," Gray said.

Kenna pumped a victorious fist. "Events coordination is too big for just one person," she told Jacob. "But now there's two of us."

"But we've got something going on every weekend," Hud said, coming back into the room, pocketing his phone. "Our next big event is Wounded Warriors, and that's only two weeks out."

"So?" Gray asked.

"So how do we know he'll even be here?" he asked without even looking at Jacob.

"I'll be here," Jacob said. "I told you, I'm on leave. I go back shortly after the event."

Hud didn't acknowledge this or take his gaze off Gray.

Gray held out his opened hand, indicating that Jacob had just answered the question.

Hud left the room again.

Okay, then. Yep, things were going just great.

Several days later, Jacob was heading to his cabin, tired but feeling good about the past three days of working as one of the Kincaids, feeling for the first time like he'd actually been of some use.

And if it was Gray and Aidan—the brothers he'd never felt like he'd fit in with all those years ago—who'd made him feel the most welcome, he told himself he could wait for the rest.

For Hud.

He eyed his refrigerator. Empty.

The same way his dock had been for three nights…

With a shake of his head, he headed out to the store. He stood in the frozen-foods aisle, trying to figure out what he could toss into the microwave that might pass for dinner when he felt compelled to look behind him. Yep, there Sophie stood in front of the ice cream section, and suddenly he was ravenous.

But not for food.

Seeing her had relief filling him. He'd been missing her, foreign as that felt to him. Missing her and worried about where she'd been staying at night, hoping she was safe, wishing she trusted him enough to stay at his dock.

She hadn't seen him yet. Her back was to him and she was on the phone, so he didn't approach her. But he wanted to.

Stand down, soldier, he told himself. *You already know she's not for you. Or more accurately, you're not for her.*

Chapter 12

Sophie stood in the frozen-foods aisle at the grocery store, staring at a two-gallon tub of ice cream. She was doing her damnedest to stay upbeat, but between her and the very tiny bathroom mirror on *The Little Lucas*, she was having a hard time.

She was on the phone with her parents, and her dad didn't sound happy. But then again, he never did. She wished she could find the magic button to cheer him up, wished—

"How's the hotel chain management job going?" he said.

Her stomach sank. "I was fired from that one." She paused. "A month ago."

The deafening silence made her wince. Being fired was the ultimate failure in her dad's eyes. After all, it was after he'd been let go from the job at NASA that he'd hit rock bottom.

"You've got to work harder at things," he said. "Like being married. Like your job. Look at Brooklyn. She has it all: a husband, kids, a good job with benefits."

"You didn't finish college because it wasn't for you," her mom said. "You left your great almost-a-paralegal job? Sophie…"

She closed her eyes at that and *thunk*ed her forehead right there on the glass door in the frozen-foods aisle.

"You've got to hold yourself to a higher standard," her dad said quietly.

"It's not what you think," she said, not quietly. That had always been part of the problem. Her parents were calm, internal people.

She didn't have a calm bone in her damn body and she'd never been able to keep much inside. "And I do hold myself to a high standard. I'm working hard, on everything." *I want to make you proud…*But she didn't say that. Instead, she said what she always said. "You'll see."

"You're like a loose tumbleweed, twisting in the wind," her mom said. "Find what you love and the money will follow."

Right. But what if she didn't know what she loved?

Or if she even *could* love?

They said their good-byes, and Sophie loaded a gallon of chocolate fudge ice cream and then on second thought made it two. Then she called her sister.

"Hey, what's up?" Brooklyn answered, sounding irritated. "And what I really mean is 'Hey, unless you have a time machine to whisk me away from the insanity of my life, I can't talk right now.'"

Sophie could hear the sounds of kids laughing and playing in the background and also what was probably the clicking of her sister's fingers over a keyboard. "You busy?"

"I can't even. What's up?"

"Just talked to Dad."

Brooklyn sighed. "And how did that go?"

"The good news is that in the best-daughter competition,

you're still winning. The bad news is that he's still upset about the divorce."

"You've done some good things too," Brooklyn said. "Marrying a dickbag wasn't one of them. Don't feel bad about leaving him. In fact, leaving him should be added to the list of good things you've done, stat. Hang on—Kyle," she yelled, "if you shove that crayon tip up your nose, so help me, I'll—*shit*. Soph, I gotta go."

Sophie slipped her phone back into her pocket and felt a tingle of awareness along the nape of her neck that had her lifting her head.

Her gaze collided with Jacob's.

He stood at the end of the aisle in front of the frozen pizzas, wearing sexy jeans and an army-green T-shirt that fit like it'd been made for him.

Bad for you, she reminded herself. All you've done is daydream about the things he did to you in his great big bed with his great big—

"Hey," he said.

"Hey."

He smiled like maybe he knew what she was thinking about. And his smile made her remember all the things she'd been coaxed into doing the last time he'd flashed it at her.

Just keep your cool. And your clothes on. She eyeballed his section of the freezer. "Dinner?"

"Yeah. The question is three meat and five cheese or fully loaded."

"In other words, a heart attack waiting to happen?"

He slid a laughing gaze her way. "Says the woman who ate a heart attack for breakfast the other day."

She'd had something else for breakfast that day too. *Him.* Her body involuntarily softened at the memory. Dammit. "That was a hangover cure," she said. "Entirely different."

His grin made the woman behind Sophie drop her frozen chicken Alfredo casserole.

"There's healthier stuff in the fresh aisle," she said.

He gave her cart—and the ice cream in it—a long look.

"Do as I say, not as I do," she muttered.

He laughed, but grabbed a loaded pizza. "I don't really have all that long of a life expectancy," he said. "So I'm not too worried about a heart attack."

That sobered her up pretty quick. And right then and there she made yet another choice. *No regrets.* "Put the pizza back," she said. "I'm grilling spice-rubbed beef tenderloin with chimichurri for a client. I'll have extra."

"You had me at beef tenderloin," he said, making her thighs quiver. "Although I've got no idea what the hell chimichurri is."

"It's a tangy, zesty condiment that's like a cross between vinaigrette and pesto," she told him. "I'll have plenty."

"How do you know how hungry I am?"

The words—not to mention his voice—gave her a shiver in the very best kind of way. "How hungry are you?" she heard herself whisper.

He let five solid beats go by, during which time he just looked at her. "Frighteningly hungry," he finally said.

Another woman promptly ran her cart into Sophie's. "Oh, sorry!" the woman gasped, face red as she hurried off.

"You're making quite an impression," Sophie managed dryly.

He shook his head like he disagreed and stepped closer to her, right inside her own personal little space bubble. Now she was in his orbit and in danger of being sucked in and going up in flames.

But she didn't make a move to a safer zone. In fact, all she could think of was how he'd felt moving over her, *in* her, his voice a low, sexy murmur in her ear. She knew the texture of his skin, the dips and valleys of his beautiful body, the sounds he made when he came…

Something flashed in his eyes. Heat for sure. And maybe humor. "I like what you're thinking about," he said.

"You have no idea what I'm thinking about."

"Wanna bet?" he asked, running one hand up her back until the pads of his fingers slid beneath her hair and brushed the sensitive skin at the nape of her neck.

Her very long few days vanished in the flame of hunger flickering to life at his touch. She'd thought she could stay away, ignore him. Ignore this. She'd been delusional.

Jacob lowered his head so that his mouth was a fraction of an inch from hers and they were sharing air. He wasn't touching her anywhere but with those rough fingertips, and yet she could *feel* him, big, warm, strong. So strong.

Yearning washed over her in waves, and she was the one to make the move, fisting her hands into his shirt and yanking him in. She who kissed him. She who planted her mouth on his and, at the taste of him, moaned.

The last time they'd kissed, he'd made her feel wanted, made her feel sexy, vibrant. *Alive.*

She wanted that feeling again, that sensation of flying without a net, knowing that he'd catch her…

Kissing him gave her all that, and when he slid his hands into her hair and cradled her head, it also gave her more.

She heard something crash and tried to pull free. Jacob, not so easily startled, was much slower to lift his head, keeping his hands on her when he turned his head to look.

Another woman had come down the aisle and had run her cart into the display of pie crusts. She wasn't alone. She had a much older woman at her side, holding on to the cart like it was a walker.

"Wow," the older woman said. "Haven't seen a kiss like that in a long time."

"Mother," the younger woman hissed. *"Shh!"*

"Just calling it like it is," the older woman said, not *shh*ing. "And look, it gave her a healthy glow. Wouldn't mind a glow like that," she said wistfully.

While the woman rushed her mother out of the aisle, Sophie drew a shaky breath and ordered herself to get a grip. "So," she said, trying to remember what they'd been talking about.

"So," he said. "You done working for the day?"

"No. I'm temping for a property management company, opening up one of the vacation homes for some English duke and duchess on a secret American getaway. I have to unload all their supplies and check that everything got cleaned and set up." Her lips were tingling.

They wanted another kiss.

She gestured to the huge cart in front of her, filled with high-end wines, fancy cheeses and crackers, and other things like caviar and stuff that cost more than she'd spend for herself in a month. "I'm filling their fridge from their list of requests," she said. "But I'm having trouble finding"—she consulted her phone again for the list—"goat-cheese ice cream."

He winced. "Who eats goat-cheese ice cream?"

Still eyeballing her list, she shrugged. "Apparently the duchess. Also, it needs to be whiskey and pecan flavored." She tried not to gag at the thought.

"What else do you need to find?"

Detecting a note of humor in his voice, she lifted her head. "Are you laughing at me?"

"I wouldn't dream of it."

She narrowed her eyes. "Uh-huh…" She eyed the list

again. "The duke wants condoms. Ribbed for her pleasure." She managed to control her grimace on that one. The duke was eighty-five if he was a day, and although he was tall and…duke-like, gravity hadn't been kind. He'd been a rugby player in his day and all that muscle had atrophied, so he now resembled something like a plucked rooster. "He also wants massage oil, but it has to be organic. And…" She paused, unable to say the next item with a straight face.

"What?"

She shook her head. Nope. Couldn't do it.

Jacob came up behind her to peer over her shoulder at the list. He left no space between them, his arms brushing each of her sides as he rested his hands on the cart handle in front of her.

She pretended to study the list. But the truth was, she'd forgotten how to read. She'd forgotten how to breathe.

"'A battery-operated massage gizmo,'" he read for her, and nuzzled her ear. "I've got a gizmo. No batteries required."

She closed her eyes. "This isn't my list."

He laughed softly, and since he remained in place at her back, she felt the laugh reverberate through his chest to hers. "Interesting job. I think we should take this discussion to the lake."

She opened her mouth to say absolutely not, but her body went to war with her brain and all that came out was a sigh.

Someone came around the corner and down the aisle.

"Kenna," Jacob said, not sounding thrilled.

"I saw your truck and *knew* I'd find you in the freezer aisle." Kenna eyeballed them both with great interest. "So you two are a *thing*."

"No," Sophie said.

"None of your business," Jacob said at the same time.

They looked at each other.

Kenna laughed. "Never mind. I've got my answer." She turned to Sophie. "You've temped at the resort a couple of times, right?"

"Yes. I've worked a couple of your events when you've been short-staffed."

"You helped us manage the mountain biking event we did a couple of weeks ago," Kenna said. "And did a hell of a job too. She saved the day," she told Jacob. "The promo was all screwed up, and she managed the social media and crazy phones, doing the work of, like, ten people. It was awesome." She smiled at Sophie. "Hope you'll join us for some of our upcoming events, specifically the Wounded Warriors. We need all hands on deck." She hugged her brother and then looked in his cart. "Seriously? What are you, twelve?"

"Hey, I've missed having some things from home," he said.

"Like what, clogged arteries?" She pointed at Sophie. "Talk some sense into him."

Sophie was fascinated by the relationship between brother and sister. Obviously, there was love and affection. And irritation. It was...normal, so much so that it made Jacob seem all the more human to her. "Have you ever had any luck telling him what to do?" Sophie asked Kenna.

His sister laughed. "Good point."

Jacob watched as Sophie moved on, heading down the aisle a bit, referencing her list, her mouth moving as she read it to herself. There were shadows beneath her eyes. She was tired and probably working too hard.

Just watching the way all those sweet, warm curves moved, the way her hair seemed to shift in counterpart—she was absolutely unaware of her beauty—made him want to haul her in close until she let out one of those sexy, helpless little murmurs and pressed herself up against him.

"I've never seen you look at anyone like that before," Kenna said. "You look at her like she's…"

He slid her a look. "What?"

"Like she's a double-fudge brownie, warm from the oven."

"You're wrong." He wasn't looking at her like she was a double-fudge brownie. She was more important than dessert. She was a main course, the base of the food chain.

And hell.

He hadn't seen her coming.

Kenna set a hand on his arm, bringing his gaze back to her. Her expression was much more serious now, her voice quiet. "You going to fall for her, Jacob?"

"Do I look insane?"

"Yes," she said immediately. "Sometimes."

He gave her hair a soft tug.

She let him lighten the mood, doing her part by sending him into the freezer doors with a well-placed shove. Apparently they'd made up and were back to normal.

Normal.

There was a word Jacob hadn't thought about for a long time and hadn't realized he even missed feeling.

Sophie was in the bread aisle, trying to find the duchess's gluten-free, salt-free, taste-free brand, when Jacob caught up with her.

Sans Kenna, he leaned in and sniffed her. "God," he said on a clearly heartfelt sigh. "You smell better than a double-fudge brownie."

She'd started to melt until he said "brownie" and instead gave him an elbow to the gut.

His hands went to her hips while he laughed and smelled her again, his face plastered into the crook of her neck. "Seriously, yum. You smell amazing. I want to eat you up, Soph. Come on, let me eat you up."

Well, hell if that didn't have her good parts standing up and waving their hands in the air like they just didn't care. "Stop it." *Don't stop…* "I'm working."

"You smell amazing and you *are* amazing." He was pressing hot, openmouthed kisses to her throat, accelerating her heart rate. "I couldn't do what you do," he said conversationally while his mouth wreaked havoc with her self-control. Her nipples were trying to break free of their confines.

And he just kept talking in that easy way of his while simultaneously arousing her with little to no effort at all.

"I'd have a hard time doing what you do," he said, and kissed the spot where her shoulder and neck met. "You work too hard."

It took her a moment to locate her tongue. And he'd noticed that she worked hard. That shouldn't have made her feel good, but it did. "Stop that. I can't think when you do that."

He nipped her and then soothed it with a hot kiss, taking his time before finally letting her go.

She let out a shaky breath and tried to remember what she was saying, when what she really wanted was to yank him down and have her merry way with him. "And then I need to check and rearrange the royals' schedules so that certain things don't…overlap."

"Overlap?" he asked.

"Well, for one, the duke's girlfriend doesn't like the duchess," she said, "and the feeling's mutual. Last time they managed to run into each other in that twelve-thousand-square-foot home, there was a huge catfight. The duke stepped in to break it up and lost his toupee."

Jacob grinned. "I'd have to shoot myself if I had your job. No, scratch that. I'd shoot the royals."

"The client's always right," she said, repeating her mantra, the one she'd sang to herself a thousand times today. But the truth was, she liked doing these temp jobs. She got to meet a lot of people, she never had to do the same thing twice, and she also got to see firsthand that it didn't matter which side of the railroad tracks you parked your head at night; everyone had problems. "I like doing my job."

"You have a more positive attitude than I do. I wouldn't last a day," he said. "Hell, I wouldn't last five minutes. You're a much better person than me."

She froze, caught off guard, not to mention flat-out surprised. How long had it been since anyone had said anything like that to her? Uncomfortable with the praise, she blindly grabbed a loaf of bread and turned to go.

But Jacob wasn't deterred. She had a feeling nothing could deter him when he'd set his mind on something.

"You know you're something else, right?" he asked. "Something really wonderful. Handling all you've been through with grace and courage. I mean, you didn't even try to kill your ex for what he did to you."

That made her smile, albeit grimly. "How do you know I didn't?"

"Because you're smart, resourceful, and determined. If you'd wanted to kill him, he'd be dead. And there wouldn't be a body."

Surprised again, she laughed. He got her. "You should remember that," she said, and started to walk off.

"You're being cautious."

"I'm trying," she said. "Join me, won't you?"

"Where's the fun in that?"

She stared at him. "Is that what we're doing? Having fun?"

His gaze met hers and held for a long moment. "Among other things."

She gulped.

"What are you afraid of?" he asked quietly.

"The list is long."

He shrugged. "Try me."

"Fine," she said, ticking off the bullet points on her fingers. "Getting hurt. Trusting again." She stopped and shook her head, feeling way too exposed.

"I'll never hurt you," he said. "Ever. We're both in this, eyes open. We know what this is and what it isn't. I'll never hurt you," he repeated, taking a step closer. "And you can take that to the bank, Sophie. I'm a lot of things, but a liar isn't one of them."

Her brain was on overload. It was just too much to process. "I've gotta go." It took a moment for her feet to obey her brain, but eventually she did walk away, thinking, Holy cow, he was potent. She needed to remember that and stay out of his force field range.

A few minutes later she got to the checkout just as Jacob was walking out the door of the store. The clerk was staring at his ass. "That is one fine specimen of man," the woman said, taking a long sip from her bottle of water like she was parched. "I mean what kind of woman wouldn't follow that man anywhere, no matter what job he lands for himself?"

"He's got a job," Sophie said. "He's military—"

"I mean after the military."

"Maybe he'll come back to doing what he's doing now, lake patrol."

The clerk stared at Sophie for a beat and then burst

out laughing. "Honey, that man's as hot as they come, and badass to the core. But he don't wear no badge."

Sophie blinked. "He's not lake patrol?"

"No way. No how."

She thought of how they'd met, when he'd made her move *The Little Lucas* that night. And the second night…Or when she'd asked if he was on duty…He'd let her make a fool of herself. *I don't lie, Soph, ever*…Funny, but she'd actually believed him. Which made her the ass, not him.

Chapter 13

Sophie grinded her teeth as she unloaded the royals' groceries in their mansion, cooked their dinner, and left. She'd told Jacob she'd bring him some dinner, but now all she wanted to do was roast him over an open fire.

That night she didn't go to his dock.

Or the next night.

The following morning she was called in to work for a local florist. The owner was Alexa, Lucas's sister. Not wanting to turn down the work, Sophie hoofed it over there.

Alexa sat behind the counter. Once upon a time she'd been nice and kind to Sophie, but that had stopped during her contentious divorce. Alexa didn't greet her, just pointed to the huge bouquet on the counter. "Needs to get up to the resort, like, ten minutes ago. You're going to have to rush it."

"To rush it, I'll need to borrow a car," Sophie said.

Alexa sighed. "You haven't gotten your own car yet?"

"I had my own car," Sophie said. "Your brother stole it."

"My brother *bought* it. You divorced him, Sophie. You don't get to have your cake and eat it too." But she pulled out a set of keys. "My Lexus. Take better care of it than you did your husband."

Biting her tongue, Sophie took the flowers and the keys. She glanced at the order slip and was shocked at how much Alexa was charging these days. She got the niggling thought that she could have supplied the flowers far cheaper and with better service too.

She drove up to the resort, and carrying the flowers, made her way to the offices and asked for Kenna Kincaid, to whom the flowers were addressed, along with a card that said simply:

> *Give me another chance…Best, Mitch*

Men, Sophie thought with an eye roll, and had to laugh to herself when Kenna Kincaid came out of an office and approached the bouquet like it was a lit fuse.

Seemed she wasn't the only one with man troubles.

"Hell," Kenna muttered. "It'd better not be from—" She let out a whoosh of air when she read the card. "Shit. It is."

Sophie smiled. "I'm guessing these flowers aren't going to get your guy out of the doghouse."

"He's not my guy, although he lives in the doghouse." She picked up the flowers and dumped them into the trash bin on the side of the counter. "Don't take that personally," she said.

"Nope," Sophie said. "I'm just the delivery girl. Is Mitch as big a jerk as my ex?"

Something crossed Kenna's face. Guilt? "No," she said finally. "He's not a jerk at all. We had an accidental one-night thing not too long ago and…well, he's just way too sure.

And I'm not sure. I'm planning on keeping him on his toes for a while until I sort stuff out in my head. That's the secret, I think, keeping a guy on his toes."

"Seems safer to do without," Sophie said. "Smarter too."

"Maybe." Kenna shrugged. "Probably. But I'm not all that smart when it comes to men."

"Hear, hear," Sophie said, and turned to go.

"Oh, wait. While you're here, can we book your services for the Wounded Warriors event?"

"Yes, of course," Sophie said. "Just call the temp agency."

"You're still with them? I thought maybe you were running your own gig."

Sophie felt something shift from deep within her. "No," she said slowly, thinking how much the idea, one that had been lurking lately, appealed to her. "I'm not running my own concierge service." She paused. "Yet."

Kenna smiled. "Keep me up to date on that."

"Oh, I most definitely will." Sophie started to go, then hesitated. "Listen, I know Jacob's hugely private, but there's someone I bet he'd love to see at the Wounded Warriors event." And then, hoping she wasn't crossing a line, she told Kenna about Chris Marshall, how he'd been injured in the same explosion that had killed Brett.

Kenna didn't speak for a long moment, and Sophie took a step back. "You know what? Scratch that. I shouldn't have said anything. I—"

"Shut the front door." Kenna grabbed her hand, lifting her face to Sophie's. Her eyes were misty. "I'm so very glad you said something," she said fiercely. "If Chris Marshall's stateside, my brother Hud will find him."

Sophie nodded. "Thanks."

"No, thank *you*." Kenna's voice was soft and a little watery. "It's so good to have him back, you know? But he's still struggling with it a little bit. We could use all the help we can get to reach him."

Before she could ask what that meant, a guy came out of one of the offices wearing a cop uniform, and Sophie's mind stuttered to a halt.

Jacob.

He glanced at Kenna and then at Sophie with a polite smile, and she instantly realized her mistake. This was Hudson Kincaid, Jacob's *twin*. She let out a shaky exhale.

Hud's eyes warmed. "I'm sorry. Didn't mean to give you a jolt. I forget that I look just like him."

Looked like him. Smiled like him. Sounded like him...

Except their eyes were different. Hud was charming and...open. Jacob's eyes were shuttered, and though he could just as easily charm when he chose to, Sophie got the impression he didn't choose to all that often.

"How's he doing?" Hudson asked.

Remembering that night they'd demolished that bottle of Scotch, when Jacob had told her about not being sure how to reconnect with his family, she met Hud's eyes. "Maybe you could ask him."

"That's not a great idea," Hud said.

"Why not?"

"Interesting question," someone said behind them.

Jacob.

He'd come in the door so stealthily that none of them had noticed. But Sophie was noticing now, big-time. He stood there in some seriously sexy guy jeans and a black T-shirt that only a few days ago would've made her want to spread him on a cracker and gobble him up.

But she was mad at him.

He stood there arms crossed, face carefully neutral, and she realized she wasn't the only mad one.

"Since when do we gossip about each other?" he asked Kenna and Hud.

Not mad, Sophie realized, but...unhappy, frustrated... sad? She'd never seen him anything less than one hundred and ten percent confident, but here, with the people he should have felt the most at home with, he was off his axis. Dammit. Dammit, that made her want to hug him.

Kenna bit her lower lip and looked at Hud.

Hud hadn't taken his gaze off Jacob.

Say something to make him feel welcome, Sophie found herself wishing. *Anything*.

Hud's mouth tightened. "Since one of us vanished without a word."

Sophie's heart fell a little bit.

"We had plenty of words," Jacob said. Still acting neutral. But he wasn't, and how the hell was it that only she could see it?

"Before maybe," Hudson said. "Not since."

Jacob nodded his head in agreement.

Sophie's chest felt too tight. She wanted to step in front of Jacob, face down his siblings, and yell, "Don't you know coming here was hard for him? That he just lost someone near and dear to him and he needs you?" But she didn't. Couldn't. It wasn't her place.

And besides, she was holding on to her own mad. By a thread.

Kenna blew out a large sigh and looked at Sophie. "I'm so glad I don't have a penis. It seems like such a handicap." She turned back to her brothers. "I don't care about *before*. I care about *now*." She came around the counter and gave Jacob a kiss on the jaw, having to go up on tiptoe to do it. "And in my opinion, now is looking pretty good." She turned to Hudson. "Yeah?"

Hudson's gaze never left Jacob. "It's looking up anyway."

Jacob headed over to Sophie, pulling her aside. "Hey. What are you doing here?"

She schooled herself not to melt because, hello, *she was still mad at him.* "Delivering flowers to Kenna."

Both Hud and Jacob did a double take.

"From who?" Hud asked.

Kenna sighed. "It's no big deal—"

"*Who?*" Hud asked again.

"Mitch," Kenna said, and seemed satisfied when both Hud and Jacob narrowed their eyes.

"*Why?*" they asked her in unison.

Kenna laughed in delight. "Ask him," she said. "Maybe you could do it together."

"I'll do it," Hud said so darkly that Sophie actually felt a little sorry for this absent-but-clearly-about-to-die Mitch.

It was another two hours before Sophie was off work. She'd paid for a day pass at the campground, but when she got to the boat at North Beach, she had a ticket because the pass apparently wasn't good for the dock she'd chosen. Furious, she left the dock and walked along the embankment above the beach. She was exhausted and pissy. She was spoiling for a fight and knew it. Just as she knew who she wanted to fight with—Mr. Not Lake Patrol.

The smarter thing would be to get back on the boat, go lie down, pull the covers over her head, and sleep until a better day came along. That's not what she did. She headed toward the first cabin.

Jacob's.

That's when she heard it, a rhythmic *thunk*ing. She recognized the sound as someone chopping wood. Her dad had chopped wood. They hadn't needed it much, since the Dallas winters were usually mild, but he'd found comfort in the mindless work. Or so he'd said. Sophie had never seen it lift his depression. But then again, nothing had lifted his depression, nothing had ever made him happy, and she had a deep-seated fear of ending up that way, never happy.

She knew her dad's depression wasn't his fault, but that hadn't stopped her from being profoundly affected by his condition. There'd been no more smiles and cuddles. No more love or even basic interest in her life other than to express disappointment. She told herself she understood. He was ill. He'd suffered. She got it.

But deep down, she didn't really quite get it. Inside she was still that pathetic little girl looking for her daddy's approval.

And if that didn't put her in a mood…And it didn't stop her from making her way to the edge of Jacob's property, where she found Mr. Not Lake Patrol himself.

He wore those sexy jeans, now so low-slung from his steady, economical movements that they were just about indecent. His entire body swayed with easy grace as he wielded the ax, his broad, smoothly muscled back moving so fluidly that she found herself sitting right there on the wild grass embankment above the beach. Because her feet hurt, she told herself, and kicked off her heels.

She needed a break, that's all, and she leaned back on her hands to watch. In spite of her pissiness, all that hot and sweaty man flesh made her a little gooey inside. The only thing that could've improved her view would've been a *Scandal*-size glass of wine and a big bowl of popcorn.

Jacob stopped and swiped his brow, and then tensed and turned, finding her in one sweeping glance. It was as if he'd felt her the same way she always seemed to feel him, and at the realization, she froze.

Damn.

She really had no idea what drew her to him. Okay, scratch that, she knew. He had a way of looking into her eyes and really listening when she spoke that made her feel... important. But he was also dark and brooding and so effing sexy he set her every nerve ending on fire with just one look.

When was the last time that had happened? Never, that's when.

Too bad she wasn't planning to forgive him.

Ever.

Once a jerk, always a jerk, and she knew that firsthand, thank you very much. Been there, bought the T-shirt, been raked over the coals.

Jacob lifted a hand to shield his eyes, presumably to get a better look at her. His other hand came up in a wave.

She sucked in a breath and didn't wave back. No way, no how. Lucas had been charismatic and charming too. She wasn't going to let her guard down, or relax.

You were pretty relaxed after having him buried deep inside you...

She sighed. It didn't matter what kind of a man he was beneath the sexy skin.

It didn't.

Not from the moment he'd let her think he was something he wasn't.

Chapter 14

Jacob had been chopping wood for about two hours, using some of the wood rounds he'd found lying in a huge pile on the side of the cabin.

He'd chopped more than they'd need at the resort, stocking the extra against the back of the cabin for winter—even though he'd only rented the place short-term and it was currently summer.

He stopped when he could no longer lift his arms. He'd set the ax aside and stood there catching his breath when he felt it. Her. But the dock was still empty, no *Little Lucas* and no wild tumbleweed Sophie Marren.

And then he realized she was sitting above, on the edge of the embankment, her bare feet hanging over, swinging slightly. She wore her sunglasses so he couldn't see exactly where she was focused, but he knew.

He lifted a hand in greeting, his body tightening. In hunger, he told himself. But he knew that it wasn't food he was hungry for.

She stood and made her way down to the beach. He met her just as a truck pulled up to the cabin. Hud's truck. Deciding Hud could wait a second, Jacob smiled at Sophie.

She didn't smile back.

"What's the matter?"

"Nothing," she said. "Or…you're not lake patrol."

He smiled at the idea of being lake patrol. Yeah, he'd been military for nine years and still was, but if there was one thing he'd learned about himself, he wasn't exactly a rule follower. Taking a job where he had to impose rules upon others wasn't going to work for him. Ever. "Not lake patrol," he agreed with a laugh.

She took a step back, and he realized his mistake. Never laugh at a pissed-off woman. He reached for her, but she evaded, jabbing a finger in his direction.

"You think this is funny?" she asked.

"Funny that you thought I was lake patrol? Absolutely," he said. "Funny that you're somehow all riled up at me? No. I don't find that funny at all. Unless you're looking to expel some of that energy in a constructive but down-and-dirty way. Because then I'm game."

She stared at him. "Are you talking about sex? Because you should know, I'm so not going there with you, not ever again. The thought makes me sick."

Her nipples were hard even though it was still eighty degrees out. Her face was flushed, but he'd bet the last beer in his fridge that it wasn't from heat. "That's a big fib," he said.

"No, see, that's my point," she grated out. "*You're* the fibber." She shoved her hair from her face, where it'd fallen into her eyes. "You let me think that I was going to get in trouble by parking here. More than once. You acted all…authoritative, and I believed you. You sucked me into your force field and I nearly lost—" She bit back the rest of that sentence.

"Lost what?" he asked.

"My job!"

He'd have laid another bet down that she'd nearly said *herself*. Which cut him like a knife.

"You know what?" she said. "Forget it. Forget all of it—including that morning last week, where for one teeny-tiny second I thought maybe your entire gender didn't totally suck!"

"It was more than a teeny-tiny second," he said.

She glared at him.

Okay, so she couldn't be charmed out of this. But he had absolutely zero idea what exactly was happening. "I'm going to need a hint here, Soph. I don't remember ever telling you that I was lake patrol."

"I *assumed*."

He knew better than to tell her what assuming made her. "How? I told you I was on leave."

"Yes, but you always seemed to be there when I was…illegally parking, pointing it out. And you have that whole authority presence down. I just—" She bit her lower lip. "Assumed," she whispered.

"I promise you," he said, "I had no idea you thought I was lake patrol."

"But…" She tossed up her hands, looking genuinely upset and miserable, and he felt bad about that. Really bad. He stepped toward her, but she pointed at him to stay. Clearly going for a dramatic escape, she stormed the beach, heading to the next property over, which was North Beach and the campgrounds. She stomped her way down the dock, with him right behind her. Ignoring him, she boarded the boat and slammed the door behind her as she headed belowdecks.

And caught the hem of her dress between the jamb and the door.

"Dammit," he heard her mutter from the other side of the door before whipping it open. She yanked her dress in and slammed the door for the second time, clearly making a statement that she was still mad.

As if he couldn't tell by the energy crackling off her, enough that he could have popped corn off her skin. He blew out a breath and stepped on board as well. "Sophie—"

"No," she said through the door. "You wielded around your power like…like you're some male alpha dog whipping it out to pee all over everything and mark your territory!"

"I rarely ever whip it out to mark my territory," he said, hoping to make her smile.

What he got was silence. "Soph."

Nothing.

"Listen," he said. "Did you ever think that I kept seeking you out because…well, because I wanted to talk to you?"

He waited while she processed that, waited as she hopefully remembered three truths and a lie. Or more accurately just the terrifying real truths over a bottle of Scotch. Their kiss.

The time they'd spent in his bed…something that hadn't been far from his mind. How she'd felt in his arms, the way she'd looked at him, like he really did it for her, like he was enough, just as he was, screwed up and all.

She opened the door and looked at him. Color tinted her cheeks. Yeah, she remembered everything. But there was something else going on here, something far deeper that was upsetting her. And he didn't buy that it was simply because she'd misunderstood him being lake patrol. No, she was upset because she thought he'd lied to her.

Her past was rearing up and lifting its ugly head, and he

got that. He did. But he wasn't going to let her make him the bad guy here. "I've never lied to you," he said.

He could feel her doubt and wished he could eradicate it, but only she could do that.

"I need to think," she said.

"Can you think over dinner? I'll cook so you won't have to."

She looked at him doubtfully.

"No, really, I'll surprise you." And himself…

But she shook her head. "I can't think in your presence."

"Why not?"

"Because looking at you is like…" She tossed up her hands. "It's like walking down the chips and cookie aisle at the grocery store. I can't resist you, and then I'll forget why you're bad for me."

"How about I promise to be so good to you that you'll forget the bad?"

Her gaze had started to soften, but then she apparently found her resolve, because she shook herself out of it and said, "Argh!" Then she jabbed a finger at him. "No. No more of your magical kisses that make my clothes fall off. You've got to go." To prove it, she moved to the captain's chair, started the boat, and revved the engine.

He'd have liked to push the issue and talk her down, coax her into coming back home with him, but he knew pushing her right now wasn't the smart move.

And he wanted to be smart here. Wanted to be smart with her. Careful. She needed to be in control, and he got that. "Promise me one thing," he said. "That you'll moor at my place. No more sneaking around, trying to find a place at the end of a long day when you're too tired to be behind the wheel. My dock is open to you. No fee, no paybacks, no worries. Period."

She stilled. "Okay," she murmured.

Okay. She'd be back when she needed to moor the boat for the night, and they could talk then. On her terms.

He barely got out of the boat before she hit the gas and was gone, leaving nothing but a wake.

Hud came down to the dock to stand next to him, smirking, the ass. "You've been back, what, two weeks, and you've already pissed off the hottest redhead in town. I think that's a record, even for you."

Chapter 15

Jacob shook his head. He hated letting Sophie go, but she needed a moment, and he could give it to her, knowing she'd be back tonight. "Don't start," he said to Hud, and turned his head to eye his twin—who up until now had barely given him the time of day, even though they'd spent a lot of time at the resort together.

He'd done his best not to care. He'd spent time with his mom. He'd also been working on the cabin here and there, fixing some things that had been bothering him, like a loose floorboard and some wonky electrical that made it so he couldn't run his TV and make toast at the same time.

He'd been taking long paddleboard rides, pretending not to search for one crazy hot and adorable redhead's boat.

But he was restless, spending too much time not doing what he'd come here to do.

Which was not one Sophie Marren. "What are you doing here?" he asked Hud.

"You've been visiting Mom."

Jacob stared at him. "Did you think I wouldn't?"

Hud didn't answer that. Instead he said, "You went a long time without seeing her."

This conversation was a one-way-road straight to Trouble-ville. Because he *had* seen their mom, as often as he'd been able to manage it. "Was there a question in there?" Jacob asked.

Hud didn't react to this, but there was something in his eyes, something to suggest temper even though he looked calm and patient and utterly in control.

But Jacob wasn't nearly as patient, never had been. "Why don't you just say what you came here to say."

"All right," Hud said, "but it's going to be a repeat of what Sophie Marren just yelled at you."

"You don't want any more magical kisses that made your clothes fall off either?" Jacob asked.

Hud gave him a long, level look. "You lied to me."

"What the hell are you talking about?"

"You let me think that you left here and never looked back. But you paid half of Mom's bills."

Jacob let out a breath. Not where he'd thought this was going. "You already knew that," he said. "Where's the lie in that?"

"Because I just went to pay her next month's bill online and discovered someone already paid it. In fact, someone paid it for the rest of the year. In full."

Jacob lifted a shoulder. "So?"

"I knew it." He pointed at Jacob. "That's bullshit—you know that? I pay my half, always have. I don't need you to cover my part. Just because you heard about the resort and the money troubles doesn't mean you get to show off by stepping up and playing the hero now to assuage your own guilt."

Jacob had been about to say that stepping up now was the only way he knew how to make up for things, but Hud's holier-than-thou attitude was pissing him off. He stepped closer to his brother and Hud did the same, clearly itching for a fight every bit as much as he.

The thing was, stepping up to pay his mom's bills wasn't about showing off. He'd saved just about every penny he'd made over the past nine years. In the beginning he'd been aggressive with investments and it had paid off. His money had made money, and now he had a nest egg. It gave him peace of mind to know that if something happened to him, his mom would be okay.

"You didn't write," Hud said. "You didn't call. But you sent money for Mom and…Fuck." He shoved his hands in his hair and turned in a restless circle. "How could you not even call?"

Jacob closed his eyes. "I don't know." But he did know. It'd been because of what Hud had said to him before he left, angry words that shouldn't have sliced as deep as they had, but he'd been eighteen and he'd felt gutted. And hurt. And what eighteen-year-old punk kid dealt with that well? Not him.

"And now all of a sudden you want to put money in and be a part of this family?" Hud asked in disbelief. "You want to be the big hero and think that it fixes everything? Tough shit, man. You can't buy your way back in."

Is that what Hud thought? If so, hell if Jacob would explain about Brett and why he'd come back to Cedar Ridge. "Your problem with me being home has nothing to do with me helping out," he said. "And I have the money, so why the fuck can't I use it to help? Or do you plan to hold this over me for the rest of our lives?"

Both of their phones buzzed an incoming text at the same

time. They pulled their phones from their pockets and froze at the group message from their mom.

I've fallen. I don't want either of you to worry. I'll be fine. But they insisted I let you know. XOXO, Mom.

In sync, they moved toward their vehicles. "Meet you there," Jacob said.

Hud shook his head. "I'll drive. Get in."

Jacob did just that, taking some hope from the fact that at least in the case of an emergency they could come together and do what had to be done.

"She's never fallen before," Hud said with a frown, whipping out of Jacob's driveway. "Physically, she's been really good."

Jacob was trying to reach the front desk by cell phone but was on hold. "What are you doing slowing down?"

"The light's going to turn red before I get there," Hud said.

"Since when do you drive like a grandma?"

Hud grinded his molars and hit the gas, making it through the intersection without the light turning red.

"Turn left," Jacob told him. "It's faster to go down Jeffrey Pine Road."

"I'm a cop," Hud said through his teeth. "I know the best route."

"Great. Do you know which pedal is the accelerator?"

"Shit." Hud hit the gas, and Jacob couldn't help but note with some grim satisfaction that he turned left on Jeffrey Pine, possibly on two wheels.

Five minutes later they hit their mom's room at a dead run and came to a skidding halt in her doorway.

Carrie sat in the center of her bed, her ankle propped up

on an ice pack. She had a supersized loaded pizza in front of her.

"Just in time, boys!" she said cheerfully. "Come, sit, eat while it's still hot!"

"Mom," Hud said, still breathing hard from the run up the stairs. "You said you fell."

"I did. I was leading a Jazzercise class downstairs and tripped over Yvonne. We toppled like dominos. You should've seen us. There's a pic of it. Carl said he posted it on Instagram. He's going to tell everyone that his girlfriends are more into each other than him." She laughed and reached for her phone on the bedside table.

"Mom, we don't need to see the pic," Hud said. "How badly are you hurt?"

Jacob already knew the answer to that. She was beaming at the sight of them, happy and absolutely pain free. In fact, he'd bet his portion of that pizza that she was up to shenanigans and one hundred percent lucid at the moment.

"Baby, relax," Carrie said to Hud, and patted the bed. "Come eat."

Hud pinched the bridge of his nose and took a deep breath before looking at Jacob like *WTF?*

Jacob shrugged and moved to the bed. He removed the ice pack from her ankle and eyed it closely. Slightly swollen. Relieved, he replaced the ice pack and sat, pulling her in for a hug. Then he grabbed the biggest piece of pizza and took a bite. "Good stuff," he said. "Stone's?"

Carrie nodded with a smile.

"Missed that place," he said. "I'm starving."

Hud divided a look between the two of them like maybe they didn't speak the same language as he. But he sat. "Mom, what's going on?"

She patted his knee. "Do you remember that time you traded my cat for one of the neighbor's dog's new puppies?" she asked.

Jacob remembered. He and Hud had been maybe eight and had a mutual hate affair with the love of her life, Bones the cat—who'd hissed at them and shit in their shoes at every turn, out of spite. The people in the apartment across from them had a dog who'd shown up pregnant after being missing for two days. Two months later, she'd had pups in their bathtub.

Hud and Jacob had gotten the bright idea to trade Bones for a new puppy, and aided by the neighbor's son, the switch had been stealthily made one night.

The next morning, the neighbor had blown a gasket and so had Carrie. "You made us work for the guy cleaning up after those puppies for two weeks," Jacob reminded her. "Ten puppies, each with a loose digestive track. And this one…" He jabbed a thumb in Hud's direction, "kept pretending to gag like he was going to throw up and managed to get himself excused."

"Aw," Carrie said. "He wasn't pretending. You know he's got a weak stomach." She ruffled Hud's hair. "Don't you, baby?"

Hud grumbled something beneath his breath, and when Jacob laughed, he narrowed his eyes.

And then stood up and stared at them some more.

"What?" Carrie asked him. "What is it?"

"I'm missing something," Hud said.

"Oh no," she said. "I'm so sorry. Where did you last see it? Because your room's a complete and utter wreck, Hudson. If you'd just clean it like I asked—"

"It's not a *thing*," Hud said. "It's something else." He stared at Jacob.

"What is it?" Carrie asked, but Jacob knew. He held Hud's gaze and *knew*.

"You two don't seem like people who haven't spoken to or seen each other in nine years," Hud said.

Carrie laughed. "Well, of course not, silly. I speak to him as often as I speak to you. And speaking of that, you have a big birthday coming up. You're finally going to hit double digits, the big one-oh. What should we do to celebrate?"

So this answered Jacob's immediate question. They were ten years old today. Or would be next week.

And she wasn't in the present at all…

"We don't need anything special, Mom," Hud said, and stood up. "You, I want to see you outside."

"Can't, baby," she said. "My ankle—"

"*Jacob*," Hud said.

Jacob casually reached for another piece of pizza and leaned back against the headboard. Because he knew what was outside. A fight. One he didn't want to have.

Carrie took Hud's hand. "Honey, whatever it is, just say it."

Hud pinched the bridge of his nose and then dropped his hand and looked at his mom. "You heard from him. All this time, when he was"—Hud looked at Jacob—"gone, you heard from him."

Carrie, confused on the timeline or not, knew she'd stepped in it. She bit her lower lip, her expression dialed to an unbearable sadness that Jacob couldn't take. He reached for her hand and squeezed it. "I called every week," he told Hud.

"He used FaceTime," his mom said. "And sometimes he came in person."

Hud's eyes widened as he stared at Jacob. "You came here. You came here to Cedar Ridge?"

"Yes."

"How many times?"

"Hud—"

Hud pointed at him. "How many times, Jacob?"

"I don't know," he said.

"Nine," Carrie said, and winced when both boys turned to her. "I kept count. Was I not supposed to keep count?"

Hud swore and paced the length of the room, glowering fiercely. Then suddenly his temper drained and he shoved his fingers in his hair. "Jesus, Jacob," he whispered. "You kept up with her?"

"Did you really think I wouldn't?"

Hud's eyes hardened again. "You kept up with her and not me."

Yeah, okay, that one was more difficult. He took a deep breath to speak, but Hud closed his eyes and turned away. "Forget it," he said.

Forget it. He'd said the same thing all those years ago to Jacob, turning away from him then too. *If you want to be like Dad, go. But know that if you do, we're no longer brothers.*

And Jacob, not exactly an innocent party to the fight, had let those words fester deep inside. It'd taken him a shamefully long time to realize that what Hud had said had been in anger.

But what Jacob had done, walking away, he'd done with a purposeful calm. He'd walked away.

He'd been the bigger ass.

He knew that.

What he didn't know was how to fix it.

When the pizza was gone, Hud dropped Jacob off at the lake, not saying another word.

Jacob got out of his brother's truck and turned back. "I'm still going to work at the resort."

"Fine," Hud said tightly. "We need you."

The knot in Jacob's chest unloosened a little. "Fine."

"Fine," Hud said again. "As long as it doesn't involve you writing a goddamn check." He drove off, leaving Jacob in his dust. Fair enough, since Jacob had once done the same.

He sat on the porch as the sun set, waiting for Sophie.

But she didn't come back. Not that night.

Or the next.

Or the next.

Chapter 16

Sophie stood on the deck of *The Little Lucas*, her hands on her hips, trying to control her temper as she glared at the guy standing on North Beach's public launch dock a few feet away.

His mouth was moving as he went on and on about how she'd illegally moored last night, blah, blah, blah...

What he didn't know couldn't hurt him, but the truth was, she'd been illegally moored several nights in a row now. The first night she'd stayed in a quiet cove, but she'd been awakened at four in the morning by fishermen. And five. And six...The second night she'd found what seemed like a deserted private dock. She'd learned her mistake when the moon rose and a bunch of teenagers had shown up to smoke weed.

She still had a contact high.

Last night she'd started out near the campgrounds but had left when she'd seen a bear going through the trash cans right outside the women's restrooms. She'd ended up having to move several times throughout the night, and what she needed more than anything was eight straight hours of sleep.

"I'll be moving any second now," she promised. "I'm just waiting for the rest of the fam to get here." She smiled in a way that invited him to join her.

He declined.

"It takes my sister forever to get out of the house," she said, hoping she was coming off as charming and not as bat-shit crazy as she felt. "And my mom…well, let's just say my dad's probably going nuts right about now. You know how dads are. Everything's on a timetable and no one listens, and then it's one big yell-fest instead of a good time. But no worries. They'll be here soon and we'll get going in no time."

He didn't look impressed. "It's almost dark. You can't still be here after dark."

"I promise," she said, "because that would be totally and completely illegal." She flashed another smile.

Nope, still nothing. Instead, he crossed his arms over his chest.

"Okay," she said. "Here's the truth. My family's not coming."

He gave her a *duh* look.

"But I have a really good reason to be here. I swear," she said, waiting for her brain to come up with that great reason.

"It's for the resort," an unbearably familiar male voice said from above the dock.

She turned her head and watched as Jacob lithely leapt over the railing and landed with easy agility on the dock. She hadn't seen him for three days, something she told herself she'd been relieved about. She'd been working her ass off during those three days, at a myriad of temp jobs, and knew he'd been doing the same because she'd had lunch with Kenna yesterday.

She and Jacob would be working together on a bunch of

upcoming lake events as the resort kicked their summer season into high gear.

Jacob's military-short hair was growing out. He'd gotten some sun too. He stood there in a pair of jeans and a T-shirt advertising the resort, his eyes hidden behind dark lenses. She pasted on a casual smile and tried not to whimper as she watched him come closer, the soft twilight casting subtle shadows and highlights that shifted across his muscles as he moved.

"Hey, Rob," he said to the lake patrol guy. "Been a long time."

To Sophie's utter shock, Rob-of-the-absolutely-zero-personality smiled widely and enthusiastically pumped Jacob's hand.

"Heard you were back, Kincaid. Causing a big old stir in town, man. People can't wait to see you."

Jacob nodded easily, but Sophie could see past the calm facade. That news didn't make him happy.

Not that she cared. "If this little reunion is over," she said, "maybe we could get back to the issue here, which is that I don't deserve a damn ticket because—" Well, actually, she didn't have a because.

But as it turned out, she didn't need one.

"You're not going to get a ticket," Jacob said.

She turned to him. "How do you know? You don't work for lake patrol, remember?"

Jacob turned to Rob. "You heard that we're taking over North Beach for some upcoming events?"

"Yeah," Rob said. "Everyone's looking forward to them."

Jacob smiled. "Nice. Sophie's on our staff."

"Gotcha," Rob said. "You'll need to get her a lake pass if you're going to keep her moored overnight anywhere other than a private dock."

"We've got a private dock secured," Jacob said, and pointed to the line of cabins and private docks to the far right—of which his was the first one. And then the two of them continued to speak casually for another few minutes while Sophie stared at Jacob.

He'd lied to that lake patrol guy for her...

After a minute she realized he was staring at her back and that Rob had left. She opened her mouth, but he shook his head and boarded *The Little Lucas*. Then, casual as you please, he moved to the controls, started the engine, and motored them out of the boat ramp area.

"What the hell?" she asked, the forward motion of the boat forcing her to sit in the chair next to him or fall over.

Jacob handled the boat with the ease of a man who'd been born to it. The wind beat at them and she shivered, but Jacob looked impervious to the weather. "What the hell was that?" she asked.

"Not here." They left the five-miles-per-hour zone and he hit the gas. Talking became impossible over the high-pitched whine of the engine. They zoomed along the shore for a few minutes, the wind tousling her hair, the slowly sinking sun slanting over the mountain peaks and into her eyes.

She gasped in surprise when the boat slowed without warning and would've slid forward if Jacob hadn't put out an arm to catch her. She strained against his tanned, corded forearm, righting herself as soon as she could.

Okay, maybe not quite as soon as she could. Maybe she let her hands hold on to that hard arm for a few beats longer than she needed. She was only human.

They were in a secluded cove, no other boats in sight, no one on the shore, when Jacob turned off the boat and faced her.

"What—" she started, but was effectively shut up when

Jacob rose to his feet, yanked her up as well, and into his arms. Her heart rate tripled before he even touched his mouth to hers, and then she couldn't think at all.

Tightening his grip, he kissed her long and hard and deep, and by the time they pulled apart for air, she had her hands all over him, one at the small of his back, holding him to her, the other—oh God—in his jeans. She jerked her hands around and up, putting them on his chest.

To push him away, she told herself.

But she didn't push. Instead, her fingers curled into the cotton of his shirt as a battle raged inside her. Fear and lust were in mortal combat, and she had no idea which would win. If he kissed her again, they'd end up naked on the floor of this boat, but she didn't think she could be with him like that again and not fall.

Hard.

He didn't appear to have the same internal war going on. His big, yummy hands were exploring and his mouth wasn't far behind, and she was losing her mind, not to mention her resolve. She already knew he liked to kiss and that he was a master at it, but she was starting to learn that he liked to kiss *everything*, on his own schedule. And he liked to linger.

A lot.

The memories of a Jacob-induced orgasm had been fueling her fantasies for days. And, if she was being honest, it'd fueled more than one self-induced orgasm as well.

But then they locked eyes and they froze in place, her from a sudden rush of emotions, Jacob probably from watching them play out across her face.

"I want you to know," she said. "That this…" She wagged a finger between them. "This insanity between us, it's not making any sense to me. It just isn't. I'm still…conflicted."

"Three days, Soph."

"What?"

"I let you stew for three days, but I can't do it anymore." He hauled her in again, wrapped his hand in her hair and tugged just enough to make her look at him. "You've wrecked me," he murmured against her mouth, making her heart skitter to a halt in her chest.

"I wrecked you? What about what you've done to me?"

His eyes searched hers, an unholy light coming into his.

Well, crap. Instead of putting the brakes on this disaster walking, she'd just tossed gasoline on the fire.

Pulling her in closer, he kissed her again. "So you're as utterly"—another kiss—"wrecked"—and yet another—"as I am. Good to know." The next kiss took her to another place, where the only thing that existed was his hard body and what it was going to do to hers—

"Soph."

She was too busy shoving up his shirt so she could nibble her way down his bare chest to answer.

"Soph."

She licked one of his nipples and got a thrill when he shivered.

He picked her up, and she immediately wrapped her legs around his hips. He had one big hand cradling and caressing her butt, the other across her back, holding her close. She slipped her arms around him, hoping, wishing, that she'd never have to let go.

His hands tightened on her. "Tell me we're going to wreck each other again," he said, voice low and gritty with desire.

To that end, she tore off his shirt and pushed him down to the long bench seat.

Jacob took her with him, keeping a hand in her hair and

his mouth locked on hers. With a groan, he angled his head, his tongue sliding against her, making her feel like she'd been starving for this, for him. All she could think was he seemed to crave her as much as she craved him. He told her so in each press of his lips, every soft stroke of his tongue telling her, *Yes, this, more of this, don't stop...*

"Jacob."

He had his mouth at the base of her throat and hummed a wordless response.

"I missed you."

He stilled, his eyes closing for a beat. "I'm all yours," he whispered, and flipped them so that she was flat on her back on the seat. He rose over her, his chest and hips sliding against hers so that she could feel exactly how much he wanted her.

He kissed his way down her neck, opening her blouse and then the front clasp on her bra, spreading the material to the side to get a look at her.

"Why do you have a bruise on your left side?" Jacob asked.

"Yesterday I temped at a vet's office. I had to check in a cranky goose. Do you notice everything?"

He gave her an almost smile. "When it comes to you."

"If you weren't so hot, I'd find that really annoying," she said.

That got her the full-wattage smile. He didn't use it often, which made it all the more potent and sent desire skittering through her.

He reeled her in for a brain-melting kiss, during which her hands found their way down the back of his jeans.

"If your endgame isn't finding yourself naked and under me for the rest of the night, you should stop that," he said.

She tightened her fingers, digging them into his edible ass.

"Good choice." He lowered his head, sucking a nipple into his mouth, teasing it with his tongue, his teeth, while skimming her skirt up her thighs. "You've got me burning up from the inside out," he murmured.

She'd never done anything like this outside, ever. But they were in a secluded cove and she was flat on her back, out of sight even if someone did come along. Still, a secret thrill raced through her, an illicit one, and she felt a rush of arousal.

"Tell me you're burning up for me too."

She opened her mouth, but Jacob skimmed his lips down her torso, playing with her, easily stealing her breath along with her words. She was totally burning up for him, and as his hands slid up her thighs, she could feel exactly how turned on she was.

A single push had her skirt bunched around her waist. Another stroke of his fingers scooped her panties to one side, and then she knew he could see too.

"Yeah," he said in wicked, naughty accusation. "You're burning up for me." He stroked his thumb through her wet folds. Her thighs trembled, and she whimpered incoherently, her hips writhing.

And then he slid to his knees, pushed those broad shoulders between her thighs, and kissed her.

And then licked. Nibbled. Sucked.

And drove her right out of her ever-loving mind.

When she could draw air back into her lungs, she sat up so fast she bumped the top of her head on his chin and saw stars. "Ow!"

"Easy, tiger," he said, rubbing his chin.

His hair was standing straight up—from her fingers—and his mouth was wet—from her. No shirt, jeans low and barely concealing what was quickly becoming one of her favorite parts of him. She felt her mouth go dry just looking at him. Sliding to the floor of the boat, she mirrored his position, hitting her knees. Then she shoved him onto the seat she'd just vacated.

"Pushy," he said. "I like that—" He broke off on a groan when she popped open his jeans, tugged them down enough to free him, and sucked him into her mouth.

"Oh Christ." His voice was a low, rough growl as his fingers slid into her hair. *"Soph."*

And that, her name, was the last thing he said for a while.

Boneless and sated, they sort of melted into each other, letting the cool air drift across their damp and overheated bodies while they struggled to lower their heart rates from near stroke level.

"I can't even…," he finally murmured, his voice gravelly. "That was…" When he couldn't seem to find the words, he merely tightened his grip on her like he knew she was a flight risk and he couldn't bear it.

She loved that. The gesture, tiny as it had been, kept her warm. She knew this was to have been…what? Angry sex? Makeup sex? She couldn't remember anymore, but she knew one thing.

It hadn't been just sex.

This hit her like a wave over the head, as cold as the lake water beneath the boat. Not just sex. That meant more than just sex.

She'd told him she couldn't fall, not ever again, and yet she was seriously doing just that.

This was crazy. Crazy impossible. And just thinking about it, she began to have a very quiet, very internal freak-out.

Except maybe not so internal. She didn't realize she was trembling until, with a low murmur of concern, Jacob pulled her in closer, running his big hands over her as if to warm her.

But he couldn't, because she was cold from the inside out. Cold with the certainty that she'd truly done exactly what she'd promised herself she wouldn't.

She'd fallen. And as the commercial went, she didn't think she could get up.

"What's the matter?" he asked.

"Nothing. Everything's peachy. Listen, I think we should forget this happened."

His long look suggested she was mental, and she gave a nearly hysterical laugh, because he was just now figuring that out? Sitting up, she began to re-dress. "Hurry."

"Where's the fire?"

She'd broken the hook on her bra, dammit. She slipped her blouse back on without it. Her damn nipples hadn't gotten the freak-out memo and were pressing against the thin material. It was hugely annoying, but when she glanced over at Jacob, he seemed anything but annoyed. "Okay, so I'm not in a hurry to get somewhere. I'm in a hurry to get away from any awkward…after."

He laughed. "Since when do we do awkward afters?"

She stared at him and remembered last time, in his bed, where he'd taken her to new heights. Over and over again.

No awkward after. "Fine. Whatever. I'm taking you home."

His slow, sexy smile told her she'd just played right into his big hands, but at the moment she didn't care. She took control of the boat and headed across the water at a fast clip.

The evening was truly gorgeous. The water was like a piece of glass, and she cut straight through it, loving the light spray off the front of the hull, the wind in her face…She was almost thankful that Lucas was such an asshole.

Almost.

When she got back to the north shore, she slowed down, passing the row of cabins. When she came to Jacob's, she lined up with his dock the best she could, but she wasn't good at coming in from this direction, and the wind and waves were not being her friends.

"Careful," he said. "The corner—"

"I see it." She whipped her head around, trying to eyeball the maneuver, still getting used to how differently a boat glided over water versus a car on the road.

Jacob stood up. "Sophie—"

"Sit down or jump into the water," she said. "Because I can't see around you."

He stood on the very edge of the boat, one foot on the hull, the other reaching out to work as a buoy for the dock. "You're coming in too hot," he said. "You've got to—"

"I see it." Shit. He was right. She'd overcorrected, and now she was stuck in the position of having to overcorrect an overcorrect—which never worked out.

"Sophie—"

"I got it!"

But she didn't, and in the next second she heard the boat collide with the dock. And a big, huge chunk of the dock broke off and fell into the water.

Chapter 17

Jacob took over, leaping onto the dock, the rope from the bow of Sophie's boat in his hand, which he used to tie it to the torn dock. "Got it, Andretti," he said, turning back to Sophie with a smile that quickly died on his lips.

She hadn't moved from the controls, though she'd turned off the engine. She was still white-knuckling the wheel, head bent.

Silent.

He reached for the rope at the stern to tie that as well. "You breathing over there?"

"I'm so sorry," she whispered.

Finished with the boat, he crouched on the dock, as close as he could get to her with her still behind the wheel. "Hey."

"I'll get it fixed," she said. "I promise."

"Soph. Look at me."

She lifted her head. She was pale, upset. And goddamn it all to hell, anxious. A stark difference to how she'd been looking at him fifteen minutes ago, when she'd been on her knees between his, eyes lit with erotic promise as she'd driven him wild with her mouth.

"It's just a dock, Soph," he said softly. "It won't take much to fix it. I can do it myself." He shifted closer, and she froze. Froze into a solid block of ice, every inch of her—except for her eyes, which flared with defiance, and her hands as they tightened into fists at her side.

The gesture was familiar. Jacob had seen it every time he and Hud had gone head-to-head, or with his unit when they'd bickered…She was braced for a fight. He stared at her, trying to figure out what the hell. How could she think he was going to yell at her over a mistake, or worse… *Jesus*…put his hands on her in anger?

Moving slowly, he continued with what he'd originally planned on doing. He touched her cheek, stroked his fingers over the curve of her jaw and let them sink into her hair, gently pulling her face up to his.

She closed her eyes, and he felt his heart press up too hard against his rib cage. "Sophie, please look at me."

She opened her eyes and focused them on his face, specifically just above his own eyes, probably at the scar that bisected his eyebrow. It was a trick he knew all too well from having to stare at commanding officers who were yelling right in his face. He wouldn't give them the respect of looking straight in their eyes, saying *fuck you* by looking right through them. "I once fell out of a tree trying to beat Hud to the top," he said.

Her startled gaze flew to his. "What?"

"The scar you're looking at. I got it when I was a kid. The funny thing is that Hud has one exactly like it on the opposite eyebrow. He got his when I hit him with a bat."

Her eyes widened and she gasped.

"Not on purpose," he said. "He was catcher on our high school baseball team and got caught by a wide swing."

She stared at him. "You're trying to distract me."

"If I were trying to distract you, we'd both be naked again."

She blinked. "Awfully sure of yourself," she said.

A challenge. He liked a good challenge. He also liked her pissed off instead of anxious. He got that she was afraid of getting emotionally attached and he'd thought that worked for him. He'd mistakenly assumed that her past, and her scars from that past, were none of his business. He'd been wrong. And if it was Lucas who'd taught her to fear confrontation, he'd be teaching him to drink through a straw.

"I don't care about the dock," he said. "Or the damage. What I care about is you."

She was very busy studying her feet.

She didn't fully believe him, and he did his best to not be insulted by that. "Okay," he said. "Let's try this instead." And then he pulled her face to his and kissed her. He went in quick and easy, or meant to. But even with their awkward angle, with her in the boat and him on the dock leaning over her, there was absolutely nothing quick or easy about the way their mouths clung greedily.

She pulled back first, shaking her head like she needed to clear it. She tried to speak, but either she couldn't find the words or she was still as dazed as he was, because she ended up just staring at him.

He nodded. "I'll take that as 'Why, Jacob, I care about you too.'" He rose and offered her a hand out of the boat, which she took.

"I stand corrected," she said. "You were able to distract me."

He smiled, but she pointed at him. "But I'm onto you now, so that won't work again." And with that, she headed belowdecks.

Another challenge, he thought, and he was absolutely up to the task.

Sophie went belowdecks and pressed her hands to her racing heart. God. God, what had she done?

You let him in...

And then you destroyed his dock. She plopped down on the bed and closed her eyes. Damn, her body was still trembling. From good sex, adrenaline.

Anxiety.

She'd crunched his dock, and just like that, she'd been back in her bad marriage...nervous, jumping. Upset.

The truth was, Lucas hadn't always been a coldhearted dick. Once upon a time he'd been fun. Happy.

Then he'd been hired by a cutthroat law firm, and she'd rarely seen him. He'd felt a lot of stress and pressure on himself and he'd...changed.

Suddenly everything she did irritated him, annoyed him, pissed him off. He'd lost his patience and grown a nasty temper, and she'd...hated it. She'd also allowed herself to feel responsible. Just like she had with her dad, she'd rushed to please him.

An impossible task.

But eventually she'd gotten used to always being wrong, and worse, she'd gotten used to the yelling. It shamed her just how much. She'd withdrawn, retreated inside herself, and she was only now coming back into her own. It was way too soon to think about having feelings for anyone, and yet that's exactly what she'd done—even though she'd told Jacob she couldn't have feelings, that she absolutely wouldn't.

Ever.

It wasn't too much later that there came a knock on the door. And then... "Soph."

She closed her eyes. What was it about his voice that always reached her, even when she was mad, hurt?

And that was the problem, she knew. Not that she was mad or hurt. But afraid, of her own heart, no less.

"Let me in, Soph."

*You're already in…*Not that she planned on admitting any such thing. She stared at the ceiling. "The door's unlocked."

"Let me in," he repeated quietly.

Sophie turned her head and stared at the door. Damn him. He didn't want to bulldoze his way in. He wanted her to let him in.

If he only knew.

She stood up and went to the door but didn't open it. "Are you wearing a shirt?" she asked cautiously. She didn't trust herself if he wasn't.

There was a beat of silence. "Do you want me to be?"

She banged her head against the wood a few times, sighed, and opened the door.

He'd changed his T-shirt. This one said BOMB SQUAD… IF YOU SEE US RUNNING, YOU'D BEST KEEP UP, and she laughed.

His mouth quirked, like he enjoyed the sound of her laugh. "Come up on deck?" he asked, and without waiting for her, turned and vanished.

She followed, as he knew damn well she would.

Night had fully fallen, but that wasn't what surprised her. No, it was the candles lit on the hull, shimmering in the dark. The blanket spread out on the floor of the boat.

In the center was a picnic. A bottle of wine, cheese, crackers, salami, grapes.

"My version of cooking," Jacob said. "Sophie, about before."

"I'd rather not talk about it." She kept her back to him as

she took in the spread he'd put out for her, needing a moment, needing space, because whenever she got too close to him, their mouths gravitated toward each other like magnets.

"Not that," he said, voice low. "Before that. I honestly didn't realize you thought I was lake patrol. I should have, but I'm…"

When he trailed off, she turned to face him.

"I'm people rusty," he explained, and then grimaced. "Specifically, *women* rusty."

She stared at him as that sank in. He'd spent the past nine long years as a soldier, doing and saying God knew what. Of course he was rusty.

Anyone would have been, and she should've seen that. She smiled and hoped it conveyed her apology as well. "So your plan was to what, give me orgasms until my brain cells blew so I wouldn't notice?" she teased.

He flashed a grin. "I blew your brain cells?"

"You know you did." She gave him a little push and he stepped back.

"Your choice, Soph," he said. "Always will be."

He was telling her flat-out that she was in the driver's seat here, that she had the controls. Too bad she had no idea what to do with that.

Or him.

Liar, an inner voice said. *You want to strip him and ride him like a bronco.*

When he laughed softly, it sent a bolt of heat through her that turned into a shudder racing up her spine. "What?"

"I half expected you to shove me overboard. Instead you're looking like maybe you want to eat me for lunch, dinner, and dessert."

She closed her eyes. "Well, not all three at the same time."

He laughed again, and eyes still closed, she shook her head.

"Say it," he said quietly. "Say what you need to say."

How did he know? How did he always know? "All right," she whispered. But she needed space for this, so she took a few steps back from him. "You told that lake patrol guy that we had a private dock secured." She met his gaze. "We? Is that the royal 'we,' or you and the mouse in your pocket?"

"Babe, that's not a mouse in my pocket."

She rolled her eyes. "You lied for me, Jacob. Why?"

"It wasn't a lie. You're staff for the Wounded Warriors event. And did you forget what I told you about us?"

Her heart did a slow roll in her chest. "I'm yours," she whispered. "For the duration."

"Yes, but more than that, I'm *yours*," he said, quiet steel. "That means I give you everything I can. Help. Backup. Whatever you need."

Because that was way too much for her brain to compute, she turned away and looked at the spread he'd laid out. "This looks like a date," she said warily.

"Dinner."

"So…not a date?"

He smiled. "Which will get you sitting down and eating with me?"

"Not a date," she said instantly.

"Fine." He snagged her hand, pulled her down to the bench to sit with him.

"No glasses," she said, nodding to the wine.

"No plates either."

"I can go belowdecks and—"

"No need," he said smoothly, opening everything and pulling out his pocketknife to slice the summer sausage and cheese. When he had a cracker loaded, he handed it to her and then made one for himself. He repeated that action a handful of times, until he sighed with pleasure. It was a sound she knew well, and it had her nipples tightening.

"I was starving," he said, and opened the wine, offering the bottle to her.

It was a visceral reminder of that night they'd shared the Scotch, and the memory made her hesitate.

He grinned.

"Shut up," she said without heat. "I swore off alcohol after the Scotch, but after a day like today, a girl needs a little something-something. And don't—" She pointed at him. "Don't turn that into a double entendre."

"Don't have to," he said, still grinning. "You did it for me." He watched her drink and then held out his hand. She passed the bottle.

He let his fingers drift over hers for a beat before taking a drink. There was something about watching his mouth covering the lip of the bottle where her mouth had just been that felt so…intimate.

And sensual.

As she had that night, she stared at the way his Adam's apple moved when he swallowed, at the stubble on his jaw. And then, inexplicably drawn upward, she looked into his eyes and sucked in a breath when she found him watching her watching him.

It had her busying herself with wrapping up their leftovers, which granted, wasn't much. Apparently a shitty day plus oral sex in public made a girl hungry. "I owe you dinner," she said. "And while this is very good, mine will be better."

"I'm going to hold you to that." He took another long pull of wine, and she realized something. His eyes were shadowed, and lines of exhaustion were etched in his beautiful face.

She thought of what she'd seen at the resort, him with his siblings and the unease she'd sensed in him. "You've been hanging out with your family," she said casually. "How's it going?"

He lifted a shoulder.

She smiled. "Maybe you could use some words?"

He gave her an impressive eye roll. "Could be smoother," he admitted.

She hesitated but couldn't help butting in where she wasn't wanted. "They love you, you know. Your family."

Another oh-so-expressive shoulder lift.

She set down the bottle. "You know, it's okay to give yourself a break. Sometimes you have to get things wrong before you can get them right, and that's okay."

He slid her a look. "Is that what you do?"

"Hello," she said, spreading out her arms. "Look at me. I'm a temp worker in a temp job because I excel at getting things wrong. But I'm trying."

"You think I'm not?"

"I think you need to learn to let things go," she said gently. "You came back, Jacob. You get points for that, no matter how it goes. Stop looking in the rearview mirror and start looking out in front of you. Earlier today, Hud couldn't take his eyes off you. I think he wants you to be at home here. He just doesn't know any better than you do how to deal."

One corner of his mouth quirked. "You got that all from just looking at us, huh?"

She shrugged. "I'm good at reading people."

His eyes met hers and held. "I'm getting that," he said. "I'm also getting that you had to be."

She didn't want to go there. "You could just come right out and say you're sorry for leaving, you know."

"I'm working my way up to it," he said.

"How's that going?"

"Hud's not ready," he said.

"Ever think that maybe you're projecting?"

He didn't move, didn't even breathe as far as she could tell, so she handed him the wine. "I project," she said conversationally, taking the bottle back when he'd taken a drink. "And trust me, it's not healthy. I projected all Lucas's assholery onto myself, and I let it color how I see myself. But then I realized that no one's going to like me if *I* don't like me…" She trailed off and took another sip of the wine, and when she lowered the bottle, she discovered he'd moved after all.

Closer.

He slid his fingers over her jaw and tilted her face up to his. "You're smarter than hell, sexier than hell, and I like you way more than I should," he said. "Tell me you got over that hump, Sophie, and that you learned to like yourself even half as much as I do."

She didn't realize she was chewing on her lower lip until he bent his head and kissed that lip. And then the corner of her mouth. And then the other corner…And then he stared at her, letting her see that what he'd said was true, that he liked her a whole lot more than he should. Her breath caught.

"Tell me," he whispered against her lips, making them tingle in anticipation. She knew how he kissed now, with his entire heart and soul, and it so contradicted everything about him that it always threw her off-balance.

He threw her off-balance. In the best way.

In fact, she wanted to be thrown off-balance right this minute.

As if guessing where her thoughts had gone, the very corners of his mouth turned up.

"Sorry," she murmured. "But has anyone ever told you that you're deadly up close?"

"Sophie."

She sighed. While *she* could be distracted, she should've known that he couldn't. "Yes, I got over myself. I know now that I didn't do anything wrong. That I'm a good person." She closed her eyes. "That I deserve better."

"Good." He kissed her then, until she crawled across the blanket and into his lap, sighing when his arms closed around her.

"This is a little scary," she whispered.

"A lot scary."

She tipped her head back to his. "I'm still not keeping you." As if her body didn't agree with her mouth, her fingers tightened on his shirt. "I'm not going to keep anyone, not ever again."

"I know," he said, and stroked a hand down her back, soothing her even as she did her best to hurt him.

"But you don't want to love anyone either," she said. "That hasn't changed, right?"

He didn't answer, and she closed her eyes. "Jacob."

His big hand continued to stroke up and down her spine, and she felt hot tears prick at her eyelids. "We're so screwed up," she whispered.

"In a very large way," he agreed.

He did that thing he did, where he lightly tugged at a loose wave of her hair. Then he produced chocolate chip cookies for dessert.

"I might have to rescind my no-love rule," she said, a cookie in each hand. "Cookies are my sweet spot."

He smiled. "They're not your only sweet spot."

Her "sweet spot" quivered, a fact she firmly ignored. "I miss baking. No oven."

"Tell me again why you took this boat. Or better yet, why you stay on it. You could've gotten whatever you needed, money…nice things…"

"Money and nice things didn't work out so well for me," she said. "I'm trying something new to find my happy."

He stared at her and then smiled, shaking his head.

"What?"

"You expect me to believe that being here on this boat is making you happy?" he asked, disbelief heavy in his voice. "And be careful here," he said when she opened her mouth, "because I'm the one who held your hair back while you threw up from seasickness, remember? You hate this boat."

"Yes, but…" She grimaced. "I'm still getting some mileage out of knowing Lucas is miserable because I'm living on his baby." She didn't look at him, not wanting to see what he thought of this.

But he laughed. "Okay, remind me to never piss you off."

And that was just the thing. He *had* pissed her off, several times now. And yet she didn't feel like retreating, or never speaking to him again, or strangling him with his own pillow in the dark of the night.

Well, okay, maybe she had once or twice…But she'd also felt like making up with him in ways that just thinking about made her squirm uncomfortably. In the best possible way.

Chapter 18

Jacob gathered everything back into the bag he'd brought down from his cabin and stood.

Sophie did the same. "You told me I could stay here."

A commander had once told Jacob he was the hardest sonofabitch he'd ever met, and Jacob had believed it. He'd been in some pretty ugly places and had done some pretty ugly things. People tended to give him a wide berth.

But not this woman. Nerves and fears or not, she still went toe-to-toe with him.

He fucking loved it.

Whether she knew it or not, she was comfortable with him. It made him want even more from her. Things he hadn't imagined ever wanting from anyone. Things he'd promised her he didn't want.

Which put him in the ridiculous position of either continuing to lie to her about that, or swallowing emotions he didn't know what to do with anyway in order to keep her in his life. "Yeah," he said. "I told you that you could moor here. And I meant it. Indefinitely."

Her eyes widened in surprise. "Indefinitely?"

"Yes." *Expect more from me*, he wanted to say. *Demand it from me. You deserve it.* Instead, he smiled. "No worries. I'll collect my rent."

She didn't smile. Instead she stared up at him. "I'm sorry I assumed you were lying to me." She said this quietly but also slightly begrudgingly, which made him smile. "I'm not good at letting people in."

"I think you're doing pretty damn good," he said.

She stared at him as if she wasn't sure how to take him. So while they were on that, he said, "And you should know, I don't lie." *Well, except for how I feel about you...* "Too much to remember. I'm lazy, Sophie. Very lazy. We square?"

"You're the most unlazy man I've ever met."

"Say it."

She looked at him for a long beat. "We're square," she finally said. "Are we friends?"

Is that what they were doing? He hadn't put a label on it, but if he had, *friends* would have been in the mix. *Friends. Lovers...* "Is that what you want?"

She stared into his eyes, and then her gaze dropped to his mouth and she licked her lips, nearly causing him to groan.

"I think we're a little more than that," she said.

"Is that what you want?" he asked again.

She stared at him. "It's a start, right?"

"And the end?"

"You don't seem like a guy concerned with the ending of anything."

True enough, he thought. And he had no idea why he was pushing on this. Except he did. He wanted more and yet he wasn't exactly in a position to offer it. "You know what I'm asking. I'm asking if we're going to be more than friends."

"For the duration, you mean?"

His own words, of course, put right back on him. He'd said she was his for the duration, and he was hers. He'd meant it. He just hadn't known how much…or how badly he'd want the duration to be extended.

She cocked her head and studied him, and he did his best to look like the kind of guy she couldn't live without. And maybe also the kind of guy she wanted to take belowdecks and lick from head to toe.

"I have no idea what to do with you," she said.

"I've got a few ideas."

She snorted. "Stop. I mean it."

He sobered. "I know."

"And you know it's not you, right?" she asked earnestly. "It's me."

He laughed at her use of the cliché. He couldn't help it. And she smiled and gave him a push. "It's not a line. I mean it." Her smile vanished. "We both know I've got some things to work out. In my head."

And she wasn't the only one. Reaching over, he took her hand in his, liking it when she entwined their fingers. Bringing their joined hands up to his mouth, he brushed his lips over her knuckles.

Her breath caught.

"Sophie?"

"Yeah?" she asked a little breathlessly.

"Take your time," he said.

She let out a whoosh of air as if greatly relieved, and not for the first time he wanted to hunt down the men who'd been in her life, starting with her dad, who should've protected and cherished her and not let it be the other way around.

"We don't have a lot of time," she said. "You're leaving."

True story. "What do you need?"

She hesitated.

"Talk to me," he said.

"Well…that's just it. I need you to talk to me. I need your deep, dark secrets."

"How do you know I have any?" he asked.

"All men do."

"Ah," he said, not particularly thrilled to have been looped in with her ex and her dad but getting it. "All of us, huh?"

"Every last one of you," she said, sounding very sure.

"Okay." He nodded. "Where should I start?"

"Well…" She considered. "You could tell me what you think of cats, since I'm thinking of becoming a cat lady. There's your favorite food. Your feelings on sexy undies. Things that make you homicidal," she said.

The last part did something to him deep in his gut. She'd buried her lede, afraid to ask outright if he was a dick when he got mad about something. He got that too.

"And let's throw in your worst sexual experience," she said.

He went brows up at that one. "I don't like cats," he started.

"Why not?"

"They're smug fuckers. I hope that's not a deal breaker," he said, smiling when she cracked up. "My favorite food is cereal. I can eat it three meals a day for long stretches of time without getting tired of it. As for sexy undies, I *love* them. But my favorite undies are no undies at all."

Her eyes warmed.

"As for what makes me homicidal…"

She froze. "Yeah?"

"It's people who wear flip-flops. I think it's the toes."

She sucked in a breath. "Toes."

He gave an exaggerated shudder. "I have a toe phobia."

She laughed. "You do not."

He did not… "As for your last question…I had the worst blow job of my life on a heli, though I suspect it was because she was also piloting the thing while we were going at it."

She blinked. "Wow. I can't beat that. But…" She kicked off her sandals and waved her bare foot in his direction. "Do *my* toes wig you out?"

Her toenails had been painted bright blue and there was a white daisy on one of them. "Cute," he said. "And since they make me want to start there and nibble my way up your mile-long legs and see what else I find, I can say on good authority that no, your toes do not wig me out."

"You're doing it again," she said quietly.

"Annoying you?"

She shook her head. "The opposite."

He smiled. "Good." Leaning in, he lowered his voice to a bedroom whisper. "My turn. Tell me a secret so dirty it turns you on just to admit it."

She choked on a laugh. "I…can't."

"Can't? Or won't?"

"Can't." She paused. "Because it's about you."

"Even better."

She bit her lower lip and he went insta-hard. "Your secret would be safe with me," he promised.

She pondered this seriously. "Something else to think about," she said.

Chapter 19

They ended up in Jacob's cabin, specifically in his bed where they spent several hours, but eventually Sophie left, claiming something about needing to take her vitamins and how she couldn't sleep outside her own bed. He knew why she really left.

She needed some space.

He did too. Or so he told himself. But without her in it, his bed seemed huge.

The next day Soph flew to Dallas to spend a few days with her family and his bed got bigger each night. It was late on one of those nights that his phone *ping*ed. When he glanced at it, he was surprised to find a…tweet? The only way that could happen was if someone had signed him up for Twitter.

Kenna, no doubt, the little brat. And she'd also apparently set his phone for notifications when someone tweeted about or to him. She would pay for that…

He accessed the notification and stared down at the

message, which had come from someone called
CedarRidgeNumberOneMom. It didn't take a genius to
figure out who that was.

I joined the Twitter, baby! What's up?

He laughed in disbelief. Shaking his head, he backed out
of the Twitter app—*definitely going to strangle Kenna*—and
texted his mom.

You know that Twitter isn't like texting, right? That
everyone can see what you're doing?

In less than a minute he got another Twitter notification.

So are you busy?

He had to laugh as he called her. "Mom, you can call
me whenever you want. You don't have to use Twitter to
talk to me."

"Oh, baby, I know that. But calling is passé. No one calls
anyone these days. It's all about social media."

For the first time, he wondered just how much trouble his
mom had managed to find over the years. He'd always assumed that he'd taken the much harder road than Hudson,
being in the military, living that life.

But honest to God, he had to wonder if he hadn't had it
easy in comparison to his twin. "How about we keep things
old-fashioned?" he asked.

"But, honey, you're never going to catch a girl that way."

He'd caught one fine. He just had no idea how to keep
her. "I'll manage," he said.

"Fine, but you don't have the best of tastes. You remember last year when you were into that Weston girl? She dumped you at recess and crushed your heart. I want to meet this next one and make sure she's good enough."

Kim Weston had been his sixth-grade crush. "Got it, Mom. You're in charge."

"I mean it. I'm watching you," she said, a note of teasing coming into her voice.

His heart squeezed. "Wouldn't have it any other way."

"Good. I picked a girl for your brother and he's going to marry her. So see, you can trust my judgment."

When she disconnected, Jacob stared out the window at the lake for a long time.

He knew Hud was serious about Bailey, but only because he could see it with his own eyes and because Kenna had told him so.

He hadn't known they were going to get married.

For some reason this hurt more than anything else, that they were so distanced from each other that Hud wouldn't have told him such an important thing going on in his life.

Jacob was willing to take his part of the responsibility, and yeah, his part was more than fifty percent.

But Hud wasn't giving an inch here. He needed an inch, dammit.

Ever think that maybe you're projecting?

On that thought, he picked up his phone again and called the guy who'd leased him the cabin.

"When I first contacted you about renting this cabin, you asked if I was interested in buying," he said. "I wasn't ready then, but I'm ready now."

Sophie's visit to Dallas went predictably. It'd been great to see her sister. Good to see her parents. And bad for her mental health.

Par for the course.

As she got back to Cedar Ridge, she felt…like she'd come home.

The boat itself, not so much.

She got back just in time to take an afternoon shift at the assisted-living center attached to the hospital. A flu had knocked out the girls at the front desk. Sophie sanitized the entire place and then got them all caught up on paperwork.

While on break, she wandered down to the residents' social room to see if she was needed. It was here that the residents watched TV, played games, or just sat around and talked.

Her gaze was immediately drawn to the chess table, where Carrie was currently in the middle of a game.

With Jacob.

She'd missed him.

Carrie made a move, beamed, and then rose to her feet. Leaning over the table, she cupped Jacob's face and kissed him on the top of his head.

Sophie froze for a beat, torn between not wanting to intrude on what was clearly a private moment and melting into a pile of goo at the sweetness between Jacob and his mom.

But then Jacob's gaze slid to hers and he, too, rose to his feet.

"I'm sorry," she said. "I didn't mean to—*oh*," she breathed when he smiled and she realized her mistake.

Not Jacob, but Hudson. He'd cut his hair, and she hadn't immediately seen the difference in his eyes and smile—which were friendly and warm but not…Well, she wasn't sure she could accurately describe the way Jacob looked and smiled at her. Mostly it was with the heated, personal knowledge that came from having been as intimate with her as a man could get.

"I'm sorry," she said again. "You two look so much alike…"

He smiled. "Twins."

"Maybe." She laughed a little self-consciously. "It's hard to get used to."

"I know. But maybe as the woman helping us keep Jacob in Cedar Ridge, you'll get used to it?"

She stared at him. "Oh, I'm not—we're not—" She shook her head. "I think you've overestimated what Jacob and I are to each other."

"Oh," Carrie marveled, coming closer. "You're the one my Jacob's seeing, aren't you?" She took Sophie's hand, her smile bright. "Look at you. I just knew you'd be pretty. He always did like the pretty ones."

Hud grimaced. "Mom—"

"Oh, I know, he'll kill us, blah, blah. Might as well make it worthwhile, yes?" She smiled at Sophie. "Where did you two kids meet? School? A football game? Oh, I know! You're his English tutor?" She shifted in close and spoke in a stage whisper. "Listen, honey, I read his essay and I know you must have written it for him. No way did he read enough Shakespeare to write that on his own. I realize he's charming as all get-out, but you've got to encourage him to do his own work, okay?"

Sophie glanced over at Hud, who stood there at his mom's side, tall and broad like Jacob, eyes still warm but also something else now. Challenging? Waiting for her to react to his mom's jumbled ramblings?

Well, what he didn't know was that Sophie had been judged before and found wanting, and she no longer did anything for approval. Turning her back on him, she smiled at

Carrie and squeezed her fingers gently. "I'll do better next time. I promise," she said. "And are you done kicking your son's butt in chess? Because I'd love a game."

Carrie clapped in glee and gave Hud the brush-off with a wave of her hand.

He started to object. "Mom—"

"Baby, it's okay. I know you only came by because you're feeling guilty over how busy you are lately, but as you can see, I'm busy too. Run along now. Mama's gotta kick your twin's very pretty girlfriend's tush in chess."

Hud shook his head but pulled Carrie in for a hug. This time when he turned to Sophie, the warmth was back in his eyes, along with a grudging respect. "She cheats," he warned her.

"What?" Carrie said, hand to her heart. "Well, my goodness, I do no such thing, Hudson."

"Hand to heaven," Hud said to Sophie, and to her shock he gave her a good-bye hug as well.

"What was that for?" she asked when he pulled free.

"For giving him a challenge close to home, for putting a smile on his face."

"And how do you know that was me?" she asked, a little flustered with the praise she wasn't sure she deserved.

"A twin *knows*."

She wondered what else he knew and felt her face heat.

He chuckled, for a minute the sound so much like Jacob that she blinked. And then he was gone.

Chapter 20

Jacob sat on his porch watching the sun set over the Rocky Mountain peaks and Cedar Lake. It was his first break in days. Kenna had been saying she'd been sinking, drowning in all the prep for their upcoming events.

He'd honestly believed it was her way of forcing him to interact at the resort, to be near everyone.

Including Hud.

But he should've known better. Kenna was about as up-front and frank as a woman could be. If she had a problem, everyone knew it. There was no hidden agenda with her, no pretending to be something she wasn't. She was truly over-worked, and once Jacob realized that, it was easy to jump in and help her.

As it was, they'd been working night and day to pull off the Wounded Warriors weekend, which would provide a day of water and land sports for injured veterans and their nondisabled family and friends from all over the country. It was a hell of a lot of work, and he was good with that.

But for now he sat there watching the deep, dark night sky, his brain tired.

"You okay?"

Sophie. He'd heard her coming. She had a fondness for high-heeled sandals that made her legs look like they were ten miles long. Smooth, sleek, toned—

Don't go there, soldier.

He stood up as she came into view, standing before him with a soft smile. "Hey."

He found he couldn't talk, couldn't breathe until he'd pulled her in and buried his face in her hair. The feel of her, warm and soft in his arms, felt so fucking right. Able to breathe again, he finally said "hey" back.

She'd burrowed in as well, setting her head on his shoulder and letting out a little sigh like maybe he was her happy place.

With her curvy, warm body pressed up against his, he realized she was most definitely his. "Missed you," he said.

"Me too."

"You missed you too?" he teased.

She pulled back to look into his eyes. "You know what I mean."

"Maybe I want to hear it spelled out."

Her smile faded. "I missed you, Jacob."

He let out a rough breath. "Scared me there for a beat."

She stared at him. "If you knew how much I missed you, you'd still be scared."

Knees still a little weak, he sank to the porch swing.

With a small smile, she sat, mimicking his body language by slouching down a little so she could eye the sky. "You know, I never really realized what a great view we have here. You don't know what you've got until you go anywhere else, where the smog and city lights minimize the stars. It's amazing."

"I know," he said. "There's no place like Colorado."

"You've been all over the world," she said.

"I know." He tipped his head back and stretched out his arm. "This place does it for me."

"I met your mom today," Sophie told him, pressing her face into his throat. He smelled so good—he always did. "She's…well, she's pretty damn great, but you already know that."

"Yeah," he said quietly, turning his face to press it into her hair, like maybe he thought she smelled good too. "She tell you what a punk I was?"

"*Was?*" she teased.

He smiled into her hair and squeezed her. "Smart-ass."

Laughing softly, she cuddled into him. "Hud was there too. For a minute I thought he was you. But then he smiled at me and I knew."

"We smile differently?"

"Well, when you're looking at me, you do." She winced with embarrassment. "His smile is nice, but when you smile, it's…"

"Not nice?"

She gave him a mock slug to the gut. "It's just not the same kind of smile you give me, that's all."

"How's it different?"

She bit her lower lip.

And he laughed.

She slugged him again, not so lightly this time. "You know!"

"You mean because I smile at you like I'm thinking about being buried deep inside you, so deep that you're whimpering for more, begging me to 'please, Jacob, please' in my ear?"

"I don't beg!" But she blushed because they both knew that she did.

Grinning wide, he caught her hand before she could hit him again. His reflexes were good. She knew that had been conditioned into him, a necessity with the life he'd lived. But it served him well.

Rising to his feet, he scooped her up and threw her over his shoulder in a fireman's carry and then turned as if to take her inside.

She hung over his back, giving her a great view of his spectacular ass, which she smacked.

"Remember," he said, palming her ass in his big hand. "Paybacks are a bitch."

That absolutely shouldn't make her quiver in excitement. "What are we doing?" she demanded, ruining the effect by being breathless.

"Going to make you beg."

Oh boy...

Chapter 21

The next morning Sophie awoke to find herself wrapped in Jacob's arms. They were face-to-face and she'd used his biceps as a pillow and the rest of him as her personal heater.

She'd spent the night.

Panicked at the thought, she held herself perfectly still, faking sleep for a moment while her mind raced. It was just crazy chemistry, she told herself. They'd had great sex and, exhausted, she'd fallen asleep. It happened.

But it felt like more. And she didn't want more. She *couldn't* do more.

Could she?

When his alarm went off, she nearly fell off the bed, but she forced herself to stay still, not sure what she was doing. Was she really going to feign sleep?

Maybe.

Jacob stretched a little, and because he had a muscled thigh between hers, she nearly moaned at the movement.

He leaned across her to turn off the alarm, brushing a tender kiss across her temple as he did so, before rolling out of bed.

When she heard the shower go on, she debated—run out like the demons of hell were on her heels, or wait him out?

Since the shower went off, like, two seconds later, she had no choice. She felt him watching her while he dressed, but she was extremely motivated to avoid an awkward morning after because…

She'd spent the night.

The implied intimacy of that felt far more real than even their incredible sex, and she was in the middle of a full-blown panic attack by the time she heard his truck rumble to life and drive off.

She hurriedly rushed out of his bed and found a note propped up in front of a steaming cup of coffee.

Soph—
   Help yourself to whatever you need. Clean towels in the bathroom.
   —J

Help herself to whatever she needed. That felt intimate too. She walked into the bathroom and stared at his shower. She could imagine the steam of the hot water, see it sluicing off his incredible body, picture the soap suds caressing his skin. His towel was damp and smelled like him—which she knew because she pressed her face to it like a hormonal teenager.

She was such a goner.

This didn't help her panic attack any. She couldn't breathe. She literally couldn't breathe, so she escaped to the boat, punishing herself with her trickle-of-ice-water shower.

Help yourself to whatever you need.

Was he crazy? He was letting her in. Didn't he know they were now in the danger zone? He was leaving, and the more attached she got, the more it'd hurt when he was gone.

She barely made it to the job on time, which today was manning the front desk of the Cedar Ridge Inn—luckily not the hotel she'd been fired from. The day was unseasonably warm and brought in a homeless guy, who made himself at home in the lobby. He looked to be at least ninety, so there was no way she was kicking him to the curb. When she took a quick break, she brought him an iced tea, and he gave her a grin that was missing a few teeth.

"Thanks, chicky," he said. "Marry me?"

"I would, but I'm off men." Which wasn't strictly true, since only hours before she'd been on Jacob. Literally. On him, over him, trying to crawl inside of him…

She was supposed to be answering phones and taking reservations, but she found herself having to be more of an all-around concierge service—ordering flowers, setting up cleaning services, arranging for upscale grocery shopping for people who didn't have time but had too much money…Then the little coffee shop just off the lobby was short a waitress, so somehow she ended up throwing on an apron and running around to serve there as well as at the front desk.

By noon she'd logged more than ten thousand steps on the phone app she'd downloaded to make sure she didn't get fat. That was when she realized she was better at the job she hadn't even been hired to do than any job she'd had recently.

Concierge. "I'm really doing the wrong job," she said to no one.

"True," the old guy said from his perch on a lobby couch. "With those curves, you'd be making more money standing on the street corner, I can promise you that."

"Hey," she said. "You behave."

He flashed her a gummy grin missing a front tooth. "Where's the fun in that? And besides, have you seen your legs?"

She rolled her eyes and then froze as she caught sight of the man getting out of his car in front of the place.

Lucas.

She absorbed the shock of that just as her phone buzzed an incoming text from Jacob.

Picking something up for dinner. Wanna share?

With one eye on Lucas heading her way, she quickly texted back: *Busy with a client right now.*

Lucas was wearing some fancy-ass suit that made him look like he should be on the front of *GQ*, including the blonde hanging on his arm. Crap. What the hell was he doing here? She knew he owned part of the place, maybe twenty percent, but he owned part of a lot of Cedar Ridge.

Brain racing, she quickly yanked off her apron, and with nowhere else to hide, ran out from behind the counter and plopped down on the couch.

The old man waggled a bushy white brow at her. "Knew you couldn't resist me."

"Shh!" She nudged him. "Quick, sit up straight, no slouching. Don't speak. And don't smile either!" she hissed just as Lucas strode in the front door with his latest sidepiece.

He stopped short at the sight of Sophie on the couch. "What are you doing here?"

She shrugged with what she hoped was elegance and a casual air.

"She's on a date with me," the old guy said.

Sophie jabbed her elbow into his side, coughed to cover his "oomph," and stood up. "What are *you* doing here?"

Lucas didn't answer. His blonde did. "We have a room." She ran a hand up Lucas's chest. "For the whole night this time!"

Sophie slid Lucas a look that said, *You're scum*, which Lucas ignored. He walked around her and headed to the front desk, the blonde in tow. Once there, he tapped twice on the bell.

"Where the hell is the help?" he demanded.

Sophie bit her lip. If he knew she was working here, he'd one, never let her hear the end of it, and two, have her fired.

Unfortunately for her, the manager of the place poked his head out of the back office, his beady eyes landing right on her.

With a sigh, she moved to the counter. "I'm the help," she said.

Lucas narrowed his eyes. "You? You work here? In my hotel?"

Do not overreact, she told herself. *Do not give him a thing.* "It's not *all* yours," she said evenly. Lightly even. Look at her, being all mature and grown-up.

"That's what you said about my boat, and who's living on it?" he asked.

Annnnd…she snapped. "Oh, for God's sake, get over the damn boat already! The bathroom's too small, the water's ice-cold, the single burner only works half the time, and even when it does, it's either too hot or not hot enough, and the engine sputters and coughs like an old man!"

The old guy on the couch sat up straighter. "Hey."

"No offense," she said.

"The engine sputters?" Lucas asked incredulously. "What the hell have you done to it?"

"Nothing!"

"You have to baby it," he said. "You have to let it warm up and use the choke. Are you using the choke?"

"Lucas," the blonde said, tugging on his suit sleeve. "You promised me champagne and whipped cream."

Sophie threw up in her mouth a little.

"If you've ruined the motor," Lucas said tightly, "I'll—"

"What?" she asked. "Get me fired from a job I love? Lock me out of my apartment? Take away my car? What, Lucas? What could you possibly do to me that you haven't already done?"

"What about you?" he asked. "You've been telling women"—he broke off with a quick glance at the blonde—"people that I'm dead. Frigging dead, Sophie."

"Dead to me," she said. "People always forget that part."

With a growl, he took a step toward her, and she had to force herself to hold her ground because, oh, hell no would she show him a single ounce of any emotion. Which meant she needed to get herself and her temper under control and fast.

"That was *my* apartment you lived in," he said. "*My* car you drove. I took it all away because it was mine, not yours. You leeched off of me from day one, but that parade's over, you little—"

That was it. The last straw, so to speak, and through the rushing of the blood in her ears, she ignored both the manager's horrified gasp and the fact that the front door had opened again. Putting it all aside for the red fury she couldn't see past, she grabbed the pitcher of water from the counter, the one filled with ice cubes and lemon slices for guests, and…dumped it over Lucas's head.

The blonde gasped in horror.

"Oops," Sophie said.

Dripping water from the tips of his ears and nose, Lucas

lifted his head. "This was a two-thousand-dollar suit," he ground out, and when he took a step toward her, she couldn't stop her retreat. She backed up right into the counter just as a man appeared.

Jacob.

Blocking Lucas from making any forward progress, he turned his head and looked her over, checking for what exactly, she had no idea. His mouth curved slightly and his eyes warmed with what she thought might be...pride?

"What's going on?" he asked casually, like *How's the weather*.

"I'm on a date with the hot chick," the old guy on the couch said. "The redhead, not the skank."

The blonde blinked. "Hey."

Lucas ignored Jacob. He ignored the old guy. He even ignored the blonde. He put a finger in Sophie's face. "That was no accident, and this isn't either—you're fired. I'll make sure of it."

Well, that had been a foregone conclusion from the moment he'd stepped inside the hotel, so there was really no use crying over...spilled water.

Jacob pushed Lucas's hand away from her face, added a long hard look at Lucas that would have had Sophie peeing her pants, and turned his back on the guy to face Sophie. "What do you want to do, babe?"

What do I want to do? He'd just wandered in for God knew what, waded through all the shit they'd been slinging, held off a furious Lucas—no mean feat—and then had handed her the reins, calm as you please. "I'd like to leave," she said.

He offered her a hand—which she took—and they walked out of the hotel into the hot evening. He opened the passenger door of a truck that had her stopping in her tracks.

"This isn't your new truck," she said.

"Sold it. Bought this instead."

It was still a nice truck, but it'd been around the block a few years. She turned to him. "Why?"

He shrugged. "It wasn't Cedar Ridge."

"And this truck is?" she asked, knowing damn well she was stalling with the small talk, but also knowing there was something she was missing here.

"Yes," he said.

That's when it came to her. Just about everyone knew that the Cedar Ridge Resort was in financial trouble and had a big balloon payment due this year.

Jacob was trying to do his share.

For some reason it was this act of loyalty, combined with the way he'd waded through the shitstorm of her life and temporarily rescued her from it, that had her eyes filling. "Dammit." She wasn't going to cry. She was absolutely not going to cry.

Ever.

Jacob silently helped her up into his truck, leaned over her and buckled her in. Still bent over her, one hand on the console, the other on the headrest of her seat so that his forearm brushed the side of her neck, he looked at her.

Really looked.

"I'm okay," she whispered. Or she would be.

"Yeah, you are," he said. "But you just had a bitch fight with your ex and probably lost your job. It's okay to need a minute. Or ten."

"You lost your friend and you didn't need a minute."

"Babe, I'm still taking a minute. And I'm not even close to being done taking it either."

She paused and then set her hands on him. She could feel the heat and strength of him beneath his T-shirt. The quiet, steady thump of his heart was incredibly soothing. Her hands slid over him a little, making themselves at home.

"Soph."

Not wanting to talk, not wanting to think, she went after what she did want. To lose herself in the only man she'd ever actively craved more than air. Wanting him to crave her back, to want to lose himself in her with the same intense longing, she turned to face him. Straining against the seat belt, she slid her mouth up the side of his throat.

He smelled good, so good that she had to taste. So she did, running just the tip of her tongue along the same path, smiling against him when he swore roughly, his fingers tightening on her as he shivered.

"Soph," he said again, voice low now and also a whole lot husky. "We're in a parking lot."

He was big and strong, and yet she never felt overwhelmed by him. No, scratch that. She did feel plenty overwhelmed—by his innate maleness, by the testosterone and pheromones that rolled off him in waves, by how much he cared for her. But it was the very best kind of overwhelmed. Pretending that her entire life wasn't in the toilet—again, or maybe the better word was *still*—she pulled him in as close as she could get him.

She both felt and heard the low rumble of his groan. It made every part of her react, and she couldn't hold back. She nipped at his sexy throat, and when he groaned again, she pressed her lips to the spot.

Lose yourself in me. Let me lose myself in you...

As if he could read her thoughts, his hands tightened on her, one sliding between the seat and her back, sinking low to cup her ass, his other hand fisting in her hair to hold her mouth for his kiss.

Chapter 22

Jacob pulled back first, not wanting to make Sophie the center of any more attention than necessary. He was gratified to see she'd lost the temper and nerves in her eyes, which had been replaced by a sensual daze that raised the beast in him.

Shaking it off took a shocking amount of effort, but he did just that. He walked around the truck, got behind the wheel, and pulled out of the lot.

They didn't speak, but the silence was easy now. Comfortable. And he realized it was always that way with her. He could relax with her in a way he couldn't with anyone else.

He wondered at the potential fallout from today. Not for himself. He couldn't care less about that. In fact, he and his siblings had had several business meetings with Lucas this week. He'd found him to be exactly the same guy he'd known in school—excellent at his job if not exactly a stellar human being.

But today business hadn't come into it. In fact, Lucas had barely acknowledged him at all. That was good, leaving the business out of it, because Jacob planned to do the same when he paid Lucas a visit.

He parked in front of his cabin and turned to Sophie.

"I don't want to talk about it," she said.

No big surprise there. He got that. But when he'd first walked into the inn and seen her standing there, hair practically sizzling with fury, eyes bright, holding her own, he'd wanted to both cheer her on and slay her dragons for her.

It'd been hard to let her lead, but if he wanted a shot at making this smart, warm, feisty, amazing woman comfortable around him—and he did—he had to be the man she'd never let in before. "You ever wakeboard?" he asked.

She blinked. "No."

"Your husband owns that boat and he never took you out on the water?"

"You've seen what he used the boat for," she said.

Yeah, he should've beaten the guy to a pulp. "How about paddleboarding?"

She shook her head.

"Go change into a bathing suit."

"What?"

"Preferably a really itty-bitty, tiny bikini. The ittier the better. Five minutes."

Was he serious? Sophie wondered. Five minutes to be bathing suit ready?

Did he not understand the concept of having to check if she needed to shave? Insta-tan? Wax? None of which could be done in five minutes.

While she sat gawking at him, Jacob got out of the truck and came around to open her door for her. He offered her a hand, nudged her toward her boat, and then strode off to his cabin.

Nope, correction, he went to the side of his cabin, where there were…oh God help her…two paddleboards leaning up against the siding.

Over his shoulder he smiled at what was surely a look of horror on her face. "Never pegged you for a chicken," he said.

That did it. She whirled and went running to the boat to change.

"Five minutes," he called after her in a voice she imagined had served him well in the military.

Over her shoulder she flipped him the bird. The sound of his answering chuckle had her smiling as she jumped on board. *Smiling*, after the shit day she'd had. It was a miracle, she thought.

No, wait. Not a miracle. It was Jacob Kincaid.

As it happened, she did own an itty-bitty bikini, one she'd bought on a whim during a Victoria's Secret semiannual sale. She had yet to wear it because it showed an awful lot of Sophie.

Screw that, she told herself bravely, stripping and shoving herself into the thing—and she did mean shoving. She inspected her legs and decided that yesterday's shave would have to do. As for a tan, well, that wasn't going to happen, so she might as well own her white-girl skin. At the last minute she added a short, white camisole sundress that gave her at least the illusion of coverage.

She found him waiting on the water's edge in front of his cabin in nothing but board shorts, and at the sight, she tripped over her own feet.

Good Lord.

The man was ripped. He was leanly muscled from head to toe, and his shorts had slipped dangerously low, to just beneath hip muscles that could make a grown woman stupid.

He pointed to the boards, both in the water.

"How do I do this?" she asked.

"On your knees."

She wondered if it was his voice or just the way he reeked of bad boy that made everything he said seem dirty. She went brows up.

He smiled. "Maybe later, if you're good."

She flushed and waded out until the water lapped at her calves.

"Not sure the dress is a great idea," he said.

"Trust me, it's a great idea."

He shrugged and steadied the board while she got on her knees and tested her balance. He handed her a long black paddle and showed her how to hold it. "Stay on your knees until you're comfortable," he said. "You can push to your feet when you're ready."

She nodded and then watched as he mounted his board, not going to his knees at all, but standing straight up on his feet with an ease and agility that she knew she could never match.

"Hey," she said. "Why don't you have to start out on your knees?"

"I never get on my knees on the first date."

She choked out a laugh, and he flashed her a smile that sent heat and desire, instead of blood, skittering through her veins. He pushed off ahead of her, showing her the best way to maneuver, and she watched him carefully.

Okay, so she watched his ass carefully. Hey, it was a grade-A ass!

He craned his neck and caught her staring, sending her a look that had her burning up from the inside out. Doing something with his pole, he stopped dead in the water and...she sailed right past him.

"Hey," she said, panicking.

"You're okay. Loosen your knees. Good. Watch your balance…Don't look backward." He laughed when, with a squeak, she whipped her head around to face forward again and nearly tumbled off.

"Steady," he said. "Relax, keep breathing."

She nearly told him where he could stuff his "relax," but he was right. When she controlled her breathing, it was easier. Not so much like a cat trying to figure out how to swim without getting wet.

"Ready to stand up?" he asked.

"No!" She watched him move with such masculine grace and wanted to be able to do that. "Okay, yes."

"Go down to all fours, with your paddle across the front of the board."

Once again her mind went straight to the gutter. But she went to all fours, wildly aware that he was right behind her, watching.

"Slowly push to your feet," he instructed.

Easier said than done. Her sundress was caught between her knees and the board, holding her down. As she struggled to free herself, the board began to wobble and she swore the air blue. "Damn, shit. Fuckers!"

Laughter in his voice, Jacob said, "Don't overcorrect…" just as she did exactly that and for a moment went on a wild roller-coaster ride without a seat belt, and then…

Fell face-first into the lake.

The cold water closed over her head, and she had just enough time to think, I'm gonna kill him, before she broke the surface, gasping for air.

She grabbed her board and hung on to it, narrowing her eyes at Jacob, who—smart man—wasn't laughing outright. Nope, it was all in his eyes.

"How's the water?" he asked.

Dammit, it was deliciously chilly on her heated skin, not that she was about to admit it. She waited for him to say, *I told you the dress was a bad idea*, or at least smirk at her clumsiness, but he did neither. Instead he crouched low and used his paddle to hold her board steady.

"Stay low as you pull yourself up," he instructed, sure and calm.

It kept her the same as she managed to get back on. Sitting, her legs hanging off either side of her board into the water, she wrung out her hair. "You're about to get a good look at why I keep my hair constrained," she warned.

He took in the long, wavy red strands. "I love it like that."

Okay, so maybe she wouldn't kill him after all.

Her dress, which had been light and airy around her legs when dry, now clung to her like a second skin. A *sheer* second skin, emphasizing her hard nipples.

"I'm feeling a little self-conscious," she said.

"That's not what I'm feeling," Jacob said. "You still going to try to paddle in that dress?"

Dammit. No. She pulled it off and wrung it out, sending Jacob a long look, daring him to say one word about her admittedly itty-bitty bikini.

He just smiled. "Nice. Really nice. You ready?"

"No comments on the level of itty-bittiness?"

"I was trying to be respectful, but you should know I had to roll my tongue back into my mouth to keep from drooling and that I want to worship you with said tongue from top to bottom and back."

She both laughed and felt sexy, loving that he could make her feel that way. They drifted along on the water for a time. With maybe two hours until sunset, the sunrays slanted over the rugged peaks, making the water seem like a sheet of sheer, endless glass. Far beneath the clear surface, schools of fish swam, an entire world going on parallel to hers. Birds chirped. Insects hummed. Her heartbeat and blood pressure slowly lowered.

It was the most amazing, peaceful thing she'd ever done.

They paddled across the lake to the south side, which was forestland. Here there were no houses, just secret little coves and awe-inspiring scenery. "Wow," she breathed. "This is incredible by daylight. I tried to stay here a couple of times at night but got spooked. No city lights, no one else around, and then there was the fact that the trees looks like three-hundred-foot-tall ghosts in the dark."

He didn't smile at that. Instead he looked distinctly unhappy. "Promise me you won't do that again."

"Be spooked by ghosts masquerading as trees?"

"Stay out here alone."

She looked around. "You don't think I could have done it?"

"Sophie, I think you can do anything you set your mind to. I just don't like the idea of you out here alone and so isolated."

Isolated seemed like a problem right now. In fact, like always in his company, all worries vanished. They slowed in a cove, drifting, resting. Jacob sat with his long legs hanging down over each side of the board. She lay flat on her belly and worked on her tan.

After a while, Jacob lithely jumped from his board to the shore and gestured for her to do the same. Knowing she could never do it with the same grace, she instead crawled off hers while he held the board steady, making him grin.

"There's a path up to that cliff," he said, pointing up about fifty feet above them, to a rocky overhang. "Want to jump off into the water?"

"Sure," she said, eyeing the drop-off skeptically. "The day I'm given a terminal diagnosis, that'll be the first thing I do."

He cocked his head. "What are you afraid of?"

Um…everything? "The water's cold."

"You're already wet," he pointed out.

Yes, and just his words seemed to make her wetter. And as she sucked on her lower lip, he laughed low in his throat. "I can't help it!" she said. "You have a dirty mind."

"Babe, that's all you," he said, still smiling. "But I love it. Come on."

"We don't have shoes."

"The path is smooth. It'll be fine."

Oh, dear God. They climbed the steep trail, Jacob urging her on. At the top, she stopped to catch her breath, losing it entirely when Jacob hauled her sweaty, sticky body in close to his. Palming her ass, he squeezed, smiled, and kissed her. "You're beautiful," he said, then flashed a quick smile, took her hand, and…ran with her right off the cliff.

She screamed all the way down and into the water, but was laughing when they surfaced, grinning at each other like loons.

After, they sat on the boards in the water side by side and watched the sun start its descent, making the water shimmer like a blanket of diamonds.

"Tell me a story," he said quietly.

She glanced over at him in surprise. "Why?"

"Because you owe me a story."

"How do you figure?" she asked.

"I've told you lots of stories."

She sighed. "That's not why."

"Fine. Lucas upset you today, and I guess I want to know why you let a guy who you don't love anymore get to you."

Her gaze flew to his, but there was no judgment there, nothing but genuine curiosity. "I didn't know we were at the discussing-our-past stage of the relationship," she said. "Especially since we're not having a relationship beyond checking each other for ticks."

He laughed, the sound low and sexy. In nothing but those board shorts and a whole bunch of really great muscle definition, he made her body come alive and ache, damn him.

"You want to check me for ticks right now, don't you?" he asked.

"No." Crap. "Okay, yes, fine, I want to check you for ticks."

"Too late," he said. "I want a story."

"The Lucas story."

"Yes."

She sighed. "I told you already."

"Fill in the blanks."

She shrugged. "We met my freshman year of college. He was in law school, so a few years older, wiser, blah, blah. I was a…pleaser. I'd do anything for a kind word. I'm not exactly proud of that."

Jacob shifted and started to speak, but she shook her head. "No, it's true. I'd spent my entire life trying to please my dad and that hadn't worked out, but I was determined to make someone love me." She winced at how that sounded. "Lucas came along and paid me attention, and I was in hook, line, and sinker."

"Not your fault," Jacob said.

"Of course it was my fault," Sophie said. "I don't believe in being a product of my environment. And yet I played right into that. Poor little neglected Sophie, desperately seeking attention. And I found it too. Lucas was out of my league and I knew it, but he had this really great car…"

Jacob let out a low laugh. "So I wouldn't have had a shot at you."

"Which is kinda my point," she said. "I was that shallow girl, which means I got what I deserved."

His smile faded. "Maybe you should tell me the rest, because I don't believe that for a second."

She closed her eyes and remembered. "Lucas would see me walking to class and give me a ride. He knew money was a problem for me and he'd buy me things. A pretty dress. A fancy meal. I was young and stupid and I let his charisma turn my head even though I knew he was a player. I wasn't the only one attracted to his showy ways. But I believed him when he told me I was the one."

"And you married him."

"Yes. I was twenty, way too young, of course, but no one told me I was being stupid."

"Not even your parents?" he asked.

She shook her head. "Lucas was wildly ambitious and smart. He'd fast-tracked his way through college and law school, and they thought he was my last chance at succeeding at something. At first it was good. He liked having me in the background, taking care of everything for him, the house, his life, even some of his work. I did anything and everything he needed because I was still that pleaser. And it wasn't until he got a promotion from associate to junior partner that he started to change." She frowned at the memory and put her drink down.

"Change how?" he asked.

"He'd say things, things he never would have said before, to hurt me. And he knew exactly how to do that." She hated this part. "And I let him. I'm not even sure why, but it made me try harder to please him. I should've known from experience that I couldn't, but I was stupid. I stayed."

"What happened?"

"He became unreasonable. Suspicious. A little verbally abusive. At first I thought reassuring him would work, but again, I should've known better. I couldn't get anything right, and I got so frustrated I—" She broke off and shook her head.

He reached for her hand. "Did he hurt you, Sophie?"

She let out a choked laugh and shook her head. "No, you don't understand. It was me. He'd been after me to put together this dinner party so he could impress some of the other partners at his firm. I worked my ass off on it until everything was perfect: the dinner, the decorations, the house...The next day one of the partners sent me flowers. Lucas accused me of sleeping with the guy. He'd been suspicious for a while at that point, accusing me of flirting with the mail carrier, the grocery store clerk, everyone with a penis, and it pissed me off. When it came out during that fight that *he'd* been the one sleeping with everyone in sight, I chucked the vase of flowers at him. I didn't hit him, but he called the police anyway."

"What?" Jacob said, straightening up with a frown. "Are you serious?"

"We were both arrested and hauled downtown for domestic disturbance and violence," she said, shuddering in horror at the memory. "And while we were there, he managed to flirt with one of the desk clerks. It was kind of an as-low-as-you-can-get day for me. He bailed himself out and cleaned out the account I had access to so I couldn't do the same. I had to ask my parents for bail money."

"How did that go over?"

"Not well," she said. "I'd failed at something else."

"Getting out of a marriage that was killing you slowly isn't a failure," he said.

"Says the man who's never failed at anything in his life."

He laughed. Tossed back his head and let go, and watching him, she felt her own smile curve her lips. "So you're a big, fat loser too?" she asked hopefully.

"Many times over," he assured her, and his gaze ran over her slowly, warming her up.

He was so different from anyone she'd ever known. Even when he was pissed off or hurting—and she'd seen him both ways now—he neither internalized his feelings nor put the weight of them on anyone around him.

And she was breaking her rule. Falling for him. "Jacob?"

"Yeah?"

"You remember our promise to each other, right? The one where I won't fall for you and you won't fall for me?"

He studied her a beat, giving nothing away. "Hard to forget," he finally said. "Why?"

"Just making sure."

"Are you reminding yourself, or me?" he asked.

"Maybe both."

He smirked. "Can't resist me, can you?"

She laughed in spite of herself, and he smiled. "Come over here," he said in his bedroom voice, "and I'll prove it."

Oh boy…He was most excellent at distractions, but she had to stay strong because she was missing something. She could feel it. "Just talking though, right?"

He smiled and instead of answering, hooked her paddleboard with his paddle and drew her toward him.

Chapter 23

Jacob watched Sophie sit up on her board as he towed her toward him. She was right about her hair. It had rioted, falling to her breasts in wild, fiery waves that his fingers ached to sink into.

And then there was Sophie Marren in a bathing suit.

She had curves that made his mouth water and legs that went on for days. Their boards gently bumped as he slid an arm low around her hips and leaned in to kiss her.

She put a hand on his chest, and with their mouths an inch apart, gave him a long look. "You don't look like you're about to talk."

"Caught," he said. "Is there something you wanted to talk about?"

"Well…you never said what brought you to the inn today."

He didn't really want to go there. He'd had a shit day, and his first instinct had been to be with Sophie.

"Talk," she said in an imitation of a guy's voice, which he

assumed was supposed to be mimicking his own. "Tell me what's going on."

Spending time with Hud and the others again had been pretty great but also hard. Back when he'd been a stupid punk kid, he done his damnedest to keep his distance from Gray and Aidan, but they'd gotten past his walls more than he'd thought, something he hadn't realized until he'd left.

Being back had those walls crumbling with shocking alacrity.

But not with Hud. They'd worked together all week and yet it was still…strained. So after a long day it had felt natural to hunt up Soph, because nothing was strained with her except for his zipper.

Exerting pressure on the hand she had on his chest, he leaned in past her barrier and nuzzled the sweet spot he knew was just beneath her jaw.

She sucked in a breath and…tilted her head, giving him better access. "You're trying to distract me," she murmured.

"Is it working?"

"Are you kidding? You're a walking distraction," she said. "What is it, Jacob? Your mom? Hud?"

He must have given himself away, because she wrapped her arms around him and squeezed, her wet and nearly nude body a welcome distraction.

"It'll get easier with him. It will," she said softly. "Just don't give up."

He shook his head. He wouldn't.

"Is that what brought you to my work?"

"Actually," he said with a smile at the memory, "it was your text."

"The one where I said I was busy with my client?"

"Ah," he said with a smile. "So *that's* what you meant."

She blinked in confusion.

"You had a typo," he said. "You left out the 'e' and 'n' in client."

Her brow furrowed as she worked that out in her head. He was already flat-out grinning when she gasped in horror.

"Oh, my God!" she cried. "I didn't!"

"Yep. You did. You said you were very busy with your clit. I had to come see that."

"Oh, my God," she said again, on a groan this time, and tried to push free of him. "Let go so I can sink into the water and die."

"Hey, if I were a chick, I'd be very busy with my clit too. I'd be busy twenty-four seven."

"Spoken like a *guy*." Her cheeks were red, her green eyes wide. "I can't believe my phone changed 'client' to…"

"Come on, make my day and say it," he teased.

She covered her face. "Bite me."

"I'd love to," he said. "Right on your client, minus the 'e' and 'n.'"

One hand still over her face, she used her other to point at him. "You, I could do without right now."

He burst out laughing. She dropped her hands from her face and stared at him.

He couldn't help it. People had come and gone in his life. He'd come and gone as well. But this time, with this woman, he didn't want to let go.

And yet she did. Well, so she said. And he knew she wanted to believe it. But he also knew she wasn't being honest with herself, because her eyes, mirrors to her heart and soul, gave her away. It was in every look she sent his way, in every sweet laugh, every sexy moan when he kissed her, in every slow, delicious writhe of her hot body when she wrapped it around his.

But that didn't matter if she didn't want to want him.

And he was going to be good with that. He'd promised her, and he didn't break promises. But he was one hundred percent going to have to pull back to keep it.

When the last of the sun dipped behind the mountains, the temp began to drop. "Come on," he said, "let's get you back."

"I'm fine."

"You're cold and wet, and we both know I prefer you hot and wet."

She rolled her eyes. "I'll race you home. Loser has to tell me what happened today with his twin."

"Nothing to tell," he said.

She searched his gaze. "Nothing to tell? Or nothing to tell *me*?"

Stubborn, gorgeous, a wicked smart-ass, *and* sharp. God, he loved that. "We going to argue about this?"

"Don't we argue about everything?"

"Good point," he said. "Let's settle this one like adults—in the bedroom, naked."

But she didn't smile. "I told you my stuff. It means you have to tell me your stuff."

But he couldn't. He slowly shook his head.

"Why not?"

"Let it go," he said.

"But—"

"Look, Sophie, stop, okay? You set some boundaries and I'm trying to keep them for you, but it turns out I have some boundaries too."

Her face went blank. "Right. Sorry." She turned her board away and began to paddle.

He stayed where he was for a beat, hating himself. When he realized that she was seriously moving, working hard to lose him in nothing but that itty-bitty bikini, he went after her.

She moved faster, not giving up, even when the winds

kicked in, blowing right at them, making the going all the more difficult. She simply faced the winds head-on, attacking the water with her paddle.

Much as, he now knew, she tackled life.

In any case, the view of her, slightly bent, a little bit of a wedgie going, was enough to fuel his fantasies and distract him so much that he actually forgot to beat her to the shore in front of his cabin.

She jumped off the board, dragged it up the sand enough that it wouldn't float away. Then she headed straight for her boat.

Your own doing, he reminded himself. *You had to remind her about the boundaries.*

He started to follow her, but she picked up the pace.

"I'll be in my shower," he called after her. "My very hot shower."

This made her stop short on the dock and go hands on hips. Still facing away from him, her head dropped low and she swore under her breath before kicking the boat. Slowly she turned to face him, her expression torn between lust for his hot water and a hesitation that made his heart feel a little too tight for his rib cage.

He crooked a finger at her.

She bit her lower lip in indecision—her blue lower lip—and he moved toward her, scooping up the shirt he'd left outside so he could drop it over her head.

It fell to her thighs, and she immediately hugged herself to hold the shirt closer to her chilled body. "Unlimited hot water," he said. "And I just got new towels. Thick. Sitting on a heated towel bar even as we speak."

He saw the towel lust in her eyes and he smiled. "And there's also a room heater. You can crank it up. And after, I have hot chocolate."

"You do not," she said.

"You willing to risk it?"

"The boundaries," she whispered.

Yeah, the boundaries. But here was the thing. He wasn't ready to let her go. "The shower is a boundary-free zone," he said.

She stared at him. "Are you sure?"

No, he wasn't sure. He was talking out of his ass. But he nodded, and she did an about-face and then strode straight at him.

He started to lift his arms to pull her in, but she walked right past him, heading toward the cabin at a near run.

For his hot water.

In the boundary-free zone.

He really was an idiot. Catching up, he opened the front door for her, gesturing her in ahead of him.

She was seriously shivering now, and some of the wind had gone out of her sails. Feeling like a jerk, he took her hand and led her through the place, quiet as she stopped and stared.

"You leased this place furnished," she said.

"Yes."

"But...the furniture's gone."

"That's because I took it all to Goodwill," he said. "I replaced the important stuff for now." Bed, bedding, towels, and flat-screen TV.

"But you're just leasing," she said.

"Was. I'm buying it."

She stumbled, and when he stopped, she plowed into him, all those delicious curves plastered to him. For a beat he reached back and held her there. Just until she found her feet.

And then he let her go. He considered it practice for when he had to let her go for real.

"You bought this place," she said slowly.

"I wanted to have a home to come back to after I finish my service." Dammit. Why did he feel defensive?

"You're really coming back," she breathed.

He stopped in the bathroom doorway and looked into her eyes. "Yeah," he said. "I'm coming back."

"And staying."

"And staying." He lifted a shoulder when she only stared at him. "I walked away from my family and my life here once. I'm not going to do it again."

There was something new in her eyes now. A light he couldn't read. "You should tell them that," she said very softly.

"After I earn my way back into their good graces."

"Oh, Jacob." She touched him then, the first time she'd instigated contact, lifting her hand and setting it on his jaw. "They'd be crazy not to want you."

He let out a short laugh.

"I'm serious."

"I was a real prick back in the day, Soph. I told you."

"You weren't. You were a young kid who'd been hurt by his dad, who had to raise his mom instead of the other way around, and who didn't know how to deal emotionally. And anyway, it doesn't matter what you were then. I know who you are now. You come off all big and bad and tough, and those things are true, but you'd also give a perfect stranger the shirt off your back." She spread her arms out to reveal herself wearing his shirt.

He managed another rough laugh, even though she was killing him. "Maybe I gave it to you because you look hot in it. Especially since you're cold."

She rolled her eyes.

"You're also not a stranger," he said. "Not even close."

Her breath caught. "I'm not perfect either."

From where he stood she was. He opened his mouth to say so, but her finger brushed over his mouth, keeping his words in. He closed his eyes a beat and soaked up her touch. When he felt the fine tremors going through her, he gently nudged her into the bathroom. Leaning past her, he turned the shower on hot and gestured to the towels. "There's shampoo and soap there. Use whatever you want."

"See," she said so softly he could hardly hear her. "One of the good guys."

To prove it, he left her there, gently shutting the door.

Alone in the hallway, he had to take a deep breath. He was hard, aching with it. He looked down at it. *It's not going where you think...*

Shaking his head at himself, he strode into his bedroom, sat on the bed and pulled out his phone. He scrolled through his contacts and stared at Hud's name for a long moment before pressing the button to contact him. He hit FaceTime for a video call instead of just a voice call because the two of them were having enough communication problems trying to be regular people.

And they weren't regular people.

They were twins who'd once known what the other was going to think before they even thought it, and he wanted that back, dammit. To get there, he needed to see him, needed to look into his eyes.

"Is it Mom?" Hud asked in lieu of a hello. He was sitting at a desk and looking irritated as hell.

"No," Jacob said. "She's fine. I didn't get a chance to tell you, she found *the Twitter*."

"I know. She tweeted Bailey that I couldn't come out to play today because I was grounded for lying about my grades." Hud blew out a breath and turned to look at someone, shaking his head with a low laugh. "Bailey says she'll wait for me."

Jacob tried to smile but couldn't.

Hud frowned. "What is it?"

"I'm not trying to buy my way back in. But I can't deny that I do want back in."

"I was wrong to say that," Hud said. "I shouldn't have."

Relief washed through Jacob. He didn't say anything, and for that matter, neither did Hud, but for the first time since he'd come back, the silence between them didn't seem filled with animosity but rather the kind of quiet they used to have.

"So," Hud finally said. "Wounded Warriors tomorrow. Kenna told me you've both been working your asses off on it."

"Yeah." And he'd loved it. "Going to be fun."

"I'll be there," Hud said. "We all will."

The implied support tightened his throat.

"And I've been meaning to tell you," Hud went on, voice gruff. "Bailey's been bugging me to have you over—" He broke off and again looked over at someone. He listened a minute and then rolled his eyes. "Okay, *bugging* is apparently the wrong word here."

And then Bailey's face appeared next to Hud's. "Your twin's an idiot," she said. "Finessing a conversation is beyond him."

Jacob grinned and looked at Hud. "I knew I liked your woman."

"I'm my own woman," Bailey said, but she smiled. "And I like you too. So get your ass over here for dinner sometime soon and spend some time with all of us. My other half would like that."

"Hey," Hud said to her. "If I can't call you my woman, then you can't call me your better half."

"I didn't say *better*," Bailey said.

Jacob laughed.

Hud smiled and slid his arm around Bailey. "I'll show you better. Later."

She waggled a finger in his face, and Hud leaned forward to nip it with his teeth. With a laugh, she pushed off of him.

They had a bond, a hell of one by the looks of it. He wasn't jealous. He liked knowing his brother had found that. No, what shocked Jacob was that he wanted it too.

"You don't have to stay away," Hud said. "There's plenty of room here at the resort for you with us, with all of us. And then you, too, can be annoyed as shit by the marrieds who seem to think they're entitled to have sex as many times a day as possible. Or have to deal with the mercurial moods of one evil Kenna Kincaid—"

"I can't," Jacob said.

"Right, okay, yeah." Hud's smile faded. "I get it. You're just back for…well hell, I don't even know, and then you're out again."

"I told you I was coming back," Jacob said, "and I mean it."

"Then why the hell can't you stay with us, where you belong?"

Where he belonged. For a minute this struck Jacob completely dumb. He couldn't talk. He couldn't breathe. The warmth of it washed over all the cold, hard parts deep inside of him, the change so huge it actually hurt.

"Fine, fuck it," Hud said, rising to his feet. "I've got to go—"

"I can't stay at the lodge because I bought this cabin," Jacob said. "But it's good to know you're still a hothead."

Hud didn't say anything. Not a single sound, and Jacob stared at the phone, trying to figure out if the call had gotten frozen. "Hud?"

"The cabin is yours?"

"Well, technically, it's the bank's," Jacob said, trying to lighten the mood.

But Hud wasn't interested in lightening the mood. "You bought the fucking cabin. Here in Cedar Ridge. With us."

"Yeah, well, not exactly there with you," Jacob said. "Because a little distance from the crazy would be good, but it's only six miles, so it's close enough, right?"

For the first time in way too many years, Jacob had the pleasure of seeing Hud smile. It took him only a second to realize it was mirrored on his own face as well. And hope—something he hadn't allowed himself because it felt like a luxury—bloomed in his chest. Not trusting his voice, he didn't say a word, but he knew he didn't have to. Sensing movement, he craned his head and took in the vision in his doorway.

Sophie, in nothing but the scent of his soap and his towel.

"I've gotta go," he said to Hud.

"I know that look," Bailey murmured.

Hud narrowed his eyes a little and stared at Jacob like maybe he was trying to read him the same way Jacob had tried to do to him only a minute ago. Then Hud's eyebrows vanished into the hair falling across his forehead. "Looks like maybe there's something else keeping you in Cedar Ridge besides the cabin."

"It's not what you think."

He smiled. "Wanna bet?"

Jacob blew out a breath. "I'm disconnecting now."

Bailey blew him a kiss.

Hud simply nodded and disconnected.

Jacob tossed his phone aside and turned to Sophie.

"I didn't mean to eavesdrop," she said. Then she paused and grimaced. "Okay, so I did. To be honest, I was shamelessly eavesdropping." She hugged herself, looking so hauntingly beautiful in his towel, smelling like his soap.

Jacob had to force himself to stay seated. Because if he stood up, he was going to haul her in to him, bury himself deep, and get lost in her eyes, her smile, her voice, her body...

Nope. Not standing up.

"Jacob." She came into the room, coming close, too damn close, not stopping until she stood between his legs.

Don't touch her. Don't— His hands went to her hips. "Soph—"

"I've spent a lot of time letting others make me feel like the redheaded bastard stepchild," she said, "like the easy throwaway."

"Soph." He shook his head and held her gaze. "You're not either of those things."

"Not when I'm with you, I'm not." She paused. "Do you still want me, Jacob?"

Always. He held up his forefinger and his thumb, an inch apart. "Little bit."

She bit her lower lip.

"Or, you know, this much." And he spread his arms as wide as he could.

She smiled. And then she dropped her towel.

Chapter 24

Sophie blamed Jacob's shower for her bravado. All that gloriously hot water had gone to her head—and her good parts—as she'd run Jacob's soap over herself. And then she'd used a faintly damp towel that told her the last person it had touched had been him...

By the time she'd stepped out of his bathroom, she'd been shaky with need, her heart galloping so hard that her ribs were rattling.

She'd heard the low rumble of Jacob's voice and for a crazy moment she'd wondered what would happen if she went out there and pressed herself up against his big, strong frame and begged to be held.

Touched.

Kissed.

Devoured.

Just until she felt alive again. Until she felt whole again.

She didn't have that right. Not when she'd set the boundaries.

But then Jacob had turned to face her the moment she stepped through the doorway, his expression unguarded and…and she'd needed him so much she could scarcely breathe.

When she'd admitted to eavesdropping, he'd looked amused. When she'd strode toward him with a confidence and bravado that was pure Academy Award–worthy acting, his eyes had gone molten-lava hot.

And then she'd dropped her towel.

He took her in with eyes gone dark. In just those board shorts riding low on his hips, his skin was darker than hers and stretched over enough muscle on muscle that her mouth went completely dry.

Without thinking, she straddled him, burrowing her face into his neck, taking a long, slow breath of the essence of Jacob Kincaid.

It should be bottled.

No, scratch that. She didn't want to share him with anyone. She ran a hand down over the sculpted landscape of his chest to rest over his heart, feeling the beat of it through her palm, steady. Rock steady. Her fingers stroked a little, liking the feel of his heated skin, the way his nipple hardened beneath her touch.

"Sophie." The underlying emotion in the way he said her name took her breath. His voice was low, more than a little strained, and beneath her fingers, his heart pumped a little faster.

Not so steady now. *Don't stop me…*Leaning in, she nuzzled the soft skin just under his ear, enjoying the way his hands tightened on her. She felt him take a deep breath and let it out slowly.

Please don't stop me…

"Soph."

"Please," she whispered. She sank her teeth into his ear-lobe and then flicked her tongue over it, a full-body shudder racking her when Jacob hissed in a breath. "*Please*, Jacob."

At her plea, he groaned as his hands slid to her bare ass, squeezing, making her stomach clench with anticipation. She lifted her face to say it again, but he cupped the back of her head and covered her mouth with his.

Had she been cold to the core only a few minutes ago? Because now heat suffused her, starting from her center and working its way out, tightening her nipples into two hard little beads, spreading southbound to rev up ground zero. Had she ever felt like this with anyone else? Never.

She'd been doing her best to resist him, but that was turning out to be like trying to hold back the tide. No matter what you did, it was going to come in. And something else was coming…a massive tidal wave of desire, trying to pull her under.

Jacob gently nudged her back so he could stand and drop his board shorts, and…sweet baby Jesus. She'd thought she had the image of his perfect, naked bod imprinted and permanently etched on her brain, but her recollection was flawed. He was even better than she remembered.

Smirking at what was probably a dumbstruck expression on her face, he hit his knees, his eyes dark and intense and locked on hers before traveling slowly down the length of her body. "Mmm," rumbled from deep in his throat as his hands glided up the backs of her thighs. "Pretty."

She felt such a rush she shuddered. Catching it, he smiled a very badass smile, cupped her ass in his hands, leaned in, and put his mouth on her.

Her head fell back and her mouth opened because she needed it that way just to breathe. She felt him smile against her as he worked his magic with his very talented, ingenious tongue and diabolical fingers.

In shockingly little time he had her on the edge, two fist-fuls of his hair in her hands, panting for breath while simul-taneously begging him to "pleasedon'tstop, pleasedon'tstop, pleasedon'tstop…"

He didn't. Of course he didn't. Because Jacob was a man of his word, as she was learning. Or in this case, a man of his tongue.

And, oh God, that tongue.

When she came, hard, her legs buckled, but Jacob caught her, bringing her straight down onto him, sheathing himself deep within her.

She immediately came again, completely out of control and unable to do anything but hold on for the ride. When she could unclench her toes, she opened her eyes and realized he hadn't moved. His blazing-hot gaze held hers.

"Condom," he grounded out, his entire body strained, strung tight as a bow.

Good God, for the first time in…well, forever, she hadn't given a single thought to her own protection—or his. She hadn't thought at all. "I'm on the pill," she whispered. "And I'm…safe. I had myself checked." She'd done so right after finding out about Lucas's extramarital activities and then again more recently to be doubly sure.

Jacob banded his arms around her tight and kissed her. "Before I met you, I hadn't been with anyone in two years."

She gaped at him. *Two years?* Cupping his face, she leaned in and kissed him softly. And then not so softly, get-ting a feminine rush when his breathing hitched. Letting her hands drift over every part of him that she could reach, she reveled in the low groan she wrenched from him and began to move.

He assisted, his hands at her hips, gaze locked on hers, holding her prisoner. A willing prisoner.

They ended up on the floor. Then against the door. And then last but not least in the shower, leaving her to wonder if he was even human.

By then it was dark and past her bedtime. She was rag-doll floppy, sated beyond her greatest imagination and making contented, purring noises that she couldn't seem to control.

This left Jacob to towel her off from their shower, as she was unable to lift a finger to help him. But she did manage to lift a finger—all of them, in fact—to touch him, trailing her fingertips across his chest and abs, which contracted at her touch.

When his body rose to the challenge, she had to laugh. "Aren't you tired?"

He smiled, but his gaze remained focused on the towel he had covered her with and was now slowly sliding from her. "Never too tired for this."

A soft moan escaped her when he bent his head and let his mouth follow the trail of the towel. She might have whimpered as she found a secret stash of energy in reserve...

Much, much later she found herself curled up in his bed, his arms wrapped around her. His lips were warm and soft against hers, and unlike their kisses earlier, this one was un-hurried.

"Hungry?" he asked.

"I need sleep for tomorrow..." She looked at his clock. It was two thirty. "...Today," she murmured drowsily. "The on-site boss is rumored to be a real hard-ass. If I go to sleep right now, I could still get six hours before any Wounded Warriors show up."

"You know what would be even better?" he asked, voice all bedroom husky.

"Let me guess," she said. "*Five* hours?"

He smiled. "I like the way you think." And then he rolled them, tucking her beneath him.

Or four, she thought. She could definitely make do with four…

Jacob woke up the next morning to the deafening roar of Sophie thinking too hard. She had her head on his shoulder, an arm and a leg thrown over him, holding him to the mattress, and if he wasn't mistaken, she'd drooled in the crook of his neck. The thought made him start to smile, but it vanished when he realized that she was slowly inching away from him.

Once again trying to sneak out of his bed.

She was a horrible sneak. She had her hair in his face and nearly unmanned him with her knee, but because he was amused at her utter lack of skill, he let her get to the edge of the mattress before he said her name.

She fell out of the bed.

She immediately leapt back up and whirled, clearly looking for something to cover herself. He caught her expression, so utterly anxious, it quelled his amusement.

"I'm sorry," she gasped. "Did I wake you?"

Pushing the fury at Lucas down deep for now, he rolled out of the bed and came slowly toward her. Halfway there, he scooped his T-shirt off the floor and gently dropped it over her head, smiling at her when her face peeked out and the hem fell to mid-thigh.

Having her here with him like this made his heart beat faster, made him feel worth something, and he enjoyed every second he spent with her, even when they were bickering.

Maybe especially when they were bickering. They had something here between them, something good. And he was pretty sure he could prove it to her. But if she needed to hide behind the sex until she felt safe, until she realized that he would never hurt her, that was fine. And damn if he wouldn't make sure she enjoyed herself in the meantime, because even though he had the patience of a saint, he most definitely wasn't one.

Her hair was wild and crazy, and he stroked the beautiful mess back from her face and bent to kiss her.

She put a hand between their mouths. "I haven't brushed my teeth!"

"Me either," he said, not retreating but instead smiling into her adorably worried face. Then he stayed right where he was, their mouths a fraction of an inch from each other, separated only by her hand, waiting, letting her make both the decision and the move.

She blinked once, slow as an owl, and then slowly lowered her hand.

Taking the invitation, he gave her a short, sweet kiss. "Morning," he said huskily, and then grabbed her hand and pulled her out of the bedroom.

"What are you doing?" she asked, looking hot in only his shirt and bedhead hair.

"Making you breakfast, which is what you missed out on when you played possum and then sneaked out the last time you spent the night."

"I didn't sneak."

He gave her a knowing look, and she had the grace to blush. "Well, if I'd known breakfast was on the itinerary...," she muttered.

In the kitchen, he lifted her to sit on the counter and started pulling stuff out of his fridge.

She watched with avid interest. "So you *can* cook?"

"Bacon and eggs," he said. "But my ability is born out of hunger, not raw talent."

She watched him start the bacon and then crack eggs into a bowl one-handed and gave a wolf whistle of appreciation.

He grinned at her. "Guess I do have a talent."

"More than one," she quipped, making him laugh. She'd recovered and was back to her usual sunny self, which he was beginning to get was just her invisibility cloak.

"So…today," she said. "And Wounded Warriors. I'm working beneath you."

He liked the sound of that. A lot. And at whatever she saw on his face, she rolled her eyes. "Don't go getting any ideas," she said. "No bossing me around."

"On the job? Never," he said, turning the bacon and then flipping the eggs in the pan with a flick of his wrist.

"*Or* in the bedroom," she clarified.

"I promise you'd like it."

She blushed, and he laughed softly. "I'll show you some-time if you ask real nice."

She snorted. "Like that's going to happen."

He shifted from the stovetop to between her legs, bending his head to meet her gaze head-on. "Your pace," he said softly.

"We've tried that," she reminded him.

"We'll try harder," he said, and kissed her.

Not softly.

When they broke apart for air, she stared at him. "I thought you said my pace."

"It is." He grinned. "But I never said I wasn't going to stake my claim or try to coax things to go my way." He moved back to the stove and flipped the bacon and eggs onto two plates. He handed her one of them and then went to the cabinet for two glasses, which he filled with orange juice. "How about a new game?" he said.

"Aren't you tired of games?"

"Humor me. This time we'll just tell a truth."

She regarded him warily. "That doesn't sound like a game at all."

He kissed her on the tip of her nose. "Now you're getting it."

She narrowed her eyes as she considered this, along with the ramifications. He could read each and every thought as it crossed her face. Curiosity. Worry, because if this wasn't a game, it meant he was serious.

Which he was.

Finally, she sighed. "What do you want to know?"

He was a smart enough guy to get that she was the one for him. He was also smart enough to know that he was going to have to work his ass off for it. Because she wasn't open to this. To them.

To him.

He was shocked by how much he wanted to change her mind. "You're not scared of me," he said, wanting to hear her say it.

"No," she said. "I'm not scared of you. But that wasn't a question."

"I want to know what you *are* scared of."

She held his gaze. "Me."

"Why?" he asked.

She stared at him. "I think I want to go first and ask you a question."

"Shoot."

She opened her mouth and went for the jugular. "You ever been in love?"

Chapter 25

Sophie held her breath for Jacob's answer.

He shrugged. "Thought maybe I was a few times," he said casually.

She didn't know whether to be curious or jealous. She settled for both. "A *few* times?" she asked with what she thought was remarkable calm. She knew nothing about falling in love the right way and he'd done it a few times?

"My second year in the army," he said. "Jessica was one of our IT specialists overseas." He smiled with the memory of this Jessica. "We toyed around at something for a while."

Yeah, definitely jealousy, she decided. "If you loved her, what happened?"

"I said I *thought* I loved her." He tapped a finger on the chin she'd jutted out, giving her a little smile. "How come you're braced for a fight again? Was I supposed to pretend I've never cared about anyone before you?"

She blew out a breath. "No. I'm being ridiculous. Carry on."

He eyed her. "You sure you're not going to try to kick my ass?"

"Try?" she asked coolly. "There won't be any trying. If I wanted to kick your ass, it'd be kicked, buddy."

He laughed. "I stand corrected."

"Jessica," she said, and gave him the go-ahead gesture with her hand.

He shrugged. "We were young and stupid."

"Stupid how?"

He looked away. "Stupid."

Her gut sank. What if he'd cheated on this Jessica, like Lucas had cheated on her? She wasn't sure she could understand it if he had, but she attempted to keep her cool. "Can you define 'stupid' with a word other than 'stupid'?"

He drank his OJ, taking his sweet-ass time about it too. "She didn't see a problem with being young and stupid—uh…" He searched for a word. "*Naked* with every guy who turned his head to look at her. And since she was gorgeous, that was a lot of heads."

"Wait—*she* cheated on *you*?" she asked in shocked disbelief, pissed off for him.

He laughed a little. "You're good for my ego."

"No, but seriously. Have you looked in the mirror? Why would she cheat on you?"

Slipping an arm around her waist, he palmed her ass on the counter and dragged her closer to him. "You want to beat her up for me?"

Yes. "I think you're capable of fighting your own battles," she said, and wound her arms around his neck. "Did she hurt you, Jacob?"

His answer was a soft smile and a kiss. "Not too much," he said. "Because looking back, I know I couldn't have ever given her enough of myself. I didn't have it in me to give."

She wanted to ask him if he had it in him to give now, but she'd lost the right to ask that question. Boundaries. Knowing it, she tried to pull free but was easily tugged back in.

"Not so fast," he said. "You thought I was the one who cheated."

"No, I…" She sighed. "Okay, yes."

He didn't looked thrilled at that. "I get that we're all dicks. But we're not all *cheating* dicks."

"I know," she said.

He nodded but didn't look convinced, so she changed the subject rather than let him poke at the festering wound deep inside her. "You said you thought you'd been in love a *couple* of times," she said. "Who else?"

"Mindy. Three years ago," he said, and smiled. "A sweet nurse in Germany I met when I was flown in with injuries."

She tightened her grip on him and Mindy was completely forgotten. There were lots of scars on his warrior body. She knew because she'd kissed every single one of them, several times over now. His life and the danger in which he'd lived it, terrified her.

And he was going back to that… "Were they bad? Your injuries?"

"I healed," was all he said.

Her heart actually squeezed so much it hurt. "I'm glad," she managed. "What happened with Mindy? And don't tell me she cheated on you, too, or I'll go after the both of them."

He smiled. "No," he said. "She didn't cheat on me. But she did fall in love."

She stopped breathing. "With you?"

"No. A good friend. She left me first though. So there's that."

"I'm so sorry," she whispered. He'd been hurt. He knew the pain of it, the realization of the fear that you were never enough.

He leaned in a little so that their mouths were just barely touching, ghosting together with each word. "You get it now?" he asked. "Why I'd never hurt you that way?"

"Yes," she whispered.

He gave her a little smile. "And anyway, I wasn't supposed to end up with Mindy."

Her breath caught. "No?"

"No," he said, and kissed her again. When he pulled back, his gaze had gone all heavy-lidded and sexy, and she knew where that would lead, so she laughed and gave him a shove.

"We have work," she said.

She watched lust war with responsibility in those dark eyes, and when responsibility won, she liked him even more.

"You owe me," he said.

Her pulse kicked hard. "Do I?"

"Oh yeah." He kissed her lightly. The appetizer on the menu of Jacob kisses. "Tonight."

She stared into his serious eyes. "Tonight."

It took until 10:00 a.m. to set up for the Wounded Warriors event, and Jacob knew they couldn't have done it without Sophie. He'd known from day one that she had a bossy streak a mile wide, but when she harnessed her power, miracles truly happened.

They had an entrance area complete with portable wheelchair ramp rolled out, a huge canopy over what would be the lunch spread and another over the sign-up area where the veterans would decide if they wanted to Jet Ski, ride a tube behind a boat, or, if they were mobile enough, kayak or paddleboard.

He and Kenna had arranged for the staff and the equipment, but it was Sophie and her iPad who'd mapped out the setup.

With his mom's "help." Carrie had arrived, insisting she be given a job, and Sophie had taken her hand and kept her busy, aka out of trouble.

Jacob was impressed. The woman had serious organizational skills, and before he and Kenna could so much as blink, everything was in place and ready to roll.

"Man, she's a force of nature," Hud said, coming up to stand next to Jacob, who was watching Sophie direct the delivery of food coming in from the local deli.

"Yeah." Jacob watched as Kenna hugged Sophie.

Carrie walked by and snorted. "Those two together are going to be trouble personified," she said.

Hud grinned at her. "Takes trouble to recognize trouble."

Carrie smiled at her son. "Is it like looking in a mirror?"

Hud rolled his eyes at her as she moved on to go sit with Char, Gray and Aidan's mom, who was working the entrance, accepting tickets.

Jacob watched Kenna and Sophie. They clearly had a rapport. The two of them had become close, probably recognizing the wild and crazy in each other. Together they worked on the dessert section of the canopy, apparently sampling each and every kind of dessert. Their mouths were full and they were laughing at each other.

"Just what Kenna needs," Hud said. "A partner in crime."

Jacob slid a look his way.

"What?" Hud asked.

"Are we really doing this?" Jacob asked. "Small talk?"

"Better than no talk," Hud said with more than a little annoyed irony.

Jacob shook his head. "Okay, let's have it. Exactly how long are you going to hold that against me?"

Hud shrugged. "Dunno. When are you going to stop sulking around and start acting like one of us again?"

Jacob drew in a deep breath for patience. "What do you think I'm doing here?"

"Trying to relieve some guilt."

Jacob turned and stared at him. "And what the fuck am I guilty of?"

Again Hud shrugged.

"Oh no," Jacob said. "You brought it up. Spill it."

The dessert tasting was still going on under the canopy. Bailey joined Kenna and Sophie, stuffing a big cookie into her mouth. Laughing, she caught sight of Hud and Jacob. She pointed at Hud and then at her own eyes, miming *I've got my eyes on you.*

And then she blew a kiss at Jacob.

Hud scowled, but Jacob grinned. "Your woman likes me more than you."

"She wants me to be nicer to you," Hud said.

Now Jacob out-and-out laughed. "Did you tell her us Kincaids don't do nice?"

Hud squirmed.

"Aw. She has you totally wrapped around her pinkie," Jacob said. "She believes that you *are* nice."

"Yeah, and no one's going to tell her otherwise," Hud said, and pointed at Jacob much in the same way that Bailey had just pointed at him. "Don't make me kick your ass."

Jacob laughed again. "I'll keep your secret but not because I'm afraid you could kick my ass. I just need you to keep the same one for me."

Hud's gaze slid to Sophie, and he nodded grimly. "Understood."

The rest of the Kincaids found a reason to be there as well, and not to watch him and Kenna stumble through the huge event, but to help. Everything fell into place just as people started to show up for the eleven-o'clock start time.

They had fifty disabled veterans registered from all over the country, and every one of them showed up with family or friends, so in no time the entire North Beach was taken over.

Jacob spent two hours driving the boat, whipping the guests around on tubes in the waves created by all the activity. At one o'clock, they all took a break for lunch under the big canopy.

Jacob pulled off his sunglasses and surveyed the organized chaos. The veterans and their entourages were all chowing down, the staff roaming around making sure everyone was taken care of. He caught sight of a flash of red hair and followed it, catching up to Sophie just as she greeted a latecomer.

"Heard there's room for one more," the guy said.

"Absolutely," Sophie said with a welcoming smile, paying no attention whatsoever to the prosthetic arm when he held out his ticket. "You're Chris Marshall," she said.

"I am."

"I've heard a lot about you," she said warmly.

Stunned, Jacob came up next to Sophie just as Chris slid him a look. "Can't believe a thing you hear from this guy," he said, eyes on Jacob.

Jacob was having a hard time breathing. He hadn't seen or talked to Chris since Brett's funeral. He'd tried to get ahold of the guy and had taken his silence as a sign that he blamed Jacob for not dying or losing a limb.

Chris held his gaze. "Your brother tracked me down," he said to Jacob's unspoken question of what was he doing there. "He said you'd want me here."

Jacob turned and looked at Hud, who'd come up to Jacob's other side.

"Couldn't have done it without Sophie," Hud said.

Chris looked at Sophie as he spoke. "I was glad for the invite," he said. "Needed a reason to get out and be human."

Until that very moment, Jacob hadn't realized how much the guilt had been weighing him down. He took a step toward Chris and was met halfway in a hard, back-slapping hug that brought a chestful of emotions far too close to the surface.

Chris must have felt the same way. His arms tightened around Jacob, and instead of pulling back, Jacob set his head on that broad shoulder and closed his eyes. "God, it's good to see you."

"Yeah." Chris's voice sounded as rough as ground glass. "Because I'm just a ray of fucking sunshine."

Jacob choked out a laugh, and they pulled apart and stared at each other. "You're okay."

Chris shrugged. "Working on it, anyway."

Jacob became aware that Gray, Aidan, Hud, and Kenna had all moved in close at his back. And with Sophie at his side and Chris in front of him, he felt humbled and honored to the core at all they'd done for him.

And he thought that maybe, just maybe, he had a place to belong after all.

Chapter 26

As the day went on, Sophie found her gaze automatically searching and seeking out Jacob.

He hadn't said a word to her about helping to bring Chris here and she didn't know what that meant. Had she over-stepped boundaries? Was he upset? Mad?

He was for sure busy. He and Kenna ran the event hands-on. At the moment he was checking the athletes' equipment as he assisted them each onto the back of the Jet Skis. He was laughing at something one of them said, smiling easily as he made sure their life vests were tightened properly.

He didn't look upset or annoyed. He looked…happy. It was a good look on him.

But since when was she worried about someone else's mood anyway? She'd once allowed herself to be at the whim of Lucas's moods, which had changed as fast as the weather did here in Colorado. Half the time her head had been spinning at how fast he could go from one emotion to the other, and she'd promised herself to never allow herself to be at the mercy of someone else like that again.

All this past year she'd been alone, and she'd treasured it. Being responsible for only herself, she hadn't had to worry about making anyone else happy.

And yet here she was, wanting to know that Jacob was okay.

It's not the same, she told herself. Jacob didn't require her to be at his beck and call, and he certainly wouldn't want her mood depending on his.

And he hadn't asked her for anything. Not a single thing...

One of the donations for the day had been from Nelson Rentals, who'd provided the canopy, chairs, and ramps that they'd used to ease the way for the people in wheelchairs. That company was owned by Josh Nelson, who was one of Lucas's good friends.

Josh's wife, Leanne, showed up midday to check out the event and make sure Nelson Rentals was properly represented. Sophie knew Leanne well. They'd been at many society functions together in the past, but Sophie no longer ran in those circles, and she hadn't seen Leanne since before the divorce. She wondered if Leanne was in Camp Lucas or Camp Sophie. Or maybe she was in Camp I-Don't-Give-a-Crap.

Leanne moved through the event, smiling, introducing herself to the guests, effortlessly charming everyone. That pretty smile was still on her face when she came up to Sophie. "Look at you," she said. "Looking for your next husband?"

Camp Lucas, then. "Good to see you, Leanne."

Leanne's smile didn't slip. "I'm going to tell you right up front, there's no need to pretend to be friendly. I think what you did to Lucas was despicable. And what you're doing now, stepping on his toes in this way, is even worse."

"What *I* did?" Sophie repeated. "Are you referring to me divorcing him for being a cheating liar, or for taking the high road and not taking out an ad to tell everyone he was a cheating liar?"

"For stealing his boat away from him, the one thing he loved above all else."

"Ah," Sophie said. "So you've heard his side of the story, then."

Leanne snorted. "I've heard the truth. His grandpa bought him that boat only a few months before he died. It was the only thing he had of the man who practically raised him."

So that was the story Lucas had spread to gain him sympathy. It should've pissed Sophie off, but she'd realized something over the past few months. She no longer cared about Lucas and his games. "I need to get back to work," she said, and started to walk off.

"How do you excuse what you're doing now?" Leanne asked.

Sophie turned back to her. "Which is what exactly?"

"Going after one of the Kincaid brothers. That is what you're doing, right? Though you'll have to hurry. There's only one single brother left, and I hear he's emotionally unavailable." She cocked her head. "Or maybe that doesn't matter to you."

Kenna appeared at Sophie's side, eyes on Leanne. "What's up?"

"*You*," Leanne said, transferring her carefully controlled hostility to Kenna.

Sophie looked at Kenna for an explanation on that one.

Kenna smiled politely at Leanne and turned to Sophie. "Mrs. Nelson and I had words at a charity auction last month."

"Yes," Leanne said. "And after which Gray promised me I

wouldn't have to deal with you again. Honestly, does a Kincaid's word mean nothing?"

"You can't even imagine the immensity of the fuck that I do not give," Kenna said. She turned to Sophie. "I need your help."

"Of course," Sophie said, and she and Kenna walked off.

"So what's up?" Kenna asked.

"Nothing."

Kenna gave her a long look. "Didn't look like nothing."

Sophie shrugged. "She was wondering if I was trying to catch my next husband, one with a last name of 'Kincaid.'"

"Why didn't you tell her to go to hell?"

"I was implying it with my eyes," Sophie said. "It's a new thing. I'm trying to be calm and steady. Subtle."

Kenna laughed. "Us Kincaids don't really do subtlety. Outspoken and obnoxious is our specialty."

Sophie looked at Jacob, who was in the water up to his waist, steadying a kayak for one of the guests and his brother. "Not all of you," she said.

Kenna followed Sophie's gaze to Jacob, and some of her smile faded. "You're right. He's learned to hold things in. But he's working his way back to us. It's harder than he thought it would be, I think. He's seen and done things in the years he's been gone that we can't even imagine. It's changed him. But I'm pretty sure we can bully him back to us."

Sophie couldn't help her reaction. It was instinctive, telling her that she wasn't quite over the verbal bullying she'd faced with Lucas. When she sucked in a breath, Kenna glanced at her and then frowned. "You do know I'm kidding."

"Of course," Sophie said quickly. Apparently too quickly, because Kenna stared at her for a beat and then closed her eyes and muttered something.

"What are you doing?" Sophie asked.

"Telling myself not to meddle."

"Meddle in what?"

Kenna sighed. "Okay, listen. I like you, Sophie. I like you a lot."

"Uh…I like you too?"

"No, you don't understand," Kenna said. "I don't like *anyone*."

"Not even the Mitch who sent you flowers?"

Kenna sighed again. "Well, actually, I like him too much, but that's another story." She paused. "I want to tell you something else about us Kincaids."

"What?" Sophie asked cautiously.

"Sometimes we get it into our heads that we know best about something. And then we try to solve a problem without even letting you know that there *is* a problem. You get me?"

"No," Sophie said.

"It goes back to that outspoken thing. But we also try to do the right thing, and then end up knee-deep in shit of our own making—you know what I'm saying?"

"Not even a little bit," Sophie said.

Kenna grimaced. "Men can be stupid. You know that, right?"

"Not telling me anything new."

"Well, the Kincaid men are no exception to that—except their stupidity is usually done with the best of intentions. They look big and tough, but the truth is they wouldn't hurt a fly. Remember that. The best intentions, okay?"

"Okay," Sophie said, and then found herself being pulled in for a hug. "Okay, so we're hugging it out."

Kenna squeezed her tight. "Yes."

"And what exactly are we hugging out?"

"You and Jacob are going to be good for each other," Kenna said softly. "You're going to heal each other too."

Why did she feel like Kenna had just told her something very important and she'd missed it? "Kenna—"

"Shh! He's watching us with those eagle eyes of his. Don't look! He'll know I told you. You can't tell him I told you, Sophie."

Sophie shook her head and lifted her hands. "Even if I wanted to," she said honestly.

Kenna laughed. "What you *can* tell him is that I approve. No, wait. Don't tell him that either. He's just ornery enough to do the opposite of what I want, just to spite me."

"The opposite of…?"

Kenna grinned. "You don't have brothers. I can totally tell."

Sophie laughed. "Are you speaking English? Because I swear it sounds like English, but…"

Kenna laughed, and then they were dragged into refereeing a wild game of Frisbee golf with five army vets. It took both of them to keep the group from cheating and all-out brawling as they seemed to want to do.

Halfway through the game, Sophie's attention was drawn to the wakeboarding boat buzzing the shore.

Jacob was behind the wheel, Chris riding shotgun, holding up a flag signaling they had someone in the water.

"That's Hud," Kenna said. "He's a maniac on a wakeboard. How much you want to bet that he and Jacob are in some sort of do-or-die competition?"

Sophie turned and stared at her. "Why would they do that?"

"Uh, because they each have a penis?" Kenna asked.

The guys with them burst out laughing.

"Don't even think about denying it," Kenna told them.

Sure enough, two minutes later the boat whipped past the shore towing Hud. He whooped it up, and everyone onshore whooped back at him.

Then he hunkered down on his board and flew at the boat's wake, jumping it at a jaw-dropping height.

"Nice," Kenna said.

"I could do better," a guy said, coming up on Kenna's side. His badge said MITCH, and he flashed Kenna a sexy grin.

So this was the guy, the one Kenna liked too much.

Kenna rolled her eyes at him. "Must everything be a competition?"

"Competition used to be your life," he said. "You gave it one hundred percent of you, and you were the best in the country."

"And then I learned that not everything has to be won," she said. "Some things have to be earned."

Mitch's smile warmed as he touched Kenna's nose with his finger. "Bingo," he said quietly, and walked away.

Kenna was still standing there with her mouth open when Gray came up. "What's up?" he asked. "You okay?"

"Peachy."

He started to say something, but just then Hud wiped out spectacularly on a buoy and cartwheeled across the surface of the water away from the boat.

And not on purpose.

From the beach rose a collective "Ooooh…"

Kenna winced and shook her head. "That's gonna hurt."

Jacob whipped the boat around with impressive skill and hit the gas hard to get back to his brother quickly.

"Progress," Kenna said. "In the old days, the harder they wiped out, the harder the other one would point and laugh."

The boat pulled up alongside Hud, who vehemently shook his head.

"He doesn't want to get back in the boat," Kenna translated. "He wants to go again."

"So he's crazy too," Sophie said.

"Crazy as they come," Kenna said.

Jacob stood up from the captain's chair, strode to the stern of the boat, and started pulling Hud in by the tow rope.

"And as you can see," Kenna said dryly, "Jacob disagrees with Hud."

From in the water Hud yelled something at Jacob.

Jacob kept towing Hud in.

So Hud let go of the rope.

Kenna laughed softly. "And that, ladies and gentlemen, is where the Kincaids get their stubborn-ass reputation from."

On the boat, Jacob tossed up his hands and returned to the boat's controls. A minute later, Hud was back up on the surface of the water, once again hotdogging it behind the boat.

"Remember that time we sneaked out and *borrowed* a friend's boat?" Kenna asked Gray.

"We were all punk-asses," Gray said with a fond smile.

"Hud tried for a flip on the water," Kenna told Sophie, "and face-planted instead. Jacob had to dive in and save him, then ride him to the ER on his bike's handlebars. At that time we were being raised by Char, Aidan and Gray's mom. She yelled at us something fierce when she finally got to the ER and then burst into tears."

"We thought we'd gotten off scot-free," Gray said.

"But hell no," Kenna said. "Char's got a softie side, but she's also got a spine made of sheer steel. We were all grounded from life for a month."

"I got two months," Gray said. "Because I was oldest and supposedly knew better."

Kenna laughed.

Gray smiled ruefully. "Yeah, I never knew better."

"Still don't," Kenna said.

Five minutes later the boat had made a huge circle on the lake, stopping too far out for them to see what was going on. They'd shifted positions, Sophie realized. This time Hud was driving.

Jacob was now behind the boat on a wakeboard. He was wearing a life vest and board shorts that were wet and clinging to his body, plastered against him from the wind and speed. Going what seemed like a hundred miles an hour, he maneuvered right into the boat's wake and…popped up in the air like he'd been shot out of a canon, his body fluid as he literally flew up, up, up and then…holy crap, executed a three-sixty before landing lithely back onto the surface of the water.

Stunned, Sophie stood there gaping.

"I used to be able do that," one of the guys playing Frisbee golf said from his wheelchair, voice nostalgic.

Kenna reached for his hand. "Don't even worry about it," she told him. "Girls will like you better now that you're not a show-off."

The guy slipped an arm around her with a shy but hopeful smile. "Want to prove it by going out with me tonight?"

"Absolutely," she said. "First round's on me."

The other guys groaned, and someone whispered, "Ah, man, I didn't know we could ask her out!"

Mitch, who was standing close by, looked at Kenna for a long beat, his jaw a little tight, his smile definitely not matching the fire in his eyes.

"Sorry, boys," she said to everyone else, although her gaze was locked on Mitch. "You snooze, you lose."

Mitch swore, strode straight for her and yanked her into his arms, planting a hard kiss right on her mouth. When he pulled back an inch, he said, "The move has always been yours, since the night you let me into and then kicked me out of your bed, and you know it."

"Hey, man, sorry," the guy in the wheelchair said. "I didn't know. She's all yours."

Kenna narrowed her gaze on Mitch. "We both agreed that night was stupid *and* that we'd *never tell another soul.*"

"The move is yours," Mitch repeated. "Use it or lose it." And then he walked away.

Kenna stared after him.

"You going to use it?" Sophie asked.

Kenna was still watching Mitch go, her expression filled with both longing and fear. "I can't."

Sophie reached out to touch her, but Kenna shrugged her off. "Sorry," she murmured. "I need a moment." And then she, too, was gone, leaving Sophie sure of only one thing.

She wasn't the only chicken in Cedar Ridge.

Chapter 27

When the sun began to sink in the sky, Jacob lit a bonfire and then sat with Hud and Chris. He was feeling a little sunburned and a whole lot tired, but also pumped up, like he'd been a part of something really great today, something that had reached deep inside to the heart he'd kept locked up as tight as he could get it.

He and Hud had nearly killed themselves behind the boat earlier, trying to best each other, and it had felt so much like old times that he could hardly believe it.

How had he stayed away so long?

Why had he stayed away so long? It was getting so that his reasons no longer made any sense at all.

And having Chris here today meant the world to him, showed him that in spite of not being able to see it for so long, there was life after combat.

And he wanted that life, badly.

His gaze sought out Sophie, who was with Kenna—and shit, Hud was right: That combo was guaranteed trouble.

The two of them were directing what looked like a very serious competition of horseshoes.

As if she could feel his gaze, Sophie turned her head and unerringly found him. Right in the middle of her horseshoe game, she cocked her head at him and silently but effectively asked across the span of one hundred feet, *What's wrong?*

Was she kidding? She'd given him this. Chris. Laughter with Hud. The feeling of being important to her.

Don't let your glass be half empty...

Remembering that, he shook his head and smiled at her. In response she sent her best, sexy, happy, two-hundred-watt smile before she turned back to her game.

A local band that was donating their time had set up on the dock behind them and was warming up. More food had arrived and was being barbecued and spread out for dinner. They all ate together, laughing at the pics Sophie had gone around and taken during the day and then projected with her laptop onto a makeshift screen of canvas she'd commandeered from one of the tents.

She amazed him, completely amazed him.

"You should marry her," Hud said, coming back from the food table with his second plate, sitting next to Jacob with their old ease. "Because if you don't, I know at least two guys who would."

WTF. "Who?"

Hud grinned at him.

"*Who?*" Jacob demanded.

"Mitch and Chris, for starters."

Just because Mitch was an old family friend who'd become invaluable to the resort over the past few years wouldn't stop Jacob from pounding him into the ground if he made a move on Sophie.

Chris would be tougher to beat, but he'd find a way.

The band had kicked into play and more than a few people were dancing. Chris tugged one of the resort workers out there and made a move, pulling her along to the music. Gray did the same with Penny.

Mitch approached Kenna and Jacob braced for Kenna to punch the guy, but to Jacob's surprise, she stood up. "You want to dance with me?" she asked.

"Actually," Mitch said, "I want to date you until you're convinced you're mine, something I've known forever. And then I want to put a ring on your finger so the whole world knows. But yeah, I'll settle for a dance for now."

Kenna stared at him for a long beat, and then she did the most amazing thing. She smiled a warm, sweet, adorable smile that Jacob hadn't seen for a very, very long time. And then she put her hand in Mitch's and let him lead her to the dance floor.

"What the hell?" Jacob asked.

Hud grinned. "Love's in the air, man," and with that, he went after Bailey, snatching her by the wrist, tugging her in to him.

Everywhere, guys were claiming their women left and right. Or, more accurately, their women were allowing themselves to be claimed. Jacob knew one woman he wouldn't mind being claimed by and sought her out in the crowd, finding her slow dancing with—*shit*—Chris now.

They were looking pretty cozy too. As Jacob walked up to them, Sophie was laughing at something Chris had just said while Chris held her way too close. The ass saw Jacob coming, too, and kept Sophie tight to him, shooting Jacob an innocent grin over her shoulder. "Go get your own woman, Kincaid," he said.

"That's what I'm doing. Get your mitts off what's mine."

Laughing, Chris brushed a kiss to Sophie's cheek and walked away.

Good man.

Sophie didn't move into Jacob's arms. She stood there, brow arched. "Get your mitts off what's *yours*?" she repeated with more than a hint of disbelief.

"We've had this talk." He tugged her in to him. "You *are* mine."

Her arms were still crossed. A barrier between them. "And?" she inquired.

He smiled into her chilly features. "And I'm yours."

She softened at that, letting her arms fall to her sides. "One more question," she said.

"Go."

"Were you really upset that I was dancing with Chris?"

"No," he said, and paused. "You made him smile."

She stared at him for a moment before she touched him, her hands gliding up to tighten around his neck as she pressed her face to his throat.

As she relaxed in his arms, he let the beat of the music carry them around for a few minutes. It was ridiculous, but he wanted the song to go on forever just so that he didn't have to lose contact with the feel of her skin.

She wriggled in a little, like maybe she didn't want it to end either, like she couldn't get close enough. Tightening his grip on her, he was just about to whisper a naughty nothing in her ear when he felt the wetness of tears against his skin.

And his heart dropped straight out of his chest. "Hey," he said quietly. "What's this?"

She shook her head and kept her face buried against him, clearly struggling for composure. He waited her out, holding on to her with a grip he hoped conveyed some of his feelings since his mouth had never been any good at doing that for him.

Finally she gave a last sniff and lifted her head. "You make me smile too."

"You sure? Because at the moment, it looks like I made you cry."

Her eyes filled again, but she blinked back the tears. "It's a good cry," she whispered.

She killed him. "Soph," he whispered, swiping a thumb over her cheek.

She shook her head again and looked at him, eyes clear now. "And just so we're clear, *I* wouldn't have been so gracious about you slow dirty dancing with someone else."

"No?" he asked, finding that kernel of knowledge fascinating. And also a little hot. "What would have happened?"

"Well, for starters, I'd be appropriately grief stricken at your funeral."

He burst out laughing.

Smiling, she slipped her arms around his neck. "But realistically? I'm happy to have you," she said. "For the duration."

It was the second time she'd made the distinction. Definitely time to put that to bed. "How about for as long as it works instead?"

She just looked at him for a long beat, and then without saying a word, set her head on his shoulder and sighed, cuddling in like everything was okay in her world.

And it sure as hell was in his. He opened his mouth to say so, but one of the Wounded Warriors cut in. And after that, Gray cut in. And then the music slowed again and he claimed her back with a scowl that made Gray smirk.

Flipping his brother off, Jacob tugged Sophie out onto the sandy beach for privacy. There he pulled her into his arms, where they swayed to the music drifting over them in tune to the water slapping the shore.

Pressed up against her warm, giving body, he couldn't think of another place in the entire world he'd rather be, and when she sighed in sheer pleasure, he hoped that meant she felt the same.

She smiled against his throat. "Pretty nice day," she said.

"Better than nice," he murmured, and stroked a finger along her jaw, lifting her face to his. Her eyes were deep, dark, and full of things, things she felt for him, he realized, his heart taking a good, hard knock against his ribs. "What you did for me today, getting Chris here—"

"That was all Hud and Aidan," she said.

"No," he said with a slow shake of his head. "It started with you, and I can't even find the words to tell you what it means to me that you did that. I didn't realize a part of me was broken. Not until I saw Chris looking whole and… okay."

Her eyes shimmered with emotion. "You found the words just fine," she whispered, and gave him a soft smile, holding his gaze until it was…too much, and he dropped it to look at her mouth instead.

Her lips curved slowly, and he kissed her. And then again, still moving her to the beat, his body shifting against her in a way that had her letting out a soft moan, which he caught with his mouth.

"Let's go home," he said against those lips.

"The party—"

"Is going to be fine without us."

She lifted her head and stared at him, and he did the best he could to look like something she couldn't live without. When she smiled and took his hand, he felt like he'd just won an amazing prize.

Chapter 28

Jacob brought Sophie to his cabin, a place that felt more like home to him than any other place ever had. And if he played his cards right and also got very, *very* lucky, it might someday be the place she felt that way about as well.

He left the lights off. He opened the windows so that they could hear the music from the beach but kept the shutters closed enough that no one could see in. Then he slowly pulled Sophie in to him. They spent long moments swaying to the beat before he nudged her face to his and kissed her.

When they broke apart for air, he stared into her eyes and felt his heart roll over in his chest and expose its underbelly. "You're so beautiful," he said.

"Don't." She shook her head. "You don't have to do that, Jacob. I'm here. I'm a sure thing tonight."

"Well, that's a relief," he said. "I'll cancel the string quartet and five dozen roses about to be delivered, and I'll stop wondering if you're going to be scared off by the ten cases of condoms I just bought."

She laughed, her fingers smoothing their way up his chest, around his shoulders, and into his hair, making him want to purr. "Ten cases, huh?" she teased. "Cocky much?"

"Okay, maybe just one case. And it's called 'hopeful.'"

She laughed again. "Did you think I wouldn't be?" she asked softly, nipping at his lower lip. "A sure thing?"

Truthfully? He had no idea what she was thinking, or even what *he* was thinking—other than he'd trained himself not to count on anything as a sure thing.

She stared at him for a beat and then proved she was a mind reader. "You claimed me out there on the dance floor tonight," she said with a small smile. "All cocky as hell. I mean, you might as well have peed in a circle around me. Do you want to know why that didn't make me mad?"

Since she was still running her fingers through his hair and he was quickly turning into a puddle of goo, he shook his head.

"Because I've claimed you too. Love it or leave it," she said, cracking open something deep inside of him that him hauling her in even closer. Nothing was between them now except her sundress and his T-shirt and board shorts, and even that was way too much.

She must have felt the same way because she backed away from him and, with a little smile, nudged the spaghetti straps off her shoulders so that they fell to her elbows. Then, with that smile going more than a little naughty, she turned her back on him and started walking slowly to his bedroom, hips gently swinging with casual grace as she reached behind her and unzipped her dress.

And then let it fall.

And then walked right out of it in nothing but a very tiny pair of panties and vanished into his room.

* * *

Sophie barely got past the doorway before he grabbed her hand. One thing she could say about him, he wasn't one to back down from a challenge.

And she was definitely a challenge.

Eyes locked on hers, his own dark and heated, he pulled her in to him, kicking the door shut behind them. He had her up against the closed door, hands locked around her wrists, his lips devouring hers before she had time to breathe.

That was okay. She'd breathe later. All she needed now was him, and she gave herself over to it, to him, losing herself in the power of what he made her feel.

When they finally pulled apart, panting, staring at each other, he seemed to have enough control left to assess the situation and took action accordingly, yanking his shirt over his head and shoving his shorts down and off. He immediately locked her against him again, letting go of her arms only to lift her up by the backs of her thighs effortlessly.

She wrapped her arms around his neck and her legs around his waist and held on as he turned and walked to the bed with a casual strength that thrilled her.

And then he was tumbling her down to the bed. She landed on her back, where Jacob hooked his thumbs in the sides of her undies and slowly tugged them down her thighs, sending them sailing over his shoulder.

He looked down at her and groaned. "Damn, Soph," he murmured, reverently running his hands up her legs, letting his thumbs meet in the middle to lightly stroke over her. "You're wet for me."

She let out a shaky breath. "I've been this way since watching you wakeboard earlier," she admitted.

He let out a low laugh. "Is that right?"

"Mm-hmm. You guys were hot stuff out there."

"All of us, huh?"

"Well, maybe one of you more than the others," she murmured, wrapping her legs around him so he couldn't move away.

"Maybe?" he asked.

"Or definitely."

He bent over her, bracing on his hands on either side of her head. "You take my breath, Soph. Every single time."

"Yeah?"

"Oh, yeah," he whispered, and began kissing her body, starting at her mouth and working his way south. Long before he got to where she needed him the most, she was in a state, rocking her hips, practically begging him to get inside.

"In a hurry tonight?" he asked against her skin.

As a matter of fact, yes. She could feel him hot and huge against her and couldn't stand it. "*Please*, Jacob."

"Mmm," he said approvingly, nibbling at an inner thigh, making her squirm. "Love that. More of that."

She slid her fingers into his hair and tightened her grip.

That did nothing besides elicit a chuckle from him. Out of patience, she rolled and crawled on top of him. Triumphant, she beamed down and then oscillated her hips so that she could rub the neediest part of her over the hardest part of him. This caused some creative swearing from the man as taut as a bowstring beneath her, his hands going to her hips to take over in the rhythm he wanted.

A rhythm that drove her up so high she could feel herself start to quiver. Another "please" escaped her before she could stop herself, and she gasped when he pushed up into her.

"Is that what you wanted?" he asked.

"*Yes.*"

Gripping her hips, he urged her down to him so he could kiss her while also controlling her admittedly frantic movements. Seemed he wanted her on top and he wanted it slow and steady. This worked, too, and she loved how he helped her when she faltered, slowing her when he didn't want to come.

Not being nearly as controlled as he, she came twice, his name on her lips, and when she sagged over him, he flipped her over and pinned her beneath him on the mattress and then he was even deeper inside her. Holding her face in his hands, he deepened the kiss, his fingers curling into loose fists in her hair as he moved. She arched into him with every thrust he made, spurring them both on as the deep sensations pulsed and spread through her in welcoming waves.

Neither of them smiled now. Jacob's breathing was every bit as rough and unsteady as hers, and she realized it wasn't just passion washing over her, taking her under, but something much deeper. For a minute she slammed her eyes closed, needing to hide it, but then Jacob said, "Look at me, Sophie."

Dragging her eyes up to meet his, she felt an almost fist-like clenching spread through every part of her as she came.

And took him along with her.

After, she could hear her own crazy breathing compared Jacob's, deep and even now, his eyes dark as he cupped the nape of her neck and slowly brought her mouth to his, his gaze never wavering.

Hard to hide from a man who liked the visuals.

She was still trembling, but when his lips grazed hers, she gripped him tight and kissed him back. Under his gentle ministrations she finally quit shaking and felt something inside her let go.

Her fears.

After, they both fell asleep and were jolted awake later by the sound of her phone vibrating across the bedside table—a text from her sister.

Found another job for you, this one entirely un–porn related, I swear. How do you feel about phone sales?

Sophie hit herself in the forehead with her phone a few times until Jacob pulled it from her fingers. He read the text, snorted, and then…

God bless him.

He turned off her phone and tossed it aside. "Better?" he asked.

"A little." She sighed. "I just want…"

"What?" he asked quietly. "What do you want?"

"To be in charge of my life," she said. "I want to be my own boss."

"That's easy enough," he said. "Start your own temp agency. You'd be a natural. It seems like you know how to do everything."

"No." She paused. "Well, maybe. But I know what I want to do even more than that. I want to start a concierge business." She held her breath, but he gave her a slow smile.

"You're going to rock at it," he said.

The easy confidence he had in her had her smiling back. "I am, aren't I?"

He pulled her on top of him. "You'll be good at anything you go after," he said. "I love that about you."

"You do?"

"Yeah." He slid a hand to the nape of her neck and drew her in for a quick kiss. "I love your cup-half-full, rose-colored-glasses, fight-for-what-you-want 'tude."

"I thought you liked quiet and calm," she said. "And we both know I'm anything but."

"*I'm* quiet and calm," he said, "but I don't need that in you. In you, I love the chaos. I love waking up next to you and thinking, 'Good Christ, what next?'"

She smacked him and he laughed, catching her hands in his. "You're an adventure, Sophie, and I love an adventure."

She sucked in a breath because he kept using that L word.

He took in her reaction and slid his hands down her back to cup her bottom, squeezing her cheeks. "Would you like to take a guess at what else I love?" he asked.

"Um…" Her heart was suddenly pounding in her ears. "Frozen pizzas, chopping wood, and your crazy siblings?" she asked more than a little breathlessly.

"All that," he agreed. "But something else. Something big."

"Your truck?"

He smiled and pulled her arms out from beneath her so that she fell onto his chest. "Nice try." He kissed her, short but most definitely not sweet. "You," he said against her lips. "I love you, Sophie, just as you are. Not quiet, not calm, and most definitely not easy."

She went utterly still. When was the last time she'd heard those three little words from a man who'd meant it? When was the last time the simple but devastating statement had something deep inside her welling up, filling her heart and soul?

He just continued to look at her, patient. Steady as a rock. Everything she was not. She gnawed on her lower lip. "You said we weren't going to do love."

"No, you said that. Not me."

"But you agreed," she whispered.

He shrugged. "I should've known better. Nothing goes according to plan around you. You told me not to fall for you no matter how lovable you were. I overestimated my ability to resist you. The end."

She stared at him. "There's a chance I already love you," she whispered. "But you scare the hell out of me."

His mouth quirked. "I'm aware of that."

She stared at him. "What, that I love you, or that you scare me?"

"That I scare you," he said, "but good to know you love me."

"I said there's a *chance*," she clarified.

He smiled. "I heard you."

"I don't love easily," she warned. The understatement of the year, of course.

Jacob nodded. "I get that too."

"Do you also get that I don't want to love at all?"

This he didn't say anything to, but she could read him every bit as well as he could read her, and she sighed. "Okay, that's a lie," she admitted. "I want to. I want to love you. And parts of me already do. Quite madly."

He smiled. "I'll take those parts for now," he said easily.

No frustration. No annoyance at her pace. No sign of anything but the easy acceptance of what she could give. And his patience wasn't a sham either. It was totally real. He loved her enough to let her catch up. He loved her enough to wait. No one had ever loved her like that before, and it stole her breath and her ability speak for a minute. For the first time in her life she had someone who was in just as deep as she was.

And suddenly that wasn't scary at all.

A night breeze made its way through the shutters and drifted over them, cooling their overheated bodies.

Sophie felt enveloped, protected in a way that didn't smother, and she relaxed into the mattress and sighed, heart full.

She felt him smile against her and rolled her head against his shoulder to meet a pair of warm brown eyes studying her in the low light.

"Tired?" she asked, shifting to face him, touching his jaw, dark with a beyond-five-o'clock shadow.

He shook his head. He wasn't tired.

Neither was she. "Hungry?"

His eyes revealed a smile as he watched her like maybe she was his breakfast, lunch, dinner, *and* dessert. "Not for food," he said, making her laugh.

But the laugh backed up in her throat, replaced by another wave of heat and desire when he tucked her beneath him, making it clear what he *was* hungry for.

Chapter 29

The next morning Jacob woke up like he always did, quickly and immediately. That was the military training ingrained in him—never sleep too heavily, never be caught vulnerable and unaware.

So he knew before even opening his eyes that he was alone. Reaching out to confirm, he felt nothing but cool sheets.

Sophie had been gone awhile.

Flopping to his back, he stared at the ceiling, remembering all the times they'd turned to each other in the night. Hot, erotic memories played like a movie in his mind: Soph climbing him like a tree, her going all breathless and boneless when he held her down and slowly thrust into her, the sound of his name tumbling from her lips as she came, shuddering in his arms, falling apart for him.

He'd loved nothing more than putting her back together again, one kiss, one touch at a time...

Shit. He had it bad.

He rolled out of bed, surprised she'd gotten past him. He must've been more exhausted than he'd thought. The sun was just rising as he hurriedly showered and walked down to the lake for the Wounded Warriors breakfast. According to the staff chart, he was on hotcake-flipping detail. He searched the list and found Sophie on serving detail. But since no one could serve or eat if he didn't flip, he went to work without getting a chance to talk to her.

Two hours later he'd lost track of just how many hotcakes he'd created, but he'd had a great view of Sophie serving while doing it. When everyone had all they needed to eat, he filled a plate for himself and turned to find Kenna waving him over.

She was with Hud and Mitch and a few other staff members. "The problem with this weekend," he said, nudging Kenna over to make room for himself, "is that it went so well we're going to have to repeat it annually."

"Yeah, that's not your biggest problem," Kenna said.

"No?"

"No," she said. "I tried to find you last night, but you vanished right after you danced on the beach with Sophie."

Everyone was looking at him, so he shrugged. "Got tired."

"Uh-huh," one of the staffers said. "I'd have liked to get 'tired' too."

Everyone laughed, which Jacob ignored. "So what's my biggest problem?" he asked Kenna.

"Leanne Nelson nearly ratted you out to Sophie about Lucas yesterday," she said.

Leanne was a *Housewives of* wannabe, and she'd sell her own child for a good story to tell. And he was an idiot. He'd meant to tell Sophie that the resort had hired Lucas. He really had. But it was important to do it in such a way that she didn't get hurt. The opportunity hadn't presented itself to him yet, that's all.

Or you knew it was going to be a problem...

"You never told Sophie that her ex-husband is the resort's new attorney?" Hud asked in disbelief.

"Not yet."

Both his brother and sister looked at him like he'd grown a second head.

"And here I thought *you* were the smart one," Kenna said, ignoring Hud's dirty look. "But I gotta tell you, you've made a massively boneheaded move here. *Massively* massive."

"Agreed," Hud said. "Bailey would probably kill you dead. I hope Sophie's a little more open to sleeping with boneheads."

"Massively massive boneheads," Kenna added.

Jacob shoved his fingers through his hair. It was a tell, he realized, a rare tell, and he immediately dropped his hands. "It's not that big of a deal. I mean, at first I didn't even realize he was her ex."

"Yes, but after you did?" Kenna asked in a tone that spoke volumes on what she thought about his intelligence level. Or lack thereof.

"You need to tell her," Hud said. "And when you do, I'd wear a cup. And maybe a flak vest. But for the record, why didn't you tell her again?"

How was this so hard for them to understand? "Opening my mouth never works as well as keeping it shut and minding my own business."

Hud shook his head like he'd just heard more stupidity than he had the tolerance for and slowly stood up. "What the hell is that bullshit? Are you talking about us? About you and me?"

Kenna sighed and stood too. "Are we going to need to draw a line in the sandbox here? Should I call Penny to referee?"

"No need," Hud said tightly, and turned to walk away.

Jacob grabbed his arm.

"What?" Hud said testily. "I'm only doing what you claimed to have learned from me—I'm keeping my mouth shut and minding my business."

Jacob stood up so that they were toe-to-toe. "You going to look me in the eye and tell me if I hadn't done just that, if instead I'd stayed, we'd be in a helluva better place right now?"

"Are you shitting me?" Hud asked, and took a step into Jacob's air space.

"Hud," Kenna said softly, warningly.

"No," he said. "I'm going to get this out." He poked a finger hard into Jacob's chest. "I never wanted you to shut the hell up and keep your feelings to yourself. I *never* wanted you to go. What I wanted was for you to be a part of this family, and I still want that. And if you don't get that, then fuck you."

And with that, he stalked off, shoulder-checking Jacob hard as he did.

Kenna sighed and looked at Jacob. "Do you always have to be so stoic? Can't you just once let it all out, what you feel, what you want, what you need?"

He felt himself shut down a little bit. Didn't she get it? What right did he have to impose his needs or wants here?

She stared at him, made a rough sound, and poked him in the exact same spot Hud just had, which hurt like hell. "Don't you do that," she grated out, sounding furious. "Don't you act like you don't deserve to be one of us." She poked him again, and he caught her hand.

"Stop," he said.

But she just stared up into his face, her own going from angry to crushed in zero point two. "Oh, Jacob. Is that it? Do you really think you don't deserve to be one of us?"

Dropping her hand, he pushed it away from him.

"Oh, my God," she whispered, and her eyes went suspiciously shiny. "You do think that," she breathed, her voice a little broken and doing its best to do the same to him. "Damn you, you really do." She came at him hard, and he braced himself, but she threw her arms around him and clung.

He could handle a hell of a lot of things, but a crying woman wasn't one of them. He was out of his comfort zone and way beyond his area of expertise. "Kenna, I can't—" Emotion settled into his chest like a bag of stones. "Don't cry. Anything but that, okay? You can even go back to drilling a hole in my chest if you just stop."

Kenna lifted her head and pointed at him, and he manfully held in his wince. "I want you to listen to me, you big oaf," she said. "You *aren't* alone. You have family who loves you, though God knows why. You deserve this family, Jacob. You deserve our love, every bit as much as Gray or Aidan or Hud or me. Say it."

"Kenna—"

"*Say it* or I swear to God—"

"I love you, too, Kenna."

This instantly swallowed up her frustration, and she sagged a little bit. "Wow," she breathed. "You really said it."

"I meant it."

"Good," she said fiercely, and hugged him tight. "There just might be hope for you yet. Now let's go find your stubborn-ass twin."

"There's something I have to do first," he said, looking around for Sophie. Kenna was right. He had some things to tell her, and he hoped she'd hear him out before—as Hud had put it—she killed him dead.

As Sophie had worked the breakfast, she'd known she wore a perma-smile. She simply couldn't help it. It hadn't been just the sex—though that got more spectacular each time, which was saying something.

It was that Jacob loved her. He *loved* her. He loved *her*.

And here was the thing. She knew that nothing good ever came from such a deep, potentially gut-wrenching emotion, but hope sprang eternal. And she couldn't help but think that this, with him, was different.

"Looks good on you," Chris said when she refilled his orange juice.

"What does?" she asked.

"The morning after."

She jerked and poured orange juice down the front of herself. *"Crap."*

Chris grinned.

"You," she said. "Zip it."

He mimed zipping his lips and throwing away the key.

Sophie rolled her eyes and headed toward the next table but was stopped by a voice that put her back up before she even turned.

"What the hell are you doing here?"

Lucas. Grinding her teeth, she looked down at herself. Orange-juice-splattered apron over jeans shorts, flip-flops, and a tank top. No makeup, which meant she was without her armor. She blamed all the great sex she'd been having because she'd mistakenly considered the after-sex-glow makeup enough—

"You going to turn around?" Lucas asked.

She grimaced, swallowed it, and then faced him.

He took in her appearance. "At least you spilled on yourself this time," he said.

"Why are you here?" she asked.

"There's a dent on my boat. Why is there a dent on my boat?"

"You mean there's a dent on *my* boat."

He narrowed his eyes. "We could fix that right now. I'll buy the thing from you."

"I'm not selling it to you," she said.

"Name your price."

"Fine," she said. "One million dollars."

He choked. "Are you insane? Wait, don't answer that. I already know."

She crossed her arms. "I still don't get why you are here."

"The question is why are *you* here?" Lucas asked.

"*I'm* working. Your turn."

"But servers are supposed to be nice," he said. "And sweet. And subservient."

She lifted the pitcher of OJ threateningly, and he raised his hands in surrender, laughing, the bastard. "Okay, okay, cease fire! I'm working too. I'm Cedar Ridge staff. Well, not *staff* staff. I'm the resort's attorney. I'm just here making sure everything's going well."

She narrowed her eyes. "You're a Cedar Ridge attorney?"

"Yep."

She blinked as she processed that. So Lucas worked for Cedar Ridge too. And Jacob hadn't mentioned it. Not once. "Since when?" she asked.

"Since the Kincaids hired me, shortly after our divorce."

"All of them?"

"All of them who?"

"All the Kincaids," she said. "You work for all of them?"

"The five siblings, yes."

"Including Jacob?" she asked, heart in her throat.

"Well, no."

Sophie let out a shaky breath. Okay. Okay, so this wasn't any big deal. She knew Jacob couldn't have had anything to do with hiring Lucas, as he hadn't even been in town at the time. And he must not know even now. Otherwise he'd have absolutely told her. One hundred percent, he would have told her—

"Didn't meet Jacob again until he came back to town."

"Again?" she asked.

"We went to school together." Lucas cocked his head and studied her closely.

Sophie turned away. Lucas was a people reader, and he was a master at it too. But he simply turned her around to face him again. "You're her," he said slowly, understanding dawning in his gaze. "The one he's been seeing."

She closed her eyes.

"And he didn't tell you about me." He laughed. "Oh, that's good. That's really good."

Which was funny because Sophie kind of felt the exact opposite. She'd trusted Jacob with pieces of her that she hadn't ever trusted Lucas with. And he'd shaken those pieces up and tossed them out, leaving her once again feeling like a tumbleweed in the wind. Heart in her throat, she walked away.

"Does he know you're crazy?" he called after her. "'Cuz I can tell him for you if you'd like…"

She increased her pace, blood pressure somewhere around stroke level. She moved toward the kitchen canopy to drop off the pitcher of juice and ran right into Kenna.

Kenna stopped short and took in her expression. "What's wrong?"

"Nothing."

"Uh-huh." She looked past Sophie, caught sight of Lucas walking across the beach socializing, and stilled. "I'm going to guess your idiot ex got to you before my bigger idiot brother."

Deciding she was mad at anyone named Kincaid, Sophie went straight to the donut tray and grabbed a leftover jelly donut, and on second thought also took a bear claw. It was a double-fist sort of day.

"Just do me a favor," Kenna said. "Don't leave until Jacob can explain."

Not willing to make any promises, Sophie stuffed the jelly donut into her mouth.

"Right," Kenna muttered. "Okay, you know what? New plan. You don't move. I'll be right back."

Sophie was mowing her way through her second donut when she felt her heart rate double and the nape of her neck get warm.

Jacob.

She turned and faced him, not appreciating her body's response. Her brain sent the rest of her a memo that she was no longer allowed to be attracted to Jacob. On any level.

Her body rejected said memo and did a little quiver at the sight of him in board shorts and T-shirt advertising the resort. No shoes. Bedhead hair—which should have made him look ridiculous but instead made her inner ho sigh in pleasure. And then that inner ho remembered him pulling her to the edge of his bed and then kneeling on the floor, her legs on either of his shoulders as his mouth drove her straight to heaven.

Dammit.

"Woke up without you," he said. "Didn't like it."

"Yeah, well, you're going to have to get used to that," she said, and stuffed the last of the bear claw into her mouth so she could cross her arms. It wasn't easy to maintain her pissy dignity with her mouth full, but she gave it her best shot.

Jacob nodded slowly. "I'm getting that. We need to talk, Sophie."

She had to ignore how the sound of her name on his lips always made her ache. Needing something to do with herself, she grabbed the last donut. "I'll go first," she said. "Were you laughing at me this whole time? Was it all just one big joke between you and Lucas?"

He studied her face a moment and then set down his coffee. He started to take the donut from her hand, stopping when she let out a sound that might have been construed as a growl. Changing tactics, he reached for her free hand instead.

She pulled it back, which she realized made her look like a three-year-old, but she was furious. And upset. And… shamefully embarrassed—a bad combination for her, always had been.

"Soph," he said in that low, gruff morning voice, the one that until fifteen minutes ago would have made her melt.

Well, okay, so she was still melting, but that only made her angrier. God, she'd been such a fool, a complete idiot, and the worst part was, she should've seen it coming.

Nothing good came of falling for someone.

Nothing.

Ever.

"I gotta go," she whispered.

"After we talk."

"Can't," she said. "I'm working now and then I'm gone."

He froze. "You're leaving Cedar Ridge?"

"No, just you." She turned to walk off, but he caught her and turned her around to face him.

"Hear me out. You owe me that much, Sophie. And then, if you still want to dump my sorry ass, have at it."

She gave him a push. "Fine. But hands off." She couldn't think when he touched her.

He lifted his hands but didn't back away. "I can see you've decided some things on your own about me," he said, "but you're wrong. Very wrong."

She just stared at him, doing her best to remain composed. She'd signed on to work the breakfast, help with cleanup, and get the beach cleared by noon. That meant two more hours of having to keep it together.

Or at least the pretense of.

She could do that. Hell, she'd held it together for much longer, under far worse circumstances—such as her entire childhood. And her marriage to Lucas...

She was a master at holding it together. So this, with Jacob, should be easy. Totally easy.

Now, if only she believed that... "Please move," she said. "I have work to do."

"In a minute." He lowered his voice. "We have an audience. Come back home with me and—"

"No." Hugging herself with one arm, still clenching the rest of her donut, she shook her head. "I'm on the clock."

"Fine. Shift over." He wrapped his fingers around her wrist, and not giving her much of a choice, pulled her from beneath the canopy and toward his cabin.

"Don't even think about it," she said, digging her heels in. She wasn't going to his place, no way in hell. He'd talk and she'd melt, and she'd end up in his amazing bed beneath his luscious bod, and she'd hate herself.

He quickly and easily redirected without argument, taking them down the beach instead, far past the event, until the sounds from it faded away.

Now all she could hear was the occasional squawk of a

bird, the chatter of a frantic squirrel. Insects humming. The water gently sloshing onto the rocky shore.

Oh, and the sound of her own heart breaking.

When they got to a secluded little spot Jacob presumably felt was a good enough place, he turned to face her and gestured for her to sit on a fallen log at the water's edge.

She shook her head. She'd eaten the rest of her donut on the walk here and now it sat in her gut like a heavy rock.

"Please sit," he said, sounding so weary that she took a look at him, her first real look since seeing Lucas.

He was too good to show his mood in his body posture. He stood there like he always did, calm, watchful, a little dangerous, like he was locked and loaded and ready for anything. And she knew that was probably true. But a closer look showed her that his mouth was set to grim, and he had shadows beneath his eyes, suggesting he was beyond tired.

That's what happens when you are a sex fiend, she thought, and then had a brief hot flash because she was one, too, with him. For him...

And since that made her knees weak, she sat.

He surprised her by not sitting next to her but instead crouching in front of her and taking her hand. "I didn't know," he said. "When I met you, I mean. I had no idea that the resort's attorney was your ex-husband."

She'd already figured out that much for herself. "The resort's attorney and someone you went to school with."

"True," he said. "But you're going to have to trust me when I say we didn't hang in the same circles. We were never friends, and that hasn't changed."

"But you knew he was the resort's attorney, if not when you first got back, certainly later. When did you find out?"

He didn't move an inch, but she sensed a wince that he couldn't quite hide from his eyes. "Soph—"

"When?"

He held her gaze in his for an interminable beat and then let out a breath. "Hangover day."

She stared at him as that sank in. The day she'd thrown up on him—day *two*. Rising to her feet, she started to walk past him.

He caught her by the arms. "I didn't tell you right away because at first I didn't see how it mattered."

She made a scoffing sound. "You didn't tell me at all! And we talked about him, more than once." Embarrassment heated her cheeks. "You never even blinked!"

"Fine," he said grimly. "I should have told you. I know I should have. But I didn't, because as I learned with my family, sometimes standing by your opinion of someone doesn't matter so much as keeping your mouth shut and minding your own business."

She stared at him. "That doesn't even make sense!"

"Why do people keep saying that?" he asked, tossing up his hands. He shook his head. "Put yourself in my shoes, Sophie."

"But that's the thing. *I'd* have told you," she said. "I'd have told you that your lying, cheating, scum-ball ex was my attorney."

"Not *my* attorney," he said. "The *resort's* attorney, a guy who was in place when I got here. A guy I had nothing to do with hiring, a guy whose work no one can fault."

She imagined the smoke coming out her ears. "And back to that whole keeping your mouth shut and minding your own business crap," she said. "Seriously? Your family would hate that, and for the record, so do I."

"Except I was never able to mind my own business when it came to you," he said. "Not once."

But she called bullshit on that. "I've been with someone I

can't trust," she said. "You know that. What you don't know is that I can't do it again. I *won't*. I'm making better choices for myself now, Jacob. I have to."

There was something in his eyes now, something to go along with the regret. A flash of anger to match hers.

"So tried and hanged without discussion?" he asked quietly. "Is that it?"

The barb hit home, but she just shook her head and walked away.

And this time, he let her go.

Chapter 30

When Jacob got back to the event, breakfast had ended and their guests were all packing up and leaving in small groups. He couldn't reconcile the normalcy of the scene with the wild ripping and shredding going on inside him. His heart seemed to be shattering inside his chest.

He could still feel the way Sophie had quivered with emotion as she'd stepped away from him. Their eyes had met for that one beat, and the hurt in her expression had been a sucker punch to his gut.

And then she'd turned her back on him. He'd stood there and watched as the best thing to ever happen to him walked away.

And it'd been his own fault.

Since they'd given resort staff the day off, his brothers and sister were on cleanup detail.

And Sophie.

She was on her knees in the wild grass, rolling up one of the canopies. Her head was bent so he couldn't see her expression, but he had no problem reading the fuck-off 'tude emanating from her in waves.

He stood there in rare indecision for a beat, then started toward her. When he was two steps in, she lifted her head and leveled him with a don't-even-think-about-it look that only made him all the more determined. She'd clearly tried and hung him on the assumption that he'd withheld information from her for the sole purpose of hurting her. That she'd lumped him in with her ex really sucked.

But before he could reach her, Chris stepped in front of him. "Got a minute?" his old friend asked. "I'm about to get on the road and wanted to…"

Jacob watched as over Chris's shoulder Sophie began directing the takedown of the rest of the rental equipment, pointing to the back of Gray's truck.

She'd walked out of his world, but she was still running it. That was when he realized Chris was looking at him, waiting on an answer to a question he hadn't heard. "I…Shit." Jacob shoved his hand through his hair and grimaced. "I'm sorry. What?"

Chris smiled a little sympathetically. "She got you dizzy?"

"Something like that."

Chris nodded. "She's pretty amazing, you know. You're a lucky guy."

Funny, but he wasn't feeling so lucky at the moment.

"I'd wish you good luck with her," Chris said. "But given how she was looking at you last night and then how you two vanished, you don't need it." He slid the duffel bag off his shoulders and handed it to Jacob.

Jacob stared down at it, his heart suddenly thumping hard in his chest. He knew this bag.

It'd belonged to Brett.

He opened it and stared down at Brett's personal effects. His diver's watch, which Jacob had given him for his birthday seven years ago. The beat-up DS he'd played to distraction. An old, battered book of poems that Brett hadn't actually read because he hated poetry, but it had belonged to his mom, so he'd carried it all around the planet. His lucky Dodgers hat.

That was it, Brett's life in a damn nutshell, the only things left to honor a good man who was sorely missed.

Jacob was glad to have the bag and the memories that went with them even as it pained him to imagine Hud or his mom getting a bag of his things. Through a lump in his throat, he lifted his head and met Chris's gaze.

"You really didn't hear a word I said, did you?" Chris asked. "I told you that I don't know why they sent Brett's belongings to me. I was listed second. You were first. It was a mistake, and I knew you'd want to have his things."

Jacob nodded and shouldered the bag, which felt like a million pounds. Brett hadn't had any family. He'd had no one but his unit. Jacob had felt the same way, which was part of what had bonded them so tightly. He opened his mouth to thank Chris for bringing the bag all this way, but he found he couldn't speak past the lump in his throat, the one that felt as big as a regulation-size football.

Chris clasped him on the shoulder. They hugged, and then Chris was gone. Jacob stood there, registering the low hum of everyday noise in the background. The water lapping the shore. The slight wind rustling the pines. The talk and laughter of the people nearby. A boat motor.

Normal life. And it was going on around him as if completely unaware he'd stepped off the merry-go-round.

He wanted to set the bag aside and force Sophie to talk to him. At the very least he could help finish the cleanup. He wanted to jump back into that "normal life," the one that had just started to fit him like a glove.

But it was like a switch had been flipped inside of him and normal no longer applied.

"Where's Jacob?"

Sophie turned at the question. The last of everything was loaded up and she was just about out of there. Her head hurt. Her body hurt.

Her heart hurt.

And Hud stood at her side, looking around. "Have you seen him?" he asked.

Yes, she had, and she was trying not to think about it.

"He was saying good-bye to Chris," Kenna piped up. "And it looked pretty serious. Chris handed him a duffel bag that apparently belonged to someone named Brett. He died in the line of duty during an incident where both Jacob and Chris were injured and was like a brother to Jacob." She winced a little and met Hud's eyes. "You know what I mean."

"How do you know all this?" Hud asked.

"Because I eavesdropped."

Sophie hadn't been close enough to eavesdrop, but she'd been able to read Jacob's expression.

Devastation. "He thought of Brett as a brother," she said quietly. "He feels like he's lost two brothers in his lifetime."

Hud blew out a breath and closed his eyes. "I haven't been easy on him."

Sophie thought of Jacob saying "I love you" so easily. How his eyes had told her he'd meant it. How he'd been willing to take what she could offer without asking or expecting more, all while giving Sophie everything he had. And she'd taken. And taken. Until she'd gotten spooked and let Lucas shake her, let him put doubts in her head. Doubts Jacob hadn't deserved. Yet she'd used those doubts to walk away, to keep her heart safe.

Safe but not happy—in spite of the fact that she'd promised herself she was over that. "I haven't been easy on him either," she whispered. "I need to fix that."

"Me too," Hud said.

Sophie nodded. Spinning on a heel, she headed to the cabin. To her great relief, she found Jacob in his room, zipping up one of his duffel bags. "Hey," she said.

"Hey." But he didn't look at her, and she felt her heart lurch. "What are you doing?"

He shouldered the bag and turned to her. "What does it look like?"

"Okay," she said. "I'm going to give you an ass pass because we both know I was an ass first."

He shouldered the second duffel bag like neither weighed a thing. The irony wasn't lost on her. For a very long time now, this was how he'd survived, by packing light, both physically and metaphorically.

But she also knew that he was fooling himself if he thought he could just leave. He loved it here in Cedar Ridge, and no matter what his grim, closed-off expression told the world, he wanted to be here with his family.

And hopefully her. "Don't go," she said. "Not like this. Your family—"

"I have to go."

Her heart stuttered to a stop. Her entire world stuttered to a stop. "Why?"

"I called in. Cut my leave short. I'm shipping out to finish my tour."

"You tell everyone?"

"My mom knows. I'm going to see her on the way out.

I just this very second texted Hud, so he's hopefully on his way over."

"I was with him," she said. "He's…giving me a minute with you." Or so she hoped. "Jacob, what about after? When you're finished. You're coming back, right?"

He turned to look around the cabin as if making sure he wasn't leaving anything behind. Which they both knew was ridiculous. He was always careful to leave nothing of himself behind. She tried not to resent that since this was all her own doing. "Jacob."

"The way I get through this is by not looking too far ahead," he said.

She swallowed hard. "I'm sorry I didn't listen to you on the beach. I'd like to listen now."

"I don't have time."

She nodded as her poor, abused heart took another hard tumble. "What about the cabin?"

He held out his hand. For an instant she thought he was reaching out to touch her, but he was handing her a set of keys.

She stared down at them and then lifted her head in confusion.

"You hate that boat," he said. "The cabin will be just sitting here. Stay in it. Make yourself at home."

Yes. Absolutely. If he'd been staying in it with her…But she didn't need his pity. And more than that, she was having a hard time with this conversation at all. Her ribs felt like they'd shrunk and were constricting her breathing. Her heart hurt, physically hurt. Shaking her head, she pushed his hand away.

"Sophie, don't be stubborn on this. The cabin will be empty—"

"I know." She didn't need the reminder. "I'll be fine, but thanks."

He looked at her for a long beat, nodded, and walked around her to the door. She didn't turn to watch him, couldn't believe he was just walking away—

"Soph."

She whirled around and found him there, right there in front of her. The man moved like a cat. He touched her face, his own carefully blank. Then he leaned in, brushed his mouth to hers, and was gone.

She boarded the boat in a fog. Not wanting to see Jacob drive away, she went directly belowdecks. She didn't hear his truck start and figured he was waiting for Hud.

Didn't mean she had to wait. She went straight to the tiny galley and attempted to light the sole burner. "Please," she begged it.

And surprise, surprise, it went *click, click, click* and… turned on. One thing going her way…She pulled out her pan. She needed a double grilled cheese sandwich stat, with a tall chocolate milk on the side. Maybe laced.

Cursing the small quarters, she pulled out the bread and the rest of the ingredients, during which she remembered a question Jacob had asked her all those weeks ago now.

Why did she stay on the boat?

If he'd asked her even yesterday, she would have stopped and said she honest to God didn't know. And yet here she was, constantly bitching about her circumstances. So why hadn't she done anything about it?

If he'd asked her today, just now, she'd have known the answer. Just as he hadn't thought he deserved his family, she hadn't believed she deserved to be happy.

But she did. She deserved that very much, and she had held the power to change her circumstances all along.

Once the pan was heated and she had the sandwich sizzling, she pounded out Lucas's number. When he picked up the call, she immediately said, "I'm selling the boat."

"Yeah, yeah, I heard you before. You're selling, but not to me."

"I changed my mind on that."

There was a pause. "Are you teasing me?" he finally asked.

"No. I want to find my happy, and my happy involves a hot shower and a full kitchen. And your happy is this boat." She paused and rolled her eyes at herself. "And we both deserve our happy."

Another pause. "Who are you, and what have you done with my bitch ex-wife?"

She sighed. "Fine, if you're not interested—"

"Hey, whoa, I didn't say that! I'm interested. I'm *more* than interested. Consider it sold for fair market value."

"And you'll pay me up front?"

"Hell, I'll even add in your car, free of charge."

"Wow," she said, and flipped her sandwich, the scent of melting cheese making her mouth water. "Look at you, going soft in your old age."

"Bite your tongue, woman. So…this have anything to do with you bumping uglies with Jacob Kincaid?"

She'd just taken an unfortunate sip of her chocolate milk and choked on it.

"I'll take that as a yes," he said. "You know that being with him is like going from the pan into the fire, right? Because if you think *I* can't keep it in my pants—"

"You can't!"

He let out a low laugh. "Okay, touché. But the last single male Kincaid, Sophie? Seriously? It's like you *want* to be hurt. It's like you *want* to be your dad, constantly down and depressed—"

She felt her spine snap straight. "You don't know what

you're talking about," she said stiffly. "I'm nothing like my dad. And it's not like he chooses to be sad, Lucas. It's a chemical imbalance—"

"Sophie," he said quietly. "I didn't mean to start a fight and hurt your feelings. I'm just saying, I'm...worried about you."

She blinked.

"I was an asshole," he said. "There's no doubt. Hell, I'm *still* an asshole. But why are you going after another asshole? Do you *want* to get hurt again? Is that it?"

She opened her mouth and then closed it. "Jacob's not like you," she said. "When he's with someone, he's with someone."

"Okay, so maybe he's not going to cheat on you with another woman," Lucas said. "But he's not going to be able to make you happy. He's not relationship material, and that's what you want. That's what you're looking for."

No way was she going to admit to him that she'd learned that already, the hard way. "I'll be okay," she said.

He was quiet a moment. "I'll have the accountant come up with an offer for the boat and get it to you tomorrow."

"Thanks," she said, and then paused. "Wait a minute. Did we just have a relatively decent conversation in which neither of us skewered the other?"

"Yeah," he said, sounding as surprised as she. "Do you think it means the apocalypse is coming?"

"Maybe it means we're growing up," she said.

"Don't tell anyone."

She found a laugh and disconnected, and when she did, her laughter stuck in her throat and switched to tears. Dammit. Dammit, she still couldn't find her happy. Because her happy was leaving with Jacob, like one of those duffel bags over his shoulder.

She turned back to the grilled cheese and gasped at the black smoke billowing out from beneath the pan. And in the next second, the sandwich burst into flames. It caught the kitchen towel next to the pan, and that also burst into flames.

"Oh, my God!" She whirled, mind blank. She ran to the sink, but only a trickle of water came out.

By this time, the fire had spread to the window shades. She raced over to the table and ducked down, reaching for the fire extinguisher that she always bumped her legs on.

It was heavy and she'd never used one before, which made her mad. She always hated the stupid chick, the one who in the movies didn't know how to save herself. *Don't be the stupid chick!* She yanked harder. "Come on, you motherfu—"

It broke free with enough momentum to take her down to her butt. She scrambled back up and wasted another precious few seconds trying to figure out how to use the extinguisher. All while the flames grew around her. Finally she pulled the pin and squeezed the lever.

And nothing happened.

Chapter 31

Jacob tossed Hud his truck keys. "She's all yours for now."

Hud looked down at them, swore, and then tossed them back.

"That's the second damn time today my keys have been rejected," Jacob noted far more casually than he felt.

"Maybe because the people doing the rejecting don't want you to leave," Hud said.

Jacob shook his head. He was having a hard time controlling his emotions here. Very hard. He was on a short leash and needed to get the hell out before he broke.

The two of them were standing in his driveway, next to Jacob's truck. The cabin was locked up, and he was packed and ready to go. Hud had shown up and he'd immediately gone straight to pissed off without passing go, and had spent the past five minutes telling—*yelling*—about what a bad idea it was for Jacob to leave early.

"I was always going to have to go," Jacob managed to say evenly.

"But you moved it up."

Not by much, but yeah, he had. The fight with Sophie had reminded him that he wasn't fit for society. He screwed things up and was clueless on how to make them better, so leaving felt like the obvious solution.

Hud was watching him. "Some of us aren't ready."

"Was I supposed to know that?" Jacob blew out a breath. "You've spoken more to me in the past five minutes than in the whole time I've been here."

"Ditto."

They stared at each other for an interminably long beat, and finally Jacob closed his eyes. "You're making this harder than it has to be. We've done this before."

"Say good-bye? Fuck no, we haven't," Hud said. "You left without a good-bye last time, remember?"

"How can I forget? You keep throwing it in my face."

This time it was Hud's turn to close his eyes. "Fine. That was a shitty thing to say, and I take it back. But you're evading. Why leave before you have to?"

"That's…complicated."

"You fucked up with Sophie when she came to apologize," Hud said.

"I fucked up with more than Sophie."

Hud looked at him, long and hard. "If you're talking about me," he said, "or the others, you're wrong. You didn't fuck up at all. You came home. That was all we ever wanted."

The words took a surprising load off Jacob's shoulders.

"At least look me in the eyes and tell me you're coming back," Hud said.

Jacob turned his head to meet Hud's gaze and saw the smoke and flames licking out from Sophie's boat. His heart about stopped. Dropping the duffel bags, he hit the beach at a dead run. "Call nine-one-one!" he yelled back at Hud.

"On it," Hud said right on his heels.

They hit the dock in tandem. At the boat, Hud tried to pull Jacob back from jumping on board. "It's not safe!" he yelled.

"Sophie's in there!" Jacob leapt to the deck, calling out for her.

Someone landed right next to him.

Hud.

"What the hell are you doing?" Jacob yelled at him.

Hud was tugging up the vinyl seating, and Jacob knew why. He was looking for the fire extinguisher that was hopefully on board.

"Sophie!" Jacob yelled, turning to go belowdecks. The door was open, and black smoke was pouring out. *"Sophie!"*

"Here!"

She appeared in the opening holding a fire extinguisher. Hud immediately took it from her while Jacob pulled her up and off the boat to the dock.

"Are you okay?" he demanded, running his hands over her, looking for injuries. It was hard to tell. She was sooty from head to toe.

"I'm"—she stopped to cough—"fine."

He didn't stop touching her, couldn't.

"Jacob." She cupped his face and brought it to hers. "I'm fine. I just couldn't get the extinguisher to start and the flames were quicker than me."

Still holding on to her, he turned to see that Hud had abandoned the extinguisher as well and had jumped lithely to the dock beside them. He immediately turned to Sophie and looked her over as Jacob had.

Sirens sounded in the distance, and in the next minute, the fire service had arrived, along with a sea of other first responders, including Aidan.

Twenty minutes later, Sophie was sitting in the back of the ambulance, an emergency blanket wrapped around her shoulders, being looked over by a paramedic. Jacob stood hovering, especially when Lucas drove up, ran to the shore, and stared at the shell of his boat, hands in his hair. Then he turned to Sophie.

She grimaced. "I'm sorry—"

"You okay?" Lucas asked.

"Yes, but the boat isn't."

"I know." Lucas let out a long breath. "It might be karma."

She stared at him. "You really believe that?"

"I'm working on it." He started to walk off, then hesitated. Glanced at Jacob and then back at Sophie. "You need anything?" he asked her.

She shook her head.

He nodded, looking more than a little relieved. "Take care of yourself." And then he was gone.

Hud came up next to Jacob and pulled him aside. "How is she?"

Jacob shook his head. "They were worried about shock, but she's doing well, considering what could have happened. A small burn on her arm, that's it."

Hud let out a breath of relief and nodded. "They caught the flames pretty fast, but there's also massive soot, smoke, and water damage. Probably not salvageable."

Jacob nodded. He'd known this. What he didn't know was how Sophie was going to feel about it. "You tried to hold me back from jumping on board," he said.

"Yeah."

"And yet you followed me," Jacob said.

"Yeah, and if you're about to ask why, you're going to piss me off," his twin said. "Don't you get it yet? Where you go, stupid or not, I go. And vice versa. I'll beat that into you if I have to. We do the right thing by each other, always—you got that yet?"

"Yeah, I got it." Jacob paused. "Do you really not remember our handshake?" he asked, referring to the day he'd run into his brother and Hud had acted like he'd never seen it before.

Hud blew out a sigh. "You're not the only one who can be an ass. We do share DNA."

Jacob nodded. How well he knew that. "You know I'm sorry, right? For leaving without a word. For not keeping in contact. For coming back without a word. For everything."

"I know." Hud paused. "Me too."

"Yeah? What are you sorry for?"

Hud heaved out a sigh. "For letting you walk. For holding a grudge. For using being mad at you as an excuse to not take any blame on myself."

"I hated being without you," Jacob admitted.

"Me too," Hud said. "It sucked." He didn't look particularly happy at this admission. "We don't have to keep talking about our feelings, do we?"

"Hell no," Jacob said. "I'm good now. You?"

Instead of answering, Hud held out his hand, fisted.

Throat suddenly tight, Jacob bumped it with his, and then they went through their age-old complicated handshake by rote, his body still having the muscle memory to do it without thinking.

And then they hugged.

Hud squeezed him hard. "You fucking come back this time, and I mean *right* back—you hear me?"

"I will." He turned and sought out a view of Sophie.

Hud's gaze followed. "What are you going to do there?" his twin asked.

Jacob didn't take his eyes off of her. "The right thing."

Chapter 32

Sophie felt Jacob long before she saw him. As always, that sense of awareness came in the form of a tingle at the back of her neck. She lifted her head, and her gaze locked on to his.

She was still sitting at the back of the ambulance wrapped in a blanket when he crouched at her side and put a steadying hand on her thigh.

"Hey," he said quietly, eyes warm. "How are you holding up?"

"Great." Even if she had to bite her lower lip and look away or lose it, because the look in his eyes said he was there for her.

But he wasn't.

He'd made that clear.

And damn. Damn if that didn't have a tear sliding down her cheek. She swiped at it angrily and stopped breathing so she wouldn't break into sobs.

But Jacob didn't back up. Instead he shook his head at her

and gently ran a thumb beneath her eye. "I'm going to ask you again," he said. "How are you holding up?"

She sucked in a breath. "You mean other than the boat is essentially gone and so are all of my things and—" She broke off before she could say the rest. *And you're no longer mine...*

"You'll get insurance money and find a place you love. It's a new start."

She stared at him, resentful. "Since when do you see the glass half full?"

"Since you taught me to." Without warning, he rose and scooped her up with him.

She gasped. "What are you doing? I can walk!"

Ignoring her, he turned to the paramedic. "She's all good, yeah?"

"All good," the paramedic said with a thumbs-up.

With a nod, Jacob turned and strode up the deck and toward his cabin, where some of the best memories of her life had taken place. "Jacob, put me down."

He did. On his bed. He set the keys to the cabin on the nightstand. Then he sat on the edge of the bed, a hand on either side of her hips as he leaned over her. His shoulders eclipsed the sight of the room behind him, leaving nothing to look at but him. Dark jaw set. Dark eyes serious. "I have to go," he said quietly.

Huh. Turned out her heart could break in two over and over again. She looked away. Or tried. But his broad shoulders took up all of her view. Stupid broad shoulders. "So you've said," she managed.

He brought her face back to his. "I have to, Soph," he repeated.

"There's nothing wrong with my hearing."

"It's not that I want to go," he said.

"You're the one who made the call."

"I signed up for this. It's my job and my duty, and I'll finish it. I want to finish it." He pulled her to him. "And then I'm coming back."

Her gaze flew to his as she tried to pull back, but he just held on to her. With those big, warm, strong arms around her, it took her a moment to speak calmly, but even then she shoved her face into his throat first so as not have to look at him. "I'm sure that will make your family very happy," she whispered.

With a rough sound of…regret?…he slid his fingers into her hair and pulled just enough that she had no choice but to look at him again. "My family's not the only reason I want to come back," he said.

"What else is there?" she managed.

For a long beat he said nothing, and she thought that was it, the end of the conversation.

But then he spoke, his voice lowered to the tone that always reminded her of when he was lusciously deep inside her, whispering naughty nothings in her ear.

"Thirty seconds," he said.

She blinked. "What?"

"I saw the flames on the boat and knew you were in there. It took thirty of the longest seconds of my life to run from my driveway down the dock to the boat and find you alive and kicking."

Her breath caught, but she wasn't sure what to say to that, so she tried something new and kept her mouth shut.

"I keep getting these pictures of you in my head," he said. "You lying in my bed, your hair a wild disaster all around your face."

"Hey."

He smiled. "I love the way it smells—"

"It smells like smoke."

"Shh. I love how it clings to my stubble."

She liked where this was going, but she kept still just in case she was wrong. Because it wouldn't be the first time.

"And when you're truly pissed off," he said, "it gleams like fire. Just like you." He pressed his face into her hair and squeezed her hard. "Christ, Soph, you scared ten years off my life today."

"I didn't mean to."

"I know." He touched his forehead to hers. "I was wrong about some things."

She didn't move. Hell, she didn't even breathe. "Were you?"

He smiled a little, not daunted in the least at her frosty tone. "A lot of things, actually. All of it regarding you and my ability to resist falling for you, and falling hard, Soph. You're always on my mind."

How was she supposed to hold on to her anger at a guy who wasn't scared off by her mercurial moods or her temperament, a man could see through all of her BS and still love her? "Keep talking," she said.

"I think about your eyes," he told her. "How that deep green cuts right through me, past my armor, straight to the meat of things."

"And by armor, you mean your stubborn obstinacy?"

He smiled, not insulted. "You see me," he said simply, banishing the last of her resistance.

"What else?" she whispered, soft and warm now, no longer braced for rejection.

"I love how your pulse quickens when I touch you. You tremble for more and your lips part, begging for my kiss…" He leaned in, and she stopped him with a hand to his chest.

"You sure this isn't a sex dream?" she asked.

He flashed that grin she loved. "Sometimes. Lots of times," he admitted. His fingers were loosely fisted in her hair, like he'd really missed the craziness of it. "Other times it's your laugh. And the way you have of disagreeing with everything I say—"

"I do not!"

He laughed and kissed her pouty mouth. "Okay," he said. "But you do." He touched her face, his own going serious. "When I first came back to Cedar Ridge, I didn't think I deserved to be loved by any of my family. By anyone," he said. "And I sure as hell didn't deserve you. But I realized I was wrong, that I was my own worst enemy."

She was impressed by his growth, and proud. And... envious. "When did you figure all this out?" she asked. "Was it a hammer-over-the-head moment, or was it more gradual?" She genuinely needed to know. Her entire life had been a whole bunch of clusterfuck moments until it'd all sunk in. She needed to know how it was for him. She didn't want this to be just about the boat fire, about him nearly losing her, because she didn't see it like that. Yes, the fire had been awful, and she'd be dealing with the ramifications for a long time to come, but she hadn't almost died. She would have gotten out on her own. So she didn't want him back in her arms because of a single incident. She wanted him because he couldn't live without her.

"No hammer," he said. "Just a series of gradual moments, starting that first day when you dropped a pink vibrator at my feet."

She narrowed her eyes. "That wasn't *my* vibrator!"

He laughed, and she knew it was because she was arguing with him again. "And," he went on, "I really liked it when you tried to tell me why your boat should be allowed to break the rules and moor overnight on the lake."

"It's a stupid rule!"

He was still smiling, a contagious, warm, sexy smile. "And then there was when you got trashed by the Scotch—"

"Okay, that wasn't drunk," she said. "That was…cozily tipsy."

"And watching you make friends with Kenna. Or when you gave Chris's name to Hud to get him here for this weekend. It was when you told me about your past and let me in. All those things added up to me loving you," he said. "I just couldn't imagine deserving you to love me back."

She felt her smile fade, and she reached up and set her hands on his jaw. "Jacob," she murmured, her heart breaking. "Jacob, I—"

He set a finger on her mouth, halting her words. "But then I realized something," he whispered as he slowly traced her lower lip. "I couldn't expect you to return my feelings if I couldn't let you in." He dropped his finger and replaced it with his mouth.

"You ruined me with all the openness," she murmured against his lips. "The communication."

He grinned. "I ruined you in all sorts of other ways too. And you liked them, every single one of them."

She flushed and gave him a little push that didn't so much as budge him. "Full of yourself much?"

"Just optimistic."

"How unlike you," she said.

His grin widened, and his hold on her tightened. "I learned it from this amazing, headstrong, selfless, sexy-as-all-get-out woman I've been hanging out with lately…"

"Yeah?"

"Yeah."

She was laughing as she shook her head and pulled his down to hers. "Smug bastard," she said, and kissed him.

"Does that mean you can't live without me?"

"It means that *you* can't live without *me*," she corrected.

He let out a low laugh. "Oh, baby, don't I know it." He cupped her face. "I love you, Soph. The forever kind of love that survives stupid fights and transcends time and place."

Her heart kicked hard, racing, pounding in all her pulse points. "Are you asking me to wait for you?"

"Yes," he said without hesitation.

She'd asked the question, so it was silly to suddenly need a moment, but she did. She pulled at his shirt, trying to get it over his head, but he caught her wrists in his.

"I want you to stay," he said. "Here. In the cabin." His eyes were fierce, his body hard. He wasn't playing.

Leaning in, she kissed his stern mouth. "I don't really know how to do this, Jacob. Just because it's hard for me to speak my feelings doesn't mean I don't feel them. Because I do. I love you."

His eyes softened, but nothing else did. "And…?"

"And I know you have to go, but I want my good-bye."

His gaze held hers, revealing the heat, her need. "Babe, I'm on borrowed time here," he said regretfully.

"Then you should hurry."

He groaned and kissed her, but it wasn't the hard, heated kiss she'd expected. It was slow, leisurely, like they had all the time in the world.

And only when she'd forgotten herself and the fact that he was indeed leaving, only when she could think of nothing but the sensual desire sliding through her belly, did he lower her to his bed and strip her piece by agonizing piece, his fingers skimming over her as he did, slow, reverent. Loving. He removed her panties last, slowly pulling them over her hips and down her legs like he had all the time in the world.

Like her pleasure was of the utmost importance to him.

Still bent over her, he looked up into her face as he brushed a kiss over her breast. And then just below her belly button.

She quivered. The things he could do to her with one look, one kiss...

Rearing up, she got to her knees and shoved his shirt up and over his head. And though she'd seen him shirtless many times, her mouth still went dry as she watched each beautifully defined muscle ripple as he pulled off the shirt.

She splayed her hands over his heart, feeling the comforting steady pound of it beneath her palms. Smiling, she slid her hands down to his ripped abs and leaned in to stroke her tongue over one of his nipples. His stomach. And southward bound—

The breath rushed out of his lungs as he toppled her to the mattress.

"Back to being in a hurry?" Sophie asked.

"You make me lose control," he said and made her laugh breathlessly.

But then he slid inside her, filling her as only he could, making it impossible to do anything but cry out his name and wrap her arms and legs around him, desperate, hungry. Unlike him, she had no control, none at all and as he moved inside her, hungry sounds ripped from her throat, needy and desperate, and she didn't care. "Jacob."

His muscles bunched and released under her hands as he took the both of them right to the very edge, leaving her so close that her lungs burned for air. *"Jacob."*

He pushed up on his arms, his hands braced on either side of her head to hold his weight, and she moaned at the sight of the carved muscles of his chest, shoulders and arms straining as he took her even deeper, harder, and then sent her skittering into a hard climax before following her over.

When she could breathe again, when she could open her eyes and focus, she found him propped up on an elbow at her side, watching her with an intensity that took her breath.

"I need this with you, Soph," he said. "But more that, I need *you*. You make me laugh. You keep me in the moment and yet you also make me believe in a future. I want you to know all this before I go because life's short. Way too short to let go of something you know you want to keep forever."

Her heart caught. "Forever?"

"Say you'll think about it," he said. "Think about moving in here, at least until you can replace your things, until you figure out where your home is."

"And if I figure out that my home is you?" she asked in a low whisper.

"Then that's the first thing I want you to tell me when I get back."

She smiled. He had a way of making clear what he wanted, what he hoped for, without pressuring her for more than she could handle. "Kiss me good-bye," she demanded. "Kiss me so I won't forget."

He hauled her to him and held her tight before burying his hands in her hair and kissing her until they were both shaky and more than a little desperate.

She clutched at him and managed to ask, "How much longer do we have?"

He looked at the bedside clock. "An hour at most."

"Then let's make the most of it," she said, and using his weight against him, pulled him down to her.

Chapter 33

Three months later

It was two in the morning when Hud pulled up to the cabin on the lake. Next to him, Jacob took a deep breath of the Rocky Mountain air and for the first time in three months felt alive.

And hopeful. "Have you seen Sophie?" he asked. "Is she staying here?"

Hud didn't answer that. No one had and Jacob hadn't pressed, not sure if he was ready to know.

"Feels good to have you back," was all Hud said.

Two arms came around Jacob tight from behind. Kenna in the backseat. "*So GOOD!*" she whispered fiercely, hugging him for what must've been the hundredth time since they'd picked him up at the airport in Denver two hours ago.

He twisted and did his best to hug her back. She tightened her grip and...didn't let go.

"I thought maybe we'd had enough hugs," he managed to croak out past the arm around his neck.

She still didn't let go.

Jacob loved her. Ridiculously. But he needed to get inside, needed to know if Sophie was in there. Seeking help, he looked at Hud.

"He's turning blue," Hud told Kenna.

She sniffed.

Hud winced and backed up against the door, hands up.

Shit. Jacob wrapped Kenna up as tight as he could. "Hey," he said. "I'm done. I'm out. I'm not leaving again."

"You swear it?"

"I swear it."

"And you'll buy me breakfast?" she asked soggily. "At least twice a week?"

Ah, there she was. "You're wearing a ring. You have Mitch for that now."

"It's just a promise ring and he's a boy, which means he could muck it all up at any moment. You're my brother. Say it, Jacob. Promise me."

"I promise to buy you breakfast two times a week."

"In perpetuity."

"In perpetuity," he said.

"And you'll take over as events manager?" she asked. "And be codirector with me of the ski school, seeing as the resort has been saved and so have our asses?"

Jacob pulled back. "What?"

"Oh yeah," she said. "Forgot to tell you. Lucas went on a whole fix-his-bad-karma thing and was able to work out a deal with the bank so we'd have more time and lower payments. All will be paid off in two years, with the resort still making a comfortable profit if we're careful. We're rebuilding and we need you. Plus, we already had the plaque made for your office door."

Jacob looked at Hud in the dark ambient light of the truck's cab. "You know about this?"

"We all do," he said. "We want you back where you belong. With us. And if those jobs don't appeal to you, then we'll find something that does."

"They appeal," Jacob said. More than he'd imagined they could.

He got out of the truck.

He entered his cabin, tension curling through him. He was beyond exhausted after traveling for the past seventy-two hours to get back here and had no idea what to expect. He and Soph had communicated via email and Skype here and there, but connections had been spotty and she'd been vague about her plans.

Terrifyingly vague.

Was she here? Would she stay? And if so, for how long? He wanted forever, but he didn't very often get what he wanted.

The cabin was dark, and he didn't turn on any lights as he dropped his duffel bags and walked straight through the living room to his bedroom.

The glow of the moon slanted in through the window, casting the room in blue shadows. He moved to the bed, his knees nearly giving out when he saw the mass of long red hair scattered across his pillow.

Sophie lay sprawled in the center of the bed, deeply asleep, taking up all of the space. It took him a few seconds to realize what was different about the room.

The closet was open, filled with her clothes. She had several pairs of shoes scattered on the floor. One peek into the bathroom assured him that she'd taken over there as well, bottles and brushes…How many brushes did one woman need?

Moving back to his bedroom, he noticed the blanket on the bed was hers. There was a plant in one corner and her jewelry box was on the dresser. And a pair of undies on the floor by the bed gave him hope she was in there naked.

That she was there at all was a miracle on its own.

His hand shook as he shut and locked the door, doing the same for the window, making them safe for the night.

Then he sat down heavily on the chair by the bed and just watched her breathe. She was here.

She was his.

And he was absolutely hers…He closed his eyes for a second and then opened them.

And found her looking at him.

Sophie had been waiting for this moment for so long she could scarcely breathe. She'd done her best to go on with her life and continue to make it as good for herself as she could. She'd started her concierge service and had more business than she knew what to do with.

She'd spent time with Kenna and the other Kincaids. She'd settled into Jacob's cabin, feeling warm and safe and deeply attached to the place, unlike anywhere else she'd ever lived.

That was all Jacob.

He wasn't there, but she could feel his presence, and she thought about him a lot. Thought about what it would be like when he returned home.

And here he was, leaner than he'd been, tanned from long days in the sun, hair once again military short, eyes dark and filled with things that caught her breath.

"You're a sight for sore eyes," he said.

"You too. Jacob—" She broke off, nervous. He seemed content to wait for her to gather herself. He was excellent at that. God, she'd missed him. "Just so you know," she murmured, her heart pounding hard. "I did as you sug-

gested. I made myself at home." She trailed off as…
victory? satisfaction?…flickered across his face. Maybe
both, but what caught her by the heart and wouldn't let go
was the intensity of his eyes and a smile that warmed her
to the bone.

"You've made another choice," he said.

"Yeah," she breathed. "I'm home."

He stood and strode straight for her, leaning over her to
kiss her long and deep, one hand sliding up her spine to cra-
dle the back of her head.

She gripped him tight, her fingers running up his arms,
bared thanks to his T-shirt. His skin was chilled. "You're
cold," she said. "Come in here. Let me warm you," she whispered, and lifted the covers in invitation.

Holding her gaze, he stripped and climbed into the bed,
pulling her into the circle of his arms. A low, rough, heartfelt
groan escaped him as he pulled her naked body to him.
"We're *both* home now," he said.

Epilogue

Six months later

Sophie had never been so happy and so miserably sick at the same time. Currently she was kneeling on the floor in the bar's bathroom, trying to decide if she was done. She hadn't had any alcohol, but upon reflection, the second order of hot wings might've been a serious error in judgment.

Kenna was helping to hold her hair back. "Honey, you should've canceled tonight if you were sick."

"I'm not." Pretty sure she was over this latest bout, she sat back and eyed the diamond wedding band on her finger. Jacob had put it there two months ago, on a week-long vacay in Hawaii, where they'd stood together and exchanged vows. It still gave her a thrill to see the ring. "I'm okay now."

"You're not," Kenna said. She brought Sophie some dampened paper towels while simultaneously speaking into her cell phone. "Sophie's sick," she said. "Yeah, she's thrown up, like, four times."

"Three," Sophie corrected weakly, "and are you really

tattling on me?" She rinsed her mouth in the sink. "What are we, twelve?"

Ten minutes later Jacob came barging through the women's bathroom door looking very much like a warrior soldier ready to kick ass, making another woman squeak and rush out.

Jacob didn't even glance at her. All he had eyes for was Sophie. He dropped to his knees next to her where she was sitting on the floor, leaning against the wall. He pulled her in, hugging her tight, and Sophie found herself laughing and crying at the same time as she clutched at him.

"Why didn't you tell me?" he demanded incredulously.

"I didn't know until this morning, I was going to tell you later tonight, after I warmed you up to the idea…"

"Babe…" He stroked her hair from her damp forehead. "Why would you need to warm me up to the idea of having a baby?"

"You don't remember?" she asked on a low laugh. "Last week at the ball game, the woman next to us had a two-year-old who kept having a temper tantrum. And you said, 'Let's never do that.'"

"I meant because she had him dressed up in a mini Raiders uniform. No kid of mine is going to wear anything other than a Broncos jersey."

Kenna dropped to her knees next to them. "Okay, someone needs to tell me right here, right now…We're *having a baby*?"

Sophie felt her eyes fill again at the look on Jacob's face—pure, radiant joy.

"Yeah," he said, leaning in, pressing his forehead to Sophie's, his own eyes suspiciously misty too. "We're having a baby."

"*That's* why you wouldn't drink!" Kenna grinned. "Even

when I said vodka was made from potatoes and potatoes are a vegetable, which practically makes vodka a salad."

Sophie smiled. "No alcohol for eight more months."

"We're having a baby," Kenna repeated in marvel, a wide grin on her usually taciturn face.

"Well, I don't know much about the 'we' part," Sophie said wryly. "Seems to me most of the work is going to be mine."

"I'll be right there with you," Jacob vowed, voice deep and rich with the promise. "You won't ever be alone in this."

Her heart nearly burst it was so full. Him. His family. A baby...It was all so much more than she could've ever hoped for. "You might feel differently when the pregnancy hormones kick in," she warned.

He cupped her face. "I fell hard for you, Soph, and I haven't gotten up since. Never will. We're in this together, heart and soul."

She couldn't think of anything she'd ever wanted more.

The hottest property in Cedar Ridge is Aidan Kincaid—firefighter, rescue worker, and heartbreaker. But when the love of his life returns, it's up to him to convince her to give Cedar Ridge—and this bad boy—a second chance...

Please see the next page
for a preview of

Second Chance
Summer

Chapter 1

After fighting a brush fire at the base of Cedar Ridge for ten straight hours, Aidan Kincaid had only three things on his mind: sex, pizza, and beer. Given the way the day had gone, he'd gladly take them in any order he could get them.

Not in the cards.

He and the rest of his fire crew had finally managed to get back to the station. They'd been there just long enough to load their plates when the alarm went off again.

"What the hell!"

"Gonna break the damn bell and shove it up someone's—"

"This is bullshit…"

Whoever said no one could outswear a sailor had never lived in a firehouse. Ignoring the grumbling around him, Aidan pushed his plate away and met his partner Mitch's gaze.

"Gotta be a full moon bringing out the crazy," Mitch said.

"Maybe the crazy just follows you," Aidan suggested.

In turn, Mitch suggested Aidan was number one. With his middle finger.

They'd been playing this game since first grade, when Mitch had stolen Aidan's lunch and Aidan had popped him in the nose for it. As punishment they'd had to pick up and haul trash for the janitor for two weeks.

The two of them had become best friends and had spent the next decade being as wild and crazy as possible.

Eventually they'd grown up and found responsibility, going through the fire academy and now working as Colorado Wildland Firefighters for their bread and butter, volunteering on the local search-and-rescue team as needed. And here in Cedar Ridge they were needed a lot. Lost hikers, overzealous hunters, clueless novice rafters—you name it, they'd been called to save it.

Tonight's fire call came in as a possible suicide jumper off the courthouse, which at five stories high was the tallest building in town.

As they pulled up, they could see a woman had climbed out a window on the fifth floor. She stood on a ledge that couldn't have been more than a foot wide, wearing nothing but her bra and panties.

"Well, at least Nicky left her Victoria's Secrets on this time," Mitch noted.

Nicky was a bit of a regular.

And Mitch was right. The last time Nicky had gotten upset was after finding the town councilman she'd been sleeping with going at it on his desk with his assistant. She'd stripped all the way down to her birthday suit before covering herself in Post-it notes. Aidan wondered what had set her off this time.

"I changed my mind," she screamed, jabbing a finger down at them. "I don't want to die! He's not worth it!"

No Post-it notes this time. A bonus. The police had blocked off traffic, but the scene was still chaotic.

"Somebody get up here and save me!" Nicky yelled. "If I fall and die, I'm going to sue every one of you for being so freaking slow! Honest to God, what does a girl have to do to get a rescue around here?"

"So she's changed her mind," the captain said dryly to Aidan and Mitch. They exchanged glances. No one could reach her from inside the window. And climbing out on the ledge wasn't an option; it was too narrow—and decomposing to boot. And thanks to the layout of the building and the hillside, their truck couldn't get close enough to the building to be effective either.

They all knew what this meant. One of them was going to have to follow the half-naked crazy chick out onto the ledge. There were a few problems with this.

Aidan and his team had a reputation for being unflappable and tough as nails, but the truth was, plenty unnerved them—including a half-naked crazy chick on a ledge five stories up. They'd just learned to do whatever needed to be done, no matter what.

"Let the fun begin," Mitch muttered.

Plan A was for the captain to head inside and attempt to talk Nicky back inside the window. Since Plan A had a high potential for going south, Plan B was to be run simultaneously—head to the roof and begin setting up rigging for an over-the-roof retrieval.

Through it all, Nicky never stopped screaming at them, alternately begging them to hurry and hurtling insults their way.

Then came the cap's radio message. "Yeah, so she's declining to crawl back in the window because there's no press here yet. Last time she was front-page news."

Onward. The team found a good anchor spot on the roof. As Mitch and Aidan were the two most senior members of the unit, one of them always took lead. Mitch looked at Aidan. "Okay, go make like Spider-Man and rescue the damsel in distress."

"Why me?" Aidan asked.

"It's your turn."

"Hey, you're the one who likes her undies," Aidan pointed out. Not that he objected to a rescue, any rescue, but this one had shit show written all over it.

"I weigh more than you do," Mitch said logically.

Only because he was six foot four to Aidan's six two, but whatever. The team got the line set up, and then Aidan got into his five-point harness and hooked himself to the first of the two lines. Mitch hooked himself up to the second one just in case Aidan got into trouble, and the rest of the unit prepared for go time.

Aidan dropped over the edge. The plan was to rappel him down until he hung ten feet above Nicky. He'd then kick out from the building at the same time that his team lowered him eleven more feet, bringing him to just below her, putting him between her and the fifty-foot drop. He'd attach a harness to Nicky, and the team would give them enough slack so that Aidan could rappel down with her.

And the team indeed lowered Aidan to just above Nicky. Aidan kicked out. But as usual, nothing went to plan. Just as he started to swing back toward the wall, Nicky leapt off the ledge like some rabid raccoon and wrapped herself around him.

Not more than a hundred and ten pounds, she clung to him like a monkey as they hurtled at neck-breaking speed toward the wall. Aidan managed to grip her tight and twist in midair so that he was the one to slam into the brick.

Even as lightweight as she was, it still hurt like hell.

"Jesus Christ," Aidan heard the captain and Mitch say in stereo as they watched helplessly—one from above, one from below, at the window.

They didn't know the half of it. With Nicky's legs wrapped and locked around Aidan's waist, her arms squeezing his head like a grape and her breasts literally suffocating him, he couldn't breathe. Somehow he managed to turn his head sideways to suck in some air, but he still couldn't see. "I've got you," he said. "I'm not going to let go, but you need to loosen your grip."

Nicky was too busy screaming in his ear to hear him, not loosening her grip at all. "Omigod, don't you fuckin' drop me or I'll sue you the most!"

Mitch had dropped over the edge as soon Nicky leapt on Aidan's back. He was rappelling down as fast as he could, laughing all the way. Aidan couldn't see shit, but he could hear him clearly, the asshole.

"Got his six," Mitch said into the radio as he came even with Aidan, still laughing. "Though I can't tell where Aidan ends and Nicky begins."

You can kill him later, Aidan promised himself. "Listen to me," he said to Nicky. "I've got you. I need you to stop yelling in my ear and look at me."

She gulped in a breath and relaxed her hold only enough to look at him. Her eyes were wide, wet, and raccooned from her mascara.

"I'm not going to let go of you," he assured her, staring into her eyes, doing his best to give her an anchor. "You hear me, Nicky? No one's falling to their death today."

She nodded and started to cry in earnest at the same time. Aidan preferred her screaming.

"She's not attached to anything," the captain reminded them via radio.

"You don't have to worry about that, Cap," Mitch responded. "She's not letting go of Aidan."

Nope, she wasn't. She'd embedded her nails into him good, and her legs were crossed and locked at the small of his back, but at least he could breathe. "Just get us down," he said.

As the team lowered them, Mitch kept alongside, offering encouragement, cracking his own ass up as they went.

On the ground, Aidan's new companion was peeled off of him and taken away for further evaluation. Aidan took his first deep breath since the rescue had begun. Aching in more muscles than he'd realized he even had, he gathered his gear.

"You okay?" their captain asked. "You took a few hard hits up there."

"I'm fine." He could feel where he'd have bruises tomorrow, and he was pretty sure his back had been scraped raw from the demolition derby collision with the brick wall, but he'd had worse.

Mitch grinned at him. "Man, you just had your bones totally jumped by a nearly naked chick. We almost had to resuscitate you. 'Fireman Asphyxiated by Boobs, news at eleven.'"

Their captain eyed Mitch and then Aidan. "You remember we have a strict no-killing-each-other policy?"

Aidan reluctantly nodded.

"I'm going to lift that rule for a onetime exception," the captain said, cocking his head at Mitch.

Mitch's smile faded. "Hey."

But the captain had walked away.

"Whatever," Mitch said to Aidan. "If you kill me, you'll never find out what I know."

Aidan slid him a glance. "You never know anything."

"I know lots, starting with a rumor that you're about to get a blast from the past."

"What?"

"Yeah. I hear Lily Danville's back," Mitch said.

Aidan froze at the name he hadn't heard in a very long time. Years. Ten of them to be exact.

Mitch raised a brow. "Gray hasn't mentioned it?"

No, Aidan's older brother had not told him a thing, which raised the question.

Why?

"How did you hear?" Aidan asked.

"Lenny. He caught the gossip at the resort. Your family runs the place. How did you not hear this?"

Lenny had gone to high school with them and now worked at the Kincaid resort as a big-equipment driver. Aidan stared at Mitch, unable to process that everyone had known before him.

Lily Danville…Damn. Turning, he started to walk away.

"It's no big deal," Mitch said. "It's not like you're seeing Shelly anymore, right? You're a free agent, so if you want to try to get Lily back…Hey, wait up."

Aidan didn't wait. And it was true he wasn't seeing Shelly anymore. Technically, they'd never been "seeing" each other. They'd had a satisfying physical relationship whenever they both felt like it, and neither of them had felt like it in more than a month now. He hadn't thought about her once since.

But Lily Danville…

He hadn't seen her in forever, and yet he still thought about her way too often.

"Hold up," Mitch called out. "Your half of the gear's still—" He broke off when Aidan kept walking. "Seriously?" And when Aidan didn't so much as look back, Mitch swore and worked to gather the load, making some of the newbies help. He was quiet on the ride back to the station but only because they weren't alone and also he was playing a game on his phone.

Aidan reached over and swiped his finger across Mitch's screen.

Mitch swore, nearly lost the phone out the window, and then turned to glare at Aidan. "You owe me a Candy Crush life."

"Tell me more about Lily being back."

"Oh, *now* you want to talk? You done pouting then?"

When Aidan just gave him the I-can-kick-your-ass gaze, Mitch grinned. "You know you were."

"It's all over Facebook," one of the guys said from the back. "The news about Lily."

"Aidan forgot his password," Mitch said. "A year ago."

Aidan ignored him, mostly because his brain was on overload. Lily. Back in town…

He'd long ago convinced himself that whatever he'd felt for her all those years ago had been just a stupid teenage boy thing.

Seemed he was going to get a chance to test out that theory, ready or not.

As a cop and head of ski patrol at the Cedar Ridge Resort, Hudson Kincaid has seen everything. But a pretty, dark-eyed novice skier stuck at the top of the mountain's most dangerous run is about to rock his world in ways he never expected...

Please see the next page
for a preview of

My Kind of Wonderful

Chapter 1

The wind whistled through the high Colorado Rocky Mountain peaks, stirring up a dusting of snow as light as the powdered sugar on the donut that Hudson Kincaid was stuffing into his face as he rode the ski lift.

Breakfast of champions, and in three minutes when he hit the top of Cedar Ridge, he'd have the adrenaline rush to go with it. As head of ski patrol, he'd already had his daily before-the-asscrack-of-dawn debriefing with his crew. They'd set up the fencing and ropes to keep skiers safe and in the proper runs. They'd checked all the sleds to make sure their equipment was in working order.

Now he had time for one quick run before they ran rescue drills for a few hours, and then he was on to a board meeting—aka fight with his siblings. One run, ten glorious minutes to himself, and he was going to make it Devil's Face, the most challenging on the mountain.

Go big or go home. That was the Kincaid way.

Just then the radio at his hip chirped news about a report

of someone in trouble at the top of Devil's Face, and Hud shook his head.

So much for a few minutes to himself.

Ah, well, it was the life, his life, and he'd chosen it. At the top of the lift, he hit the snow at a fast clip. He'd seen a lot here on their mountain and even more on his monthly shifts as a cop in town. It was safe to say that not much surprised him anymore.

So when three minutes later he found a girl sitting just off-center at the top of Devil's Face, her skis haphazardly stuck into the snow at her side, he didn't even blink.

Her down jacket was sunshine yellow, her helmet cherry red. She sat with her legs pulled up to her chest, her chin on her knees, wearing ski boots as neon green as neon green could get and staring contemplatively at the heart-stopping view in front of her.

Hud stopped a few feet away so as to not startle her, but she didn't budge. He looked around to make sure this was the person of interest. Sharp, majestic snow-covered peaks in a three-hundred-sixty-degree vista. Pine-scented air so pure that at this altitude it hurt to breathe. There was no one else up here. They were on top of the world.

Not smart on her part. The weather had been particularly volatile lately. Right now it was clear as a bell and a crisp thirty degrees, but that could change in a blink. High winds were forecasted, as was another foot of snow by midnight. But even if a storm wasn't due to move in, no one should ski alone. And especially no one should ski alone on Devil's Face, a thirty-five-hundred-foot vertical run that required a great deal of skill and in return promised dizzying speeds. There was a low margin for error up here, where one little mistake could mean a trip to the ER.

Even Hud didn't ski alone. He had staff all over this

place—a few of them at the ski patrol outpost only a few hundred yards away, another group at the ski lift he'd just left, even more patrolling the resort boundaries—all of them connected to each other by constant radio contact.

"Hey," he called out. "You okay?"

Nothing.

Hud glided on his skis the last few feet between them and touched her shoulder.

She jerked and craned her neck, at the same time pulling off her helmet and yanking out her earbuds. Tinny music burst out from them loud enough to make him wonder if she still had any hearing at all.

"Sorry," she said. "Did you say something?"

Not a girl but a woman, and without her helmet, Hud realized he'd actually seen her before. Earlier that morning she'd been in the parking lot, sitting on the back bumper of her car and pulling on her ski boots, all while singing along with the radio to the new Ed Sheeran song. He couldn't tell now behind her dark sunglasses, but he knew she had eyes the color of today's azure sky and that she shouldn't give up her day job to become a singer because she couldn't hold a tune. "I asked if you're okay," he said.

She removed her sunglasses and gave him a sassy look that said the question was ridiculous.

She'd worn a tight ski cap beneath her helmet, also cherry red, with no hair visible and enough layers of clothing that she was utterly shapeless. But that didn't matter. Her bright eyes sparkled with something that looked a whole lot like the best kind of trouble.

He'd been running ski patrol for years now and had been a cop for long enough that he was good at reading people, often before they said a word. It was all in the posture, in the little tells, he'd learned.

Such as all the layers she wore. Yes, it was winter, and yes, it was the Rocky Mountains, but thirty degrees was downright balmy compared with last week's mid-teens. Most likely she wasn't from around here.

And then there was the slightly unsure posture that said she was at least a little bit out of her element and knew it. Her utter lack of wariness told him something else, too, that probably wherever she'd come from, it hadn't been a big city.

None of which explained why she was sitting alone on one of the toughest mountains in the country. Maybe... dumped by a boyfriend after a fight on the lift? Separated from a pack of girlfriends and just taking a quick break? Hell, despite appearances, maybe she was some kind of a daredevil out here on a bet or a whim.

Or maybe she was simply a nut job. As he knew, nut jobs came in all shapes and sizes, even mysterious cuties with heart-stopping eyes. "So are you?" he asked. "Okay?"

Her smile faded some. "Do I not look okay?"

Hud had a sister and a mom, so he recognized a trick question when he heard one and knew better than to touch it with a ten-foot pole. Instead, he swept his gaze over her but saw no visible injuries. Then again, he couldn't see much given all the layers. "You're not hurt."

"No, that's not the problem." She paused. "I guess you're probably wondering what is the problem."

"Little bit," he admitted.

She rolled her eyes. "Did you know that people who don't understand ski maps, or maps at all, shouldn't ski alone?"

"*No one* should ski alone," he said, but then her words sank in and he pulled off his sunglasses and stared at her in incredulous disbelief. "Are you saying you're on Devil's Face, the most challenging run on this mountain, because you misread the ski map?"

She bit her lip and tried to hide a rueful smile, which didn't matter because her expressive eyes gave her away. "I realize this is going to make me look bad," she said, "but yes, yes, I'm here because I misread the map. If you must know the truth, I had it upside down."

Upside down. Jesus. "We color-code the things, you know. Even upside down, green is still for beginners, blue for intermediate—"

"Well, I know that much!"

"This run is black—a double-diamond expert," he said. "It's marked all over the place." He pointed to a sign three feet away.

CAUTION: DOUBLE DIAMOND. EXPERTS ONLY!

"I saw that," she said. "Hence my thinking position, because trust me, I wasn't about to be stupid on top of stupid."

He let out a low laugh. "Good to know."

"And you should also know that I'm not a complete beginner. I've taken ski lessons before, at Breckenridge." She grimaced. "Though it's been a while."

"How long is a while?"

She bit her lower lip. "Longer than I want to admit. I thought it'd be like getting on a bike. Turns out, not so much. But if it helps, I realized my mistake right away and I really was just taking in the view. I mean, look at it…" She gestured to the gorgeous scenery in front of her, the stuff of postcards and wishes and dreams. "It's mind-boggling, don't you think?"

The wonder in her gaze mesmerized him. A little surprised at himself, he turned to take in the view with her, trying to see it through her eyes. The towering peaks had a way of putting things into perspective and reminding you that you weren't the biggest and baddest. A blanket of fresh snow stretched as far as the eye could see, glistening wherever the sun hit it like it'd been dusted with diamonds.

She was right when she said it was mind-boggling. He tried to never take this place for granted, but the truth was that he did. Interesting that it'd taken a pretty stranger to shake him out of his routine and make him notice his surroundings. He turned his head and met her gaze. Yeah. He was definitely noticing his surroundings.

She smiled into his eyes. "I figured after I got my fill of the view, I'd just head back to the ski lift and ask if I could ride it down. No harm, no foul, right? But then came problem number two."

"Which is…?" he asked when she didn't continue.

"I broke my binding, and while I've got lots of stuff in all these pockets, I'm not packing any tools. I think I just need a screwdriver or something. I thought I'd locate a ski patroller."

"I am ski patrol," he said.

Looking surprised, she ran her gaze up and down the length of him. Usually when a woman did such a thing it was with a light of lust in her eyes, but she didn't seem overly impressed.

He looked down at himself. "I'm not in my patrol jacket," he said. "I was hot from putting up the fencing—" Why the hell was he defending himself? Shaking his head, he removed his skis and walked to hers. He laid out the one she pointed to and took a look. Yep, she'd broken a binding. "The hinge failed," he said.

She crouched next to him and the scent of her soap or perfume came to him, a light, sexy scent that made him turn his head and look at her.

But what held his interest were those baby blues. They

were wide and fathomless, and he found himself utterly unable to look away.

As if maybe she was every bit as transfixed as he, she blinked slowly. "Can we fix it?"

We? "I could rig it enough to get you down the mountain if I had a piece of wire." He pulled out his radio. "I'll just call for—"

"Oh, I've got it." She rose and pulled a small notebook from one of her pockets. Clipped to it was a paper clip. She pulled it loose and waved it proudly. "I've a piece of wire right here, see?"

"Nice." He took the paper clip, straightened it, then used it to thread through the binding and twist it in place. During the entire two minutes this took, she remained hunkered at his side, leaning over his arm, her soft, warm breath against his neck, taking in everything he did.

She sucked in a breath. "You're…"

When she didn't finish the sentence, he turned his head and watched her gaze drop to his mouth, which was only a few inches from hers.

"…handy," she finished softly.

"And you're…"

She smiled. "Stubborn? Annoying?"

"Set to go," he said.

She laughed and he smiled. "I'll help you back to the lift," he said.

"Oh, I'm good now, thanks to you." Rising, she nudged her ski into place so that she could secure her boot into it. She struggled with that for a minute, unable to snap her ski in, causing her arms to tremble a little bit with the effort.

Hud started forward, but she stopped him with a raised hand and he checked himself.

Ski number two took her longer because she had a balance problem. He lasted until she started to fall over and then all bets were off. Again he moved toward her, but at the last second she managed to catch herself on her pole. When she finally clicked that second ski in, she lifted her head and flashed him a triumphant smile, like she'd just climbed a mountain.

"Got it!" she said, beaming, swiping at her brow like maybe she was sweating now. "See? I'm good."

"You were right about the stubborn," he said. "But not the annoying."

"Well, you haven't given me enough time." And with another flashing smile, she pushed off on her poles.

In the wrong direction.

Hud caught her by the back of her jacket. Even with all those layers, she was surprisingly light. Light enough that he could easily spin her around and face her in the right direction, which was a hundred and eighty degrees from where she'd started.

She laughed, and damn, she really did have a great laugh, one that invited a man right in to laugh along with her. "Right," she said, patting him on the chest. "Thanks. *Now* I'm good."

At his hip, his radio was buzzing. His guys were checking in, getting ready for their high- and low-angle rope rescue drills. Hud was supposed to run the exercise, but he wanted to make sure the woman got safely on the lift first.

"Sounds like you have to go," she said.

"I do." But when he didn't move, her brows went up. "You're cute," she said. "But you do know that even an intelligent person can screw up reading a map, right? That despite whatever it looks like, I really don't need a keeper."

Wait a minute. Did she just call him *cute*? He'd never once in his life been called cute.

Taking in his expression, she laughed, like he was funny. "It was a compliment," she said.

Not in his book. His radio crackled again. Dispatch this time, making sure he'd located the "troubled" skier. "I've got her," he confirmed, eyes narrowed in on the skier in question. "It's handled."

The dispatcher went on to fill him in on two other incidents. Hud told her how to deal with them both and then replaced the radio on his hip.

"Okay," his wayward skier said. "I stand corrected. You're not cute. You're kinda badass with all that bossy 'tude. Happy now?"

Happy? More like dizzy. "Let's just get you to the lift," he said. Calm. Authoritative. The same tone that people usually listened and responded to.

Usually...

"I'm good now," she said, and with a wave pushed off on her poles, thankfully heading directly toward the ski lift.

Not surprisingly, she wasn't all that steady. This was because she kept her knees locked instead of bending them, incorrectly putting her weight on the backs of her skis. Whoever had given her those lessons at Breckenridge should be fired.

But she hadn't asked him for tips. And he no longer worked at the ski school.

She'd be fun to teach though. The thought came unbidden and he shrugged it off. All he cared about was that she was on the right path now, leaving him free to take Devil's Face hard and fast the way he'd wanted.

Except...Her helmet lay in the snow at his feet, forgotten. He had no idea how anyone could forget the eye-popping cherry-red thing against the white snow, but she had.

And so had he, when he rarely forgot anything. It was

those pretty eyes, that sweet yet mischievous laugh, both distracting as hell. "Hey," he called after her. "Your helmet."

But she must have put her earbuds back in because she didn't stop or turn back.

Hud scooped up the helmet and, giving Devil's Face one last longing look, headed toward the lift as well, catching up with her halfway there.

She'd stopped and had her weight braced on her poles. Bent over a little bit, she was huffing and puffing, out of breath. They were at well over eight thousand feet and altitude could be a bitch. It affected everyone differently, but breathlessness was the most common side effect.

Although an uncomfortable and worrisome thought came to him that maybe it wasn't the altitude at all. When he'd lifted her before, she'd been light, almost…frail. People didn't realize it took a lot of strength and stamina to ski, and he was nearly positive she didn't have either. He put a hand on her shoulder.

She whirled to face him, saw the helmet dangling off his finger, and pulled out an earbud with an apologetic smile. "Sorry, I think the altitude's getting to me. I really should've gotten some caffeine down me before facing the mountain." She slid on the helmet. "Thanks, Prince Charming."

"Huh?"

"You know, Cinderella," she said. "The prince had her slipper and you had my helmet…Never mind," she said with a pat to his arm when he just stared at her. "Ignore me. Probably I should've put far more practical things on my list than skiing in the Rockies."

And then, before he could ask her what the hell she was talking about now, she'd tightened the strap beneath her chin, put her hands back into the handholds at the top of her ski poles, and pushed off.

He watched her head for the lift that would carry her back to safety, thinking two things. One, he really hoped she knew how to stop. And two, she was definitely a nut, but possibly the prettiest, most bewildering nut he'd ever met in his entire life.